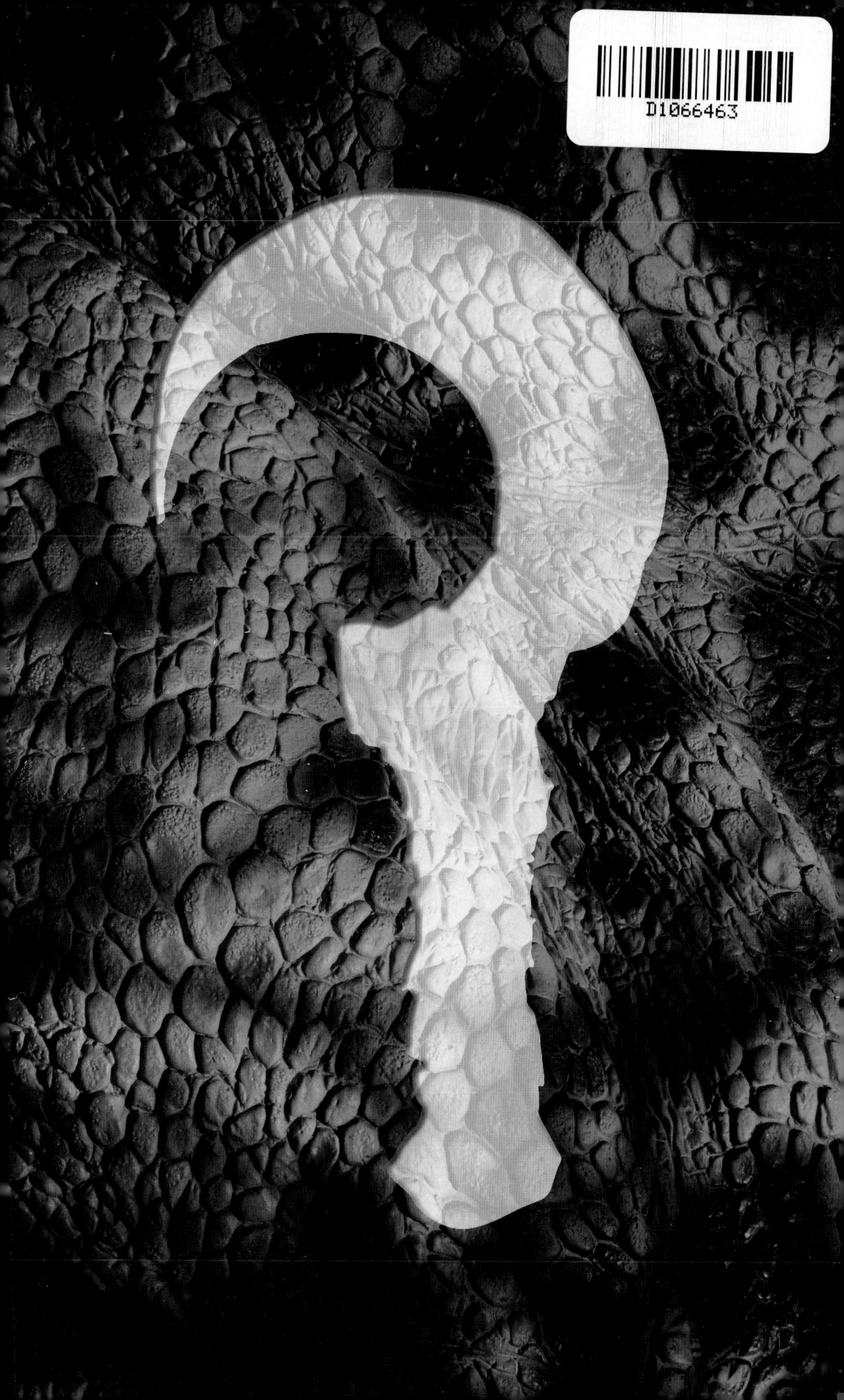

# SAVAGE ™

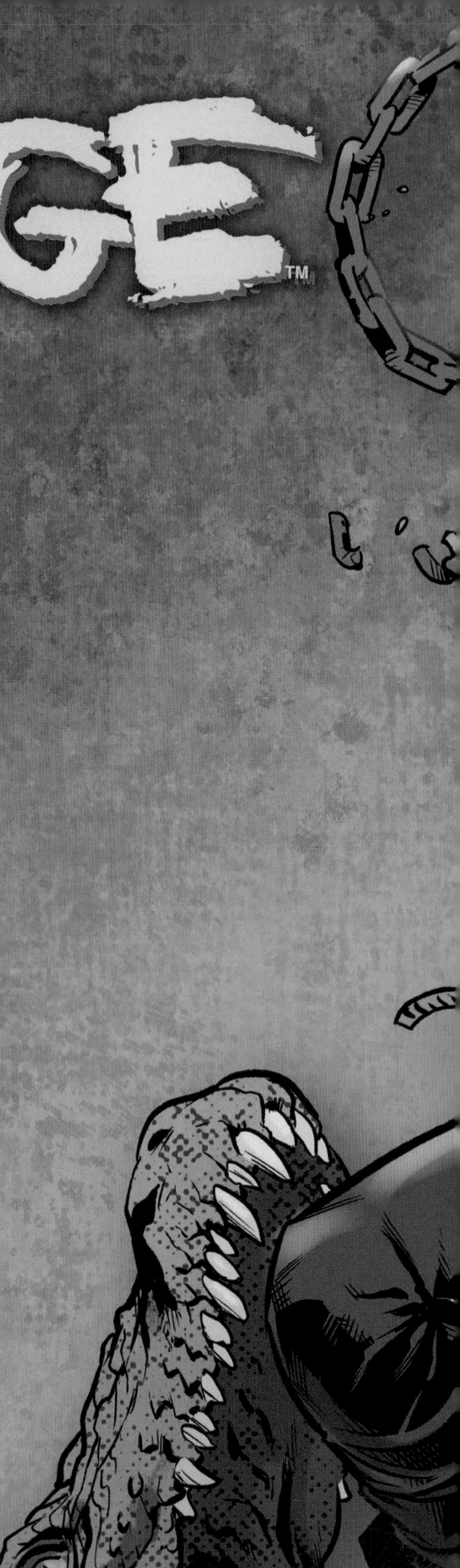

**WRITER**
MAX BEMIS

**ARTIST**
NATHAN STOCKMAN

**COLORIST**
TRIONA FARRELL

**LETTERER**
HASSAN OTSMANE-
ELHAOU

**COVERS BY**
MARCUS TO with
RICO RENZI

**EDITOR**
DAVID MENCHEL

**SENIOR EDITOR**
HEATHER ANTOS

**GALLERY**
PACO DIAZ
STACEY LEE
DAVID LOPEZ
JOE QUINONES
NATHAN STOCKMAN
CHRISTIAN WARD

**COLLECTION BACK
COVER ART**
MARCUS TO with
RICO RENZI

**COLLECTION
COVER ART**
GIUSEPPE CAMUNCOLI
with ULISES ARREOLA

**COLLECTION
FRONT ART:**
MARCUS TO with
RICO RENZI
PAULINA GANUCHEAU

**COLLECTION
EDITOR**
IVAN COHEN

**COLLECTION
DESIGNER**
STEVE BLACKWELL

## VALIANT ®

**Dan Mintz** Chairman  **Fred Pierce** Publisher  **Walter Black** VP Operations
**Travis Escarfullery** Director of Design & Production  **Peter Stern** Director of International Publishing & Merchandising
**Lysa Hawkins** & **David Wohl**  Senior Editors  **Jeff Walker** Production & Design Manager
**John Petrie** Senior Manager - Sales & Merchandising  **Danielle Ward** Sales Manager  **Gregg Katzman** Marketing & Publicity Manager

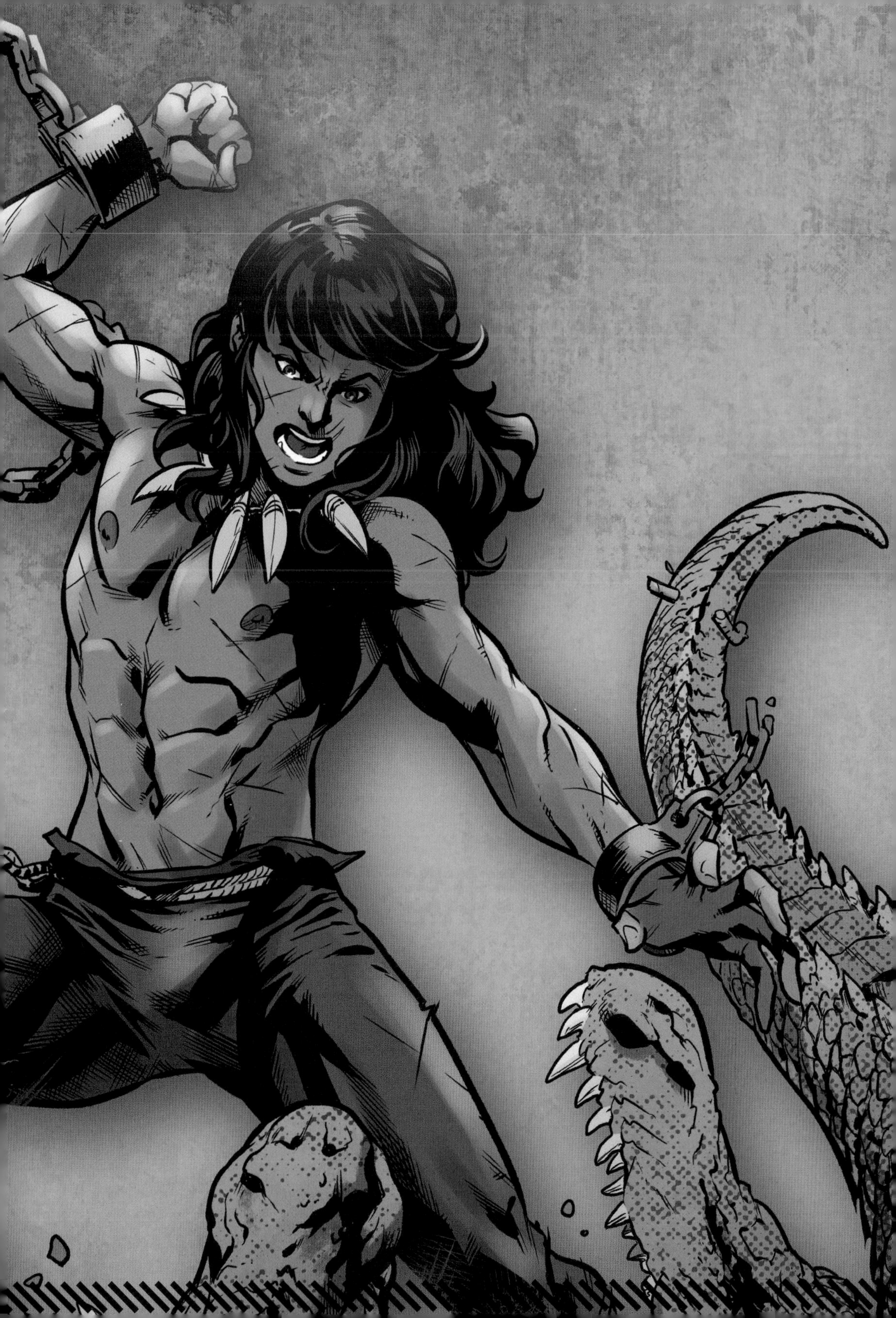

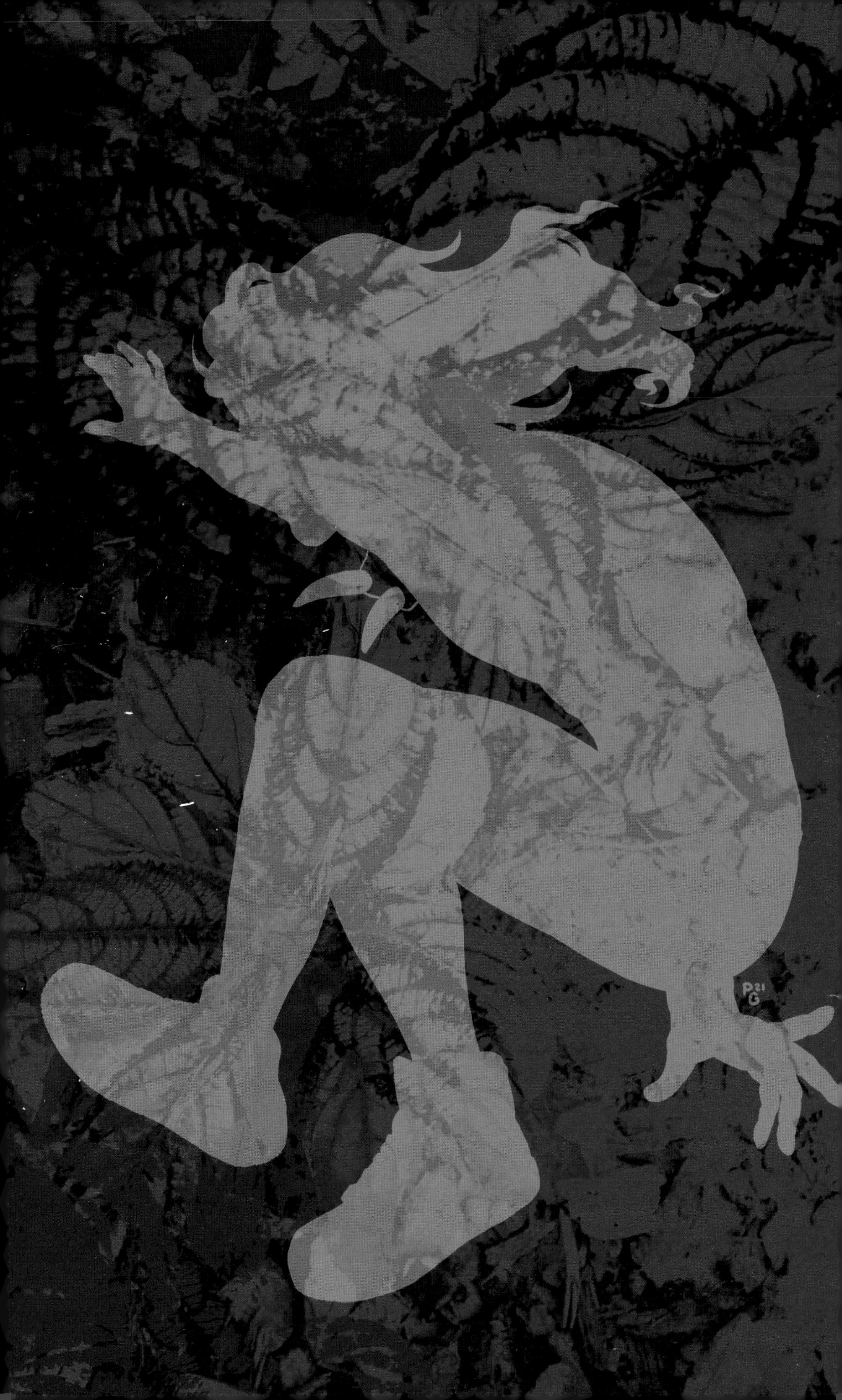

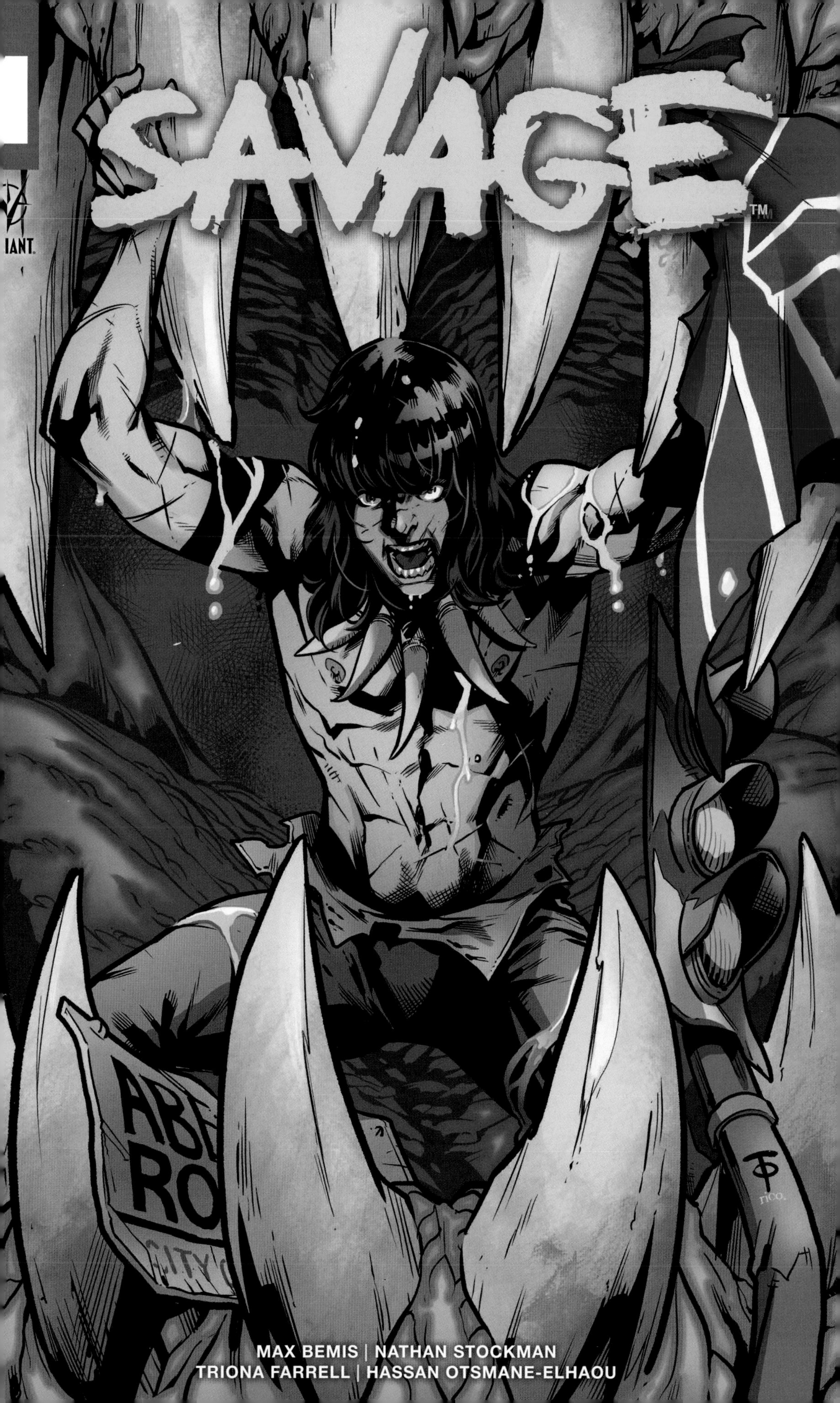
SAVAGE™
MAX BEMIS | NATHAN STOCKMAN
TRIONA FARRELL | HASSAN OTSMANE-ELHAOU

**SAVAGE #1**

*WRITER:* Max Bemis
*ARTIST:* Nathan Stockman
*COLORIST:* Triona Farrell
*LETTERER:* Hassan Otsmane-Elhaou
*COVER ARTISTS:* Marcus To with Rico Renzi
*EDITOR:* David Menchel
*SENIOR EDITOR:* Heather Antos

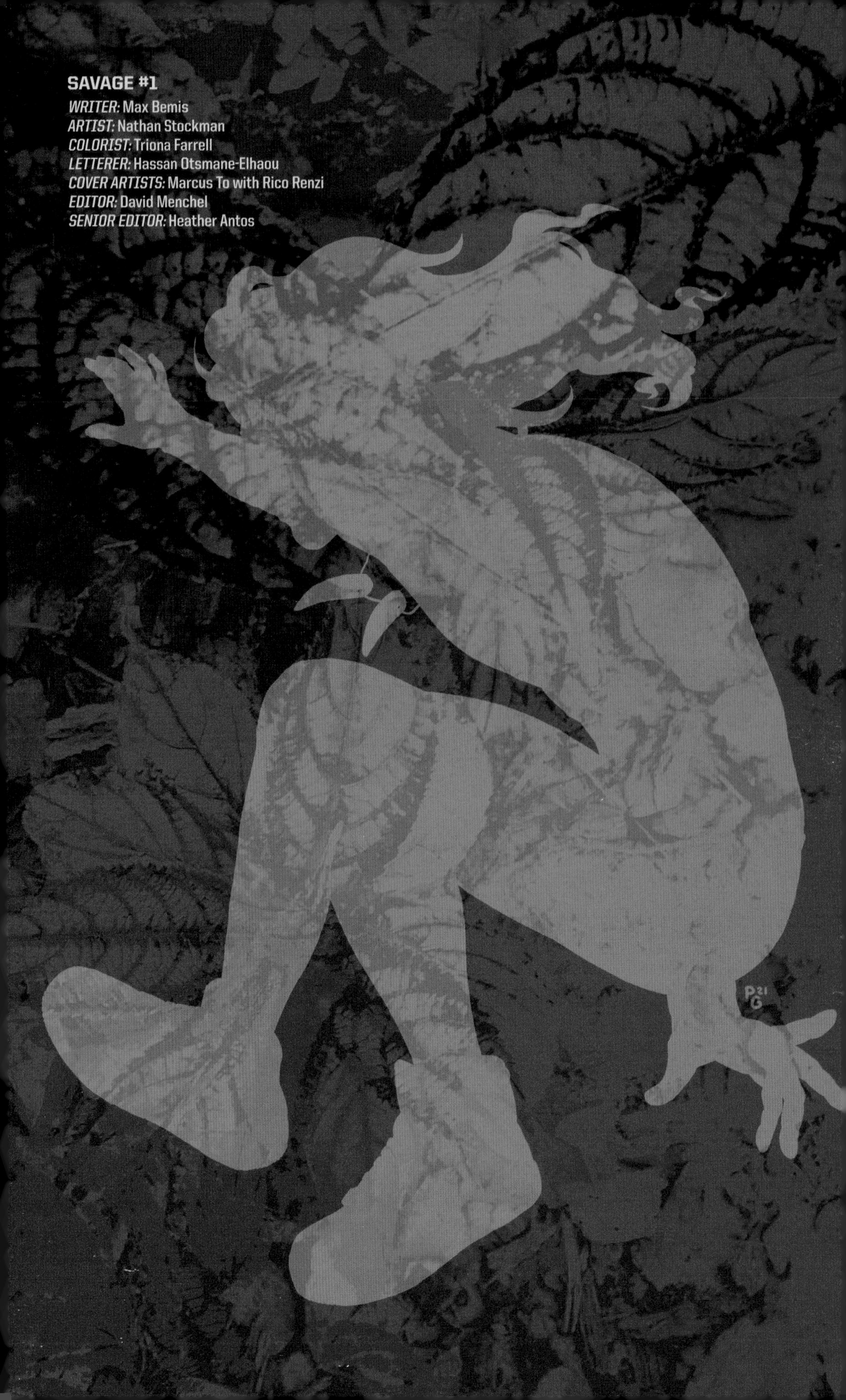

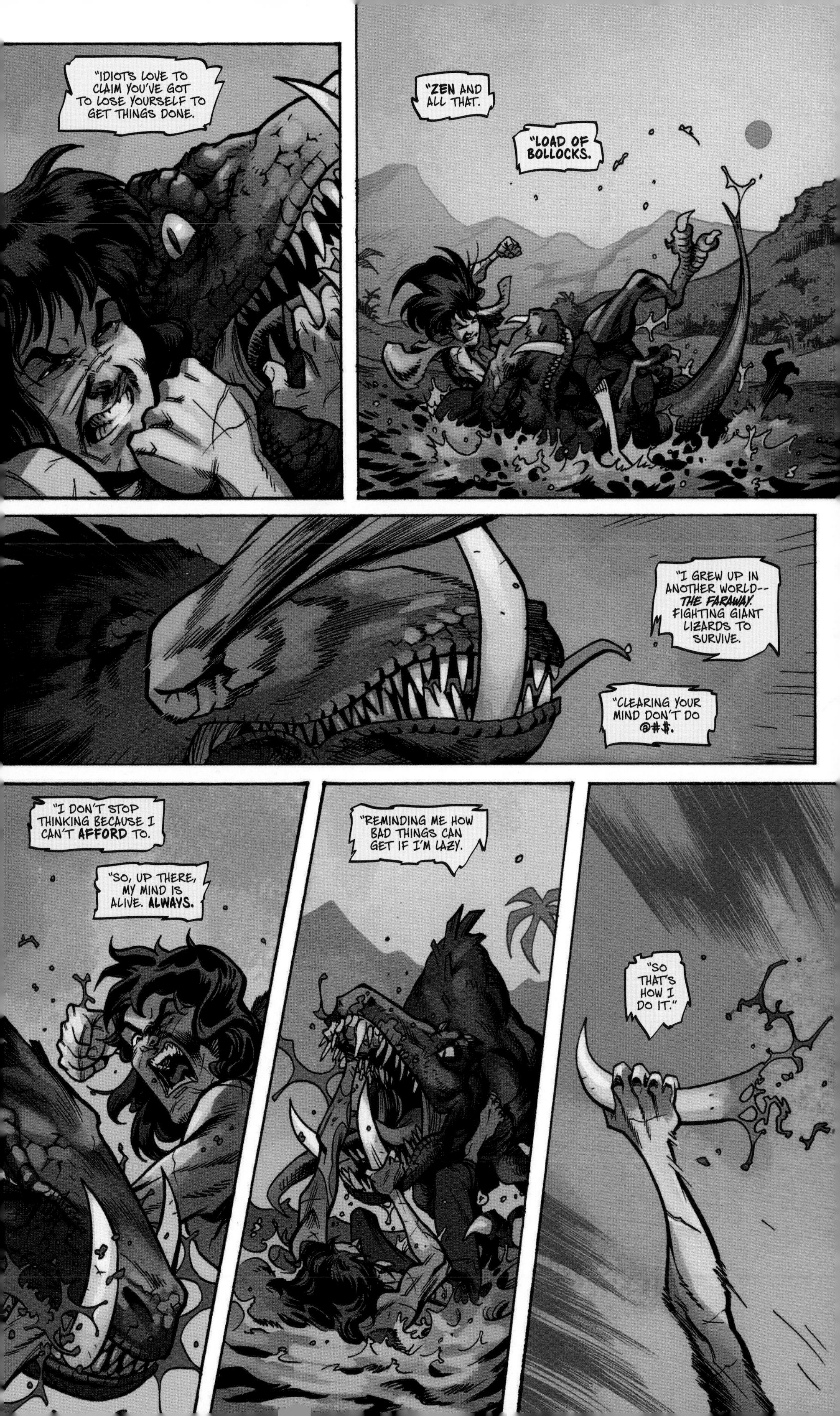
"IDIOTS LOVE TO CLAIM YOU'VE GOT TO LOSE YOURSELF TO GET THINGS DONE.
"ZEN AND ALL THAT.
"LOAD OF BOLLOCKS.
"I GREW UP IN ANOTHER WORLD-- *THE FARAWAY.* FIGHTING GIANT LIZARDS TO SURVIVE.
"CLEARING YOUR MIND DON'T DO @#$.
"I DON'T STOP THINKING BECAUSE I CAN'T **AFFORD** TO.
"SO, UP THERE, MY MIND IS ALIVE. **ALWAYS.**
"REMINDING ME HOW BAD THINGS CAN GET IF I'M LAZY.
"SO THAT'S HOW I DO IT."

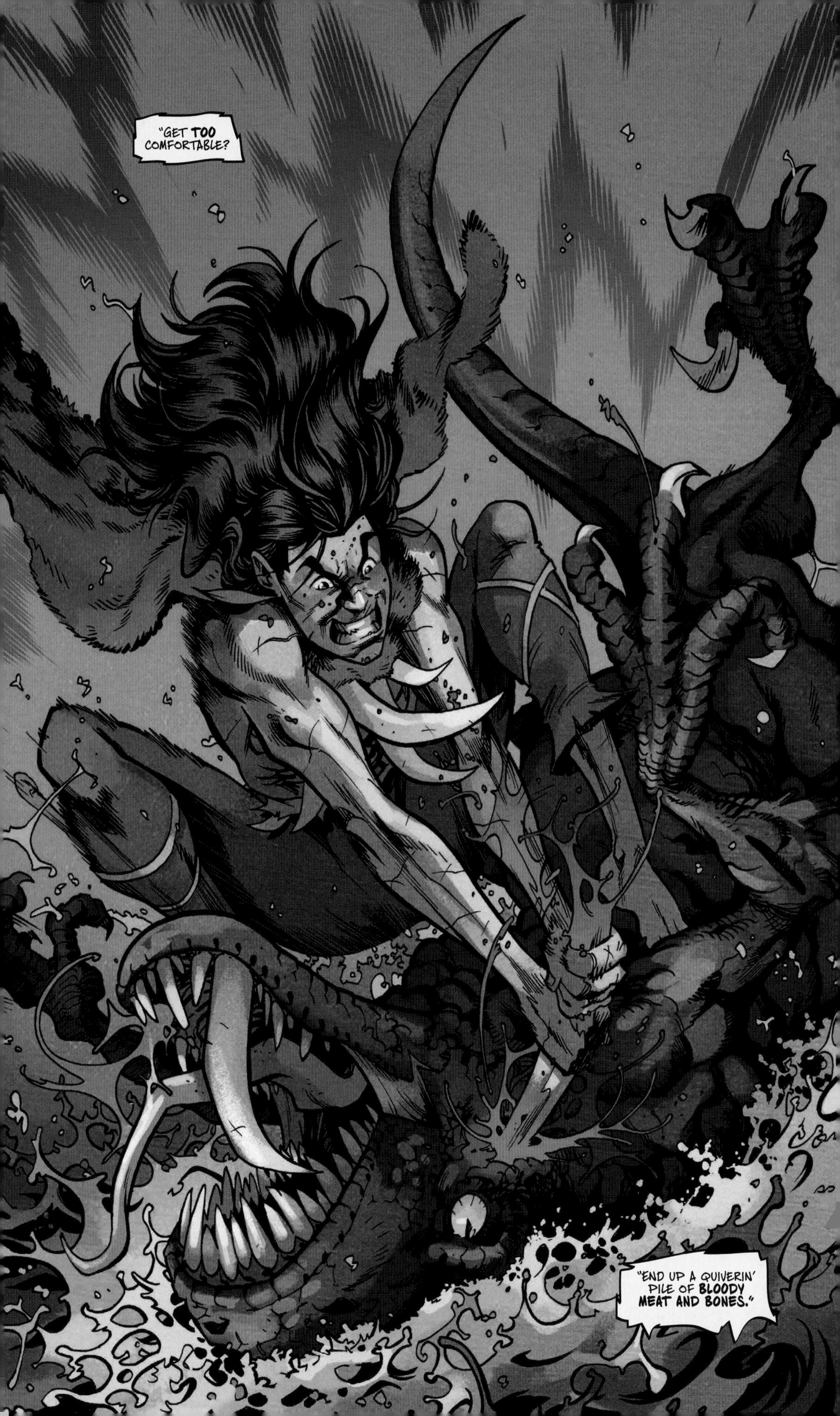
"GET TOO COMFORTABLE?
"END UP A QUIVERIN' PILE OF BLOODY MEAT AND BONES."

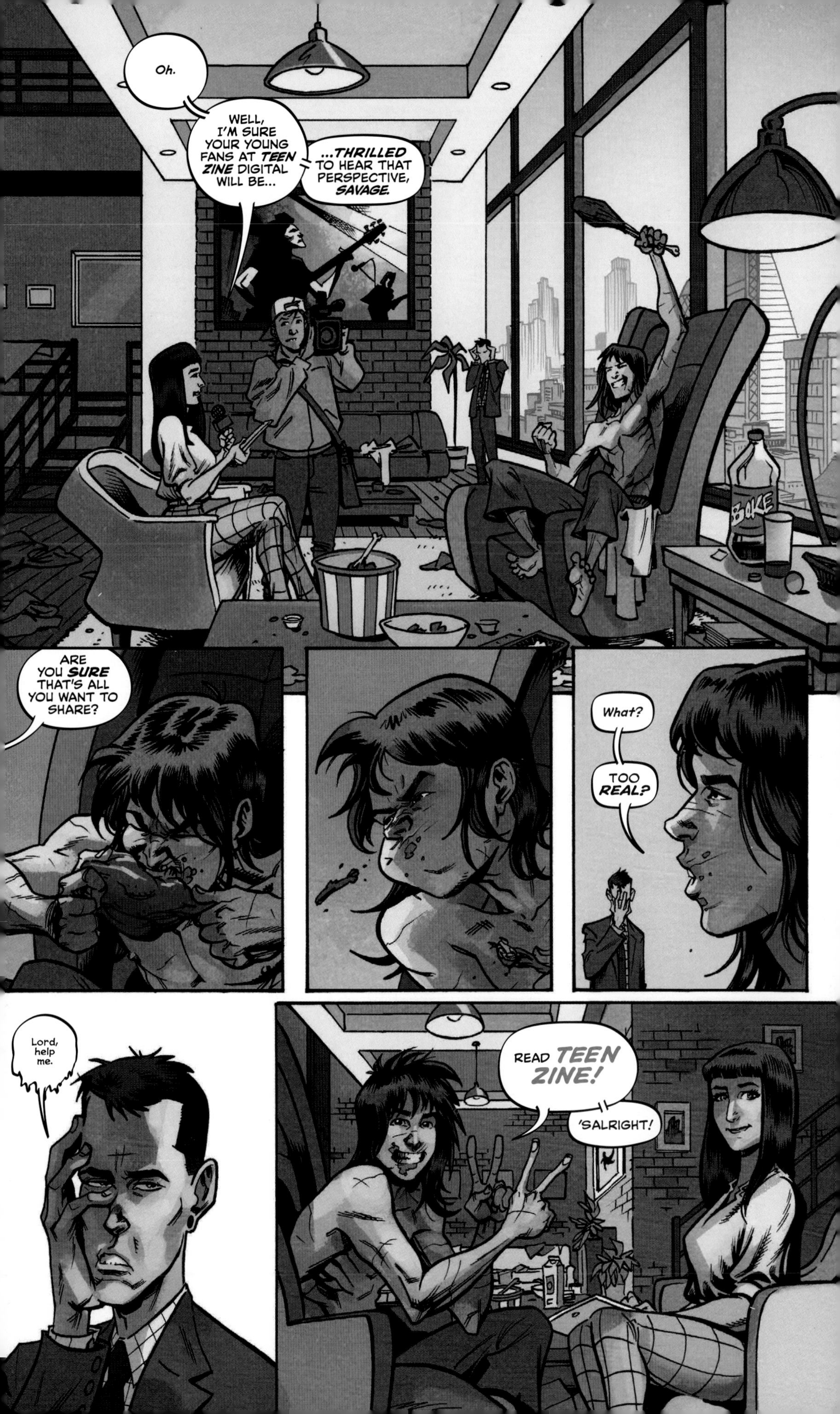
Oh.
WELL, I'M SURE YOUR YOUNG FANS AT TEEN ZINE DIGITAL WILL BE...
...THRILLED TO HEAR THAT PERSPECTIVE, SAVAGE.
ARE YOU SURE THAT'S ALL YOU WANT TO SHARE?
What?
TOO REAL?
Lord, help me.
READ TEEN ZINE!
'SALRIGHT!

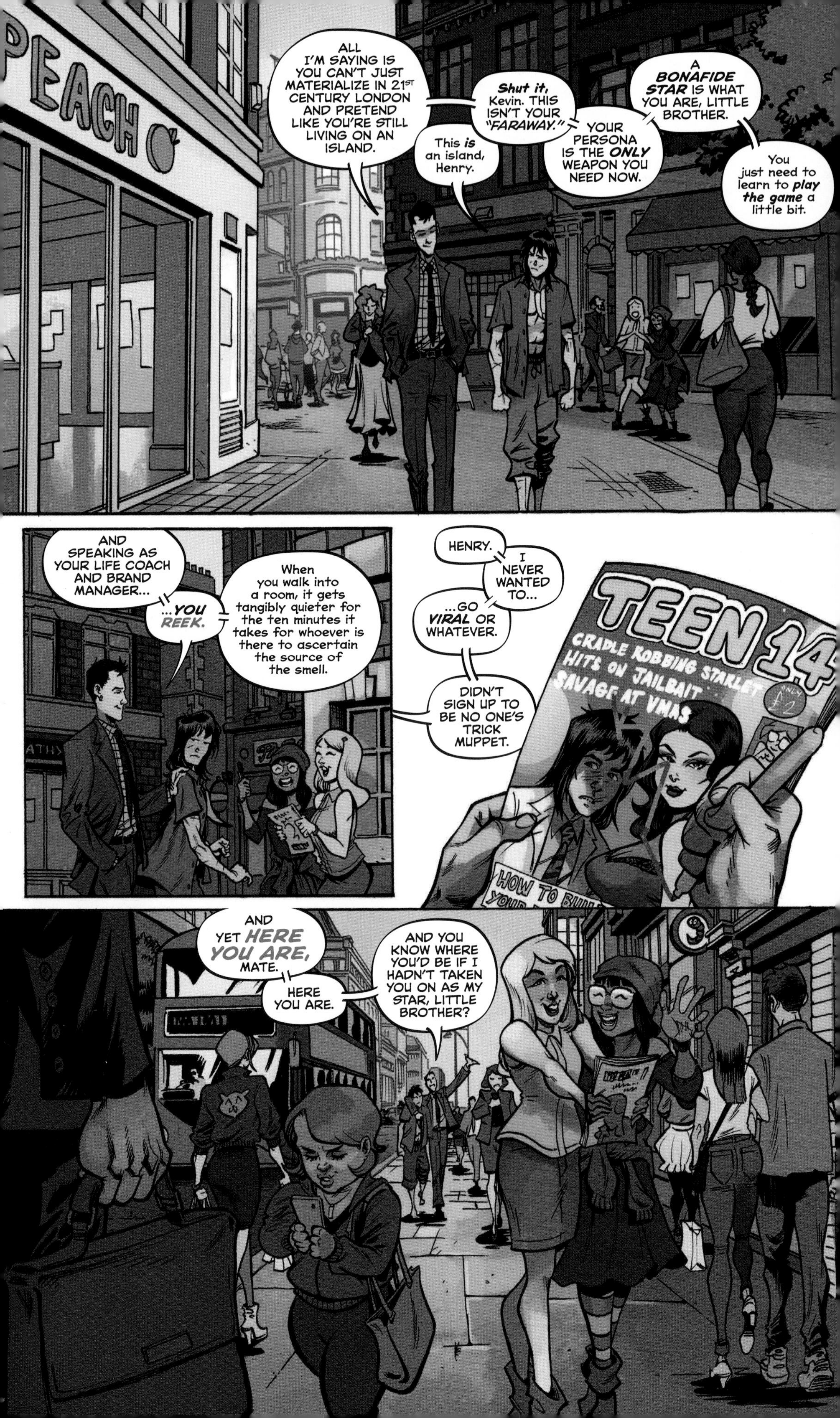
PEACH
ALL I'M SAYING IS YOU CAN'T JUST MATERIALIZE IN 21ST CENTURY LONDON AND PRETEND LIKE YOU'RE STILL LIVING ON AN ISLAND.
This is an island, Henry.
Shut it, Kevin. THIS ISN'T YOUR "FARAWAY."
YOUR PERSONA IS THE ONLY WEAPON YOU NEED NOW.
A BONAFIDE STAR IS WHAT YOU ARE, LITTLE BROTHER.
You just need to learn to play the game a little bit.
AND SPEAKING AS YOUR LIFE COACH AND BRAND MANAGER...
...YOU REEK.
When you walk into a room, it gets tangibly quieter for the ten minutes it takes for whoever is there to ascertain the source of the smell.
HENRY.
I NEVER WANTED TO...
...GO VIRAL OR WHATEVER.
DIDN'T SIGN UP TO BE NO ONE'S TRICK MUPPET.
TEEN 14
CRADLE ROBBING STARLET HITS ON JAILBAIT SAVAGE AT VMAS
ONLY £2
HOW TO BUIL
AND YET HERE YOU ARE, MATE.
HERE YOU ARE.
AND YOU KNOW WHERE YOU'D BE IF I HADN'T TAKEN YOU ON AS MY STAR, LITTLE BROTHER?

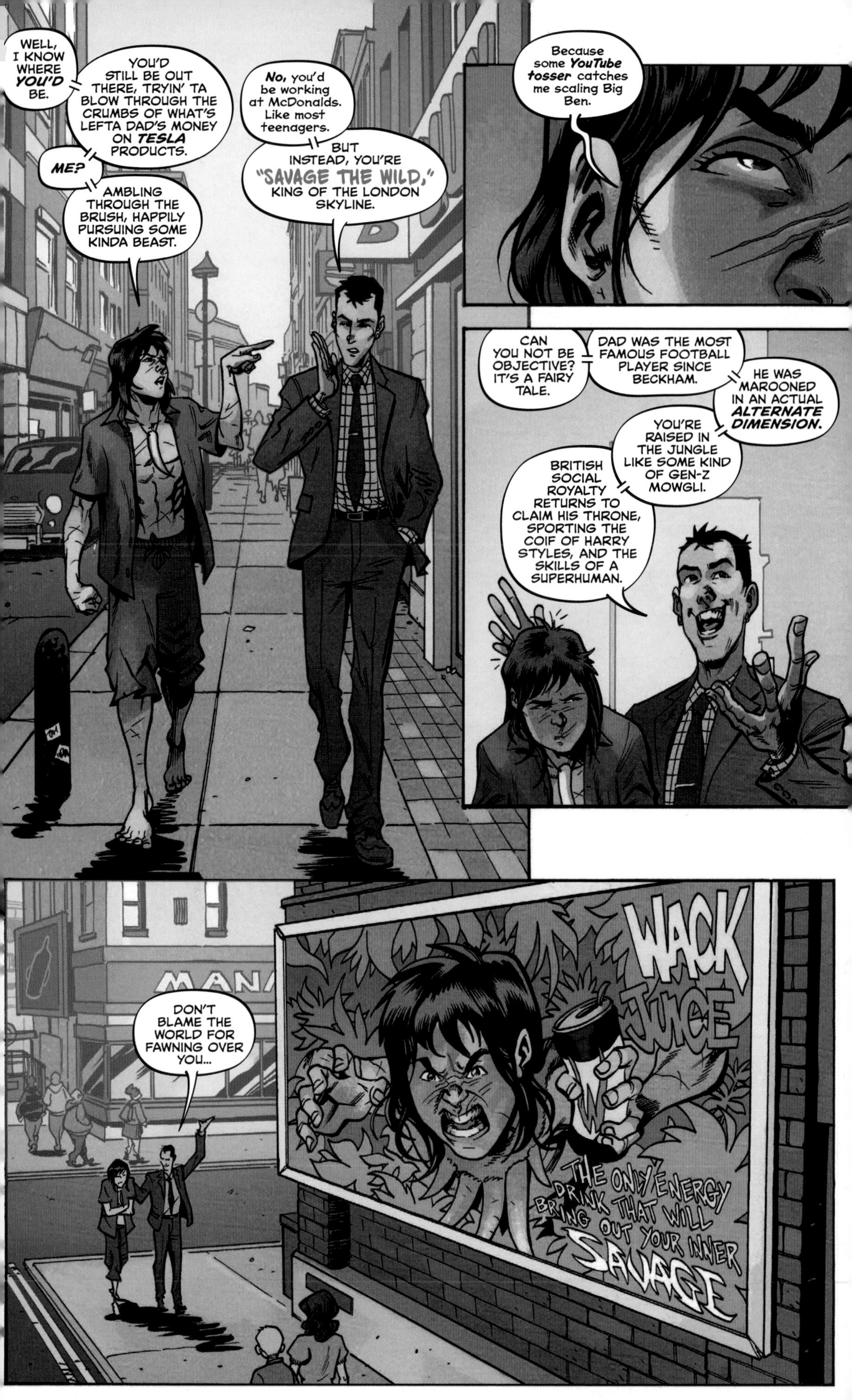

WELL, I KNOW WHERE ***YOU'D*** BE.
YOU'D STILL BE OUT THERE, TRYIN' TA BLOW THROUGH THE CRUMBS OF WHAT'S LEFTA DAD'S MONEY ON ***TESLA*** PRODUCTS.
***ME?***
AMBLING THROUGH THE BRUSH, HAPPILY PURSUING SOME KINDA BEAST.
***No,*** you'd be working at McDonalds. Like most teenagers.
BUT INSTEAD, YOU'RE "SAVAGE THE WILD," KING OF THE LONDON SKYLINE.
Because some ***YouTube tosser*** catches me scaling Big Ben.
CAN YOU NOT BE OBJECTIVE? IT'S A FAIRY TALE.
DAD WAS THE MOST FAMOUS FOOTBALL PLAYER SINCE BECKHAM.
HE WAS MAROONED IN AN ACTUAL ***ALTERNATE DIMENSION.***
YOU'RE RAISED IN THE JUNGLE LIKE SOME KIND OF GEN-Z MOWGLI.
BRITISH SOCIAL ROYALTY RETURNS TO CLAIM HIS THRONE, SPORTING THE COIF OF HARRY STYLES, AND THE SKILLS OF A SUPERHUMAN.
MANA
DON'T BLAME THE WORLD FOR FAWNING OVER YOU...
WACK JUICE
THE ONLY ENERGY DRINK THAT WILL BRING OUT YOUR INNER SAVAGE

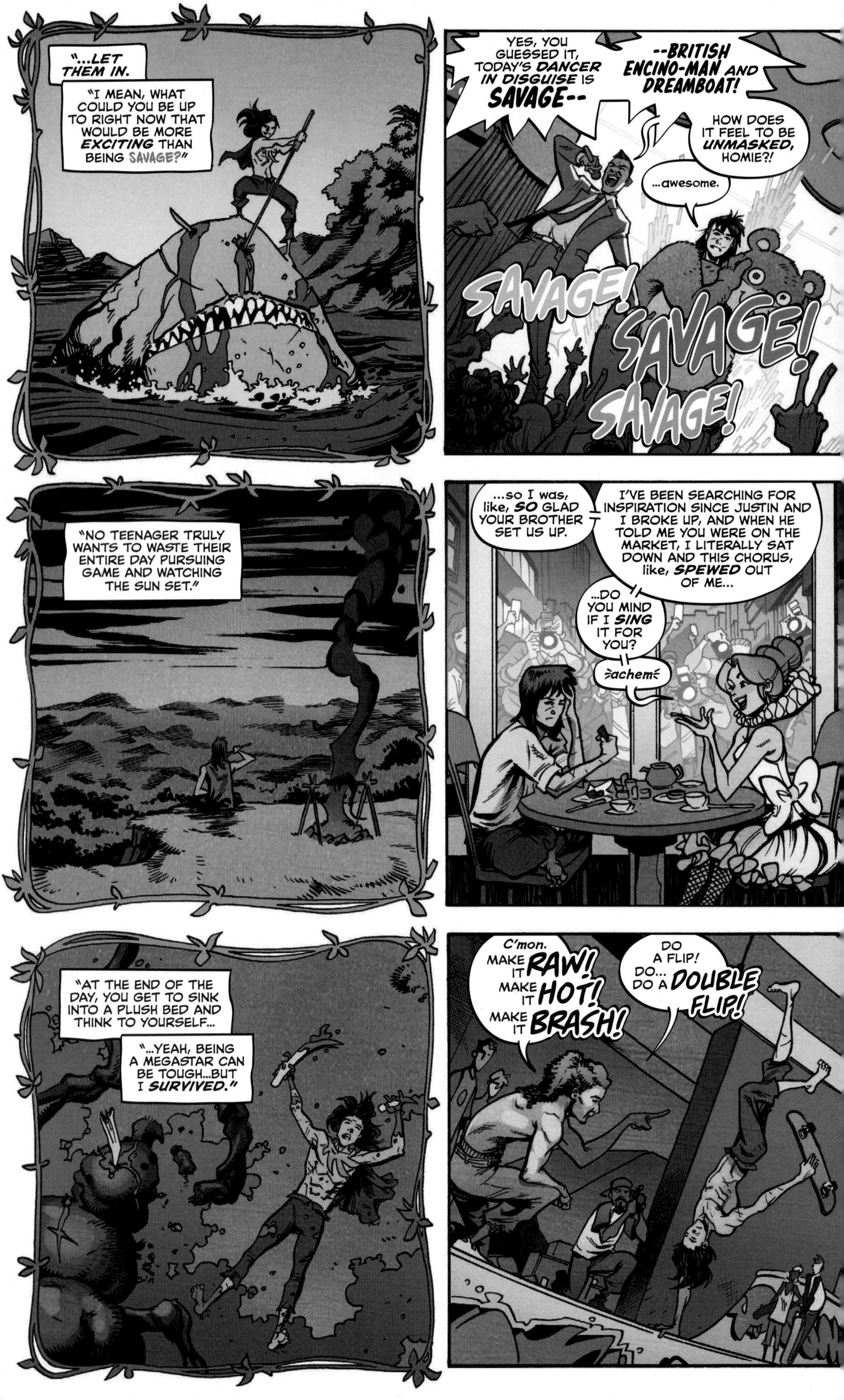
"...LET THEM IN.
"I MEAN, WHAT COULD YOU BE UP TO RIGHT NOW THAT WOULD BE MORE EXCITING THAN BEING SAVAGE?"
YES, YOU GUESSED IT, TODAY'S DANCER IN DISGUISE IS SAVAGE--
--BRITISH ENCINO-MAN AND DREAMBOAT!
HOW DOES IT FEEL TO BE UNMASKED, HOMIE?!
...awesome.
SAVAGE! SAVAGE! SAVAGE!
"NO TEENAGER TRULY WANTS TO WASTE THEIR ENTIRE DAY PURSUING GAME AND WATCHING THE SUN SET."
...so I was, like, SO GLAD YOUR BROTHER SET US UP.
I'VE BEEN SEARCHING FOR INSPIRATION SINCE JUSTIN AND I BROKE UP, AND WHEN HE TOLD ME YOU WERE ON THE MARKET, I LITERALLY SAT DOWN AND THIS CHORUS, like, SPEWED OUT OF ME...
...DO YOU MIND IF I SING IT FOR YOU?
achem
"AT THE END OF THE DAY, YOU GET TO SINK INTO A PLUSH BED AND THINK TO YOURSELF...
"...YEAH, BEING A MEGASTAR CAN BE TOUGH...BUT I SURVIVED."
C'mon. MAKE IT RAW! MAKE IT HOT! MAKE IT BRASH!
DO A FLIP! DO... DO A DOUBLE FLIP!

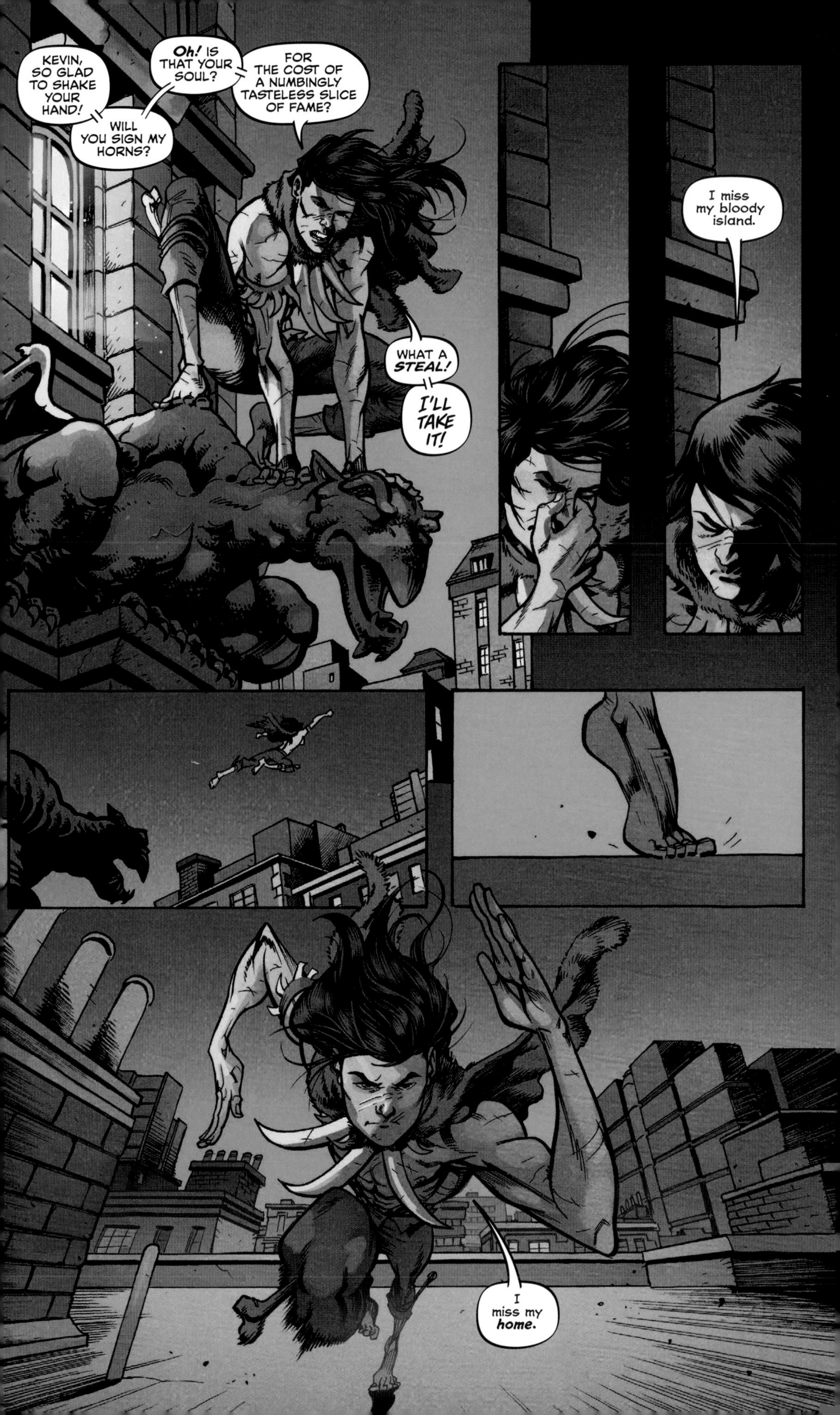
KEVIN, SO GLAD TO SHAKE YOUR HAND!
WILL YOU SIGN MY HORNS?
Oh! IS THAT YOUR SOUL?
FOR THE COST OF A NUMBINGLY TASTELESS SLICE OF FAME?
WHAT A STEAL!
I'LL TAKE IT!
I miss my bloody island.
I miss my home.

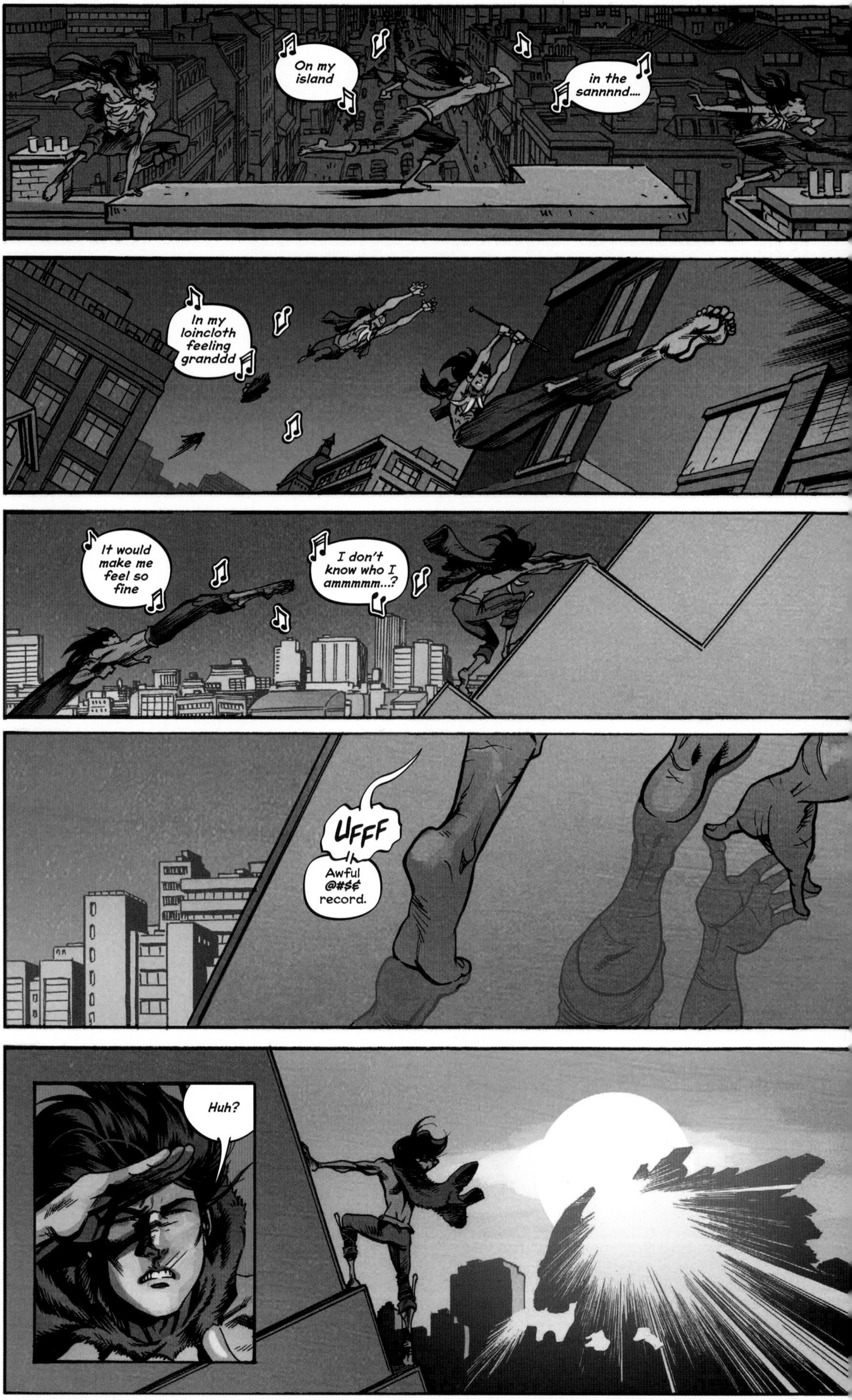
On my island
in the sannnnd....
In my loincloth feeling granddd
It would make me feel so fine
I don't know who I ammmmm...?
UFFF
Awful @#$¢ record.
Huh?

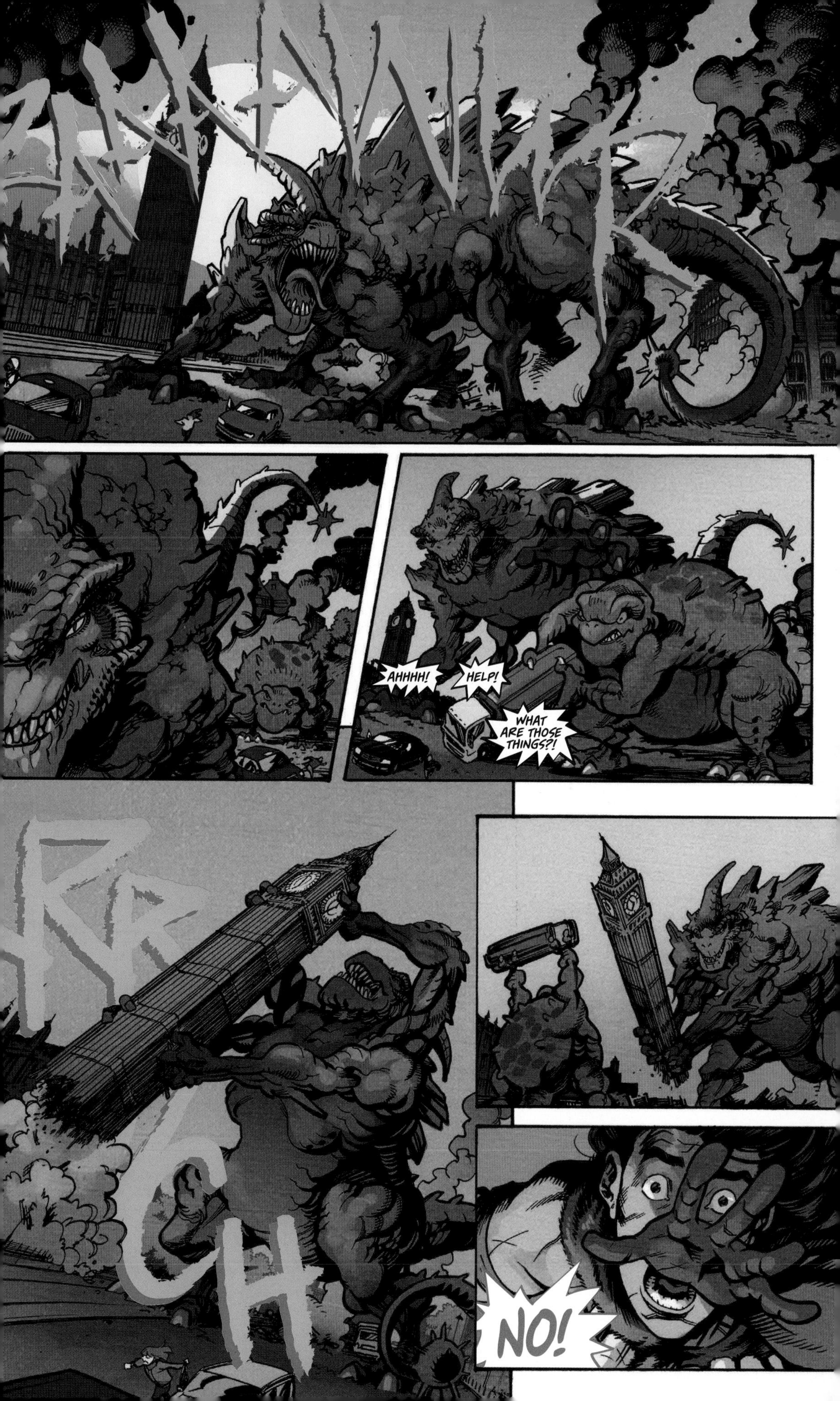
AHHHH!
HELP!
WHAT ARE THOSE THINGS?!
NO!

WHOO

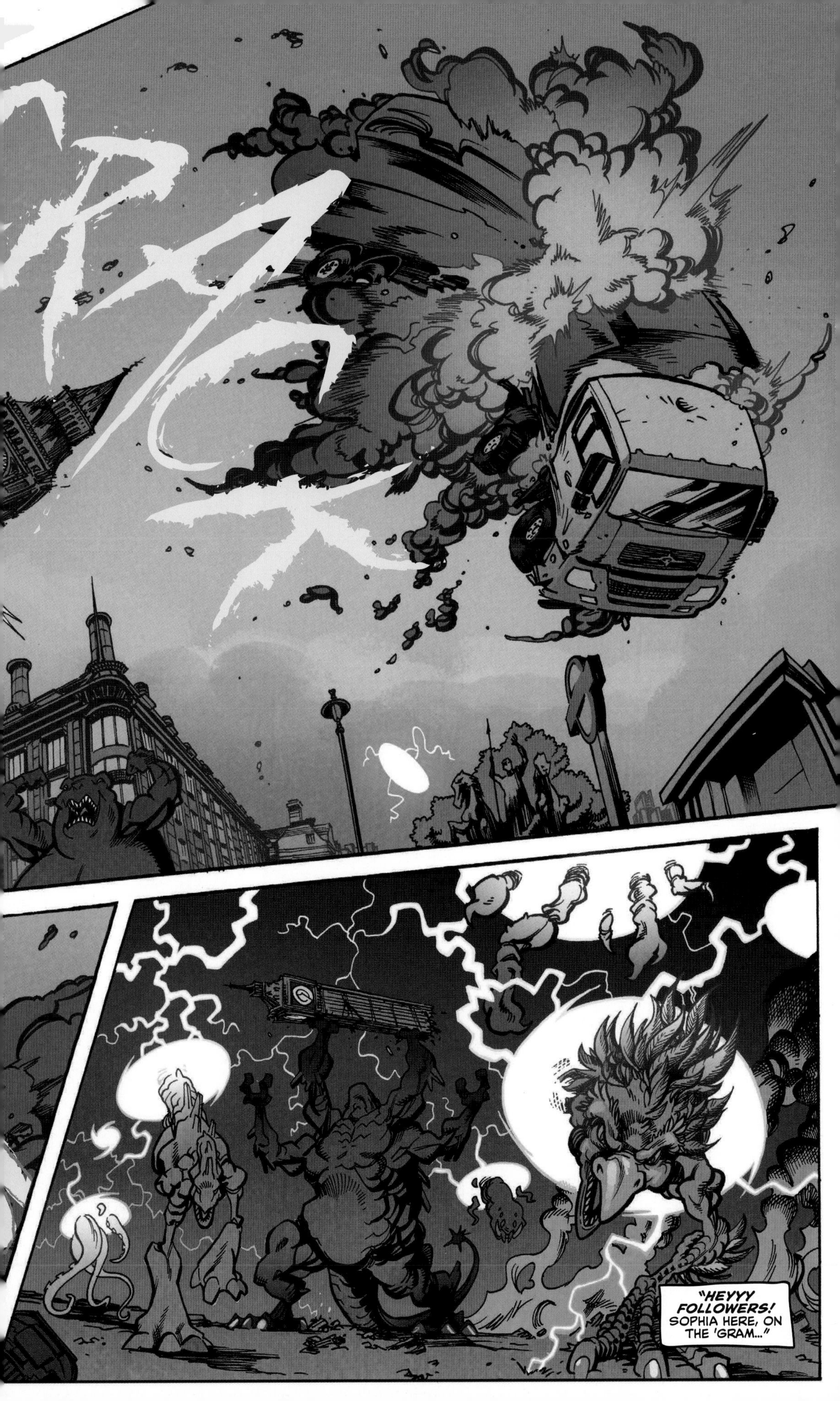
"HEYYY FOLLOWERS!
SOPHIA HERE, ON THE 'GRAM..."

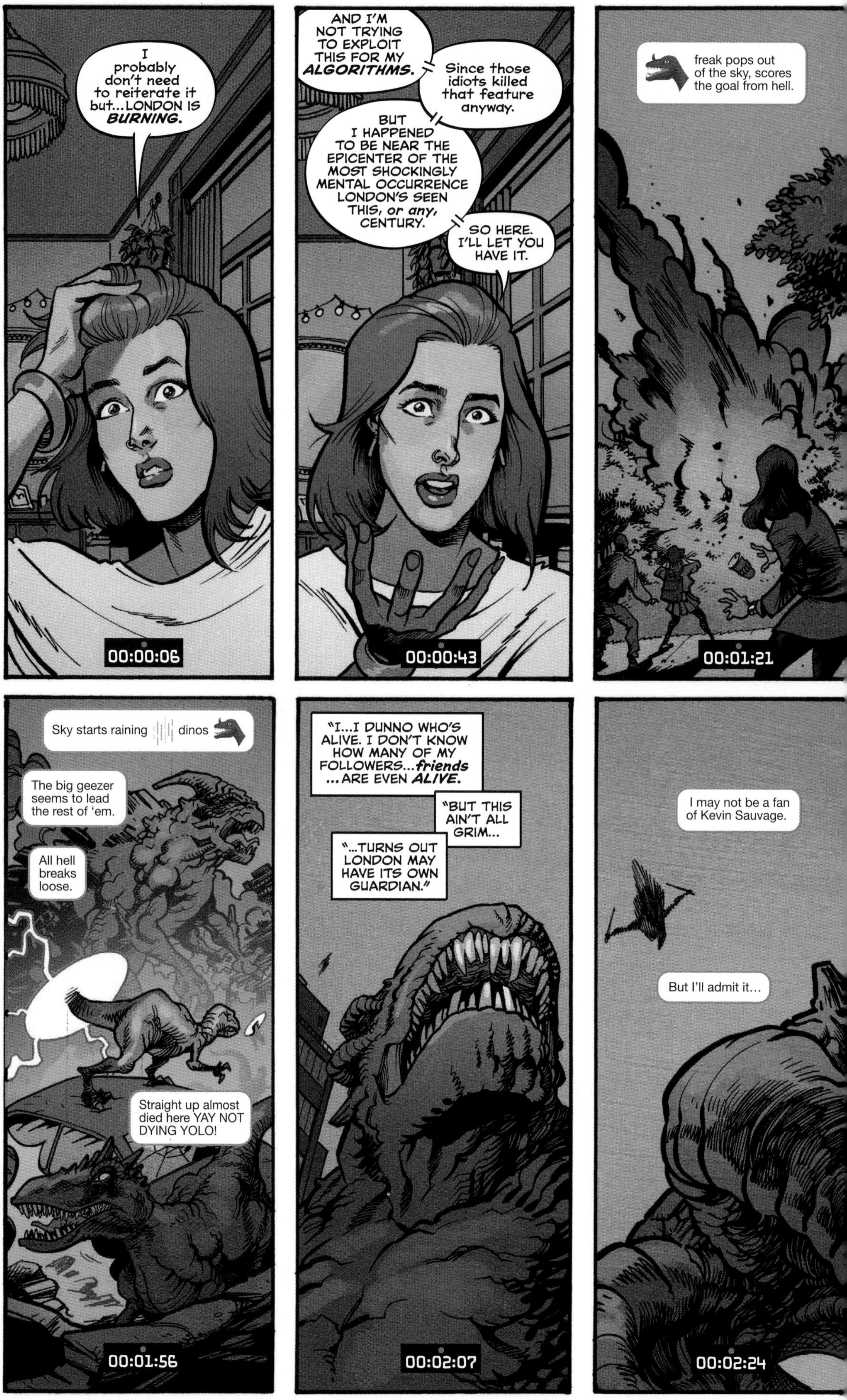
I probably don't need to reiterate it but...LONDON IS BURNING.
00:00:06
AND I'M NOT TRYING TO EXPLOIT THIS FOR MY ALGORITHMS.
Since those idiots killed that feature anyway.
BUT I HAPPENED TO BE NEAR THE EPICENTER OF THE MOST SHOCKINGLY MENTAL OCCURRENCE LONDON'S SEEN THIS, or any, CENTURY.
SO HERE. I'LL LET YOU HAVE IT.
00:00:43
freak pops out of the sky, scores the goal from hell.
00:01:21
Sky starts raining dinos
The big geezer seems to lead the rest of 'em.
All hell breaks loose.
Straight up almost died here YAY NOT DYING YOLO!
00:01:56
"I...I DUNNO WHO'S ALIVE. I DON'T KNOW HOW MANY OF MY FOLLOWERS...friends ...ARE EVEN ALIVE.
"BUT THIS AIN'T ALL GRIM...
"...TURNS OUT LONDON MAY HAVE ITS OWN GUARDIAN."
00:02:07
I may not be a fan of Kevin Sauvage.
But I'll admit it...
00:02:24

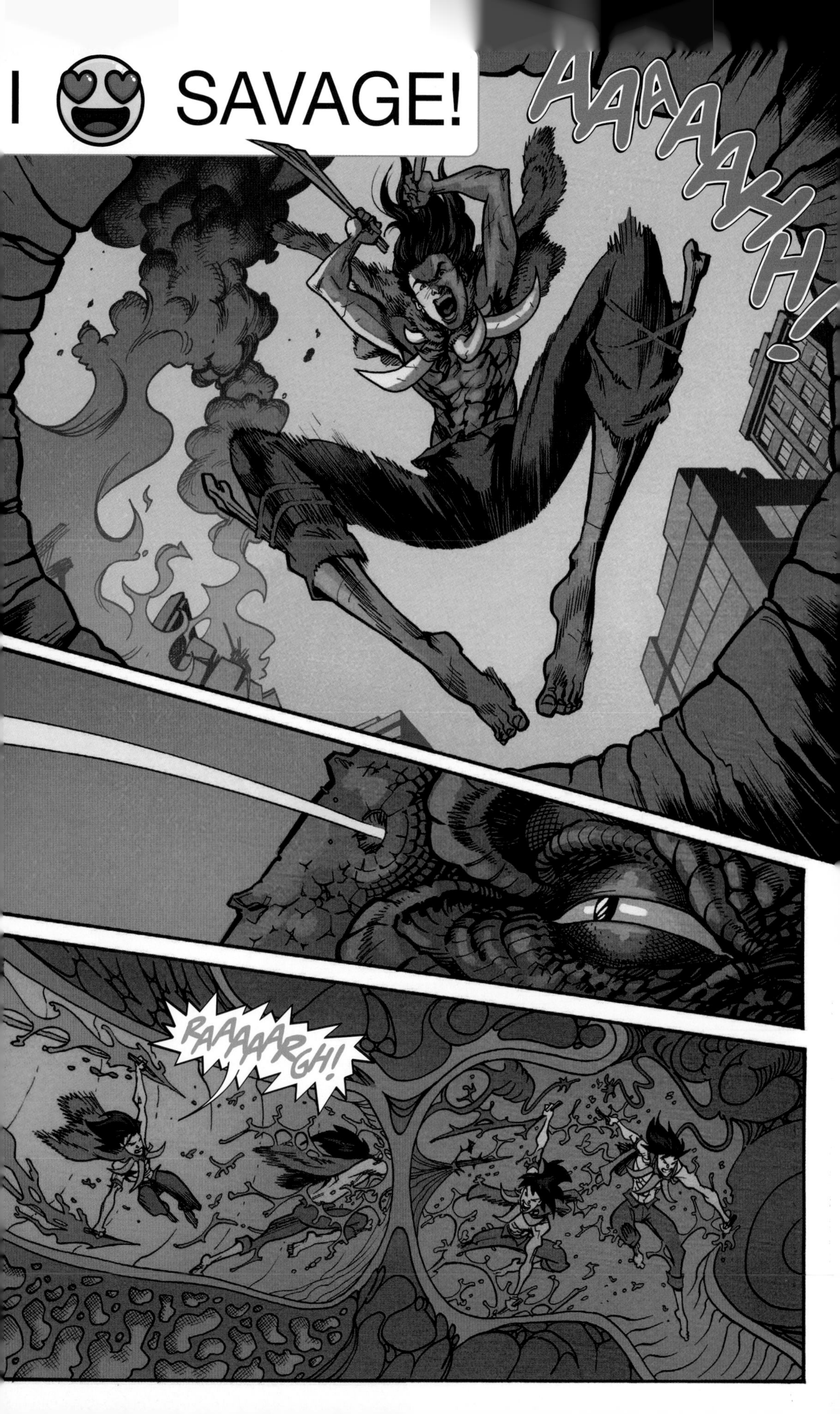
I 😍 SAVAGE!
AAAAAKH!!
RAAAAARGH!

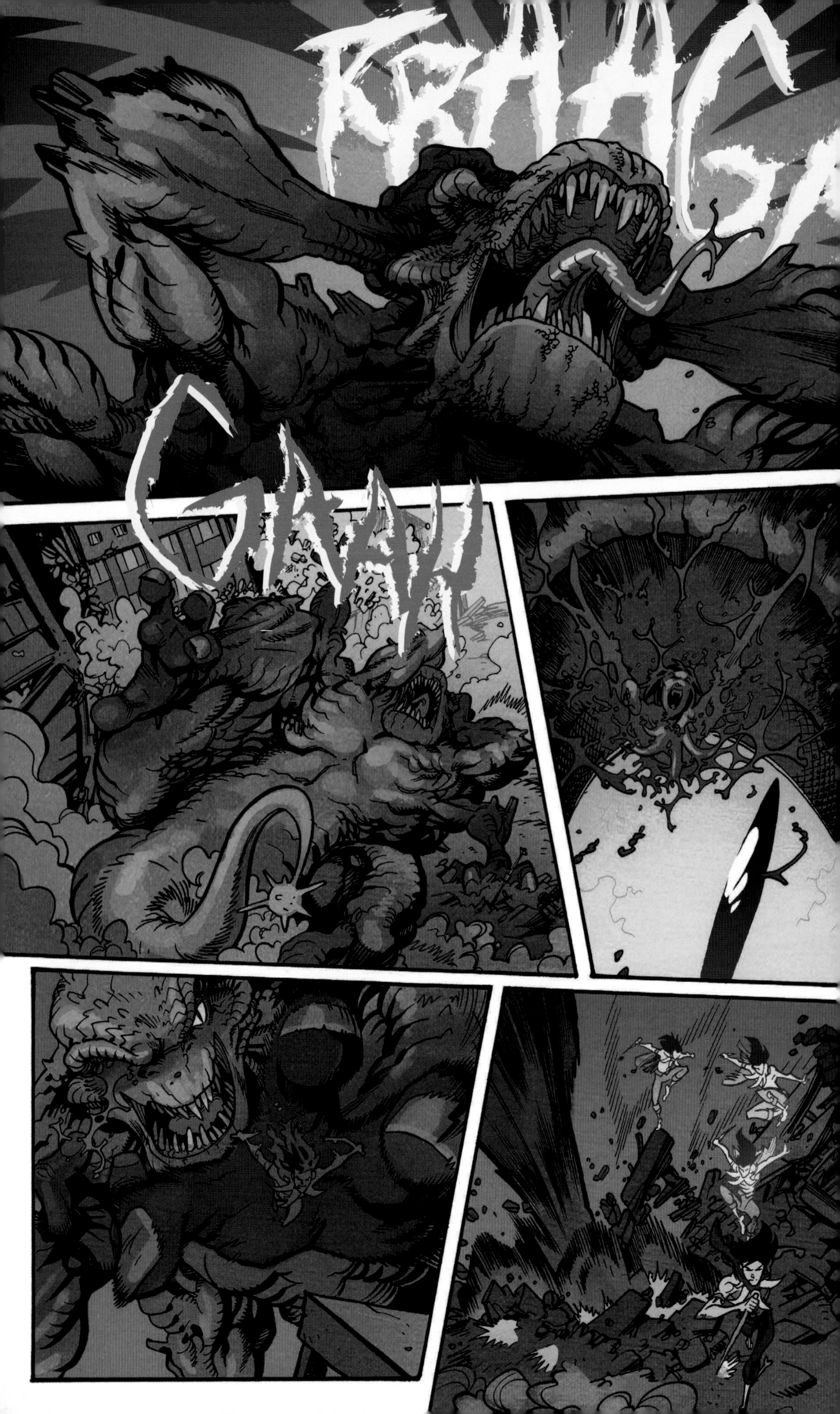

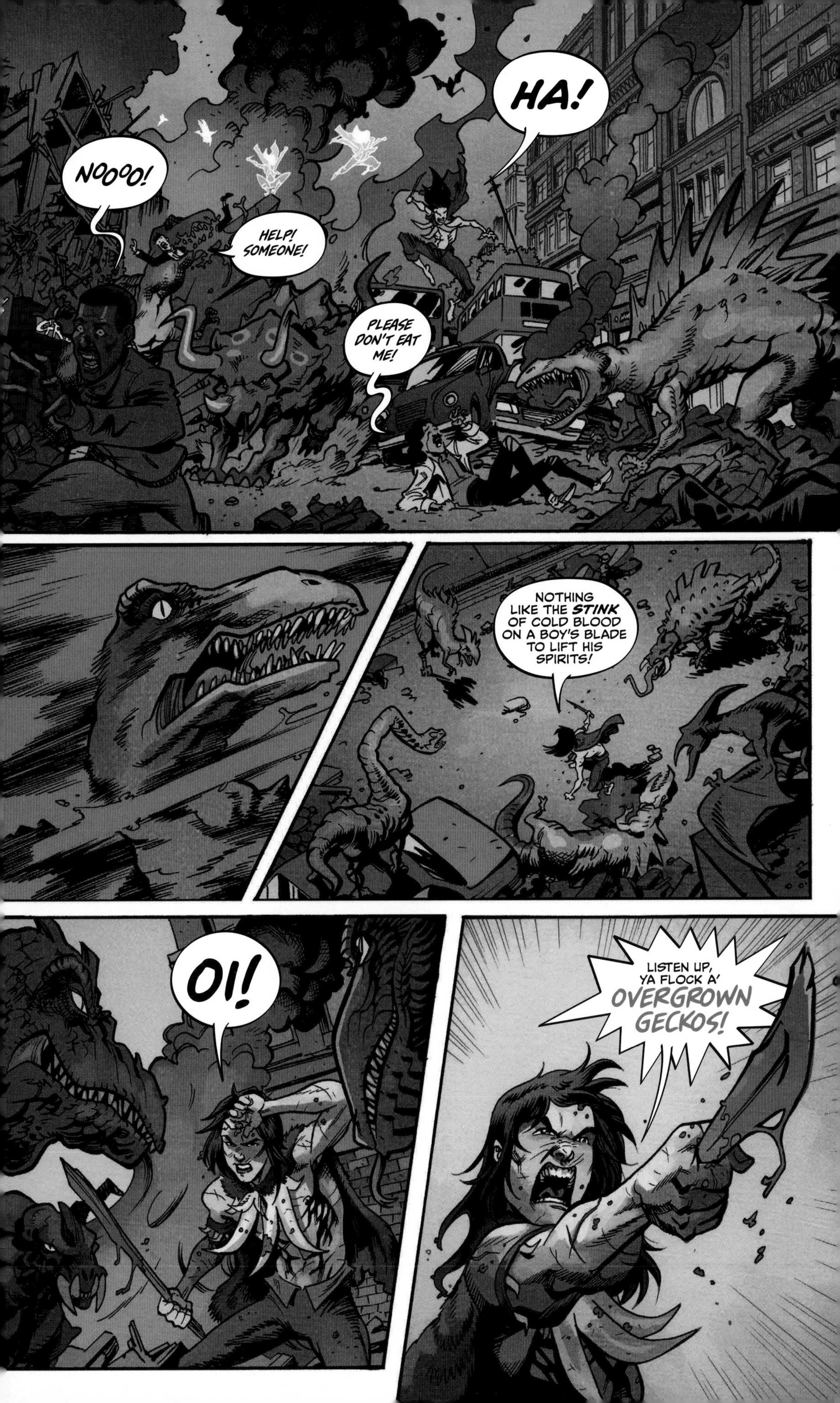
HA!
NOOOO!
HELP! SOMEONE!
PLEASE DON'T EAT ME!
NOTHING LIKE THE STINK OF COLD BLOOD ON A BOY'S BLADE TO LIFT HIS SPIRITS!
OI!
LISTEN UP, YA FLOCK A' OVERGROWN GECKOS!

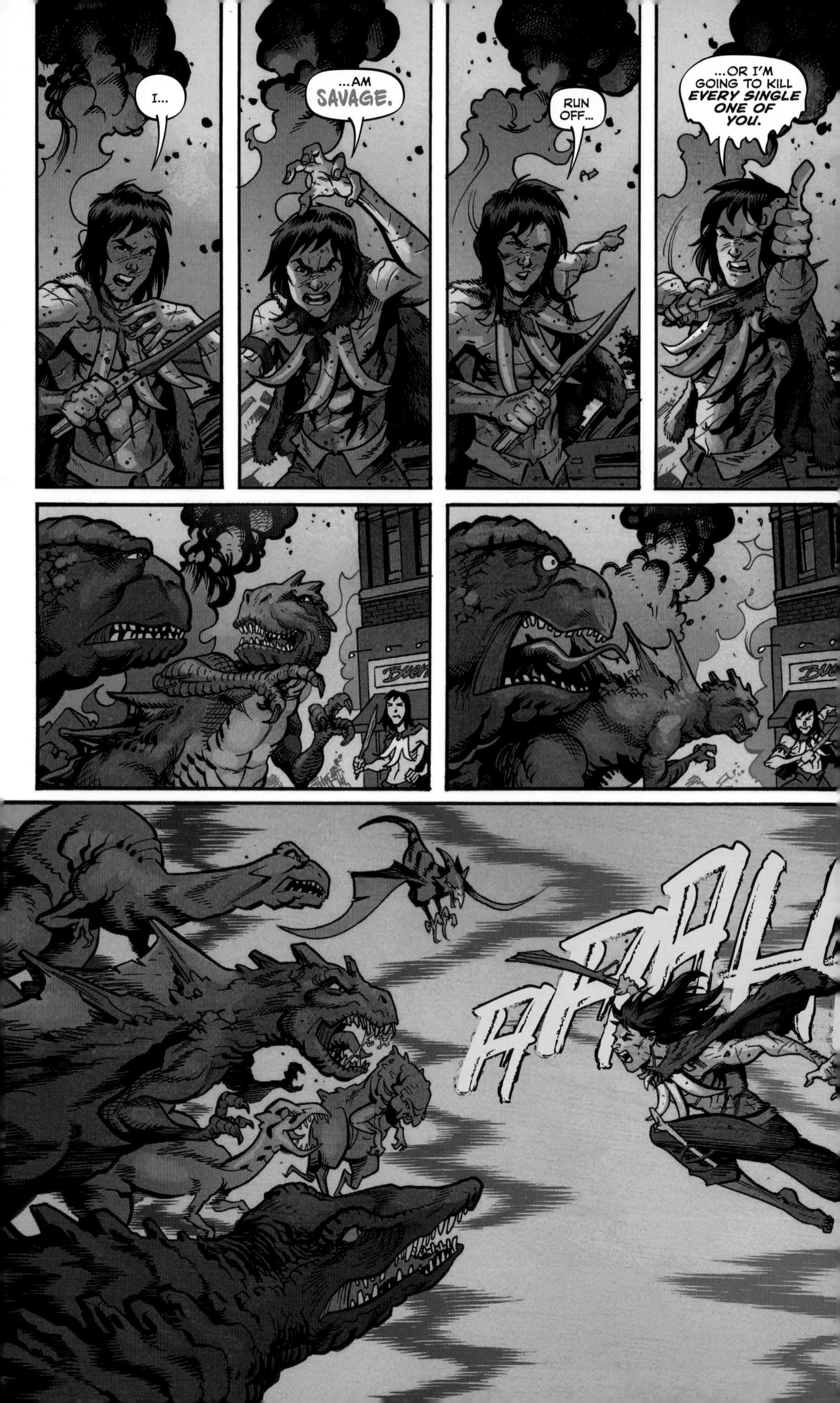
I...
...AM SAVAGE.
RUN OFF...
...OR I'M GOING TO KILL EVERY SINGLE ONE OF YOU.

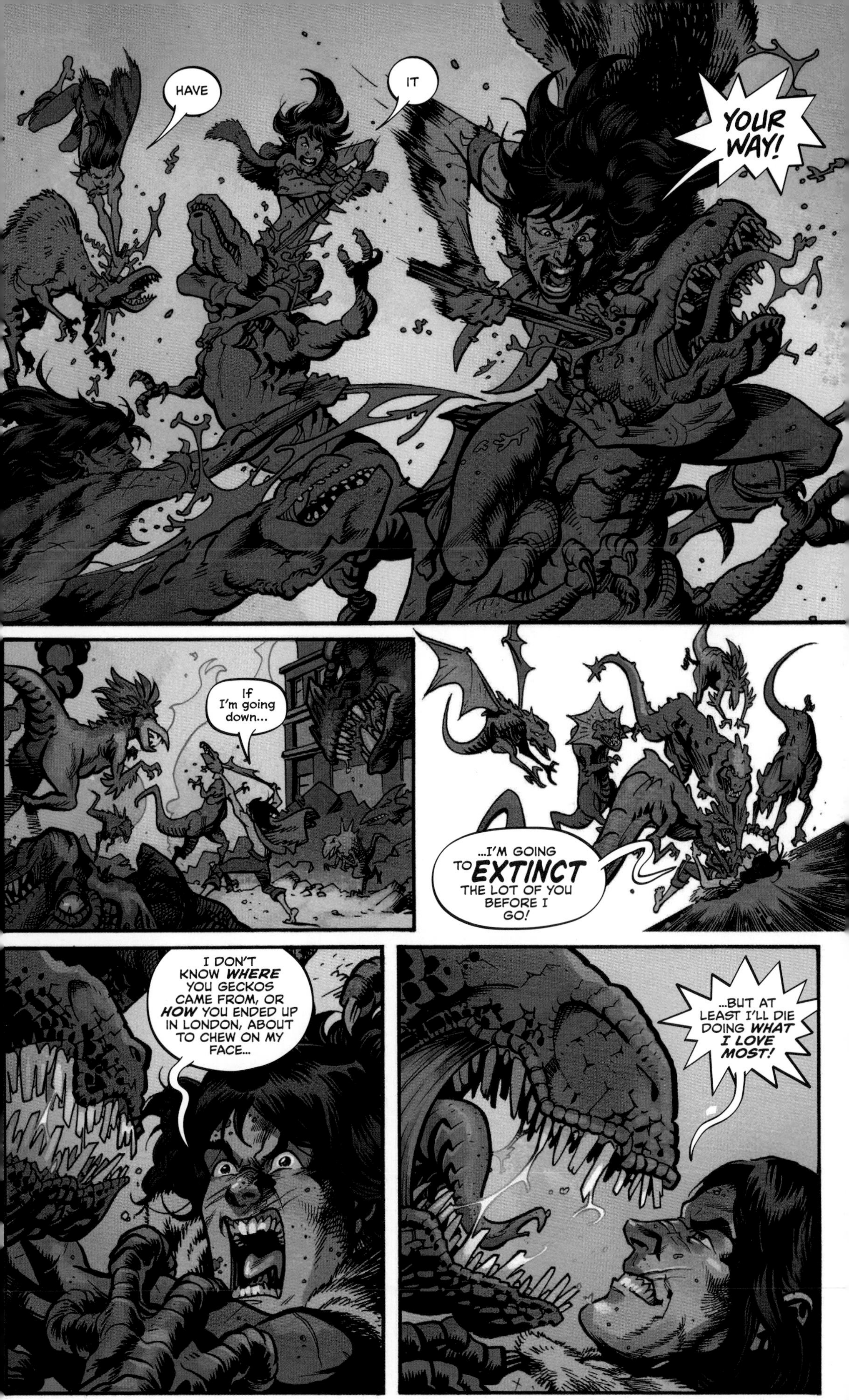
HAVE
IT
YOUR WAY!
If I'm going down...
...I'M GOING TO EXTINCT THE LOT OF YOU BEFORE I GO!
I DON'T KNOW WHERE YOU GECKOS CAME FROM, OR HOW YOU ENDED UP IN LONDON, ABOUT TO CHEW ON MY FACE...
...BUT AT LEAST I'LL DIE DOING WHAT I LOVE MOST!

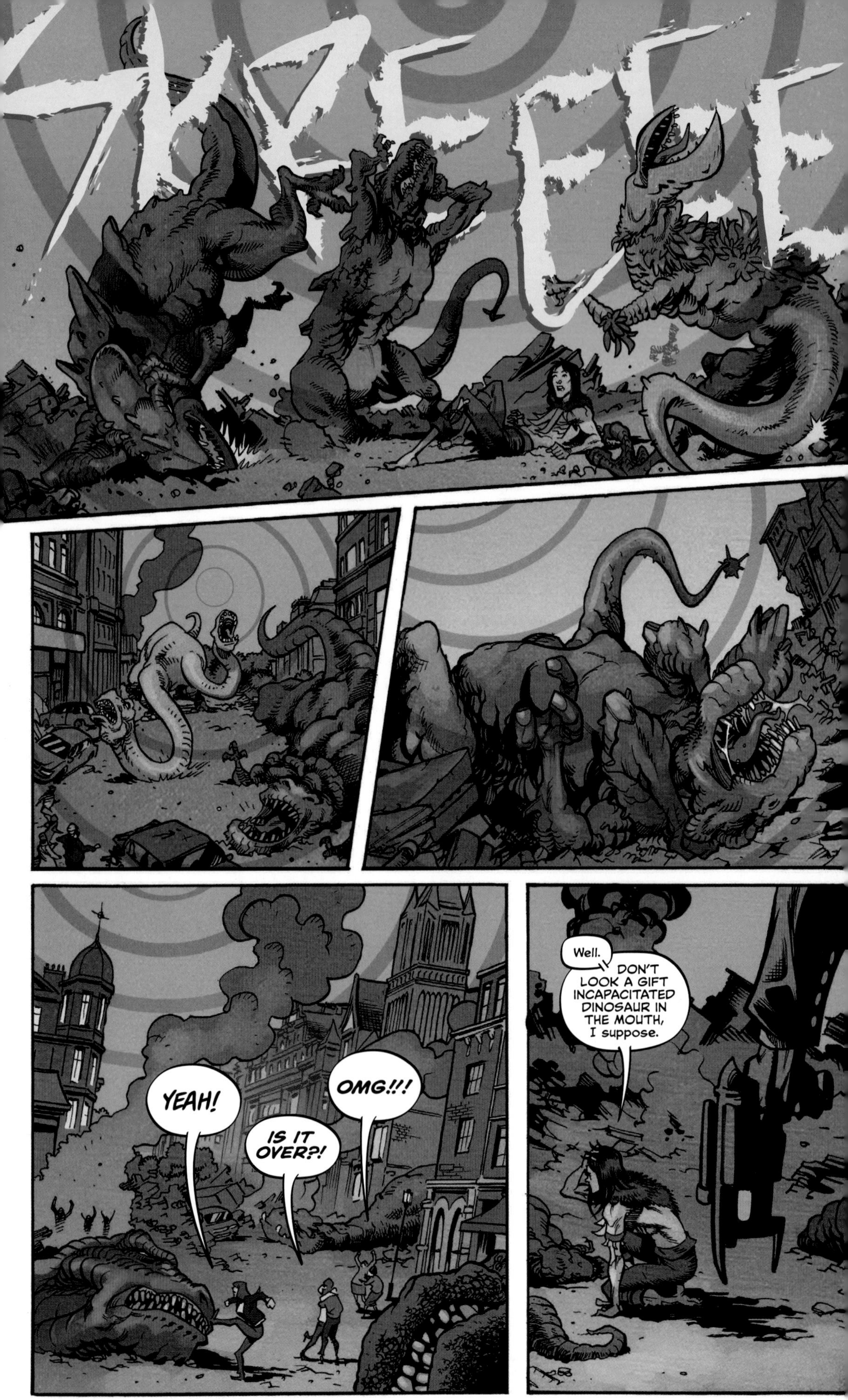
YEAH!
OMG!!!
IS IT OVER?!
Well.
DON'T LOOK A GIFT INCAPACITATED DINOSAUR IN THE MOUTH, I suppose.

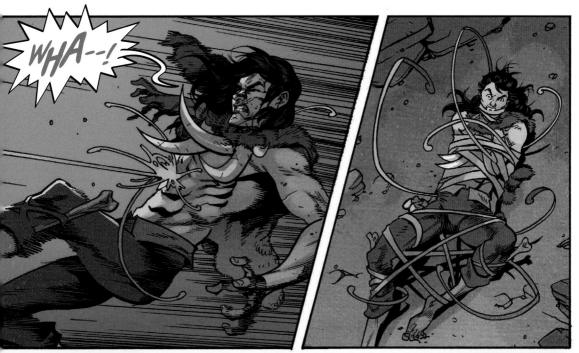

WHA--!

WELL, HE'S CERTAINLY MORE DIMINUTIVE THAN THE AVERAGE LIVING WEAPON.

YES, SIR. And what a *distinctive reek.*

STILL, HE MANAGED TO CONSIDERABLY THWART CONTROL GROUP A.

*FASCINATING.*

MR. SAUVAGE.

WE'RE *BIG* FANS OF YOUR YOUTUBE CHANNEL. SURVEILLANCE ON A SUBJECT HAS NEVER BEEN SO *EASY.* PITY YOU HAD TO RUIN TODAY'S LITTLE... *EXPERIMENT.*

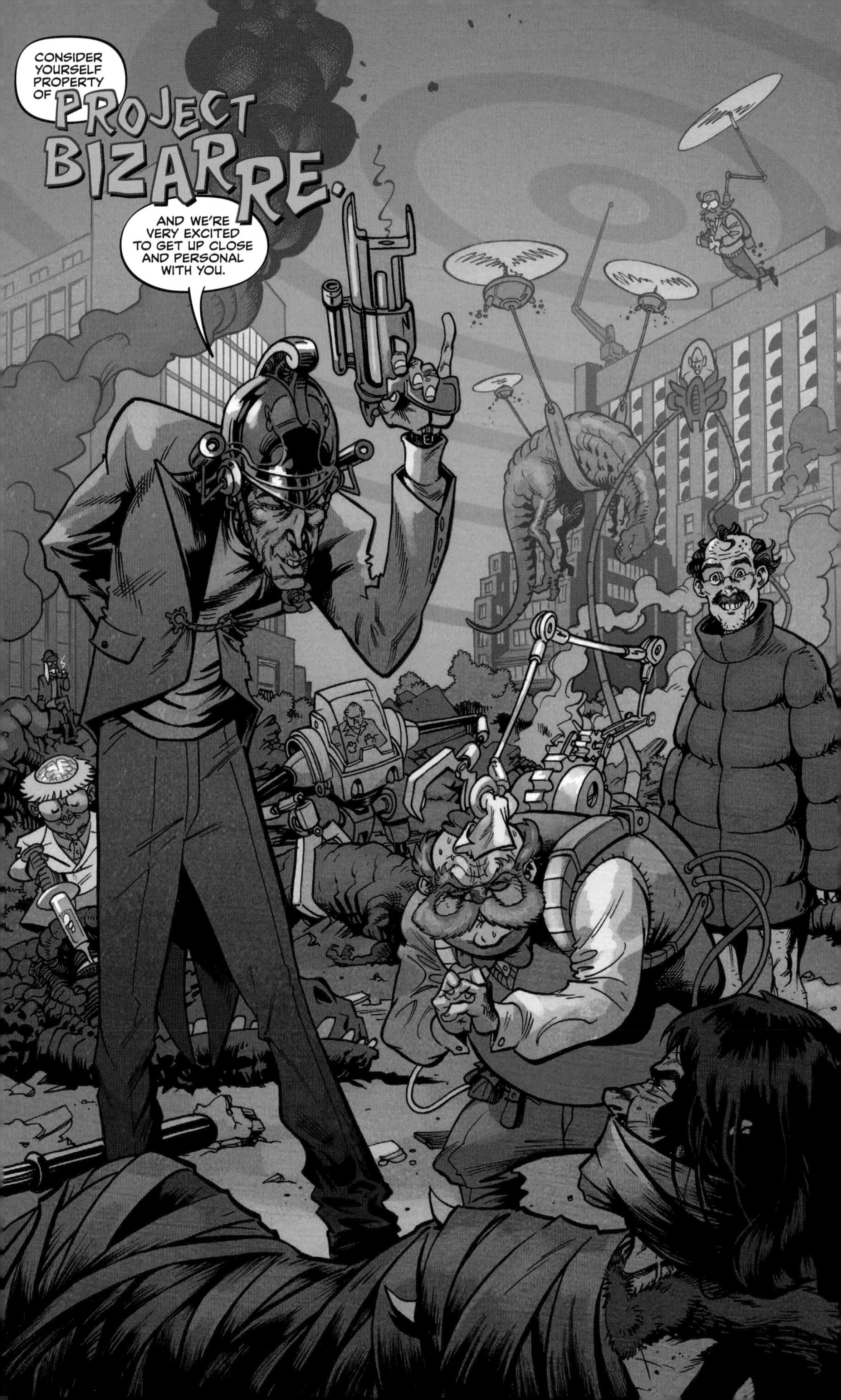
CONSIDER YOURSELF PROPERTY OF PROJECT BIZARRE.
AND WE'RE VERY EXCITED TO GET UP CLOSE AND PERSONAL WITH YOU.

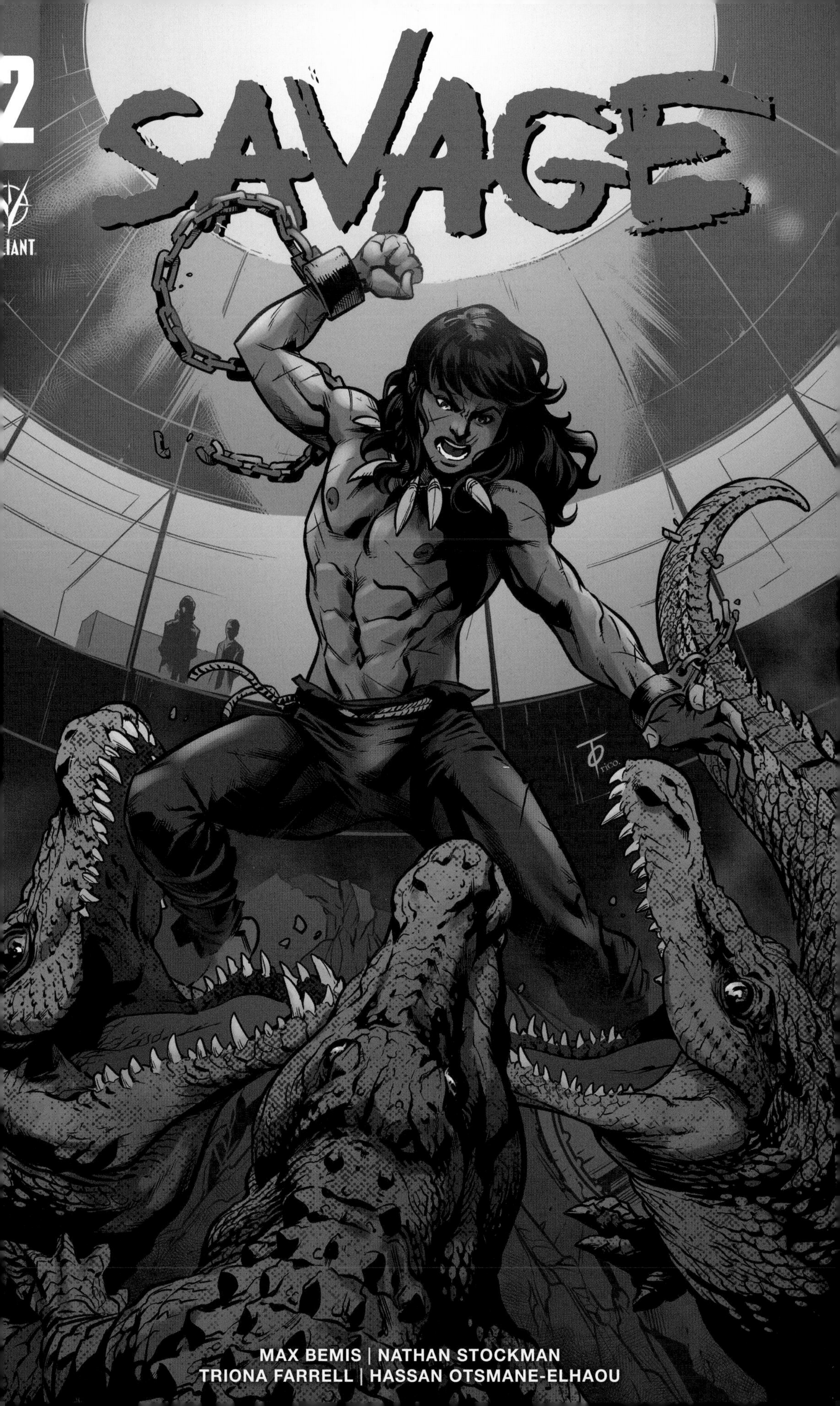
2
SAVAGE
VALIANT
MAX BEMIS | NATHAN STOCKMAN
TRIONA FARRELL | HASSAN OTSMANE-ELHAOU

**SAVAGE #2**

*WRITER:* Max Bemis
*ARTIST:* Nathan Stockman
*COLORIST:* Triona Farrell
*LETTERER:* Hassan Otsmane-Elhaou
*COVER ARTISTS:* Marcus To with Rico Renzi
*EDITOR:* David Menchel
*SENIOR EDITOR:* Heather Antos

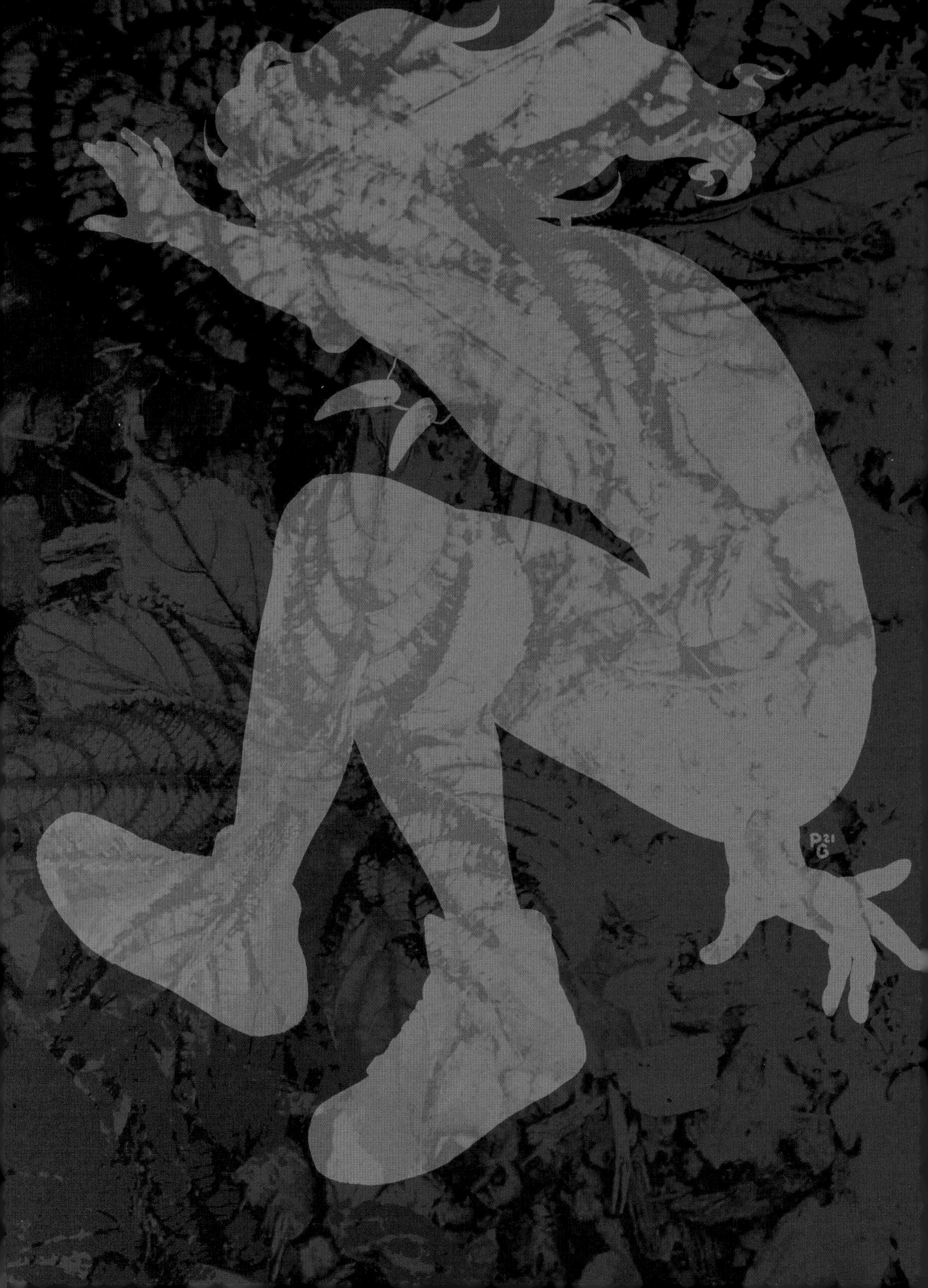

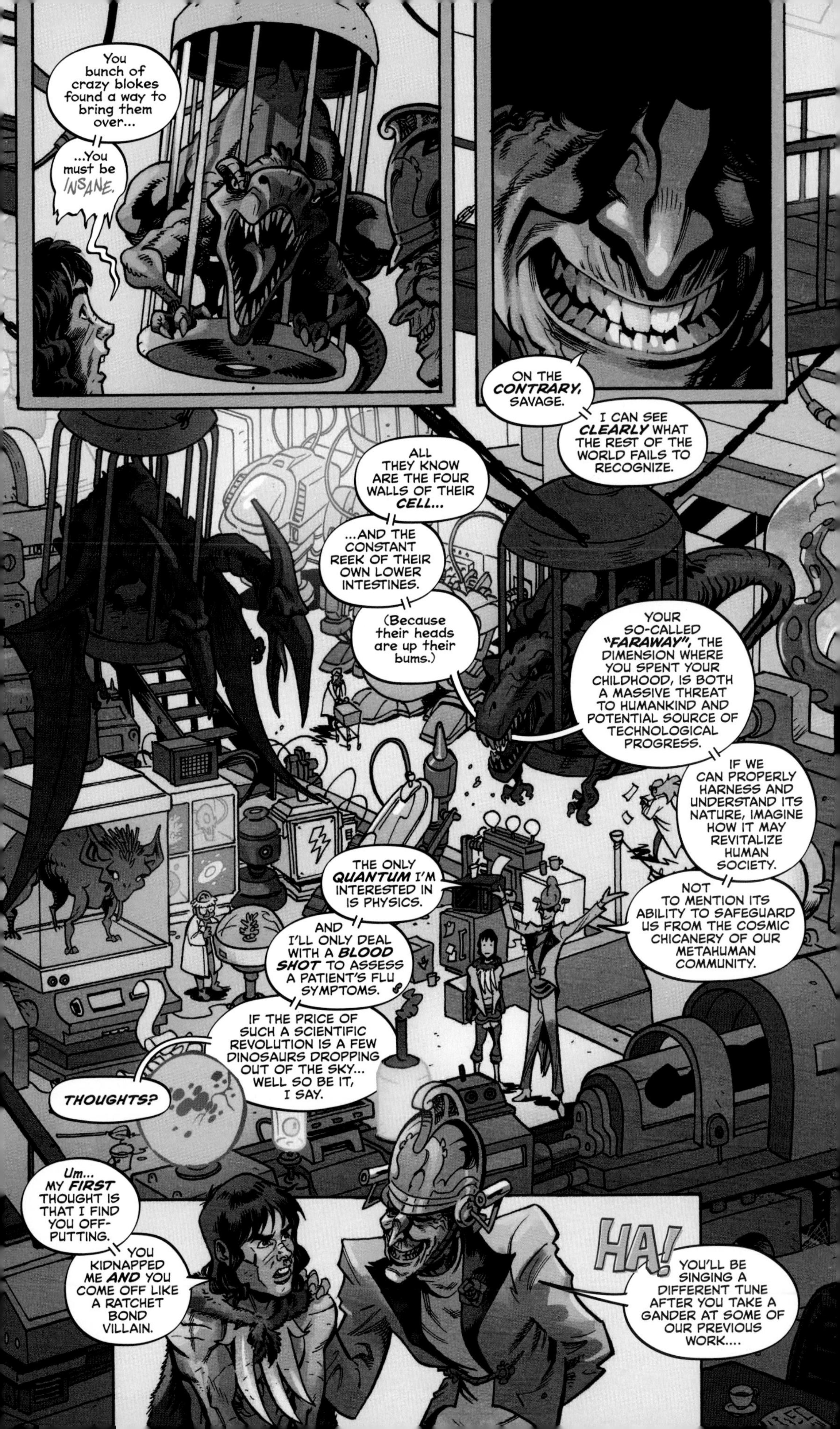

You bunch of crazy blokes found a way to bring them over...
...You must be INSANE.
ON THE CONTRARY, SAVAGE.
I CAN SEE CLEARLY WHAT THE REST OF THE WORLD FAILS TO RECOGNIZE.
ALL THEY KNOW ARE THE FOUR WALLS OF THEIR CELL...
...AND THE CONSTANT REEK OF THEIR OWN LOWER INTESTINES.
(Because their heads are up their bums.)
YOUR SO-CALLED "FARAWAY", THE DIMENSION WHERE YOU SPENT YOUR CHILDHOOD, IS BOTH A MASSIVE THREAT TO HUMANKIND AND POTENTIAL SOURCE OF TECHNOLOGICAL PROGRESS.
IF WE CAN PROPERLY HARNESS AND UNDERSTAND ITS NATURE, IMAGINE HOW IT MAY REVITALIZE HUMAN SOCIETY.
NOT TO MENTION ITS ABILITY TO SAFEGUARD US FROM THE COSMIC CHICANERY OF OUR METAHUMAN COMMUNITY.
THE ONLY QUANTUM I'M INTERESTED IN IS PHYSICS.
AND I'LL ONLY DEAL WITH A BLOOD SHOT TO ASSESS A PATIENT'S FLU SYMPTOMS.
IF THE PRICE OF SUCH A SCIENTIFIC REVOLUTION IS A FEW DINOSAURS DROPPING OUT OF THE SKY... WELL SO BE IT, I SAY.
THOUGHTS?
Um... MY FIRST THOUGHT IS THAT I FIND YOU OFF-PUTTING.
YOU KIDNAPPED ME AND YOU COME OFF LIKE A RATCHET BOND VILLAIN.
HA!
YOU'LL BE SINGING A DIFFERENT TUNE AFTER YOU TAKE A GANDER AT SOME OF OUR PREVIOUS WORK....

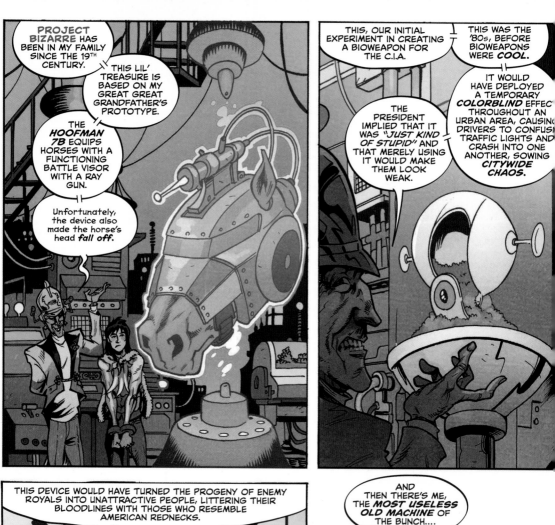

PROJECT BIZARRE HAS BEEN IN MY FAMILY SINCE THE 19TH CENTURY.

THIS LIL' TREASURE IS BASED ON MY GREAT GREAT GRANDFATHER'S PROTOTYPE.

THE *HOOFMAN 7B* EQUIPS HORSES WITH A FUNCTIONING BATTLE VISOR WITH A RAY GUN.

Unfortunately, the device also made the horse's head *fall off*.

THIS, OUR INITIAL EXPERIMENT IN CREATING A BIOWEAPON FOR THE C.I.A.

THIS WAS THE '80s, BEFORE BIOWEAPONS WERE *COOL*.

THE PRESIDENT IMPLIED THAT IT WAS *"JUST KIND OF STUPID"* AND THAT MERELY USING IT WOULD MAKE THEM LOOK WEAK.

IT WOULD HAVE DEPLOYED A TEMPORARY *COLORBLIND* EFFECT THROUGHOUT AN URBAN AREA, CAUSING DRIVERS TO CONFUSE TRAFFIC LIGHTS AND CRASH INTO ONE ANOTHER, SOWING *CITYWIDE CHAOS*.

THIS DEVICE WOULD HAVE TURNED THE PROGENY OF ENEMY ROYALS INTO UNATTRACTIVE PEOPLE, LITTERING THEIR BLOODLINES WITH THOSE WHO RESEMBLE AMERICAN REDNECKS.

UNFORTUNATELY, BOTH THIS EFFORT AND THE MACHINE WERE DEEMED REDUNDANT, AS THIS HAS BEEN THE CASE 75% OF THE TIME ANYWAY.

AND THEN THERE'S ME, THE *MOST USELESS OLD MACHINE* OF THE BUNCH....

*PROFESSOR HANLEY NEALON.*

(That was just a joke. I'm actually *vital* to this organization.)

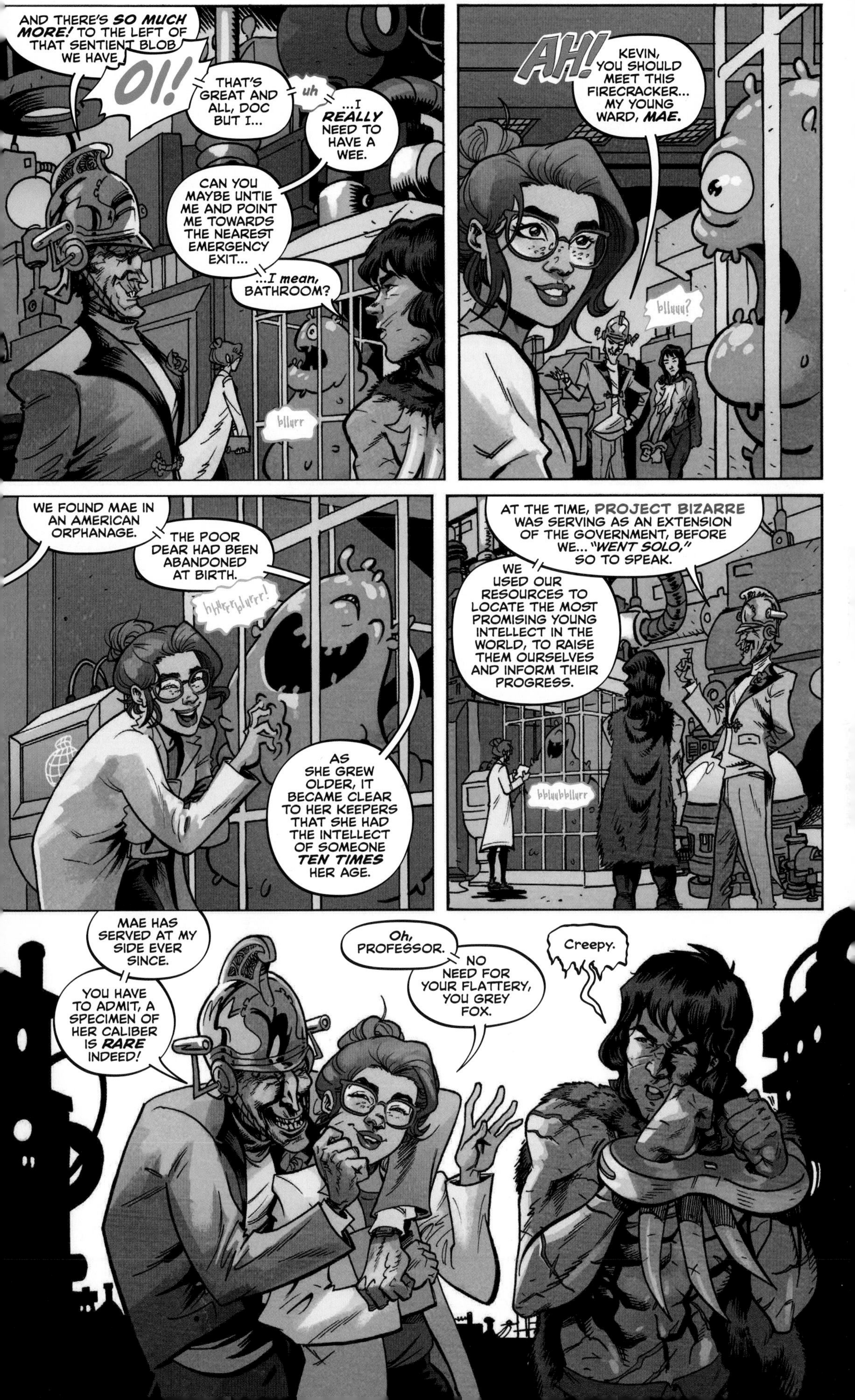

AND THERE'S SO MUCH MORE! TO THE LEFT OF THAT SENTIENT BLOB WE HAVE...
OI!
THAT'S GREAT AND ALL, DOC BUT I...
uh
...I REALLY NEED TO HAVE A WEE.
CAN YOU MAYBE UNTIE ME AND POINT ME TOWARDS THE NEAREST EMERGENCY EXIT...
...I mean, BATHROOM?
bllurr
AH!
KEVIN, YOU SHOULD MEET THIS FIRECRACKER... MY YOUNG WARD, MAE.
blluuu?
WE FOUND MAE IN AN AMERICAN ORPHANAGE.
THE POOR DEAR HAD BEEN ABANDONED AT BIRTH.
bbbrrrblurrr!
AS SHE GREW OLDER, IT BECAME CLEAR TO HER KEEPERS THAT SHE HAD THE INTELLECT OF SOMEONE TEN TIMES HER AGE.
AT THE TIME, PROJECT BIZARRE WAS SERVING AS AN EXTENSION OF THE GOVERNMENT, BEFORE WE... "WENT SOLO," SO TO SPEAK.
WE USED OUR RESOURCES TO LOCATE THE MOST PROMISING YOUNG INTELLECT IN THE WORLD, TO RAISE THEM OURSELVES AND INFORM THEIR PROGRESS.
bbluubbllurr
MAE HAS SERVED AT MY SIDE EVER SINCE.
YOU HAVE TO ADMIT, A SPECIMEN OF HER CALIBER IS RARE INDEED!
Oh, PROFESSOR.
NO NEED FOR YOUR FLATTERY, YOU GREY FOX.
Creepy.

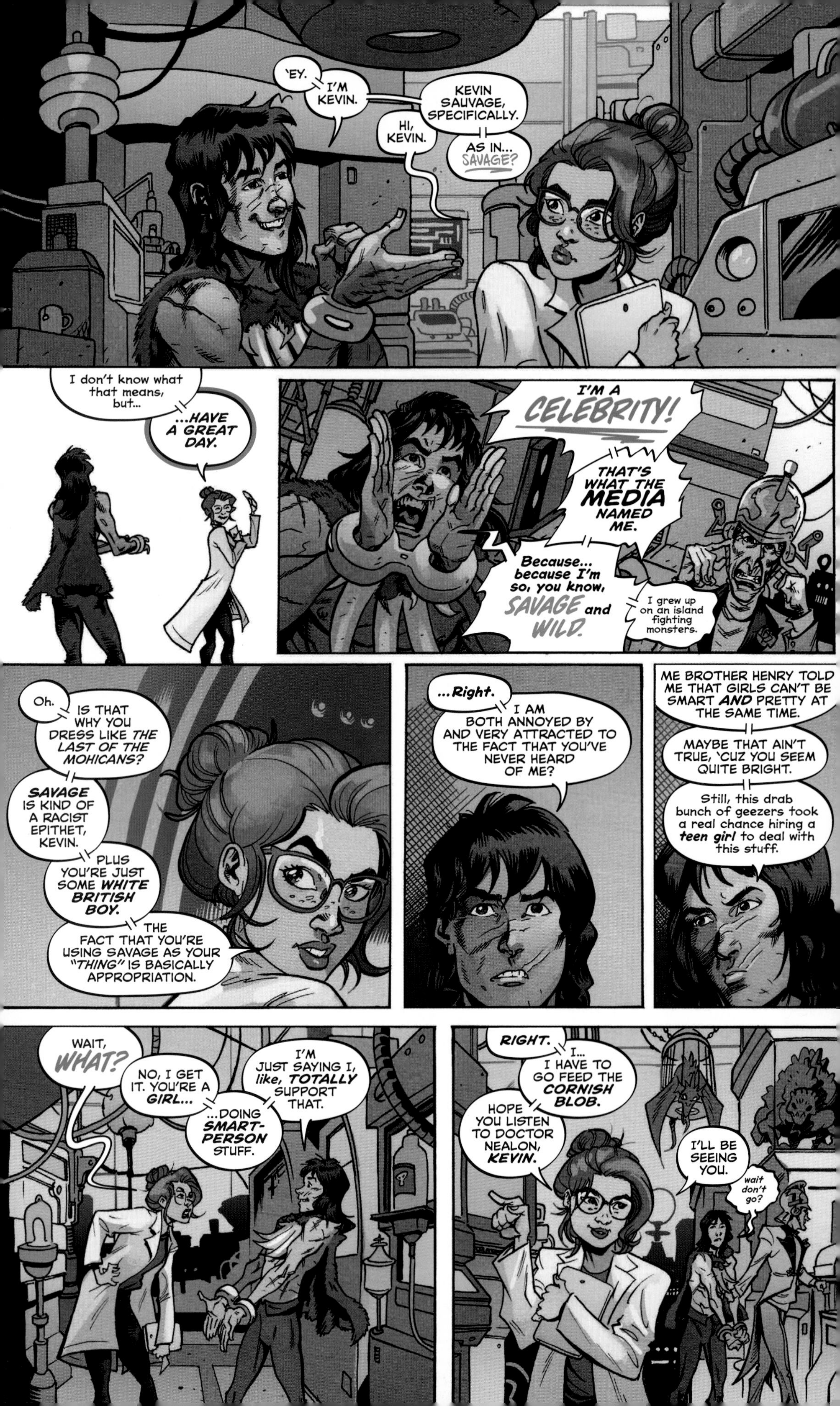

'EY.
I'M KEVIN.
KEVIN SAUVAGE, SPECIFICALLY.
HI, KEVIN.
AS IN... SAVAGE?
I don't know what that means, but...
...HAVE A GREAT DAY.
I'M A CELEBRITY!
THAT'S WHAT THE MEDIA NAMED ME.
Because... because I'm so, you know, SAVAGE and WILD.
I grew up on an island fighting monsters.
Oh.
IS THAT WHY YOU DRESS LIKE THE LAST OF THE MOHICANS?
SAVAGE IS KIND OF A RACIST EPITHET, KEVIN.
PLUS YOU'RE JUST SOME WHITE BRITISH BOY.
THE FACT THAT YOU'RE USING SAVAGE AS YOUR "THING" IS BASICALLY APPROPRIATION.
...Right.
I AM BOTH ANNOYED BY AND VERY ATTRACTED TO THE FACT THAT YOU'VE NEVER HEARD OF ME?
ME BROTHER HENRY TOLD ME THAT GIRLS CAN'T BE SMART AND PRETTY AT THE SAME TIME.
MAYBE THAT AIN'T TRUE, 'CUZ YOU SEEM QUITE BRIGHT.
Still, this drab bunch of geezers took a real chance hiring a teen girl to deal with this stuff.
WAIT, WHAT?
NO, I GET IT. YOU'RE A GIRL...
...DOING SMART-PERSON STUFF.
I'M JUST SAYING I, like, TOTALLY SUPPORT THAT.
RIGHT.
I... I HAVE TO GO FEED THE CORNISH BLOB.
HOPE YOU LISTEN TO DOCTOR NEALON, KEVIN.
I'LL BE SEEING YOU.
wait don't go?

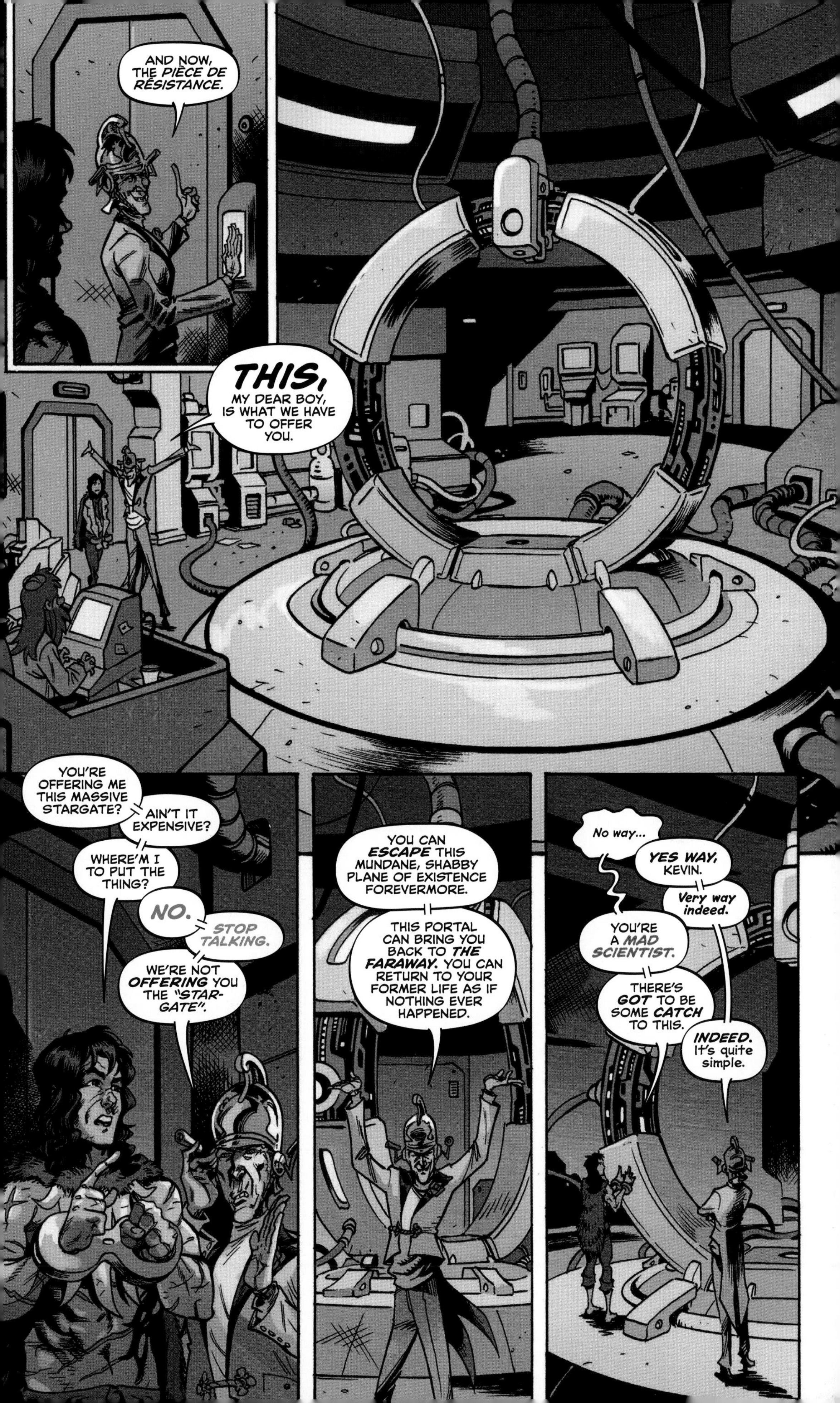
AND NOW, THE *PIÈCE DE RÉSISTANCE*.
*THIS,* MY DEAR BOY, IS WHAT WE HAVE TO OFFER YOU.
YOU'RE OFFERING ME THIS MASSIVE STARGATE?
AIN'T IT EXPENSIVE?
WHERE'M I TO PUT THE THING?
*NO.*
*STOP TALKING.*
WE'RE NOT *OFFERING* YOU THE "STAR-GATE".
YOU CAN *ESCAPE* THIS MUNDANE, SHABBY PLANE OF EXISTENCE FOREVERMORE.
THIS PORTAL CAN BRING YOU BACK TO *THE FARAWAY.* YOU CAN RETURN TO YOUR FORMER LIFE AS IF NOTHING EVER HAPPENED.
No way...
*YES WAY,* KEVIN.
Very way indeed.
YOU'RE A *MAD SCIENTIST*.
THERE'S *GOT* TO BE SOME *CATCH* TO THIS.
*INDEED.* It's quite simple.

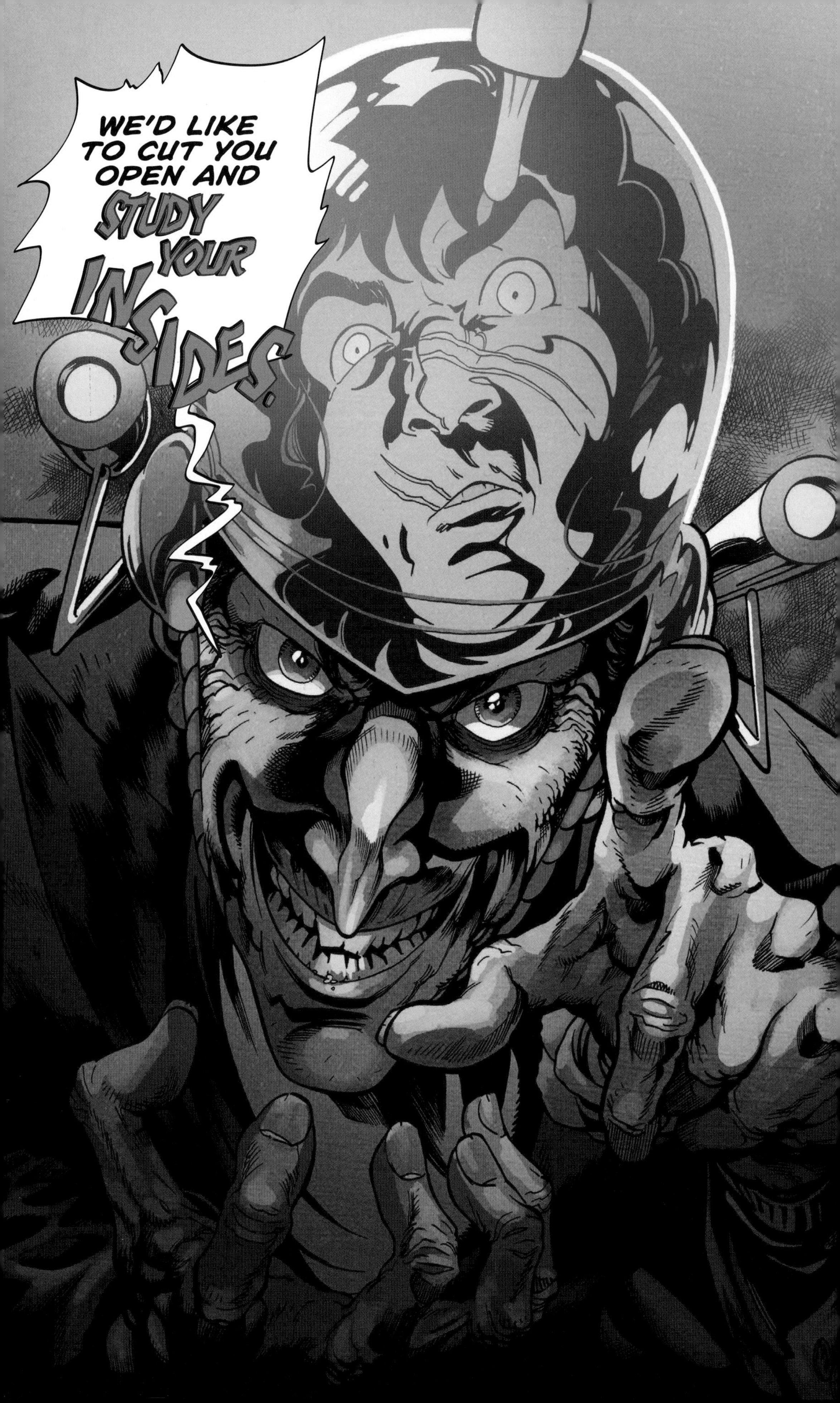
WE'D LIKE TO CUT YOU OPEN AND STUDY YOUR INSIDES.

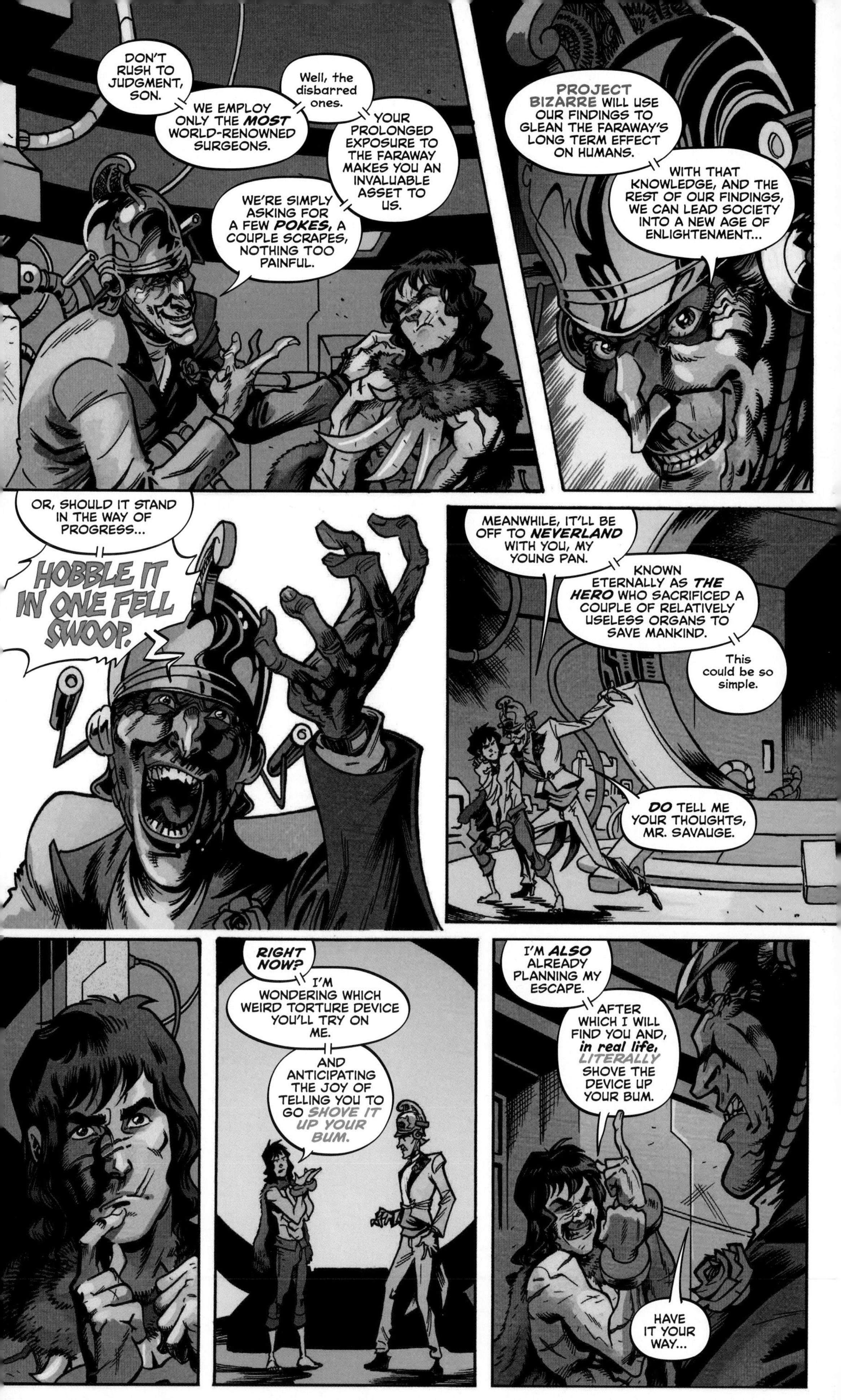
DON'T RUSH TO JUDGMENT, SON.
WE EMPLOY ONLY THE *MOST* WORLD-RENOWNED SURGEONS.
Well, the disbarred ones.
YOUR PROLONGED EXPOSURE TO THE FARAWAY MAKES YOU AN INVALUABLE ASSET TO US.
WE'RE SIMPLY ASKING FOR A FEW *POKES,* A COUPLE SCRAPES, NOTHING TOO PAINFUL.
PROJECT BIZARRE WILL USE OUR FINDINGS TO GLEAN THE FARAWAY'S LONG TERM EFFECT ON HUMANS.
WITH THAT KNOWLEDGE, AND THE REST OF OUR FINDINGS, WE CAN LEAD SOCIETY INTO A NEW AGE OF ENLIGHTENMENT...
OR, SHOULD IT STAND IN THE WAY OF PROGRESS...
HOBBLE IT IN ONE FELL SWOOP.
MEANWHILE, IT'LL BE OFF TO *NEVERLAND* WITH YOU, MY YOUNG PAN.
KNOWN ETERNALLY AS *THE HERO* WHO SACRIFICED A COUPLE OF RELATIVELY USELESS ORGANS TO SAVE MANKIND.
This could be so simple.
*DO* TELL ME YOUR THOUGHTS, MR. SAVAUGE.
*RIGHT NOW?*
I'M WONDERING WHICH WEIRD TORTURE DEVICE YOU'LL TRY ON ME.
AND ANTICIPATING THE JOY OF TELLING YOU TO GO *SHOVE IT UP YOUR BUM.*
I'M *ALSO* ALREADY PLANNING MY ESCAPE.
AFTER WHICH I WILL FIND YOU AND, *in real life, LITERALLY* SHOVE THE DEVICE UP YOUR BUM.
HAVE IT YOUR WAY...

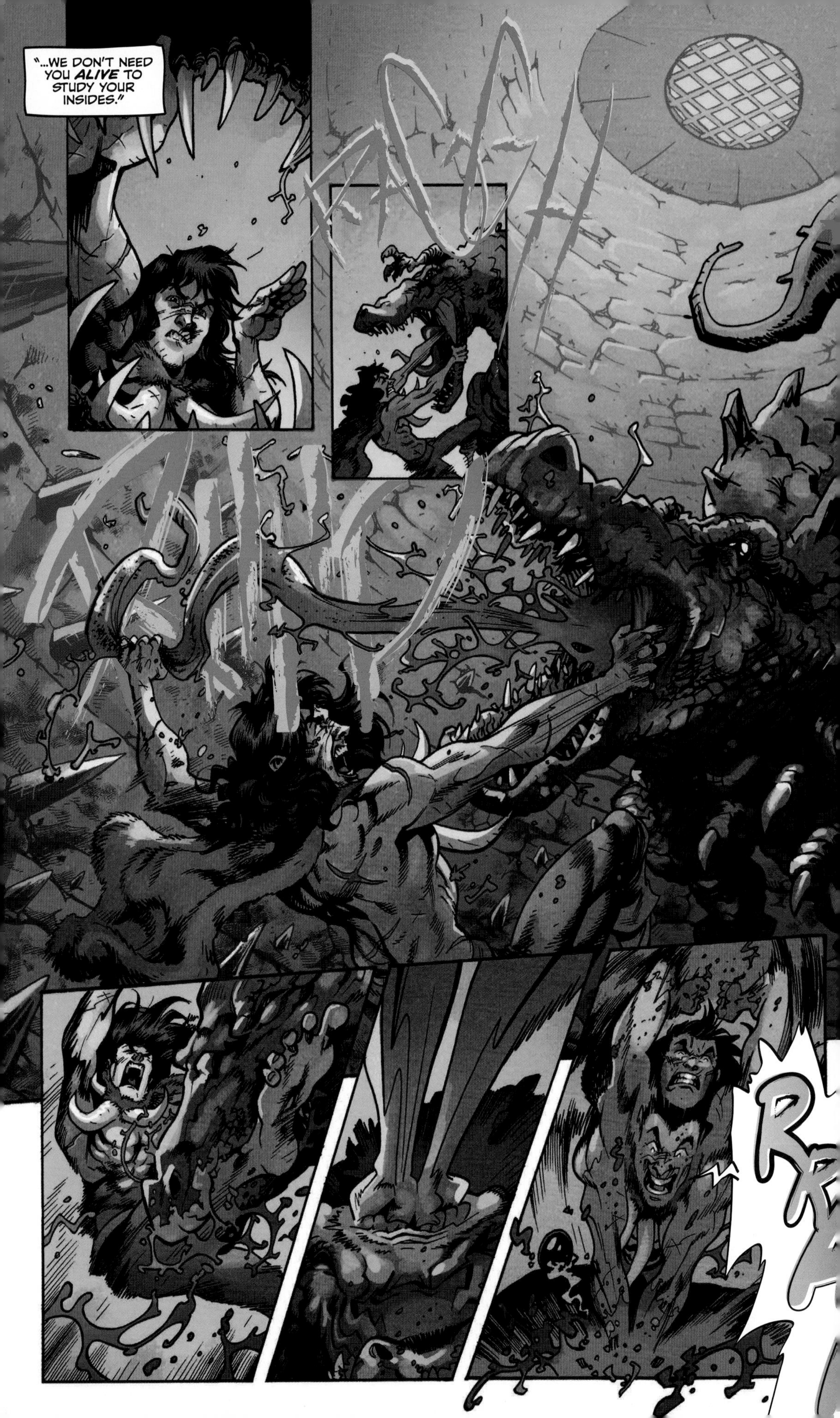
"...WE DON'T NEED YOU *ALIVE* TO STUDY YOUR INSIDES."

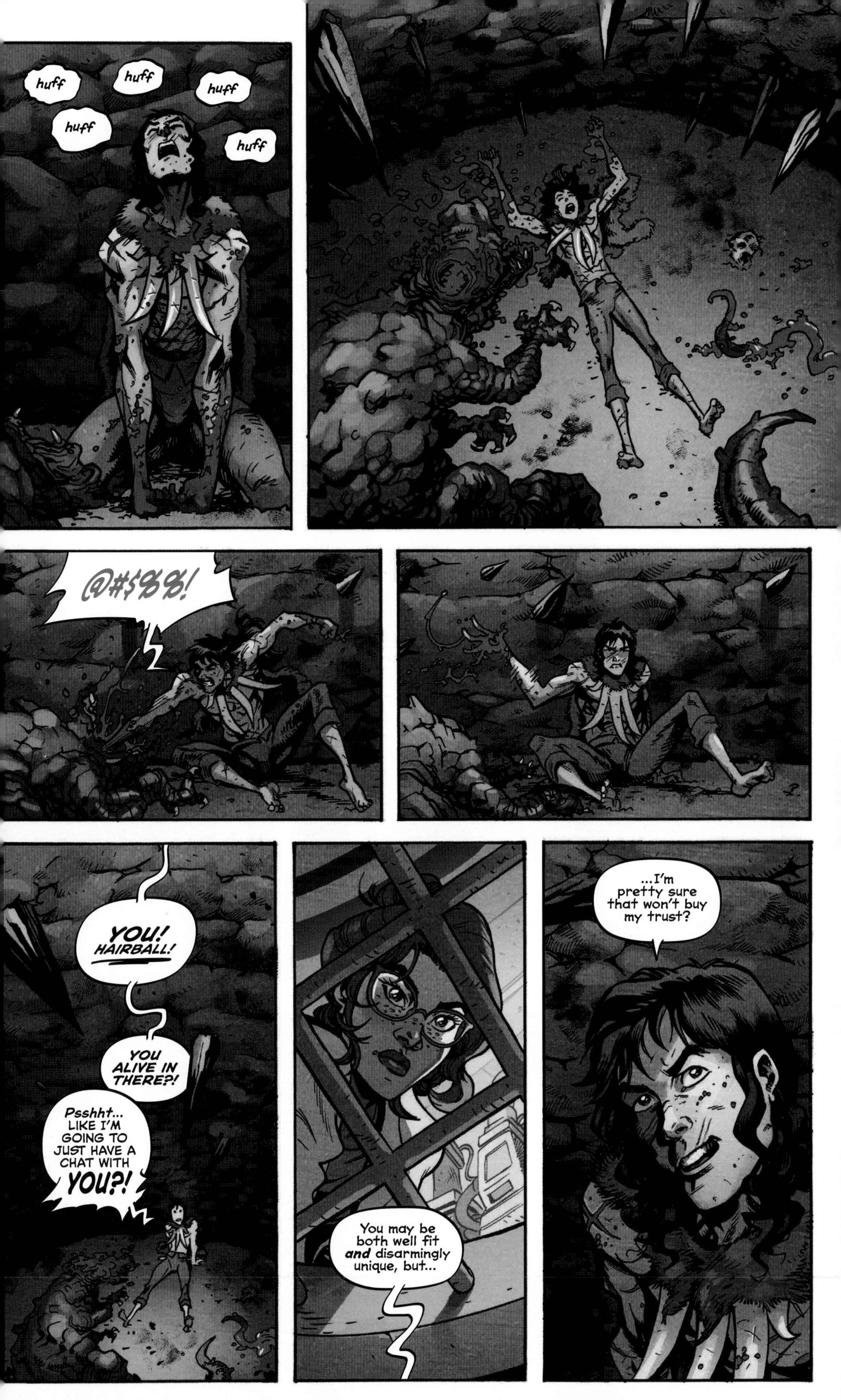
huff
huff
huff
huff
huff
@#$%%!
YOU! HAIRBALL!
YOU ALIVE IN THERE?!
Psshht... LIKE I'M GOING TO JUST HAVE A CHAT WITH YOU?!
You may be both well fit and disarmingly unique, but...
...I'm pretty sure that won't buy my trust?

YOU JUST WALTZ IN HERE AND TRY TO ASSASSINATE MY BENEFACTOR AND FATHER FIGURE?

I HOPE THEY FEED YOU TO THE PANTHER SNAKES!

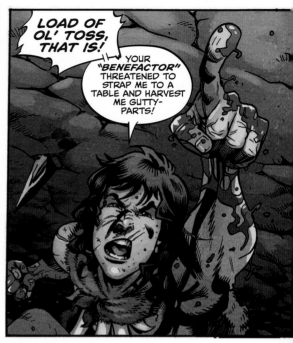

LOAD OF OL' TOSS, THAT IS!

YOUR "BENEFACTOR" THREATENED TO STRAP ME TO A TABLE AND HARVEST ME GUTTY-PARTS!

Okay, okay...just shhhh!

THERE'S A FALSE LEAD LOOPING IN THEIR SECURITY FEED BUT IT WON'T LAST MORE THAN A FEW MINUTES.

YOU RISKED YOUR LIFE TO SAVE LONDON, AND YOU STOOD UP TO NEALON.

NOW, I'M GONNA TRUST THAT YOU CAN KEEP A SECRET, SAVAGE.

I'LL HAVE YOU KNOW I WON A TEEN CHOICE AWARD FOR KEEPING SECRETS.

I'VE KNOWN ABOUT NEALON'S NEFARIOUS QUEST TO MERGE THE FARAWAY WITH EARTH...

...AND I'M SABOTAGING THIS NUTHOUSE FROM THE INSIDE.

REALLY? SO YOU STAY HERE ON PURPOSE, AMONGST THESE *MENTAL CASES?*

I HATE TO BREAK IT TO YOU, BUT MANKIND AIN'T REALLY WORTH IT.

BUDDY, I DON'T GIVE TWO @##*S ABOUT WHAT *YOU* THINK.

LET'S FOCUS ON GETTING YOU OUT OF HERE BEFORE I BLOW MY COVER.

You're like the teen British Kid Rock.

THAT HAPPENS? We're lunchmeat.

UNFORTUNATELY, MY GENIUS DOESN'T REALLY EXTEND TO TACTICAL HOSTAGE SITUATIONS.

I HONESTLY DON'T KNOW HOW TO FISH YOU OUT OF THERE.

And no offense, WE BOTH KNOW YOU'RE NOT THE TYPE TO...

*MAE.*

Please. CAN'T YOU JUST THROW ME A *BONE* HERE?

FINE, *FINE.*

PERHAPS I *HAVE* BEEN QUICK TO JUDGMENT.

It *is* one of my few faults.

YOU DO SEEM HONORABLE AND *NICE ENOUGH* FOR A BOY WHO SEEMS LIKE A GENETIC THROWBACK TO CAVEPERSON YEARS.

*MAE.*

*NO.*

I mean *literally,* THROW ME A BONE.

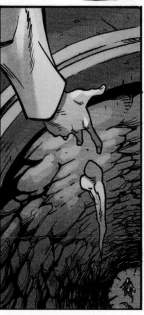

YOINK

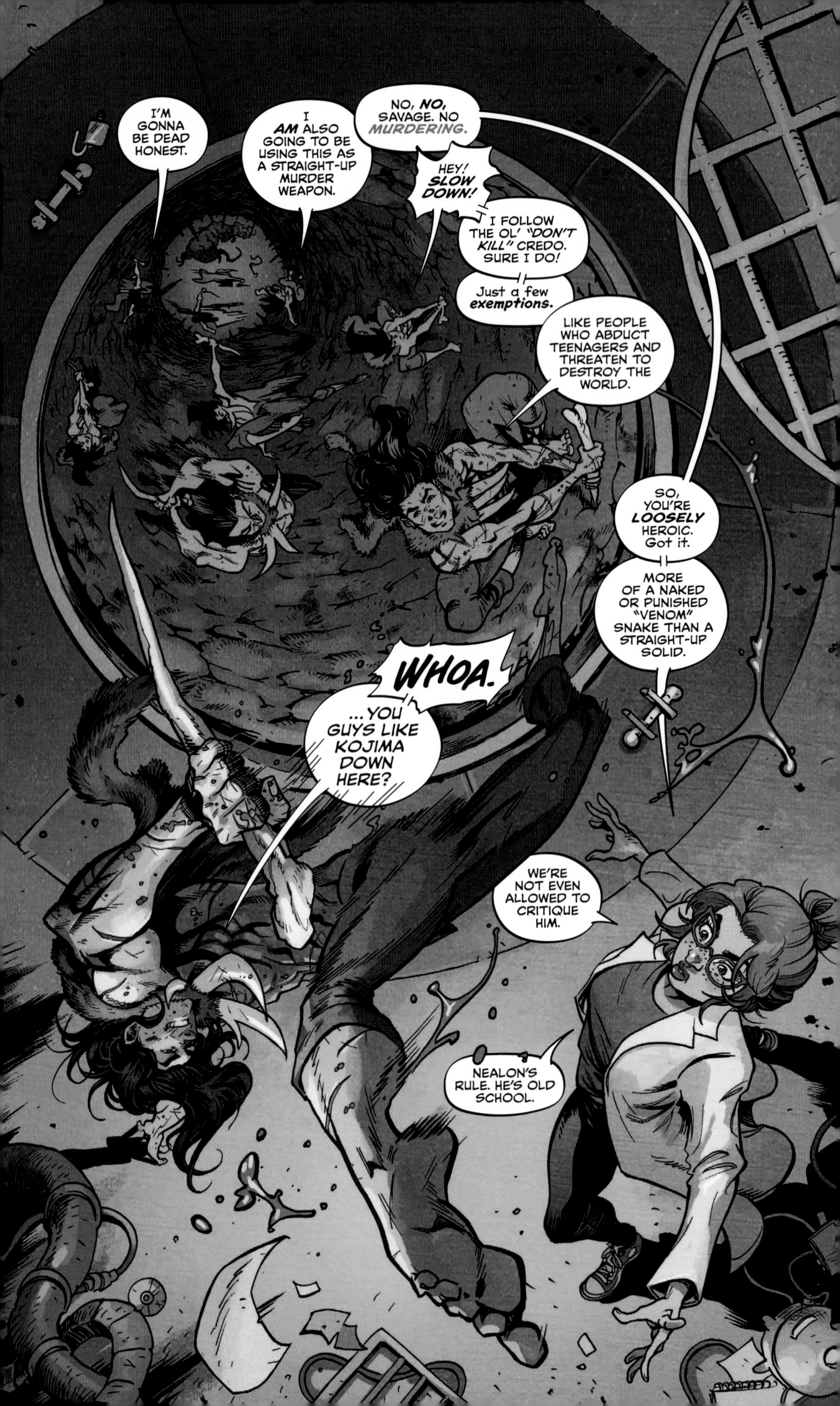

I'M GONNA BE DEAD HONEST.
I AM ALSO GOING TO BE USING THIS AS A STRAIGHT-UP MURDER WEAPON.
NO, NO, SAVAGE. NO MURDERING.
HEY! SLOW DOWN!
I FOLLOW THE OL' "DON'T KILL" CREDO. SURE I DO!
Just a few exemptions.
LIKE PEOPLE WHO ABDUCT TEENAGERS AND THREATEN TO DESTROY THE WORLD.
SO, YOU'RE LOOSELY HEROIC. Got it.
MORE OF A NAKED OR PUNISHED "VENOM" SNAKE THAN A STRAIGHT-UP SOLID.
WHOA.
...YOU GUYS LIKE KOJIMA DOWN HERE?
WE'RE NOT EVEN ALLOWED TO CRITIQUE HIM.
NEALON'S RULE. HE'S OLD SCHOOL.

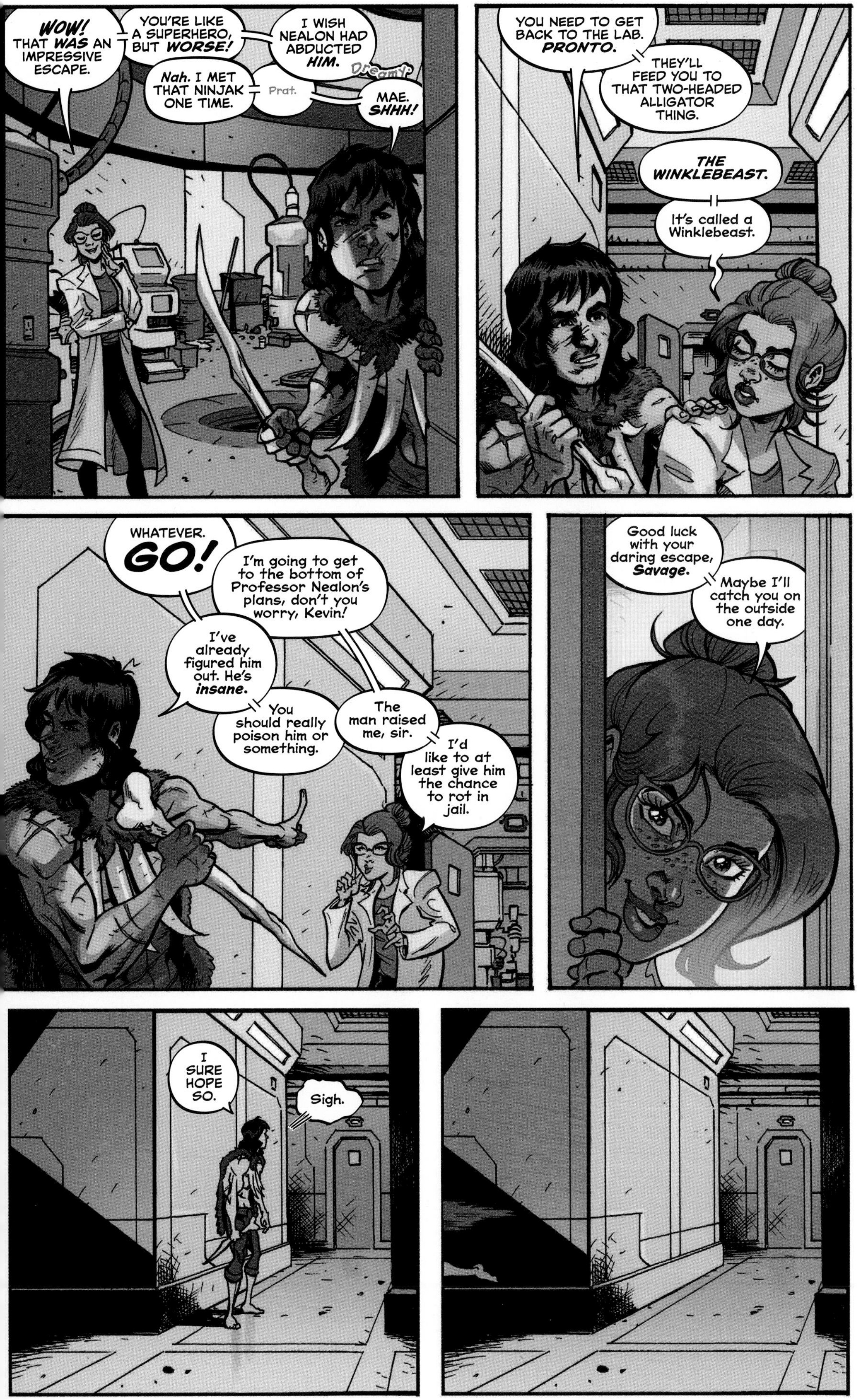
WOW! THAT WAS AN IMPRESSIVE ESCAPE.
YOU'RE LIKE A SUPERHERO, BUT WORSE!
I WISH NEALON HAD ABDUCTED HIM.
Dreamy.
Nah. I MET THAT NINJAK ONE TIME.
Prat.
MAE. SHHH!
YOU NEED TO GET BACK TO THE LAB. PRONTO.
THEY'LL FEED YOU TO THAT TWO-HEADED ALLIGATOR THING.
THE WINKLEBEAST.
It's called a Winklebeast.
WHATEVER. GO!
I'm going to get to the bottom of Professor Nealon's plans, don't you worry, Kevin!
I've already figured him out. He's insane.
You should really poison him or something.
The man raised me, sir.
I'd like to at least give him the chance to rot in jail.
Good luck with your daring escape, Savage.
Maybe I'll catch you on the outside one day.
I SURE HOPE SO.
Sigh.

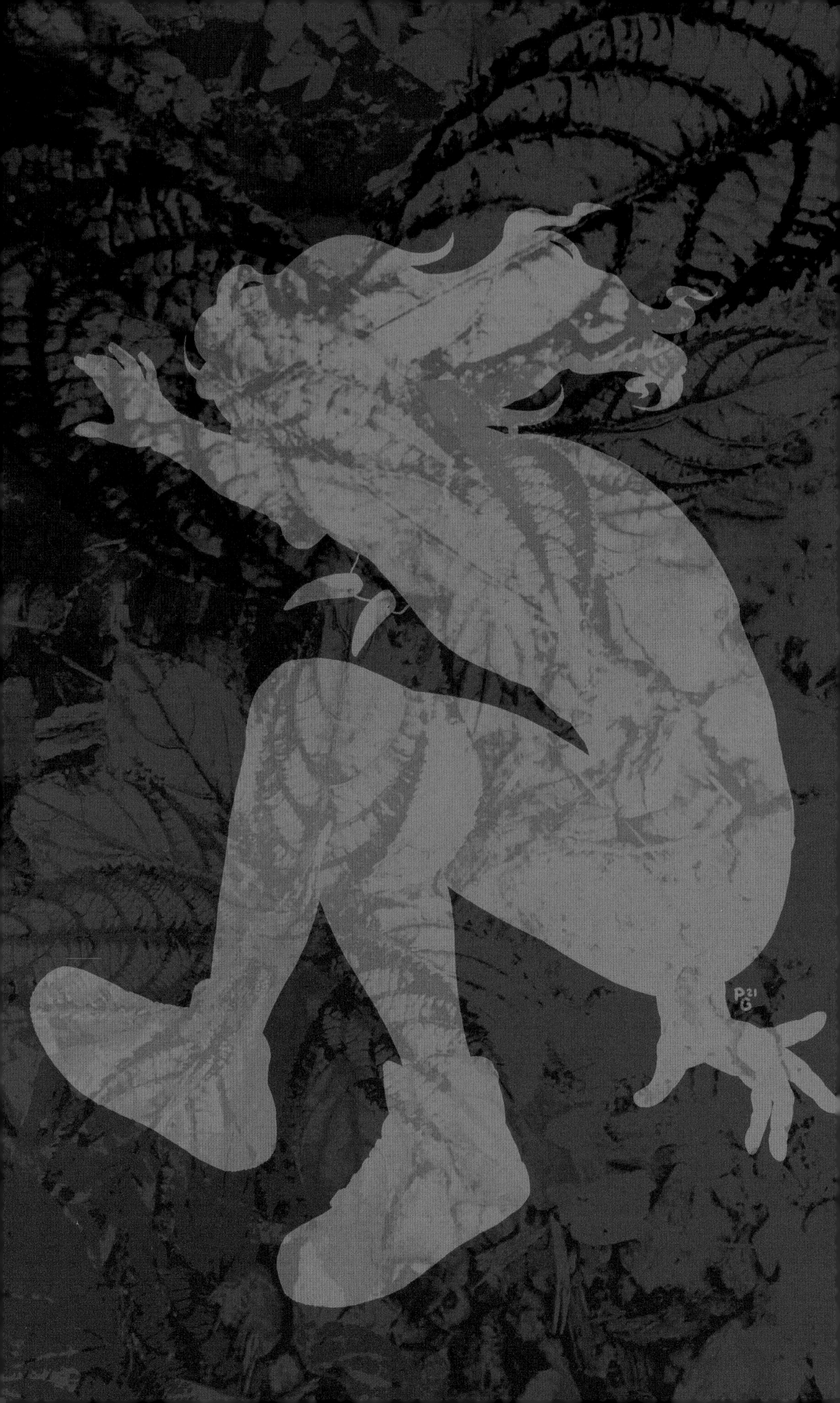

...SO I KEPT PRODDING THE DAMN THING AND WOULDN'T YOU KNOW IT... ITS HEAD **EXPLODED!**

**HA!** WHAT A JOY. ALWAYS A BONUS TO FIND NEW WAYS TO HARM THESE *HELPLESS BEASTS.*

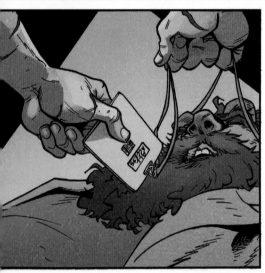

Uch.

OF COURSE.

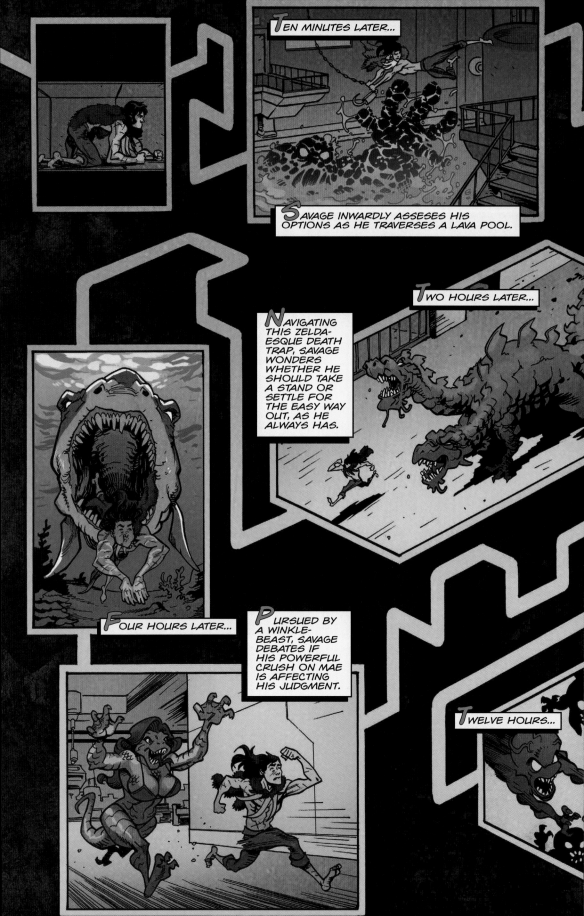

TEN MINUTES LATER...

SAVAGE INWARDLY ASSESES HIS OPTIONS AS HE TRAVERSES A LAVA POOL.

TWO HOURS LATER...

NAVIGATING THIS ZELDA-ESQUE DEATH TRAP, SAVAGE WONDERS WHETHER HE SHOULD TAKE A STAND OR SETTLE FOR THE EASY WAY OUT, AS HE ALWAYS HAS.

FOUR HOURS LATER...

PURSUED BY A WINKLE-BEAST, SAVAGE DEBATES IF HIS POWERFUL CRUSH ON MAE IS AFFECTING HIS JUDGMENT.

TWELVE HOURS...

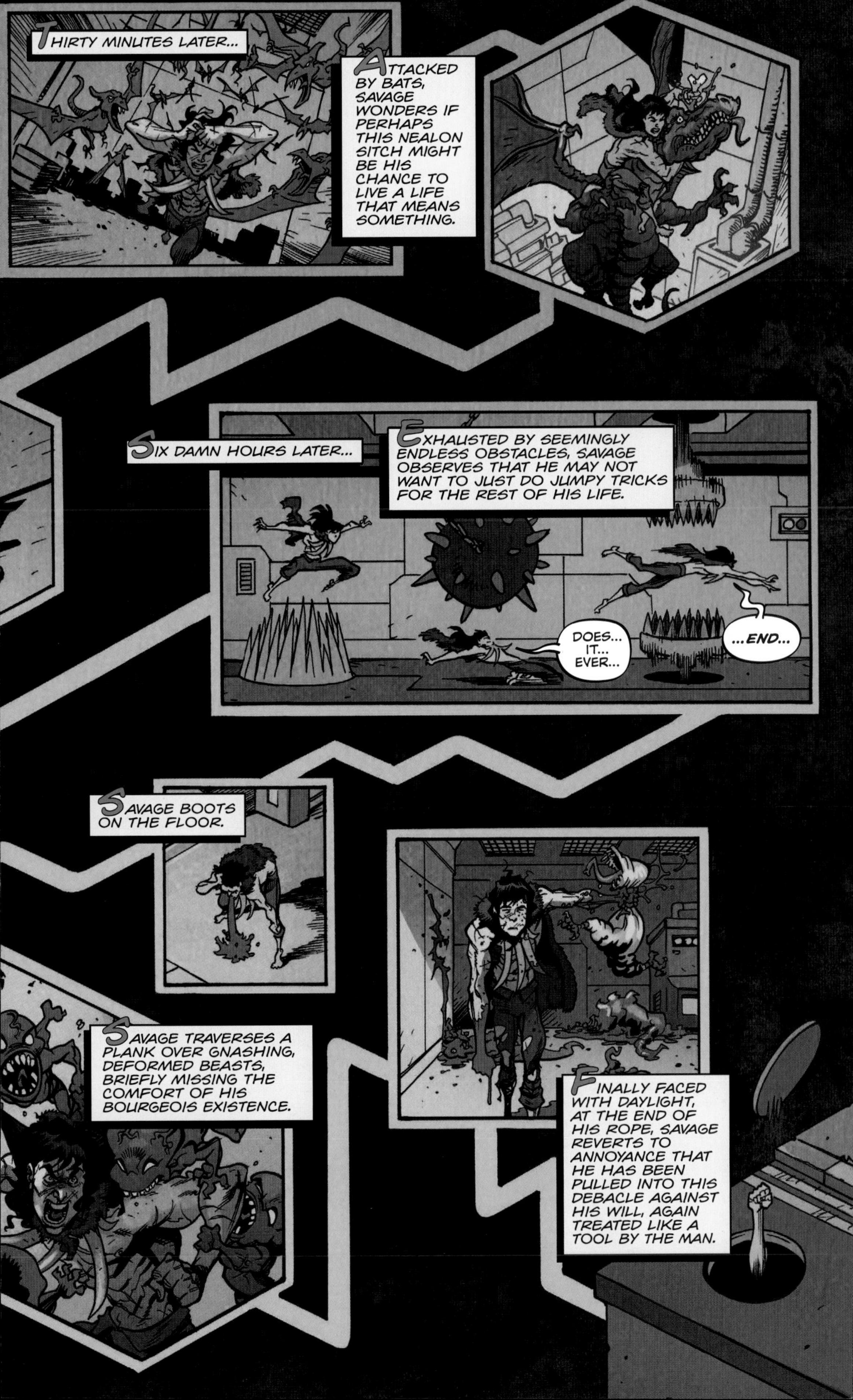
THIRTY MINUTES LATER...
ATTACKED BY BATS, SAVAGE WONDERS IF PERHAPS THIS NEALON SITCH MIGHT BE HIS CHANCE TO LIVE A LIFE THAT MEANS SOMETHING.
SIX DAMN HOURS LATER...
EXHAUSTED BY SEEMINGLY ENDLESS OBSTACLES, SAVAGE OBSERVES THAT HE MAY NOT WANT TO JUST DO JUMPY TRICKS FOR THE REST OF HIS LIFE.
DOES... IT... EVER...
...END...
SAVAGE BOOTS ON THE FLOOR.
SAVAGE TRAVERSES A PLANK OVER GNASHING, DEFORMED BEASTS, BRIEFLY MISSING THE COMFORT OF HIS BOURGEOIS EXISTENCE.
FINALLY FACED WITH DAYLIGHT, AT THE END OF HIS ROPE, SAVAGE REVERTS TO ANNOYANCE THAT HE HAS BEEN PULLED INTO THIS DEBACLE AGAINST HIS WILL, AGAIN TREATED LIKE A TOOL BY THE MAN.

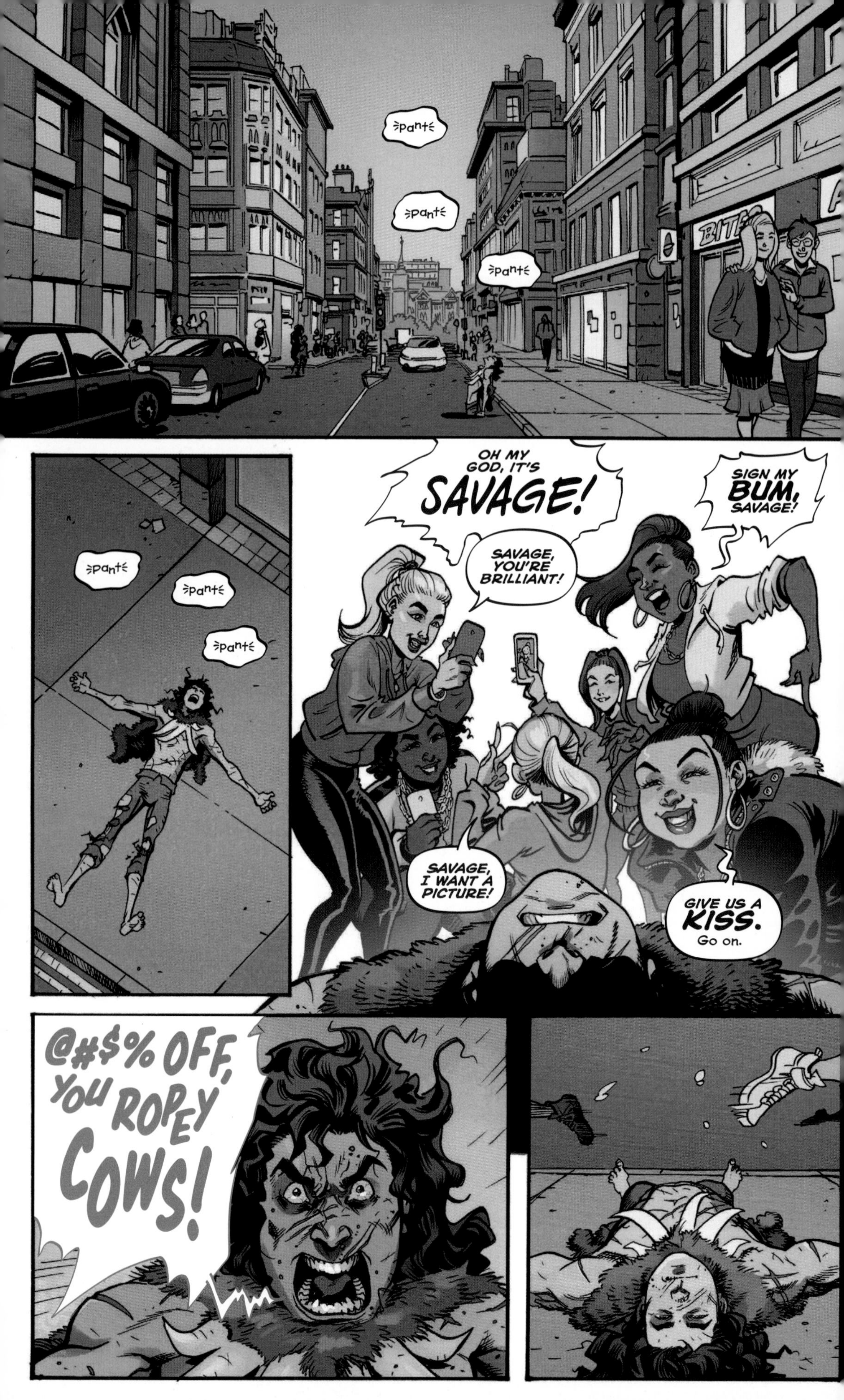
pant
pant
pant
BITE
pant
pant
pant
OH MY GOD, IT'S SAVAGE!
SIGN MY BUM, SAVAGE!
SAVAGE, YOU'RE BRILLIANT!
SAVAGE, I WANT A PICTURE!
GIVE US A KISS. Go on.
@#$% OFF, YOU ROPEY COWS!

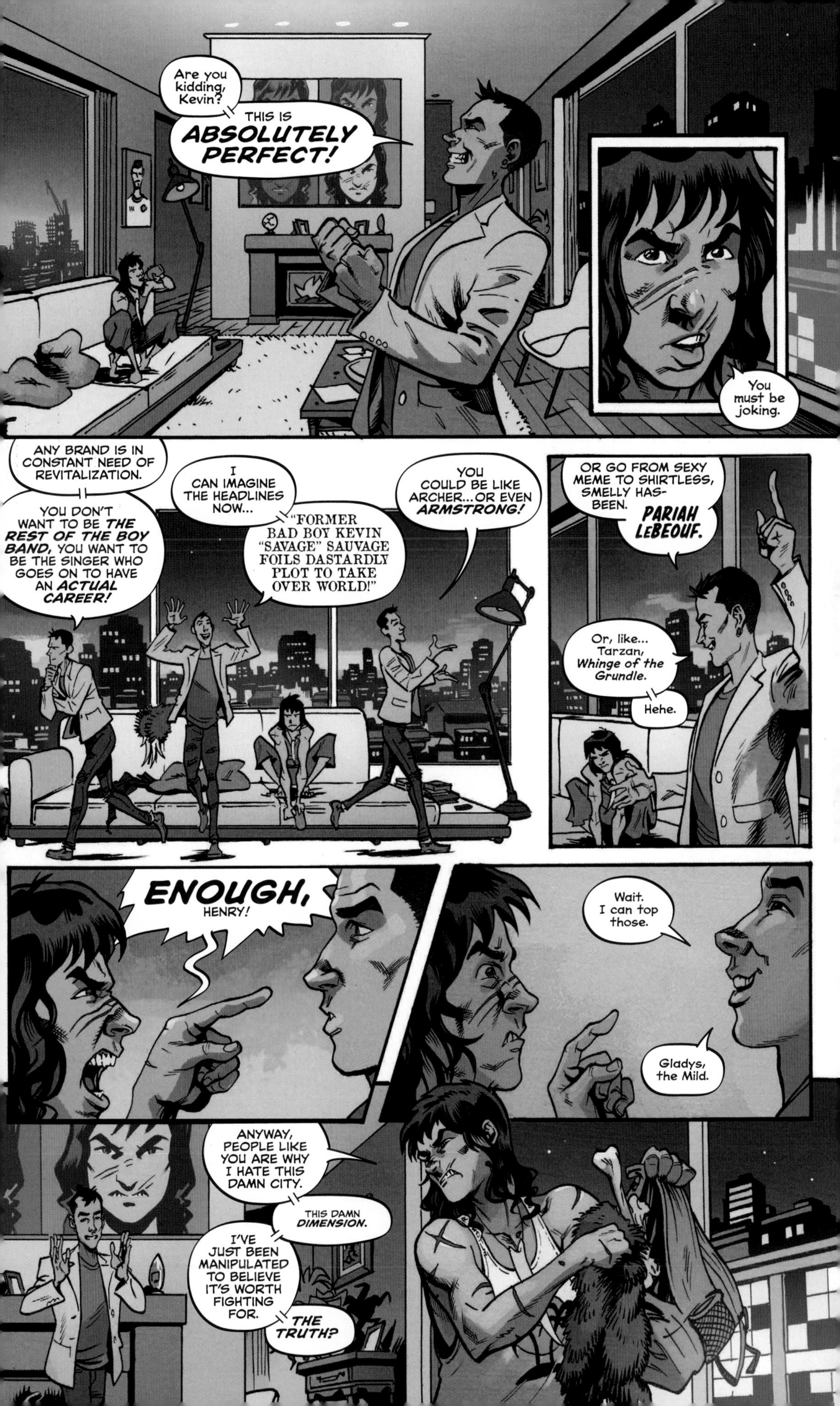

Are you kidding, Kevin?
THIS IS ABSOLUTELY PERFECT!
You must be joking.
ANY BRAND IS IN CONSTANT NEED OF REVITALIZATION.
YOU DON'T WANT TO BE THE REST OF THE BOY BAND, YOU WANT TO BE THE SINGER WHO GOES ON TO HAVE AN ACTUAL CAREER!
I CAN IMAGINE THE HEADLINES NOW...
"FORMER BAD BOY KEVIN "SAVAGE" SAUVAGE FOILS DASTARDLY PLOT TO TAKE OVER WORLD!"
YOU COULD BE LIKE ARCHER...OR EVEN ARMSTRONG!
OR GO FROM SEXY MEME TO SHIRTLESS, SMELLY HAS-BEEN.
PARIAH LeBEOUF.
Or, like... Tarzan, Whinge of the Grundle.
Hehe.
ENOUGH, HENRY!
Wait. I can top those.
Gladys, the Mild.
ANYWAY, PEOPLE LIKE YOU ARE WHY I HATE THIS DAMN CITY.
THIS DAMN DIMENSION.
I'VE JUST BEEN MANIPULATED TO BELIEVE IT'S WORTH FIGHTING FOR.
THE TRUTH?

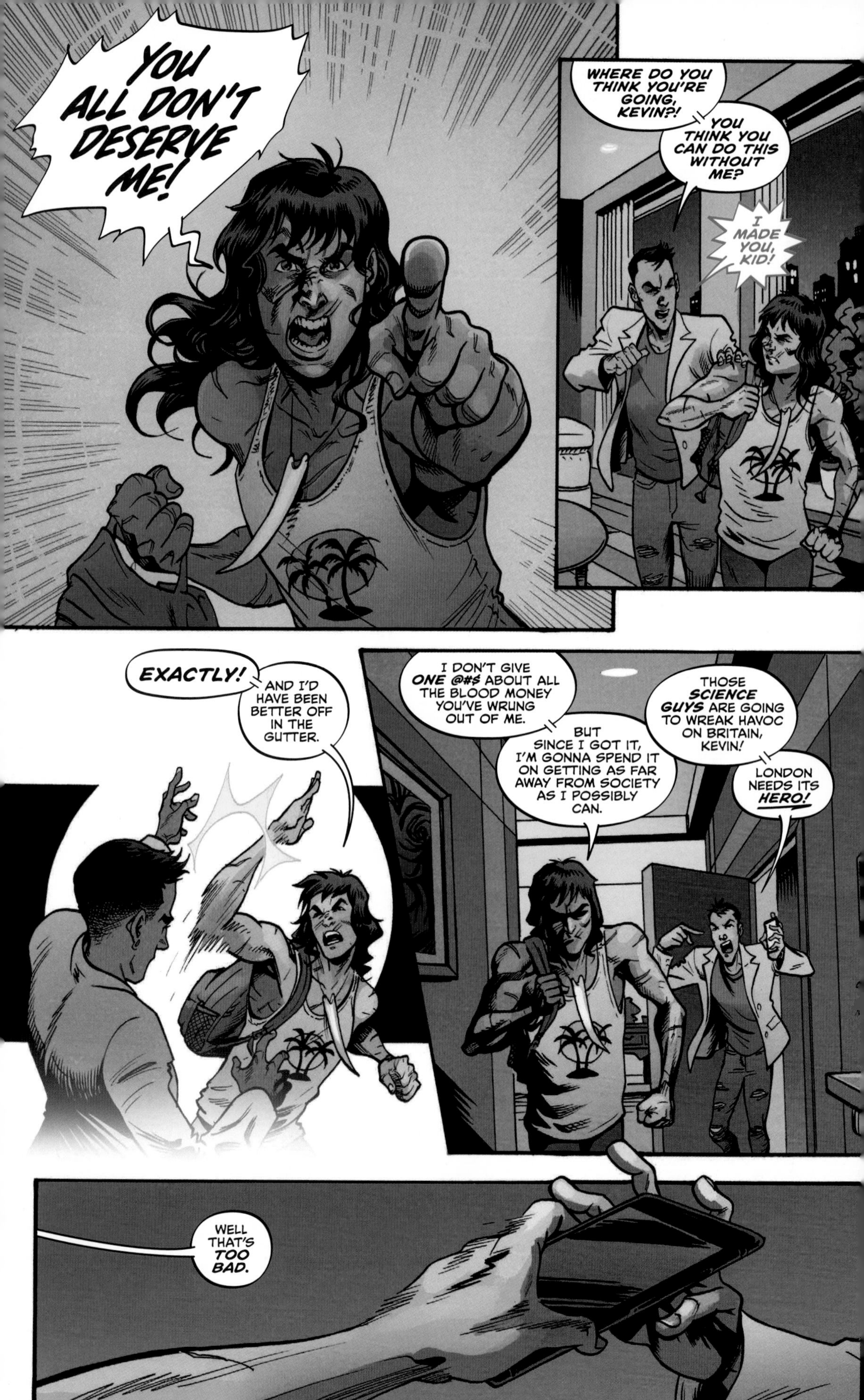
YOU ALL DON'T DESERVE ME!
WHERE DO YOU THINK YOU'RE GOING, KEVIN?!
YOU THINK YOU CAN DO THIS WITHOUT ME?
I MADE YOU, KID!
EXACTLY!
AND I'D HAVE BEEN BETTER OFF IN THE GUTTER.
I DON'T GIVE ONE @#$ ABOUT ALL THE BLOOD MONEY YOU'VE WRUNG OUT OF ME.
BUT SINCE I GOT IT, I'M GONNA SPEND IT ON GETTING AS FAR AWAY FROM SOCIETY AS I POSSIBLY CAN.
THOSE SCIENCE GUYS ARE GOING TO WREAK HAVOC ON BRITAIN, KEVIN!
LONDON NEEDS ITS HERO!
WELL THAT'S TOO BAD.

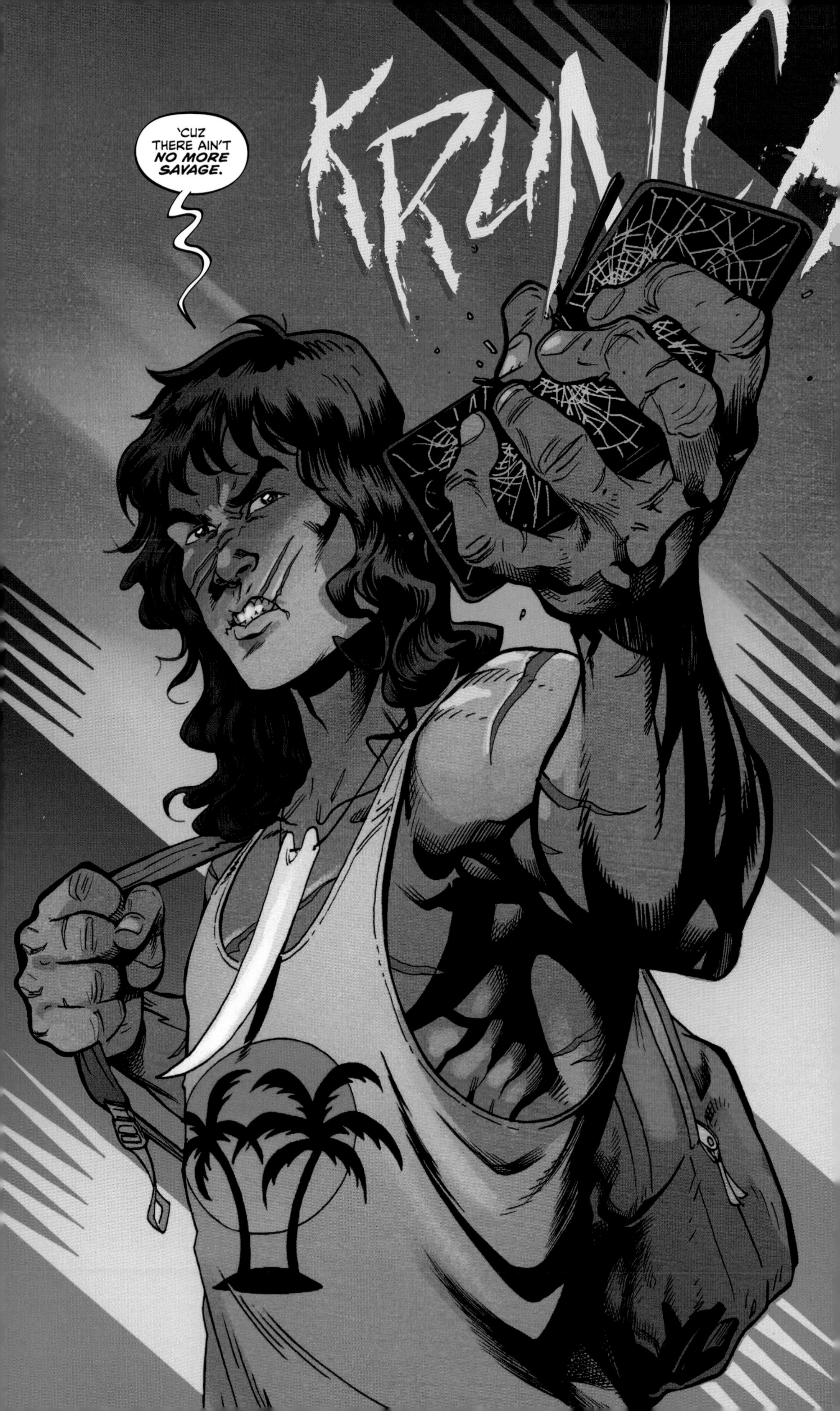
'CUZ THERE AIN'T ***NO MORE SAVAGE.***
KRUNCH

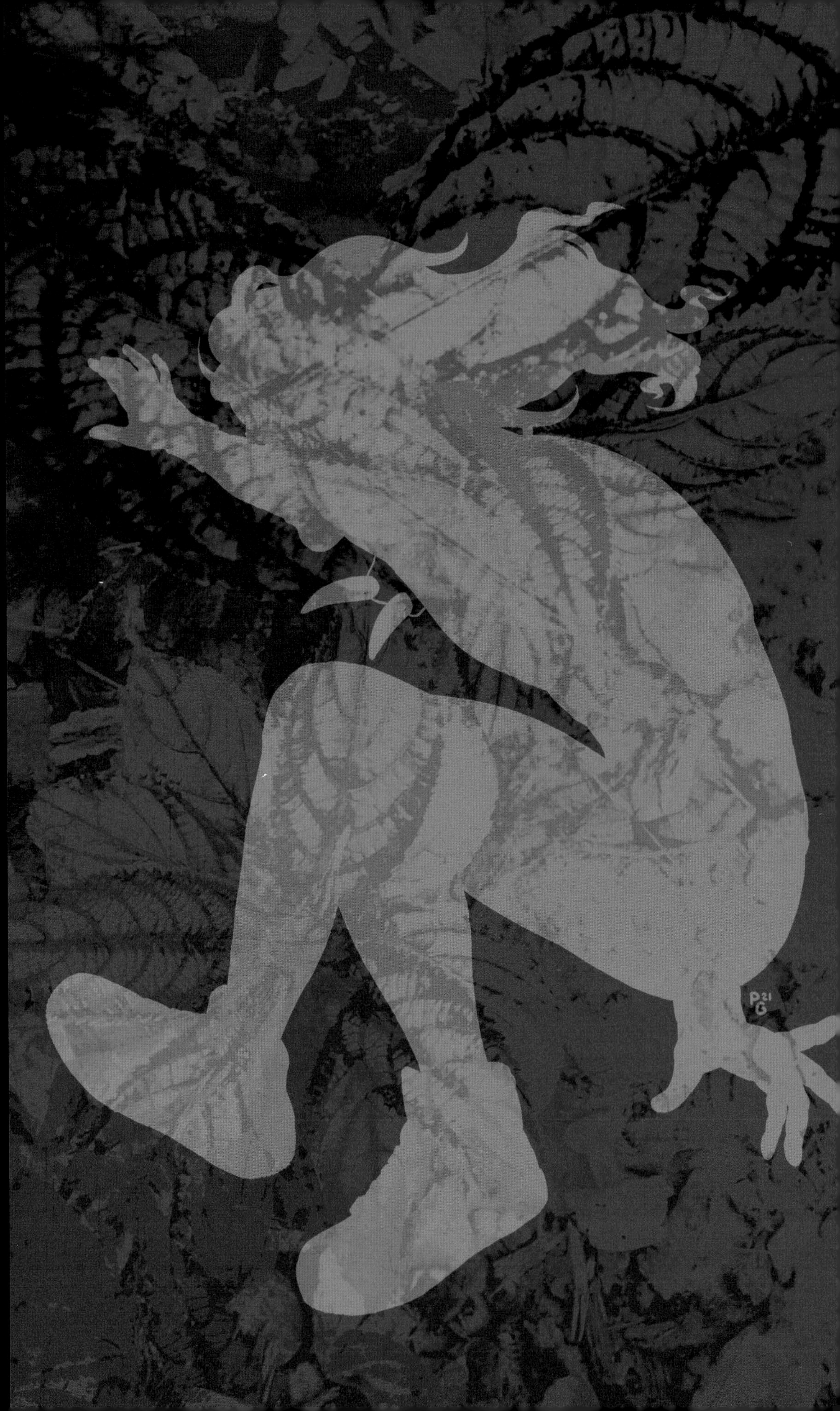

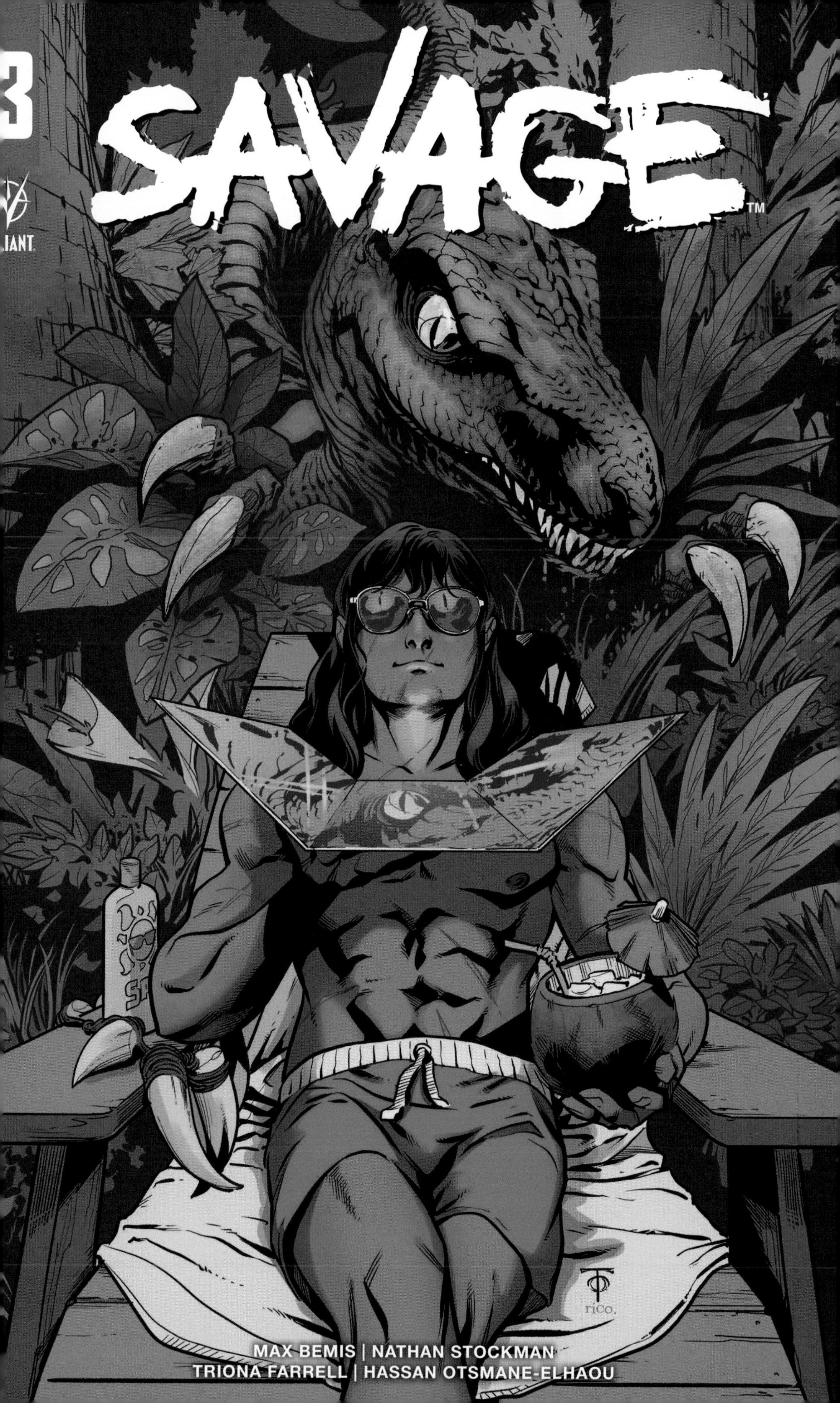
3
SAVAGE™
VALIANT
rico.
MAX BEMIS | NATHAN STOCKMAN
TRIONA FARRELL | HASSAN OTSMANE-ELHAOU

**SAVAGE #3**

*WRITER:* Max Bemis
*ARTIST:* Nathan Stockman
*COLORIST:* Triona Farrell
*LETTERER:* Hassan Otsmane-Elhaou
*COVER ARTISTS:* Marcus To with Rico Renzi
*EDITOR:* David Menchel
*SENIOR EDITOR:* Heather Antos

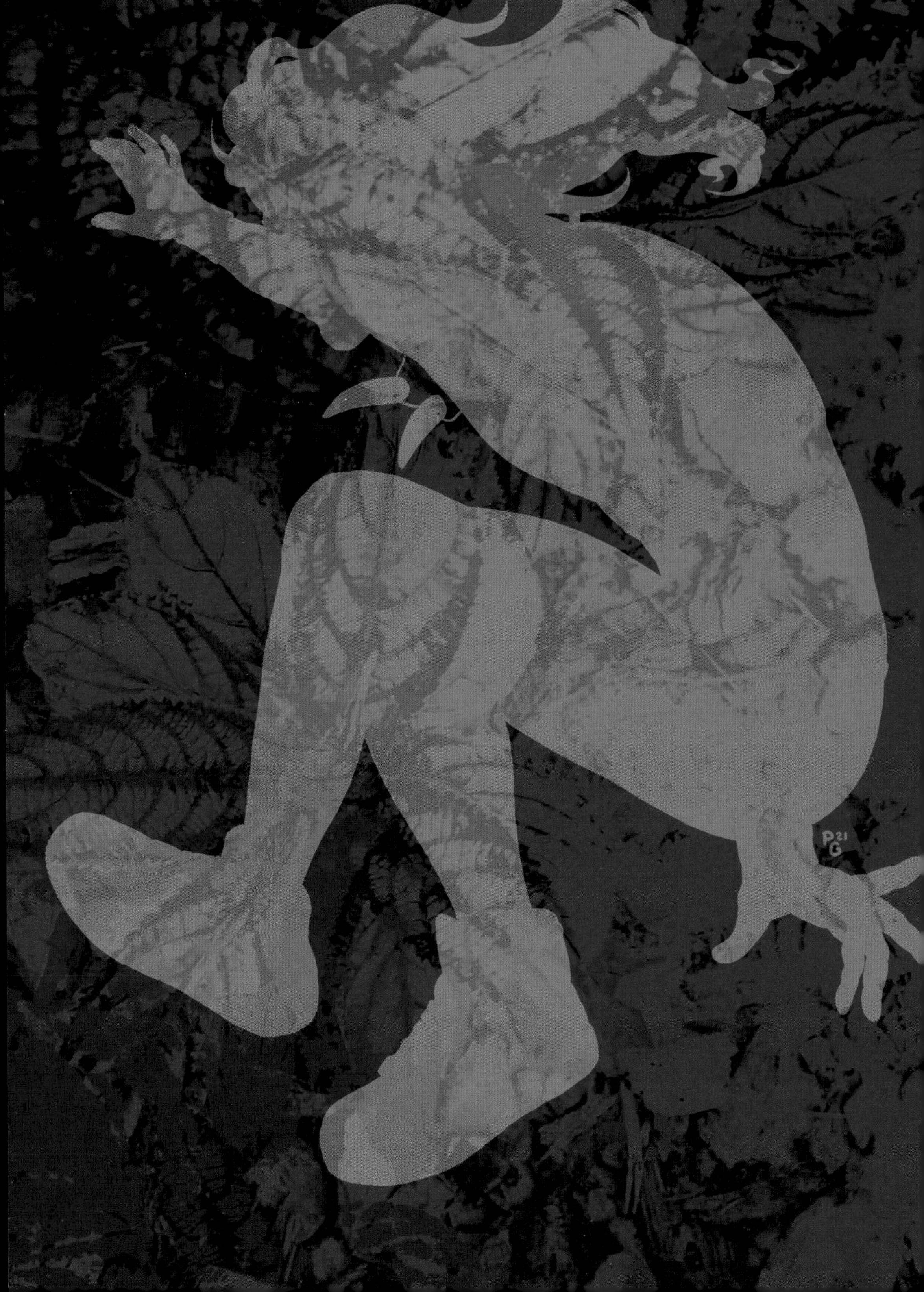

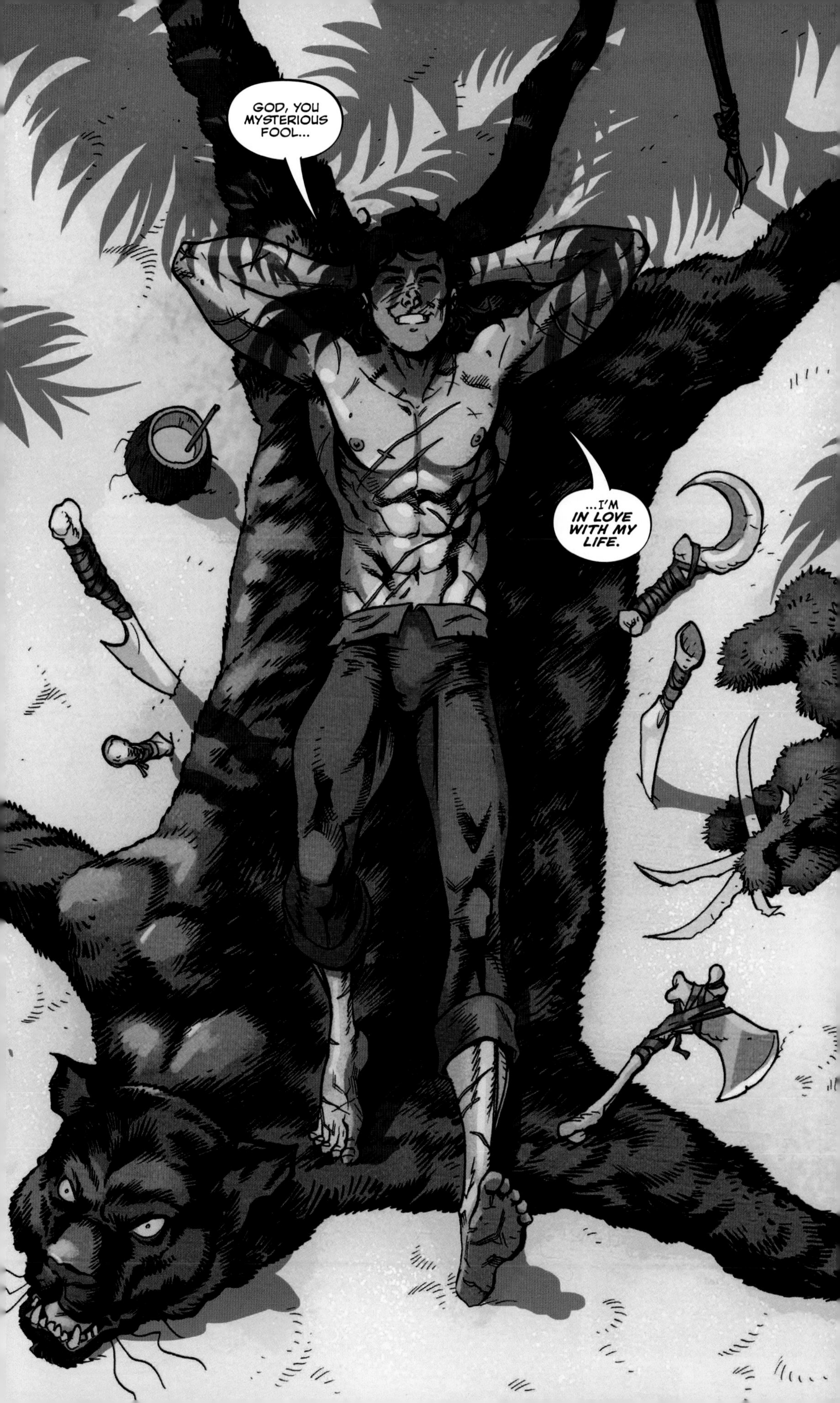
GOD, YOU MYSTERIOUS FOOL...
...I'M *IN LOVE WITH MY LIFE.*

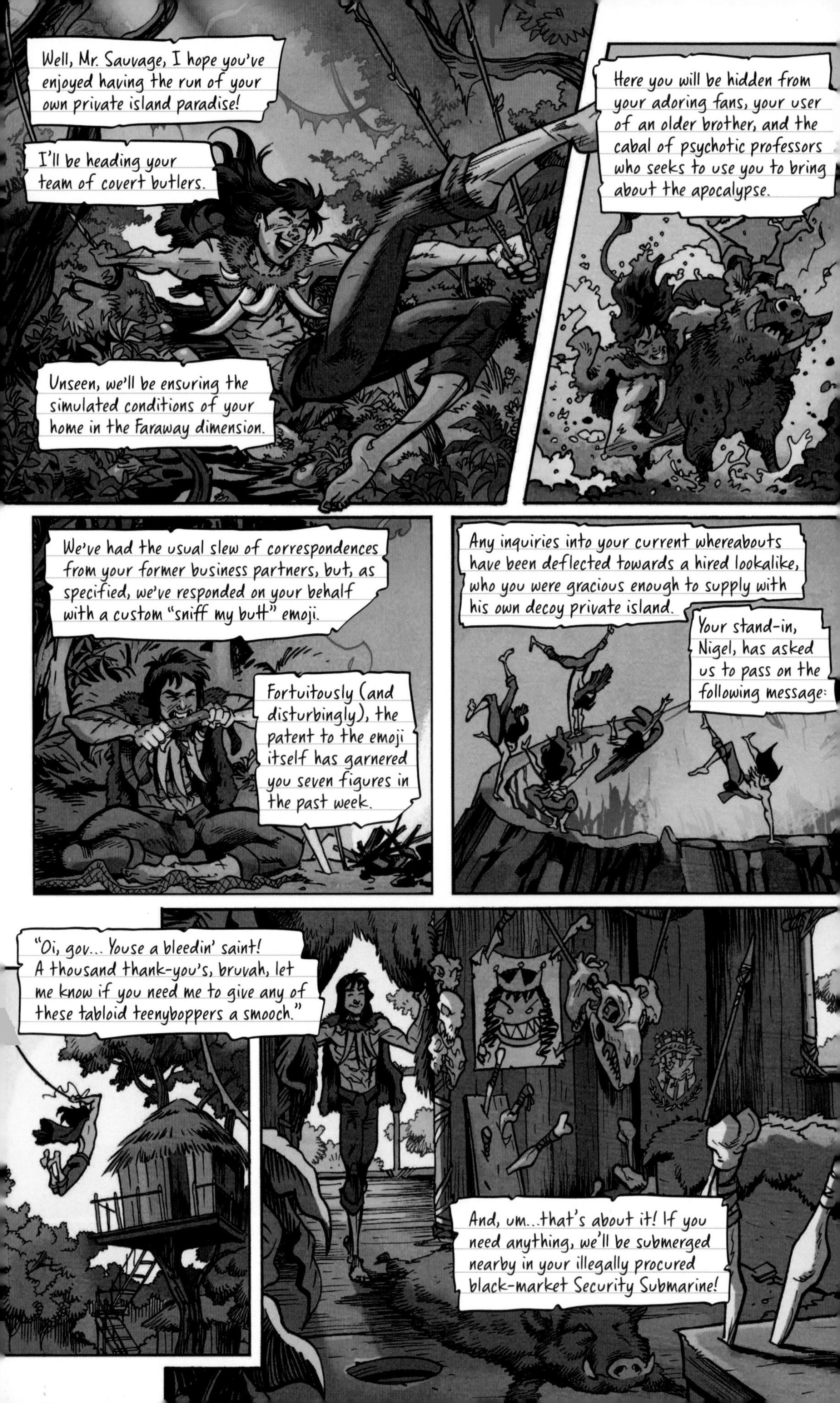

Well, Mr. Sauvage, I hope you've enjoyed having the run of your own private island paradise!
I'll be heading your team of covert butlers.
Unseen, we'll be ensuring the simulated conditions of your home in the Faraway dimension.
Here you will be hidden from your adoring fans, your user of an older brother, and the cabal of psychotic professors who seeks to use you to bring about the apocalypse.
We've had the usual slew of correspondences from your former business partners, but, as specified, we've responded on your behalf with a custom "sniff my butt" emoji.
Fortuitously (and disturbingly), the patent to the emoji itself has garnered you seven figures in the past week.
Any inquiries into your current whereabouts have been deflected towards a hired lookalike, who you were gracious enough to supply with his own decoy private island.
Your stand-in, Nigel, has asked us to pass on the following message:
"Oi, gov... Youse a bleedin' saint! A thousand thank-you's, bruvah, let me know if you need me to give any of these tabloid teenyboppers a smooch."
And, um...that's about it! If you need anything, we'll be submerged nearby in your illegally procured black-market Security Submarine!

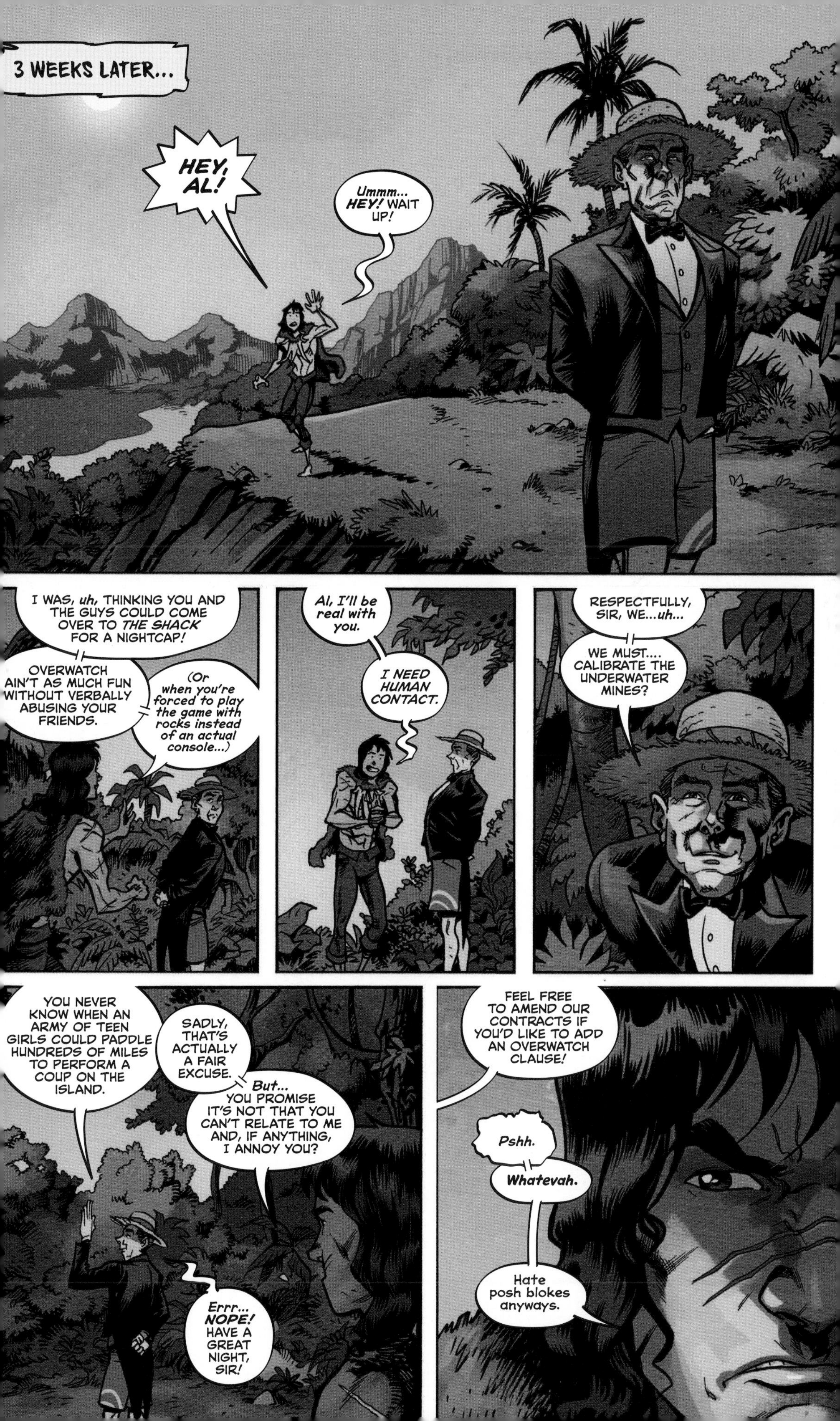
3 WEEKS LATER...
HEY, AL!
Ummm... HEY! WAIT UP!
I WAS, uh, THINKING YOU AND THE GUYS COULD COME OVER TO THE SHACK FOR A NIGHTCAP!
OVERWATCH AIN'T AS MUCH FUN WITHOUT VERBALLY ABUSING YOUR FRIENDS.
(Or when you're forced to play the game with rocks instead of an actual console...)
Al, I'll be real with you.
I NEED HUMAN CONTACT.
RESPECTFULLY, SIR, WE...uh...
WE MUST.... CALIBRATE THE UNDERWATER MINES?
YOU NEVER KNOW WHEN AN ARMY OF TEEN GIRLS COULD PADDLE HUNDREDS OF MILES TO PERFORM A COUP ON THE ISLAND.
SADLY, THAT'S ACTUALLY A FAIR EXCUSE.
But... YOU PROMISE IT'S NOT THAT YOU CAN'T RELATE TO ME AND, IF ANYTHING, I ANNOY YOU?
Errr... NOPE! HAVE A GREAT NIGHT, SIR!
FEEL FREE TO AMEND OUR CONTRACTS IF YOU'D LIKE TO ADD AN OVERWATCH CLAUSE!
Pshh.
Whatevah.
Hate posh blokes anyways.

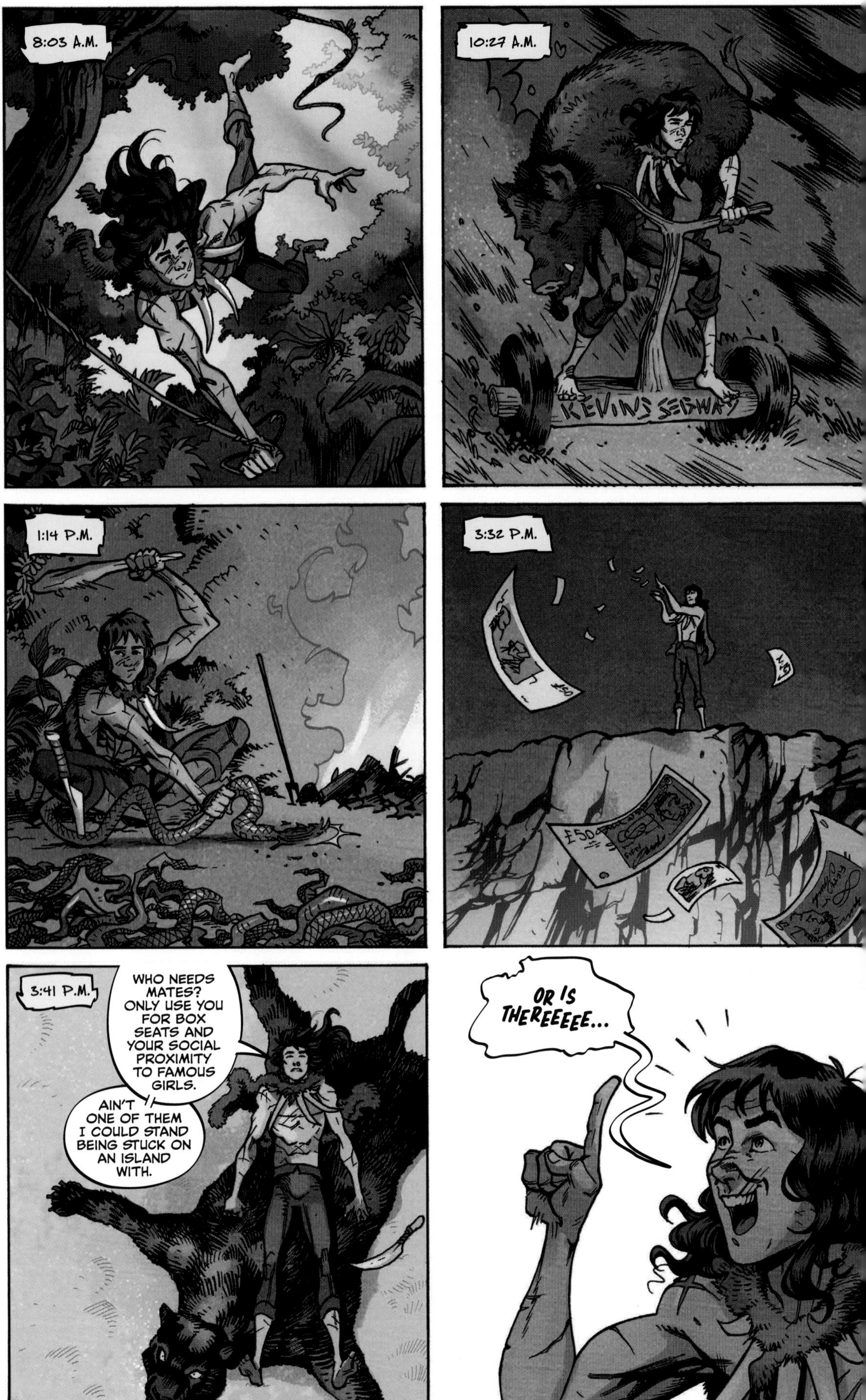
8:03 A.M.
10:27 A.M.
KEVIN'S SEGWAY
1:14 P.M.
3:32 P.M.
£50
3:41 P.M.
WHO NEEDS MATES? ONLY USE YOU FOR BOX SEATS AND YOUR SOCIAL PROXIMITY TO FAMOUS GIRLS.
AIN'T ONE OF THEM I COULD STAND BEING STUCK ON AN ISLAND WITH.
OR IS THEREEEEE...

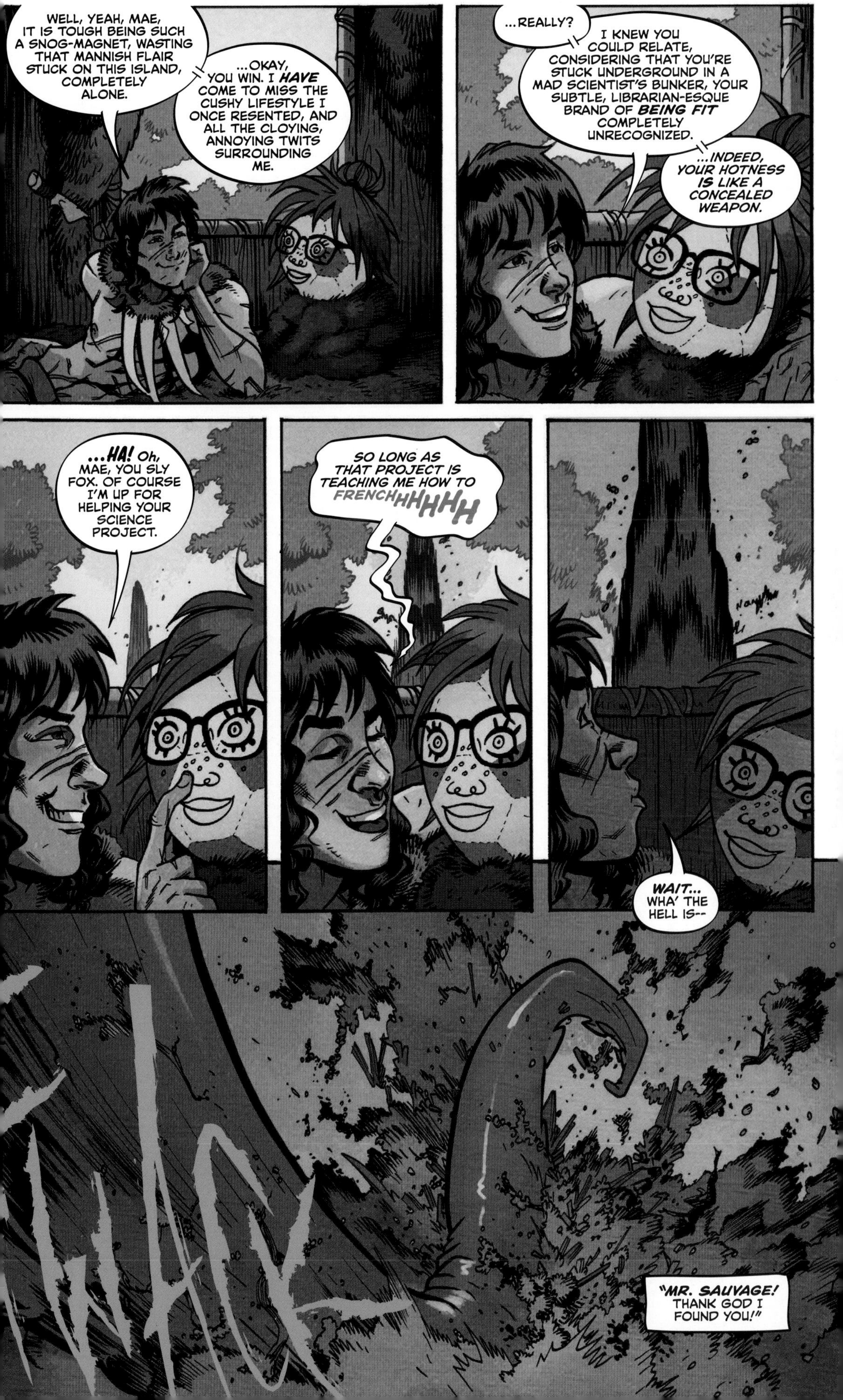
WELL, YEAH, MAE, IT IS TOUGH BEING SUCH A SNOG-MAGNET, WASTING THAT MANNISH FLAIR STUCK ON THIS ISLAND, COMPLETELY ALONE.
...OKAY, YOU WIN. I HAVE COME TO MISS THE CUSHY LIFESTYLE I ONCE RESENTED, AND ALL THE CLOYING, ANNOYING TWITS SURROUNDING ME.
...REALLY?
I KNEW YOU COULD RELATE, CONSIDERING THAT YOU'RE STUCK UNDERGROUND IN A MAD SCIENTIST'S BUNKER, YOUR SUBTLE, LIBRARIAN-ESQUE BRAND OF BEING FIT COMPLETELY UNRECOGNIZED.
...INDEED, YOUR HOTNESS IS LIKE A CONCEALED WEAPON.
...HA! Oh, MAE, YOU SLY FOX. OF COURSE I'M UP FOR HELPING YOUR SCIENCE PROJECT.
SO LONG AS THAT PROJECT IS TEACHING ME HOW TO FRENCHHHHHH
WAIT... WHA' THE HELL IS--
"MR. SAUVAGE! THANK GOD I FOUND YOU!"

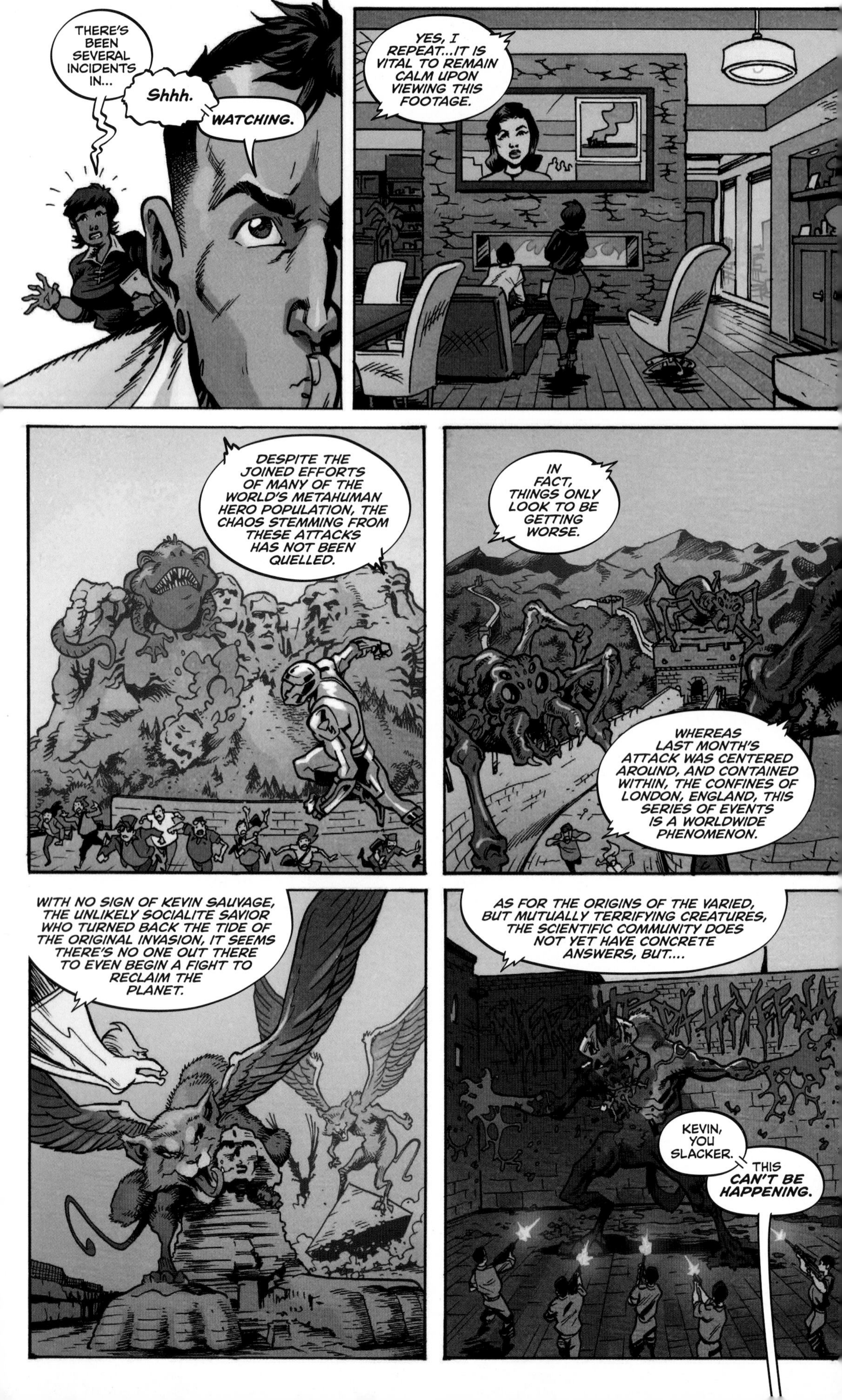
THERE'S BEEN SEVERAL INCIDENTS IN...
Shhh.
WATCHING.
YES, I REPEAT...IT IS VITAL TO REMAIN CALM UPON VIEWING THIS FOOTAGE.
DESPITE THE JOINED EFFORTS OF MANY OF THE WORLD'S METAHUMAN HERO POPULATION, THE CHAOS STEMMING FROM THESE ATTACKS HAS NOT BEEN QUELLED.
IN FACT, THINGS ONLY LOOK TO BE GETTING WORSE.
WHEREAS LAST MONTH'S ATTACK WAS CENTERED AROUND, AND CONTAINED WITHIN, THE CONFINES OF LONDON, ENGLAND, THIS SERIES OF EVENTS IS A WORLDWIDE PHENOMENON.
WITH NO SIGN OF KEVIN SAUVAGE, THE UNLIKELY SOCIALITE SAVIOR WHO TURNED BACK THE TIDE OF THE ORIGINAL INVASION, IT SEEMS THERE'S NO ONE OUT THERE TO EVEN BEGIN A FIGHT TO RECLAIM THE PLANET.
AS FOR THE ORIGINS OF THE VARIED, BUT MUTUALLY TERRIFYING CREATURES, THE SCIENTIFIC COMMUNITY DOES NOT YET HAVE CONCRETE ANSWERS, BUT....
KEVIN, YOU SLACKER.
THIS CAN'T BE HAPPENING.

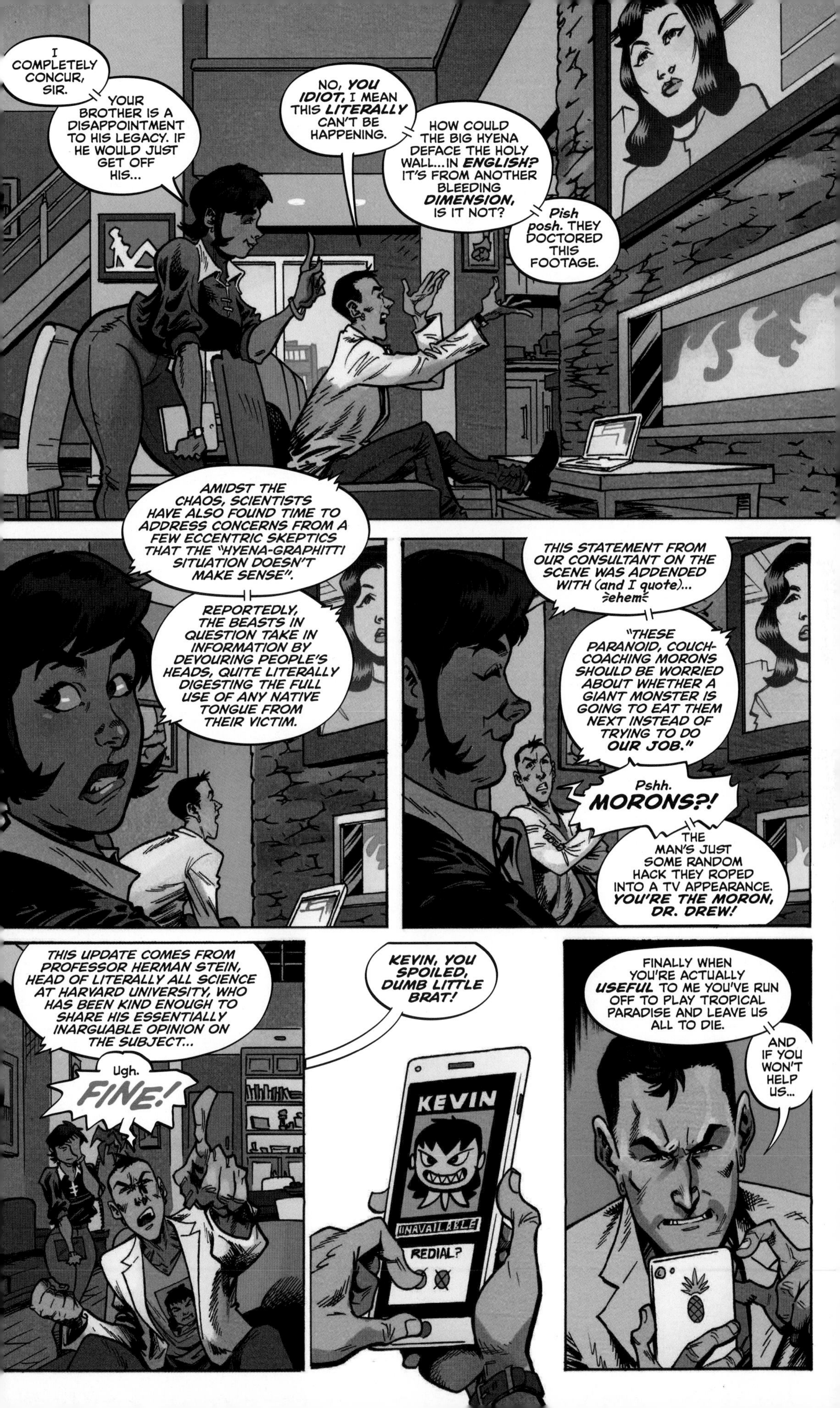

I COMPLETELY CONCUR, SIR.
YOUR BROTHER IS A DISAPPOINTMENT TO HIS LEGACY. IF HE WOULD JUST GET OFF HIS...
NO, *YOU IDIOT,* I MEAN THIS *LITERALLY* CAN'T BE HAPPENING.
HOW COULD THE BIG HYENA DEFACE THE HOLY WALL...IN *ENGLISH?* IT'S FROM ANOTHER BLEEDING *DIMENSION,* IS IT NOT?
*Pish posh.* THEY DOCTORED THIS FOOTAGE.
AMIDST THE CHAOS, SCIENTISTS HAVE ALSO FOUND TIME TO ADDRESS CONCERNS FROM A FEW ECCENTRIC SKEPTICS THAT THE "HYENA-GRAPHITTI SITUATION DOESN'T MAKE SENSE".
REPORTEDLY, THE BEASTS IN QUESTION TAKE IN INFORMATION BY DEVOURING PEOPLE'S HEADS, QUITE LITERALLY DIGESTING THE FULL USE OF ANY NATIVE TONGUE FROM THEIR VICTIM.
THIS STATEMENT FROM OUR CONSULTANT ON THE SCENE WAS ADDENDED WITH (and I quote)... ehem
"THESE PARANOID, COUCH-COACHING MORONS SHOULD BE WORRIED ABOUT WHETHER A GIANT MONSTER IS GOING TO EAT THEM NEXT INSTEAD OF TRYING TO DO **OUR JOB.**"
Pshh. **MORONS?!**
THE MAN'S JUST SOME RANDOM HACK THEY ROPED INTO A TV APPEARANCE. ***YOU'RE THE MORON, DR. DREW!***
THIS UPDATE COMES FROM PROFESSOR HERMAN STEIN, HEAD OF LITERALLY ALL SCIENCE AT HARVARD UNIVERSITY, WHO HAS BEEN KIND ENOUGH TO SHARE HIS ESSENTIALLY INARGUABLE OPINION ON THE SUBJECT...
Ugh. *FINE!*
*KEVIN, YOU SPOILED, DUMB LITTLE BRAT!*
KEVIN
UNAVAILABLE
REDIAL?
FINALLY WHEN YOU'RE ACTUALLY *USEFUL* TO ME YOU'VE RUN OFF TO PLAY TROPICAL PARADISE AND LEAVE US ALL TO DIE.
AND IF YOU WON'T HELP US...

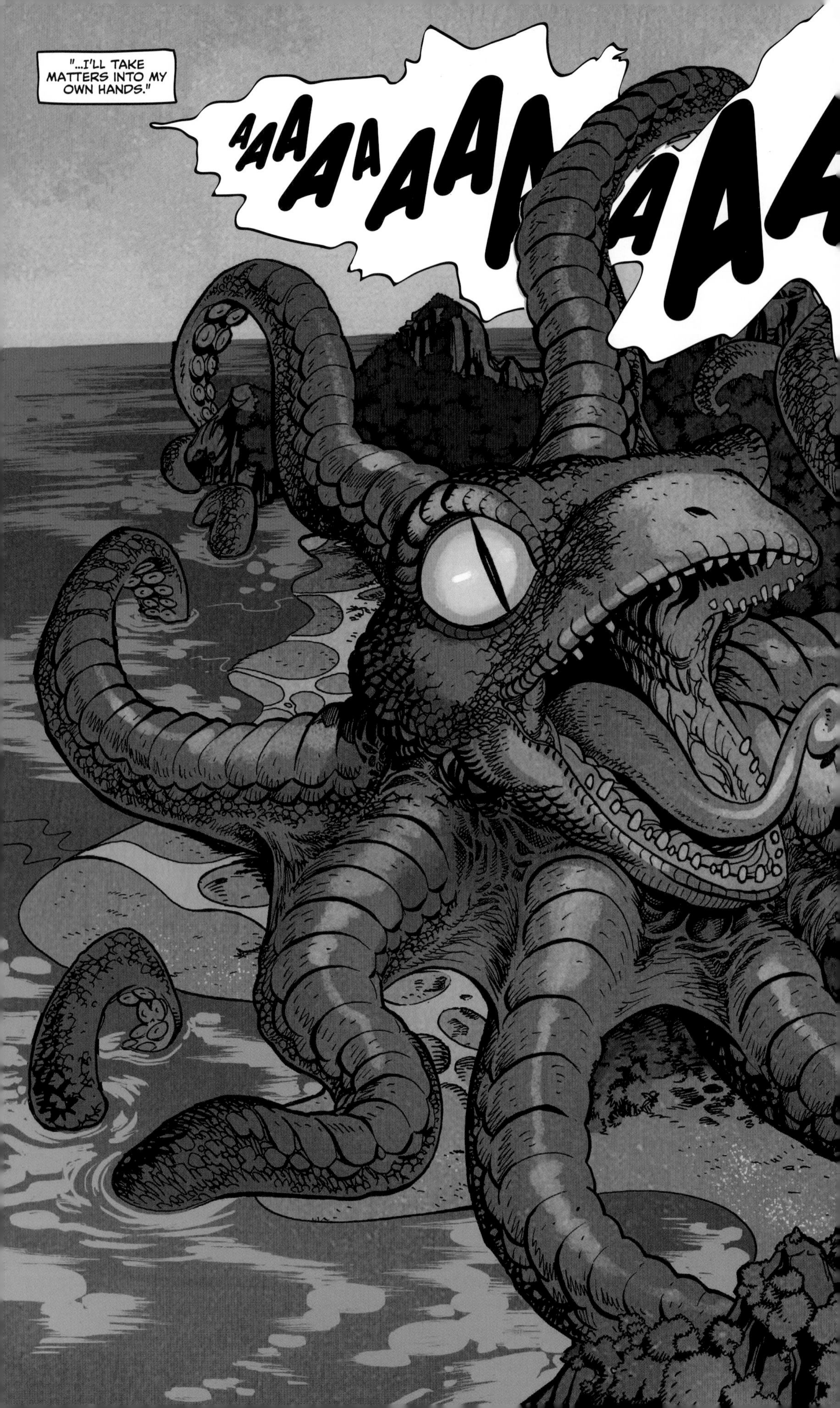
"...I'LL TAKE MATTERS INTO MY OWN HANDS."
AAAAAAAAAAAAAAA

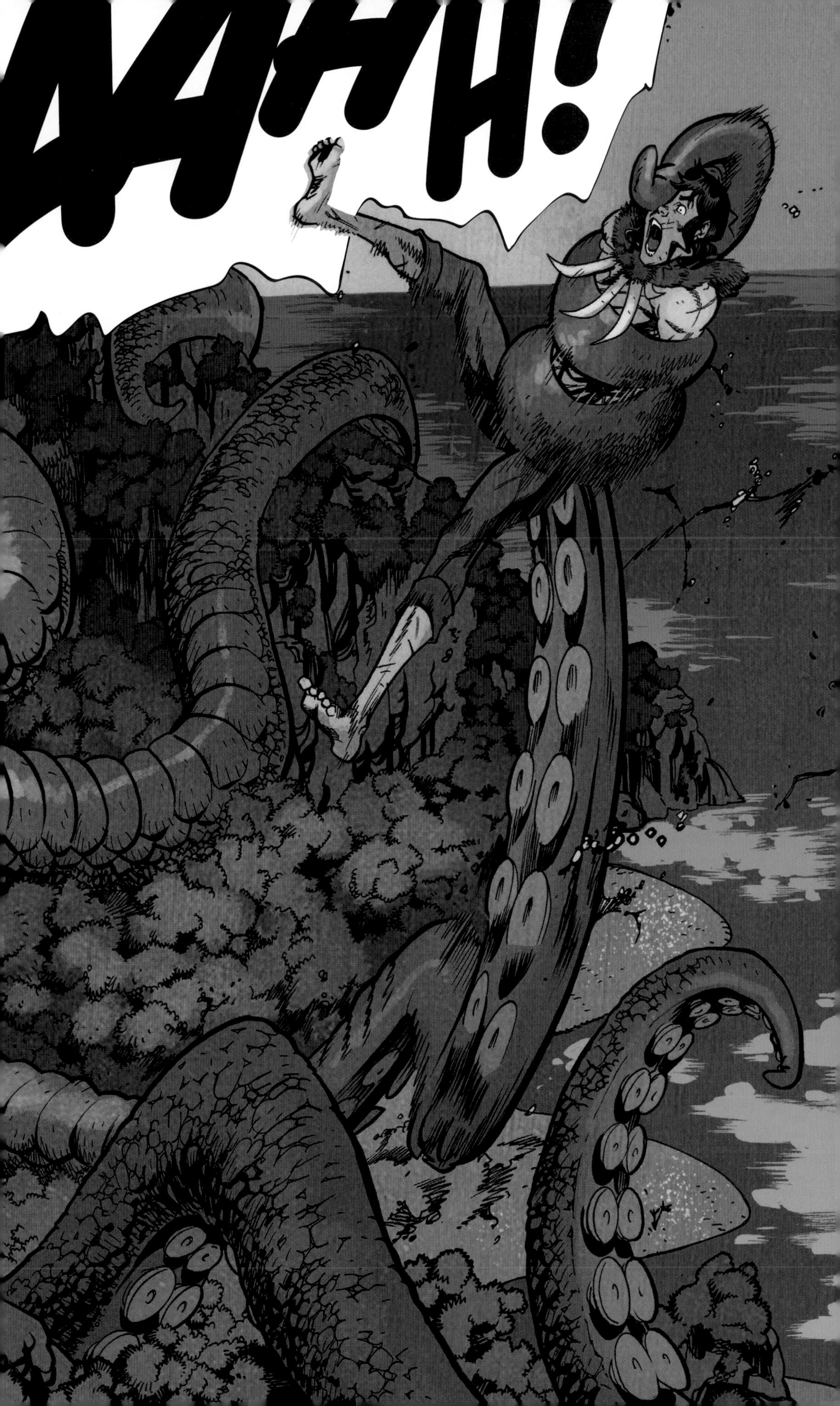
AAAHH!

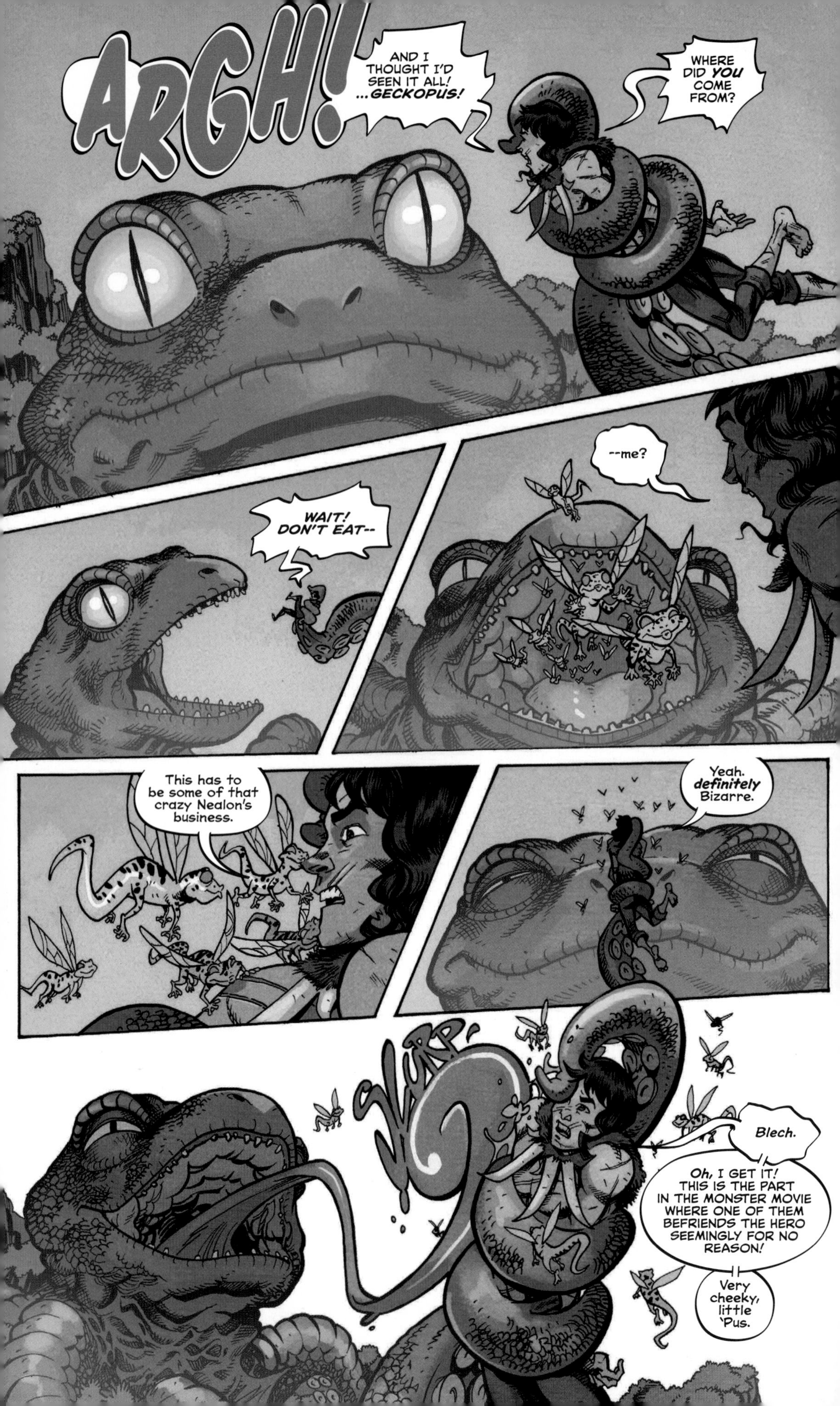
ARGH!
AND I THOUGHT I'D SEEN IT ALL! ...GECKOPUS!
WHERE DID YOU COME FROM?
WAIT! DON'T EAT--
--me?
This has to be some of that crazy Nealon's business.
Yeah. definitely Bizarre.
SHLURP!
Blech.
Oh, I GET IT! THIS IS THE PART IN THE MONSTER MOVIE WHERE ONE OF THEM BEFRIENDS THE HERO SEEMINGLY FOR NO REASON!
Very cheeky, little 'Pus.

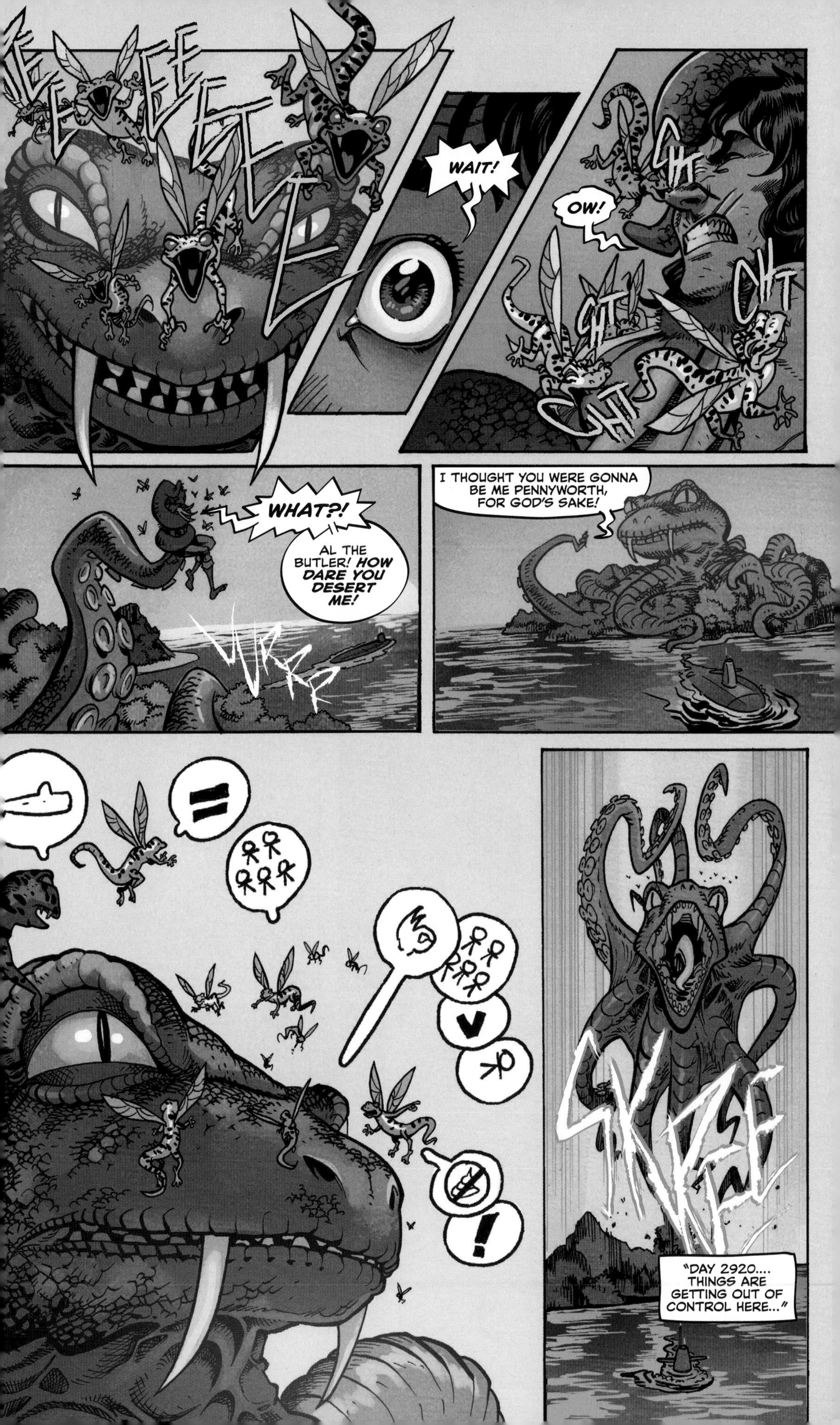
WAIT!
OW!
CHT
CHT
CHT
CHT
WHAT?!
AL THE BUTLER! HOW DARE YOU DESERT ME!
I THOUGHT YOU WERE GONNA BE ME PENNYWORTH, FOR GOD'S SAKE!
"DAY 2920.... THINGS ARE GETTING OUT OF CONTROL HERE..."

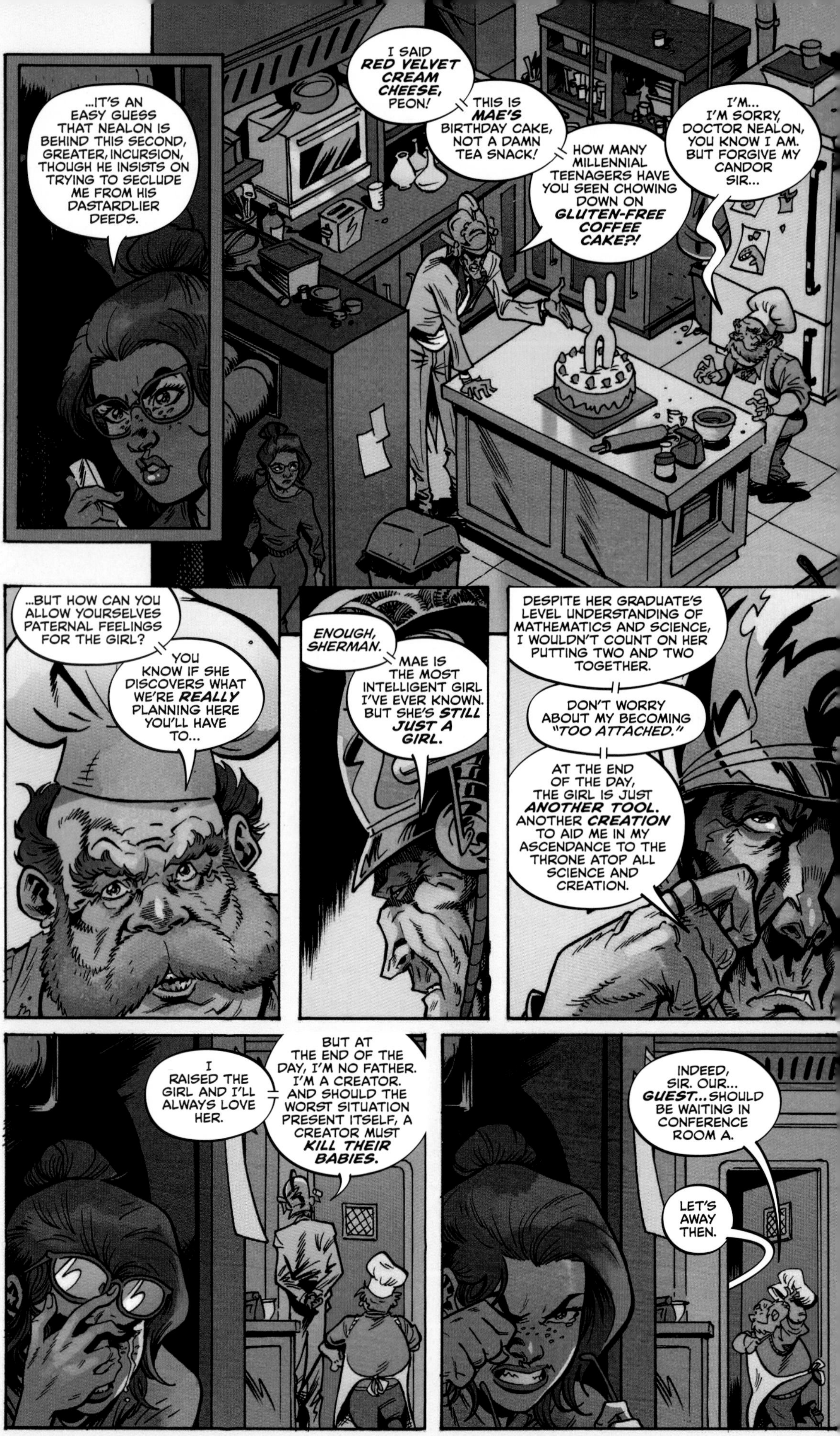
...IT'S AN EASY GUESS THAT NEALON IS BEHIND THIS SECOND, GREATER, INCURSION, THOUGH HE INSISTS ON TRYING TO SECLUDE ME FROM HIS DASTARDLIER DEEDS.
I SAID RED VELVET CREAM CHEESE, PEON!
THIS IS MAE'S BIRTHDAY CAKE, NOT A DAMN TEA SNACK!
HOW MANY MILLENNIAL TEENAGERS HAVE YOU SEEN CHOWING DOWN ON GLUTEN-FREE COFFEE CAKE?!
I'M... I'M SORRY, DOCTOR NEALON, YOU KNOW I AM. BUT FORGIVE MY CANDOR SIR...
...BUT HOW CAN YOU ALLOW YOURSELVES PATERNAL FEELINGS FOR THE GIRL?
YOU KNOW IF SHE DISCOVERS WHAT WE'RE REALLY PLANNING HERE YOU'LL HAVE TO...
ENOUGH, SHERMAN.
MAE IS THE MOST INTELLIGENT GIRL I'VE EVER KNOWN. BUT SHE'S STILL JUST A GIRL.
DESPITE HER GRADUATE'S LEVEL UNDERSTANDING OF MATHEMATICS AND SCIENCE, I WOULDN'T COUNT ON HER PUTTING TWO AND TWO TOGETHER.
DON'T WORRY ABOUT MY BECOMING "TOO ATTACHED."
AT THE END OF THE DAY, THE GIRL IS JUST ANOTHER TOOL. ANOTHER CREATION TO AID ME IN MY ASCENDANCE TO THE THRONE ATOP ALL SCIENCE AND CREATION.
I RAISED THE GIRL AND I'LL ALWAYS LOVE HER.
BUT AT THE END OF THE DAY, I'M NO FATHER. I'M A CREATOR. AND SHOULD THE WORST SITUATION PRESENT ITSELF, A CREATOR MUST KILL THEIR BABIES.
INDEED, SIR. OUR... GUEST... SHOULD BE WAITING IN CONFERENCE ROOM A.
LET'S AWAY THEN.

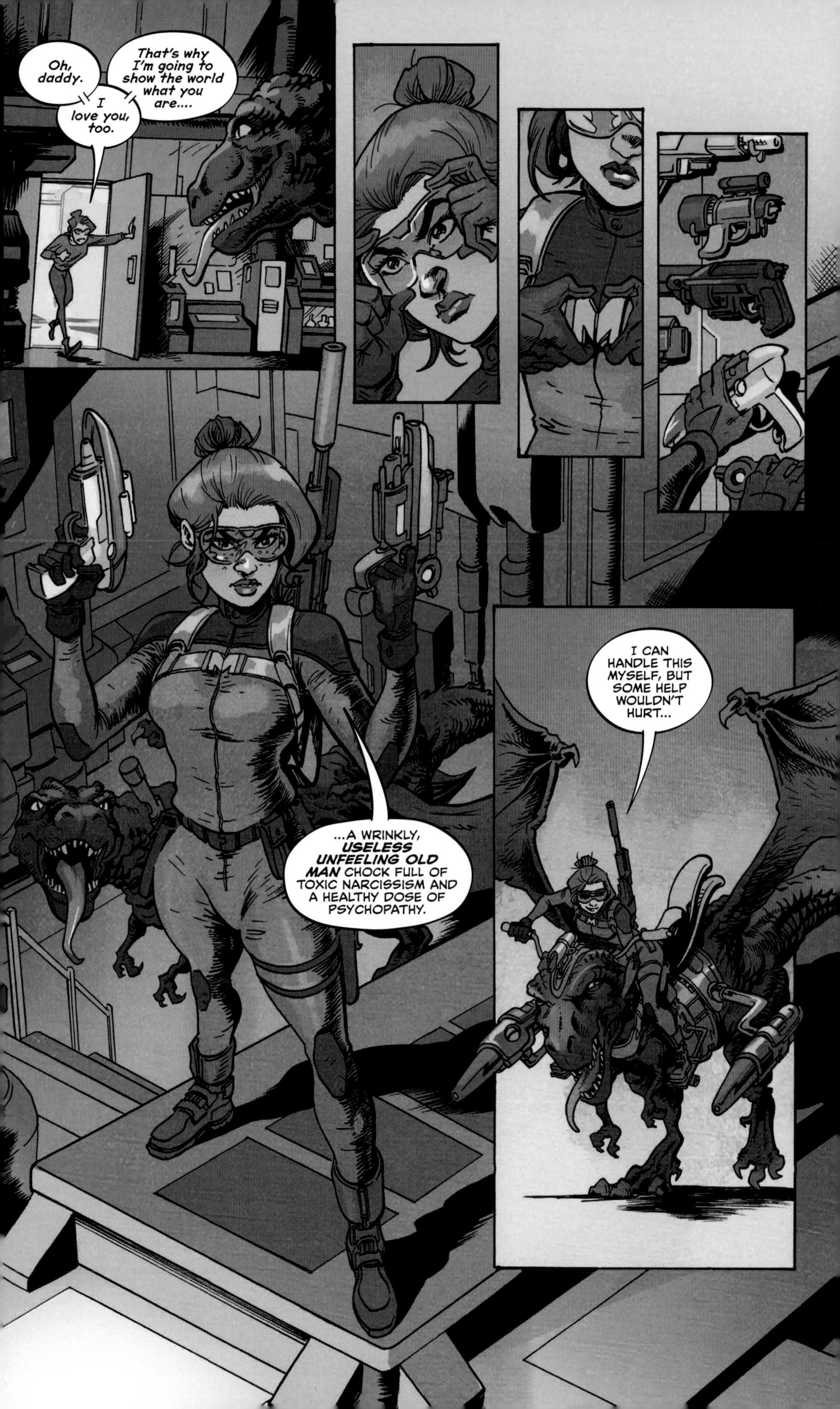

Oh, daddy.
I love you, too.
That's why I'm going to show the world what you are....
...A WRINKLY, USELESS UNFEELING OLD MAN CHOCK FULL OF TOXIC NARCISSISM AND A HEALTHY DOSE OF PSYCHOPATHY.
I CAN HANDLE THIS MYSELF, BUT SOME HELP WOULDN'T HURT...

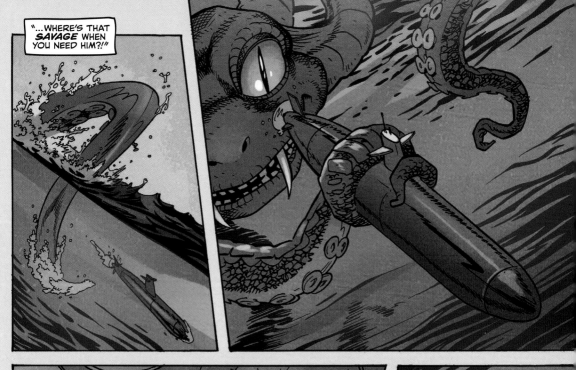

"...WHERE'S THAT *SAVAGE* WHEN YOU NEED HIM?!"

YOU KNOW, I *REALLY* SHOULD JUST LET THE BEAST EAT YOU FOR ABANDONING ME, AL.

POP!

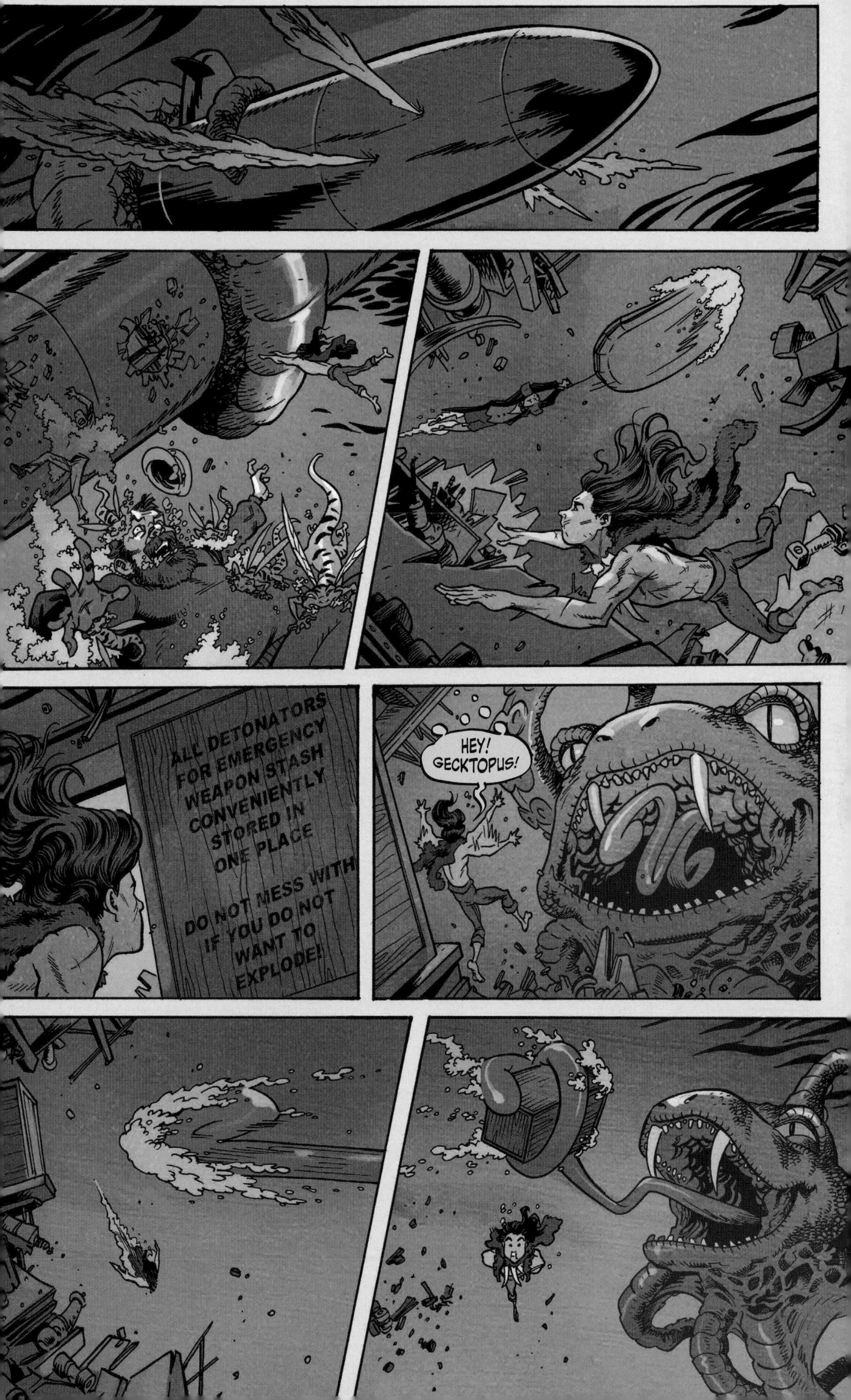
ALL DETONATORS FOR EMERGENCY WEAPON STASH CONVENIENTLY STORED IN ONE PLACE
DO NOT MESS WITH IF YOU DO NOT WANT TO EXPLODE!
HEY! GECKTOPUS!

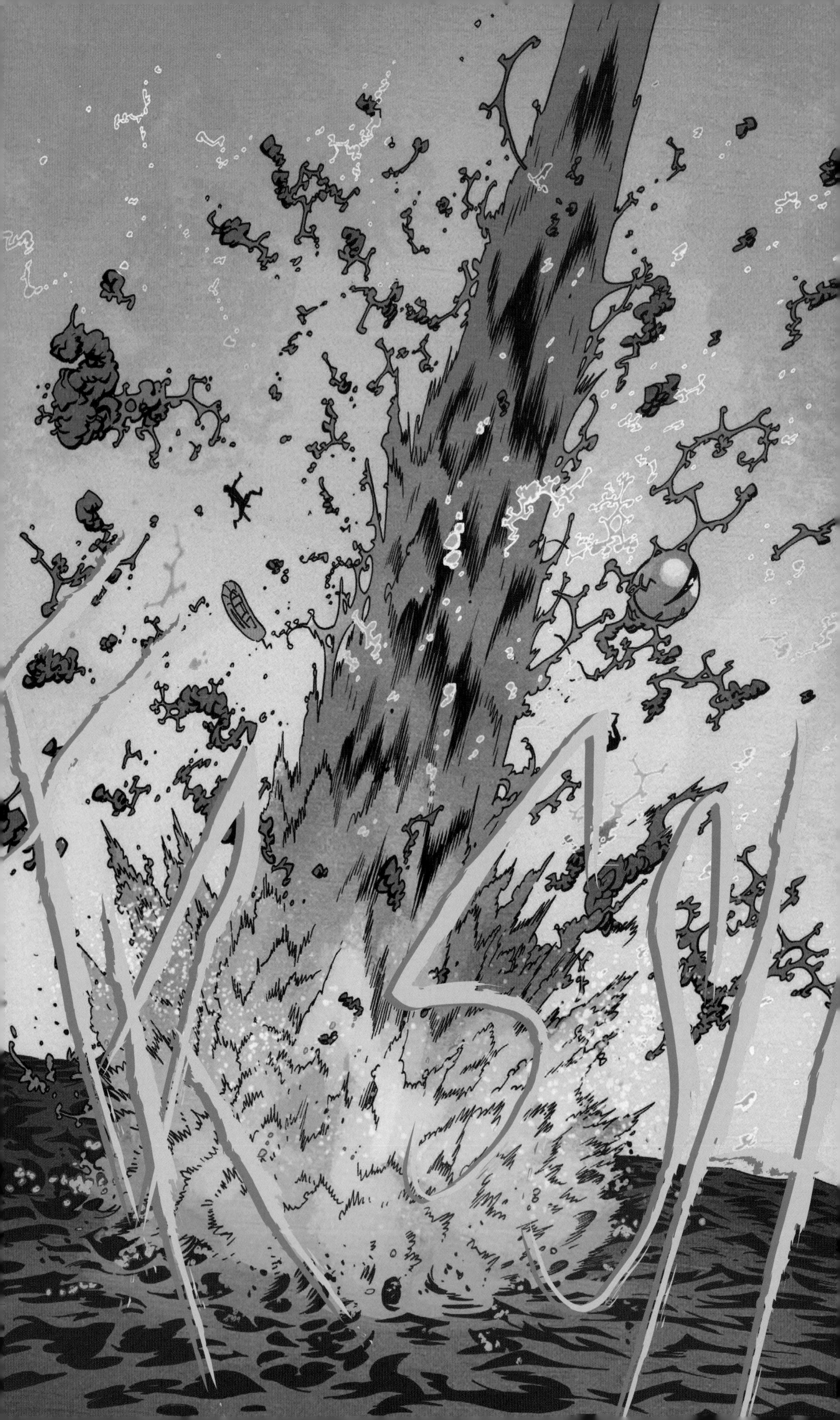

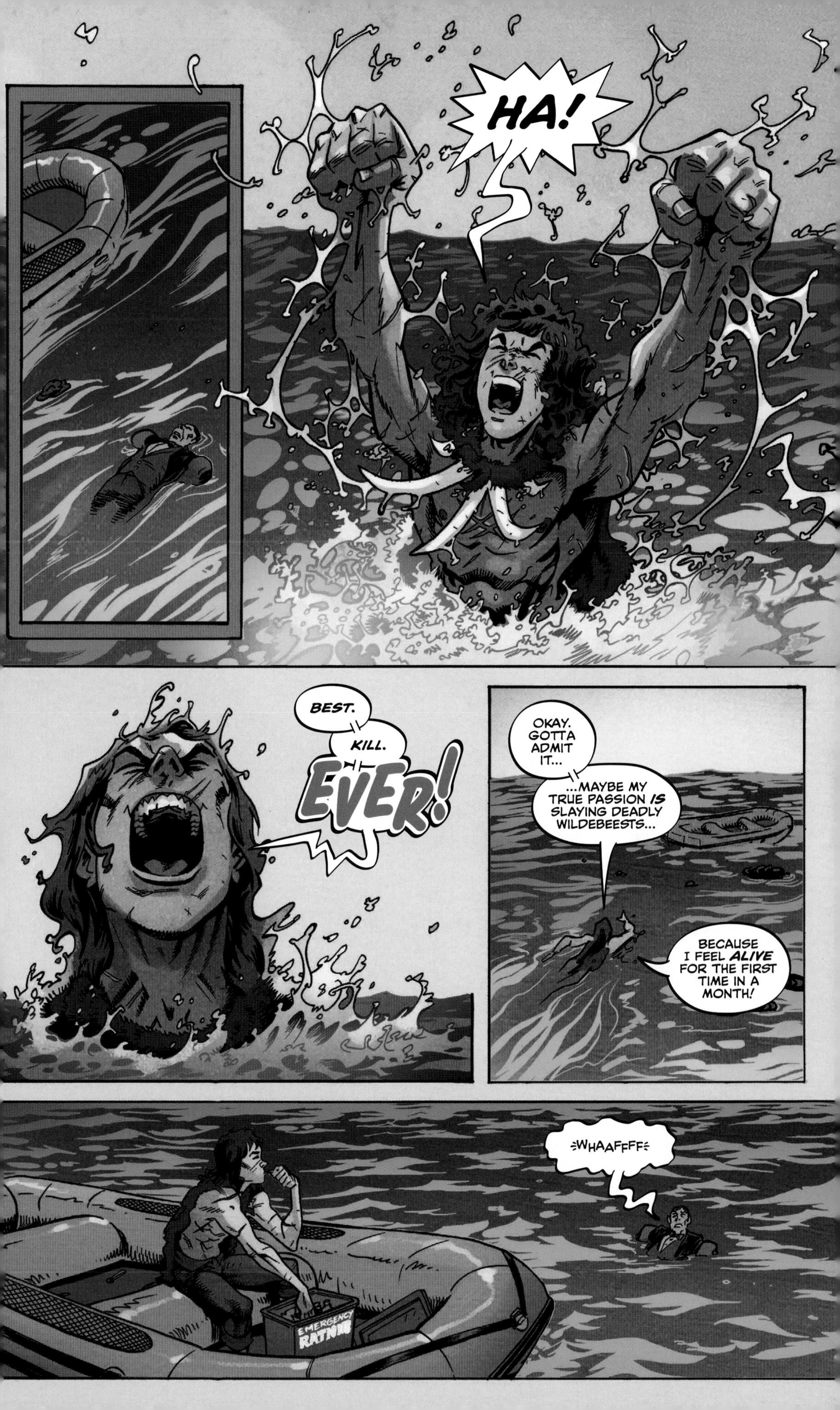
HA!
BEST.
KILL.
EVER!
OKAY. GOTTA ADMIT IT...
...MAYBE MY TRUE PASSION IS SLAYING DEADLY WILDEBEESTS...
BECAUSE I FEEL ALIVE FOR THE FIRST TIME IN A MONTH!
WHAAFFFF
EMERGENCY RATIONS

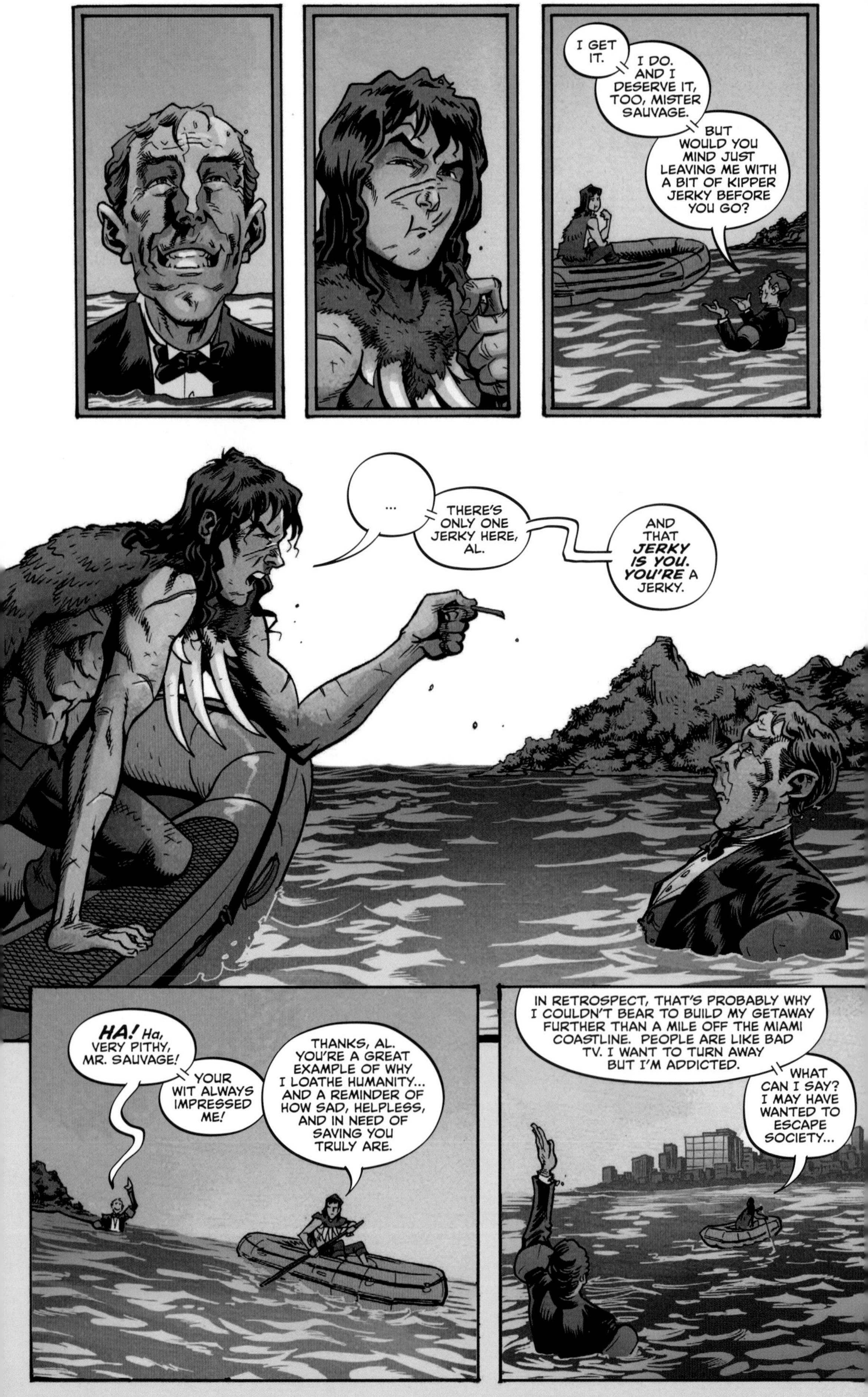

I GET IT.
I DO. AND I DESERVE IT, TOO, MISTER SAUVAGE.
BUT WOULD YOU MIND JUST LEAVING ME WITH A BIT OF KIPPER JERKY BEFORE YOU GO?
...
THERE'S ONLY ONE JERKY HERE, AL.
AND THAT JERKY IS YOU. YOU'RE A JERKY.
HA! Ha, VERY PITHY, MR. SAUVAGE!
YOUR WIT ALWAYS IMPRESSED ME!
THANKS, AL. YOU'RE A GREAT EXAMPLE OF WHY I LOATHE HUMANITY... AND A REMINDER OF HOW SAD, HELPLESS, AND IN NEED OF SAVING YOU TRULY ARE.
IN RETROSPECT, THAT'S PROBABLY WHY I COULDN'T BEAR TO BUILD MY GETAWAY FURTHER THAN A MILE OFF THE MIAMI COASTLINE. PEOPLE ARE LIKE BAD TV. I WANT TO TURN AWAY BUT I'M ADDICTED.
WHAT CAN I SAY? I MAY HAVE WANTED TO ESCAPE SOCIETY...

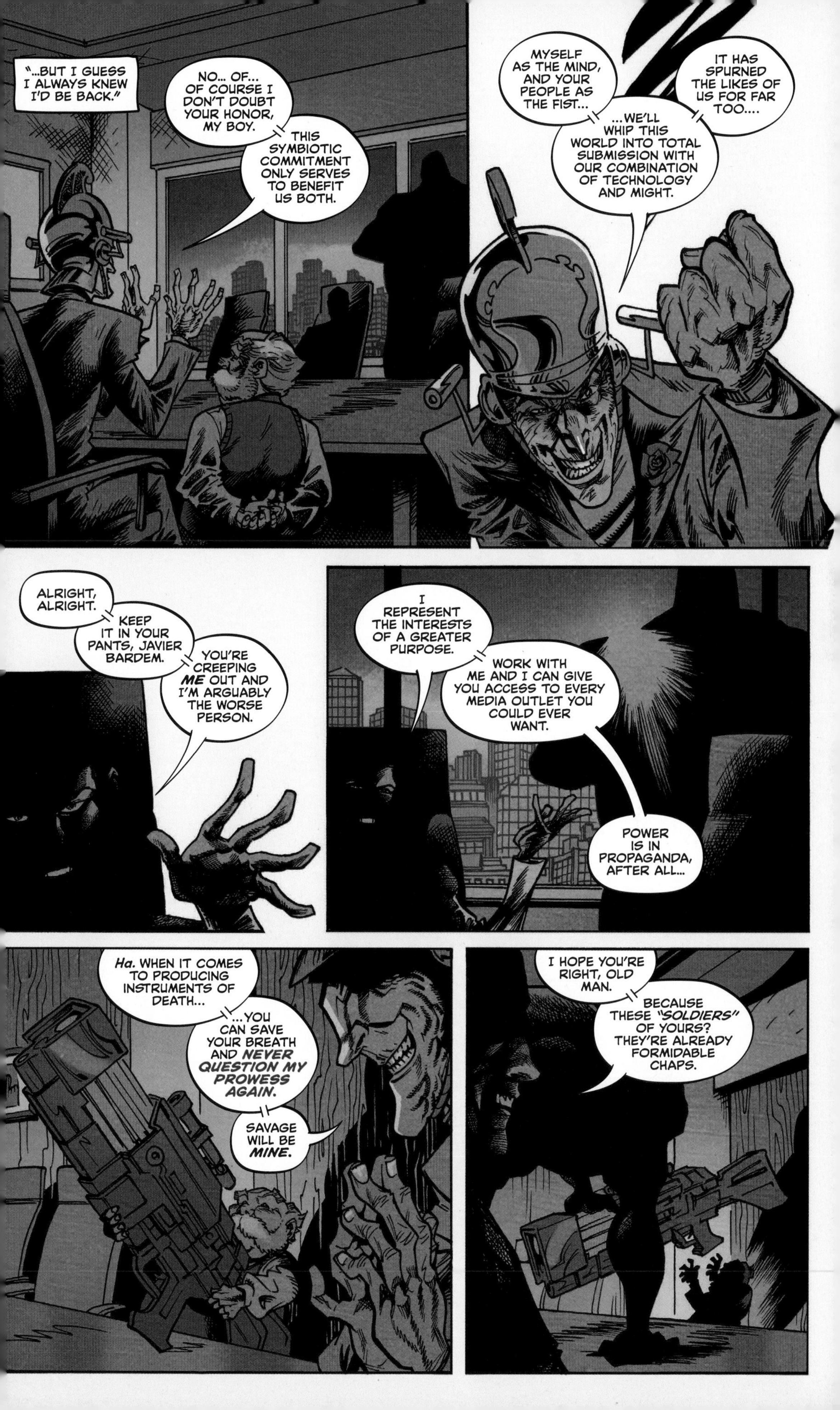
"...BUT I GUESS I ALWAYS KNEW I'D BE BACK."
NO... OF... OF COURSE I DON'T DOUBT YOUR HONOR, MY BOY.
THIS SYMBIOTIC COMMITMENT ONLY SERVES TO BENEFIT US BOTH.
MYSELF AS THE MIND, AND YOUR PEOPLE AS THE FIST...
...WE'LL WHIP THIS WORLD INTO TOTAL SUBMISSION WITH OUR COMBINATION OF TECHNOLOGY AND MIGHT.
IT HAS SPURNED THE LIKES OF US FOR FAR TOO....
ALRIGHT, ALRIGHT.
KEEP IT IN YOUR PANTS, JAVIER BARDEM.
YOU'RE CREEPING *ME* OUT AND I'M ARGUABLY THE WORSE PERSON.
I REPRESENT THE INTERESTS OF A GREATER PURPOSE.
WORK WITH ME AND I CAN GIVE YOU ACCESS TO EVERY MEDIA OUTLET YOU COULD EVER WANT.
POWER IS IN PROPAGANDA, AFTER ALL...
*Ha.* WHEN IT COMES TO PRODUCING INSTRUMENTS OF DEATH...
...YOU CAN SAVE YOUR BREATH AND *NEVER QUESTION MY PROWESS AGAIN.*
SAVAGE WILL BE *MINE.*
I HOPE YOU'RE RIGHT, OLD MAN.
BECAUSE THESE *"SOLDIERS"* OF YOURS? THEY'RE ALREADY FORMIDABLE CHAPS.

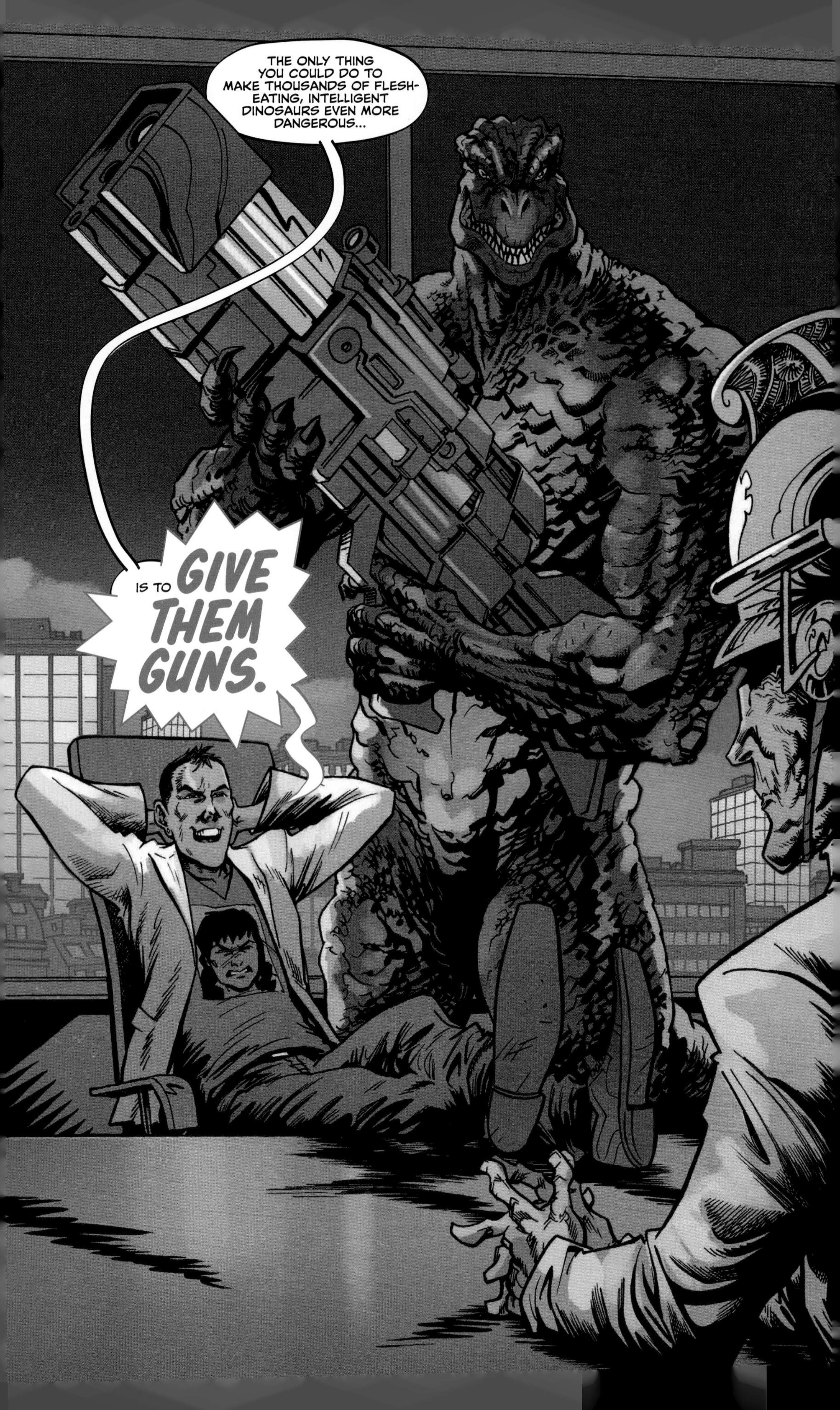
THE ONLY THING YOU COULD DO TO MAKE THOUSANDS OF FLESH-EATING, INTELLIGENT DINOSAURS EVEN MORE DANGEROUS...
IS TO GIVE THEM GUNS.

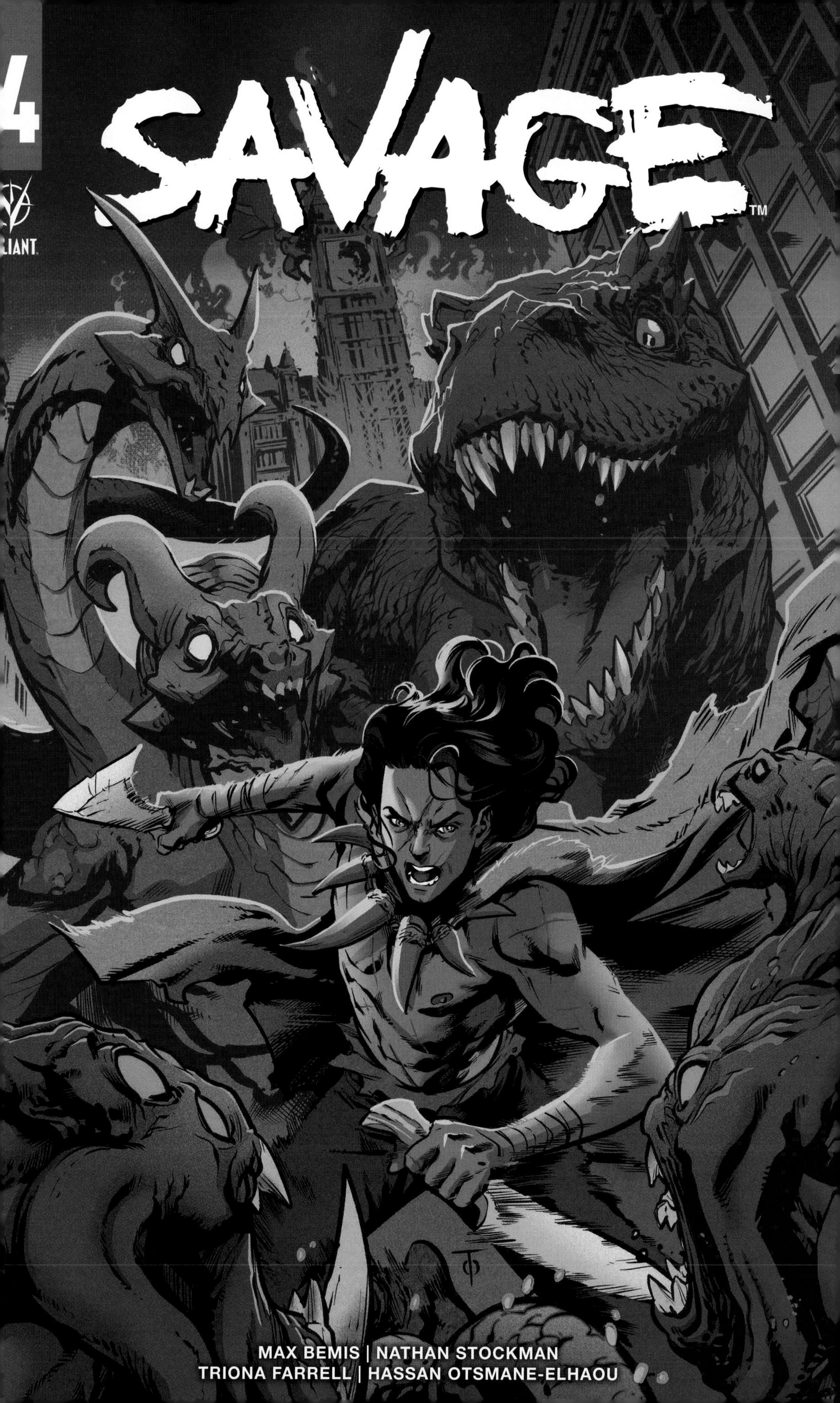
4
SAVAGE™
VALIANT
MAX BEMIS | NATHAN STOCKMAN
TRIONA FARRELL | HASSAN OTSMANE-ELHAOU

**SAVAGE #4**

*WRITER:* Max Bemis
*ARTIST:* Nathan Stockman
*COLORIST:* Triona Farrell
*LETTERER:* Hassan Otsmane-Elhaou
*COVER ARTISTS:* Marcus To with Rico Renzi
*EDITOR:* David Menchel
*SENIOR EDITOR:* Heather Antos

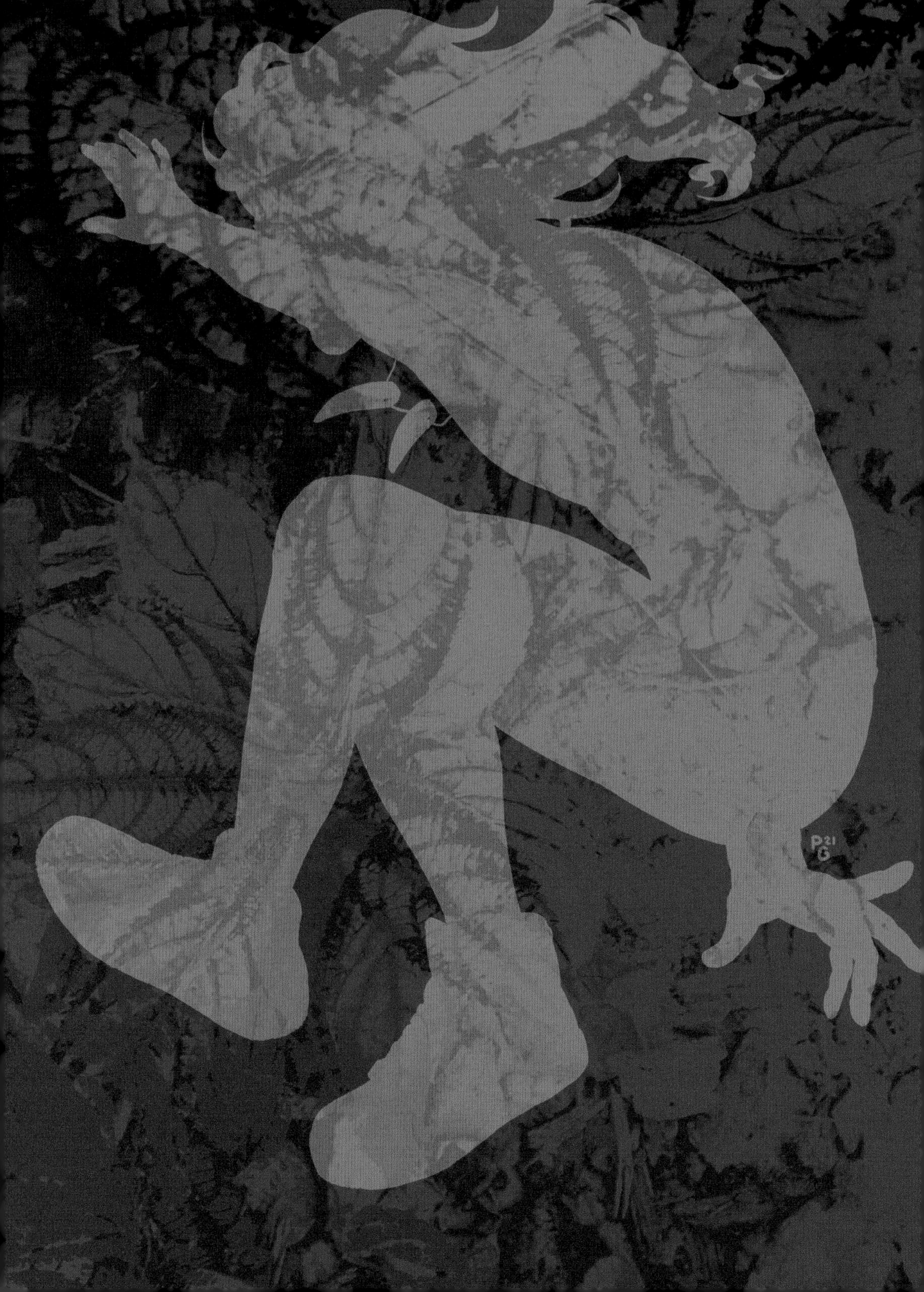

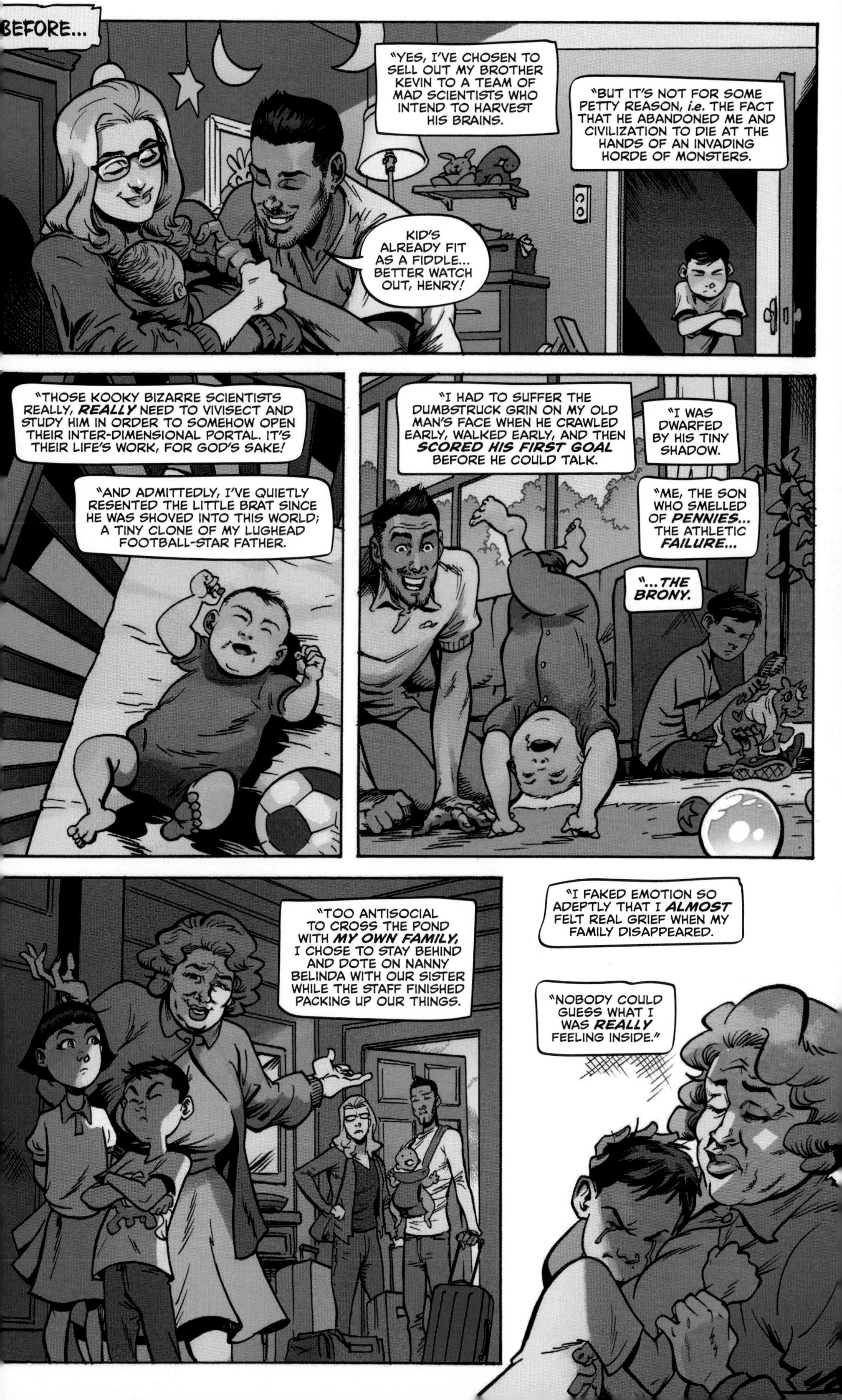
BEFORE...
"YES, I'VE CHOSEN TO SELL OUT MY BROTHER KEVIN TO A TEAM OF MAD SCIENTISTS WHO INTEND TO HARVEST HIS BRAINS.
"BUT IT'S NOT FOR SOME PETTY REASON, *i.e.* THE FACT THAT HE ABANDONED ME AND CIVILIZATION TO DIE AT THE HANDS OF AN INVADING HORDE OF MONSTERS.
KID'S ALREADY FIT AS A FIDDLE... BETTER WATCH OUT, HENRY!
"THOSE KOOKY BIZARRE SCIENTISTS REALLY, ***REALLY*** NEED TO VIVISECT AND STUDY HIM IN ORDER TO SOMEHOW OPEN THEIR INTER-DIMENSIONAL PORTAL. IT'S THEIR LIFE'S WORK, FOR GOD'S SAKE!
"AND ADMITTEDLY, I'VE QUIETLY RESENTED THE LITTLE BRAT SINCE HE WAS SHOVED INTO THIS WORLD; A TINY CLONE OF MY LUGHEAD FOOTBALL-STAR FATHER.
"I HAD TO SUFFER THE DUMBSTRUCK GRIN ON MY OLD MAN'S FACE WHEN HE CRAWLED EARLY, WALKED EARLY, AND THEN ***SCORED HIS FIRST GOAL*** BEFORE HE COULD TALK.
"I WAS DWARFED BY HIS TINY SHADOW.
"ME, THE SON WHO SMELLED OF ***PENNIES***... THE ATHLETIC ***FAILURE***...
***"...THE BRONY.***
"TOO ANTISOCIAL TO CROSS THE POND WITH ***MY OWN FAMILY,*** I CHOSE TO STAY BEHIND AND DOTE ON NANNY BELINDA WITH OUR SISTER WHILE THE STAFF FINISHED PACKING UP OUR THINGS.
"I FAKED EMOTION SO ADEPTLY THAT I ***ALMOST*** FELT REAL GRIEF WHEN MY FAMILY DISAPPEARED.
"NOBODY COULD GUESS WHAT I WAS ***REALLY*** FEELING INSIDE."

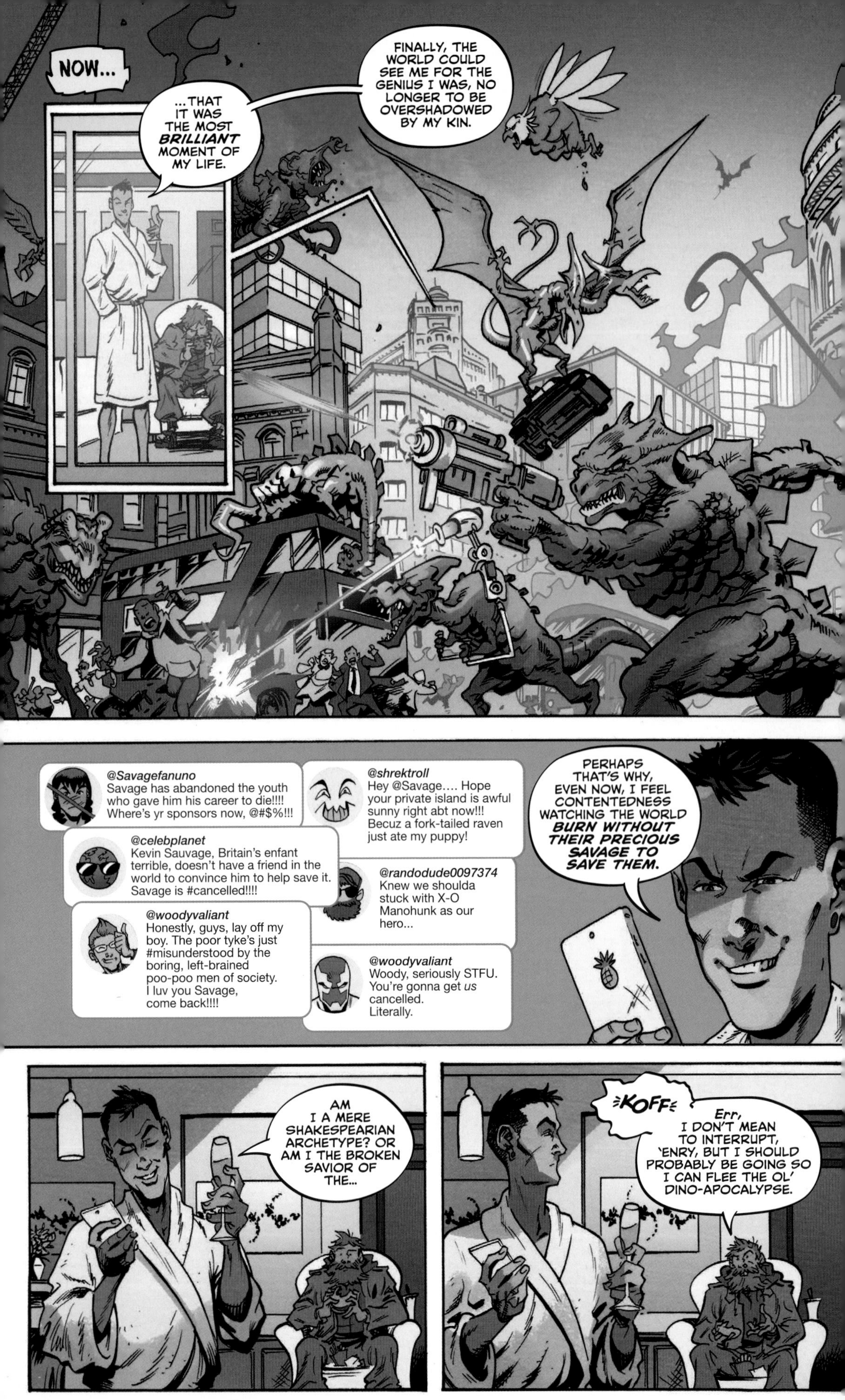

NOW...
...THAT IT WAS THE MOST BRILLIANT MOMENT OF MY LIFE.
FINALLY, THE WORLD COULD SEE ME FOR THE GENIUS I WAS, NO LONGER TO BE OVERSHADOWED BY MY KIN.
@Savagefanuno
Savage has abandoned the youth who gave him his career to die!!!! Where's yr sponsors now, @#$%!!!
@shrektroll
Hey @Savage.... Hope your private island is awful sunny right abt now!!! Becuz a fork-tailed raven just ate my puppy!
@celebplanet
Kevin Sauvage, Britain's enfant terrible, doesn't have a friend in the world to convince him to help save it. Savage is #cancelled!!!!
@randodude0097374
Knew we shoulda stuck with X-O Manohunk as our hero...
@woodyvaliant
Honestly, guys, lay off my boy. The poor tyke's just #misunderstood by the boring, left-brained poo-poo men of society. I luv you Savage, come back!!!!
@woodyvaliant
Woody, seriously STFU. You're gonna get *us* cancelled. Literally.
PERHAPS THAT'S WHY, EVEN NOW, I FEEL CONTENTEDNESS WATCHING THE WORLD BURN WITHOUT THEIR PRECIOUS SAVAGE TO SAVE THEM.
AM I A MERE SHAKESPEARIAN ARCHETYPE? OR AM I THE BROKEN SAVIOR OF THE...
KOFF
Err, I DON'T MEAN TO INTERRUPT, 'ENRY, BUT I SHOULD PROBABLY BE GOING SO I CAN FLEE THE OL' DINO-APOCALYPSE.

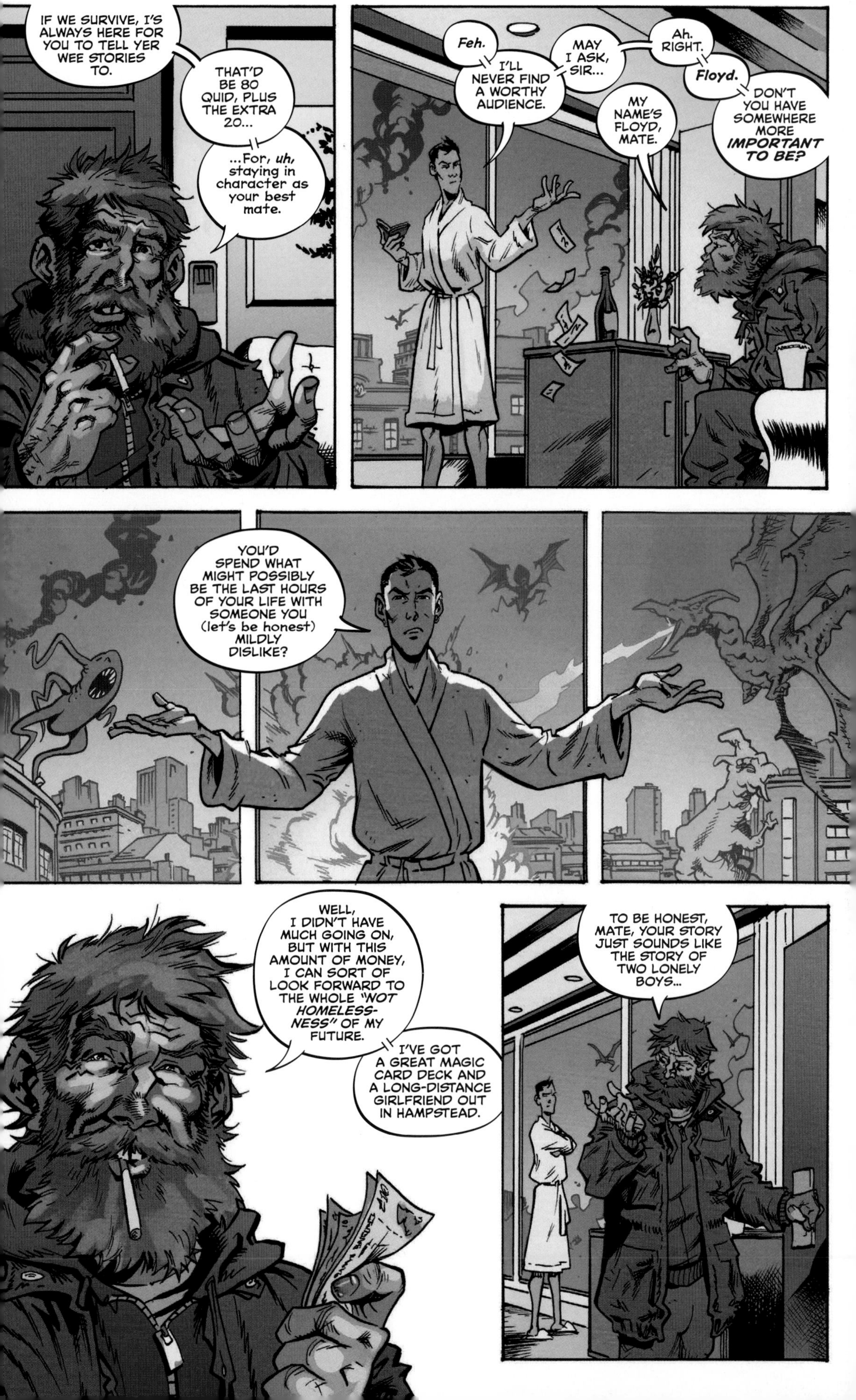

IF WE SURVIVE, I'S ALWAYS HERE FOR YOU TO TELL YER WEE STORIES TO.
THAT'D BE 80 QUID, PLUS THE EXTRA 20...
...For, *uh,* staying in character as your best mate.
*Feh.*
I'LL NEVER FIND A WORTHY AUDIENCE.
MAY I ASK, SIR...
MY NAME'S FLOYD, MATE.
Ah. RIGHT.
*Floyd.*
DON'T YOU HAVE SOMEWHERE MORE ***IMPORTANT TO BE?***
YOU'D SPEND WHAT MIGHT POSSIBLY BE THE LAST HOURS OF YOUR LIFE WITH SOMEONE YOU (let's be honest) MILDLY DISLIKE?
WELL, I DIDN'T HAVE MUCH GOING ON, BUT WITH THIS AMOUNT OF MONEY, I CAN SORT OF LOOK FORWARD TO THE WHOLE *"WOT HOMELESS-NESS"* OF MY FUTURE.
I'VE GOT A GREAT MAGIC CARD DECK AND A LONG-DISTANCE GIRLFRIEND OUT IN HAMPSTEAD.
TO BE HONEST, MATE, YOUR STORY JUST SOUNDS LIKE THE STORY OF TWO LONELY BOYS...

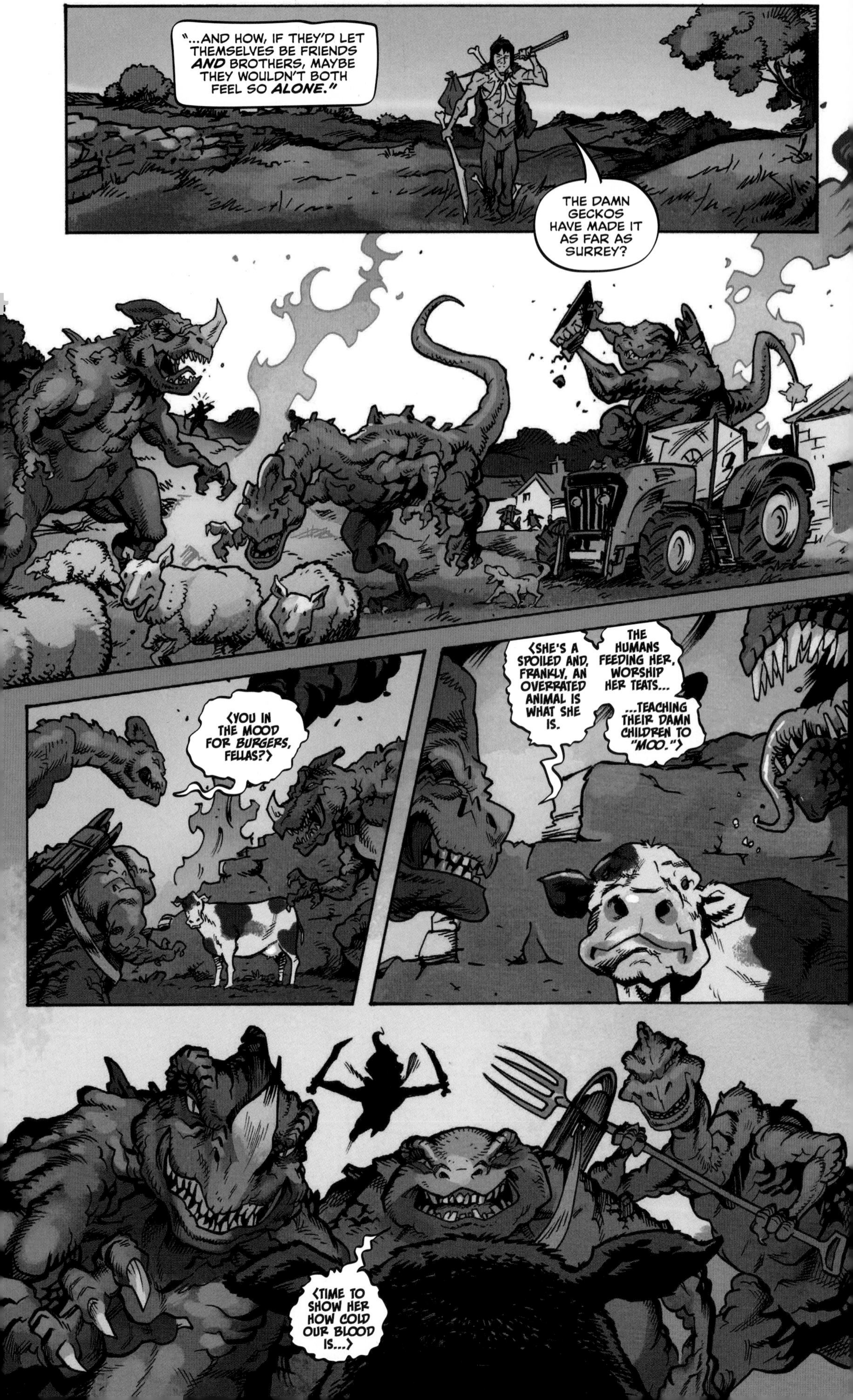
"...AND HOW, IF THEY'D LET THEMSELVES BE FRIENDS **AND** BROTHERS, MAYBE THEY WOULDN'T BOTH FEEL SO **ALONE.**"
THE DAMN GECKOS HAVE MADE IT AS FAR AS SURREY?
‹YOU IN THE MOOD FOR *BURGERS*, FELLAS?›
‹SHE'S A SPOILED AND, FRANKLY, AN OVERRATED ANIMAL IS WHAT SHE IS.
THE HUMANS FEEDING HER, WORSHIP HER TEATS...
...TEACHING THEIR DAMN CHILDREN TO *"MOO."*›
‹TIME TO SHOW HER HOW COLD OUR BLOOD IS...›

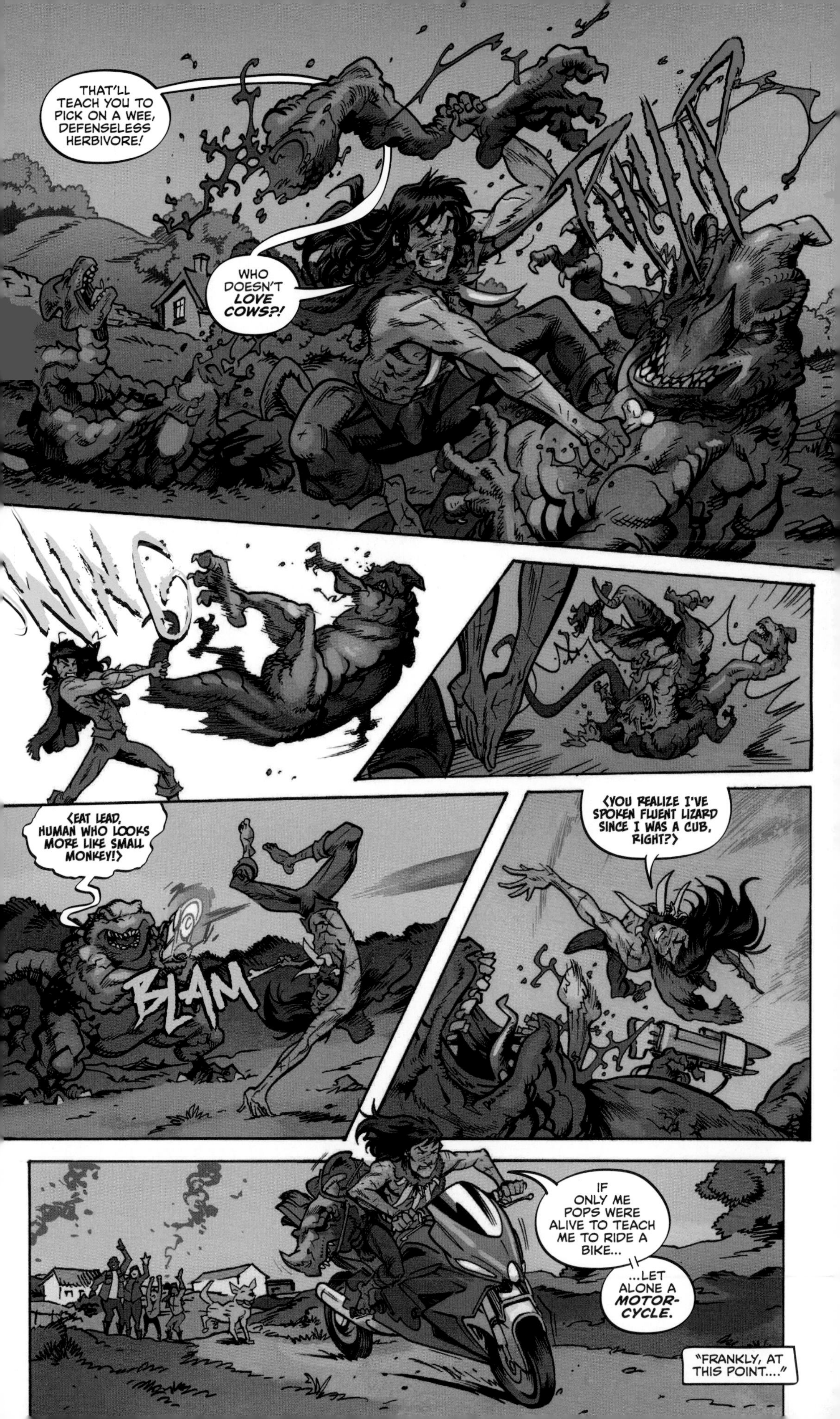
THAT'LL TEACH YOU TO PICK ON A WEE, DEFENSELESS HERBIVORE!
WHO DOESN'T LOVE COWS?!
WHAG
<EAT LEAD, HUMAN WHO LOOKS MORE LIKE SMALL MONKEY!>
BLAM
<YOU REALIZE I'VE SPOKEN FLUENT LIZARD SINCE I WAS A CUB, RIGHT?>
IF ONLY ME POPS WERE ALIVE TO TEACH ME TO RIDE A BIKE...
...LET ALONE A MOTOR-CYCLE.
"FRANKLY, AT THIS POINT...."

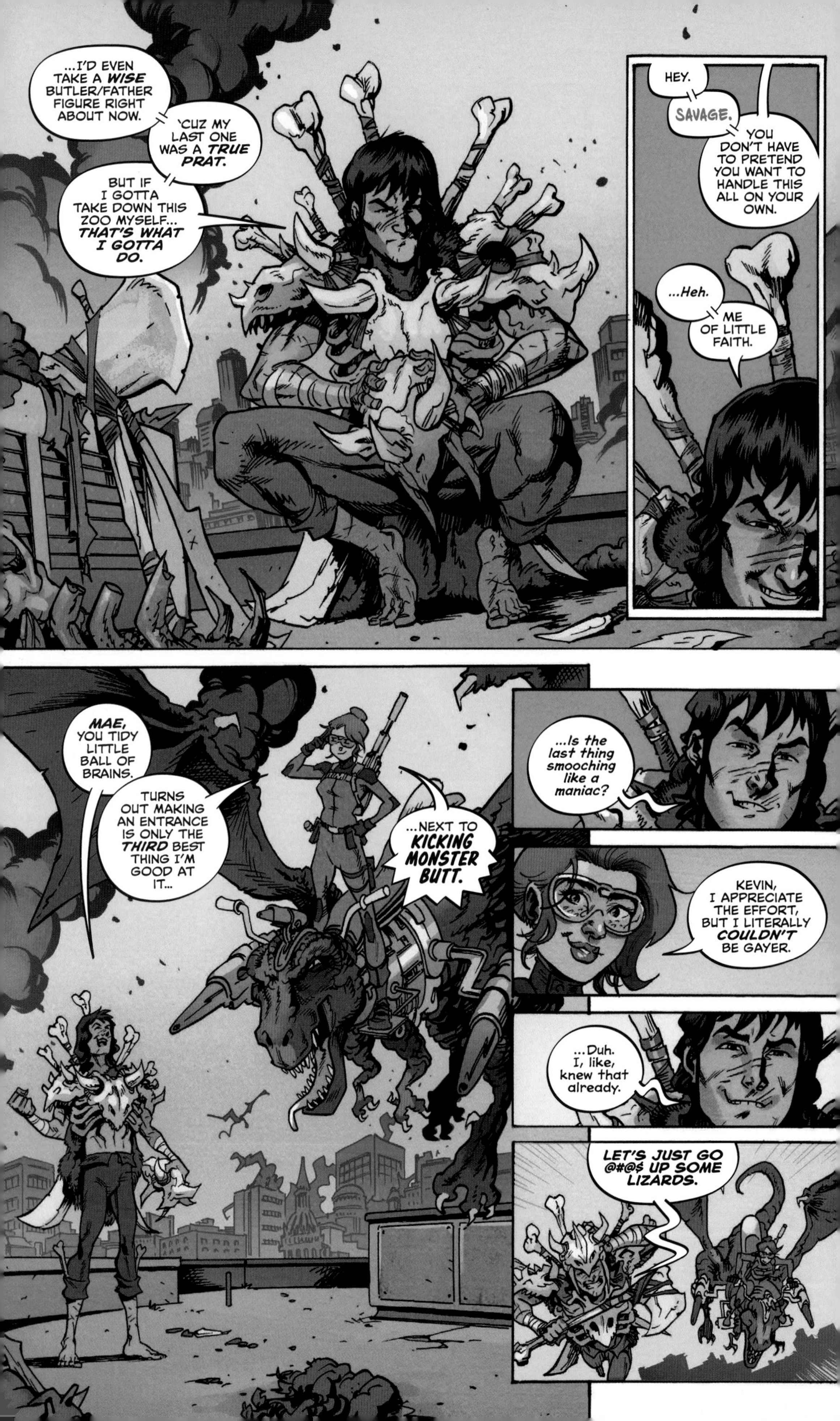
...I'D EVEN TAKE A WISE BUTLER/FATHER FIGURE RIGHT ABOUT NOW.
'CUZ MY LAST ONE WAS A TRUE PRAT.
BUT IF I GOTTA TAKE DOWN THIS ZOO MYSELF... THAT'S WHAT I GOTTA DO.
HEY.
SAVAGE.
YOU DON'T HAVE TO PRETEND YOU WANT TO HANDLE THIS ALL ON YOUR OWN.
...Heh.
ME OF LITTLE FAITH.
MAE, YOU TIDY LITTLE BALL OF BRAINS.
TURNS OUT MAKING AN ENTRANCE IS ONLY THE THIRD BEST THING I'M GOOD AT IT...
...NEXT TO KICKING MONSTER BUTT.
...Is the last thing smooching like a maniac?
KEVIN, I APPRECIATE THE EFFORT, BUT I LITERALLY COULDN'T BE GAYER.
...Duh. I, like, knew that already.
LET'S JUST GO @#@$ UP SOME LIZARDS.

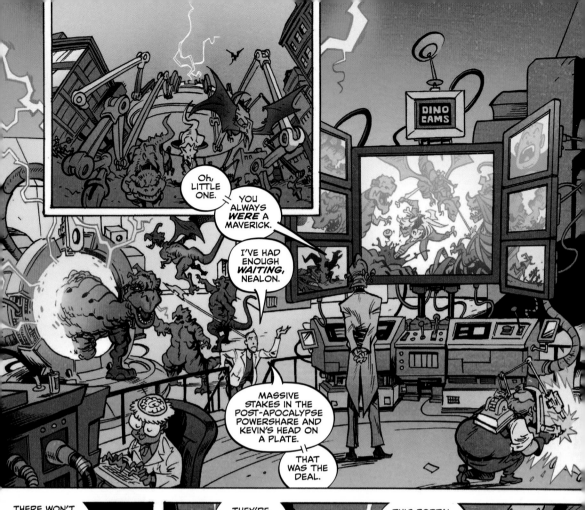

Oh, little one. You always **were** a maverick.

I've had enough **waiting**, Nealon.

Massive stakes in the post-apocalypse powershare and Kevin's head on a plate.

That was the **deal**.

There won't be anything to rule over if you can't get these **dinos** on a leash!

They're just as invested as we are.

With Kevin's genetic material and its **residue** of his... **faraway** home...

This portal will grow into a gaping **crossroads of worlds**.

It will **hunger** for his inter-dimensional duality, expand, and **rend apart** the veil between our universes.

Together, we will **rule two worlds**.

Now, just simply **hold up your end**.

No cold feet...

...Right, ol' chap?

Not even a bit, mate. **Not a bit.**

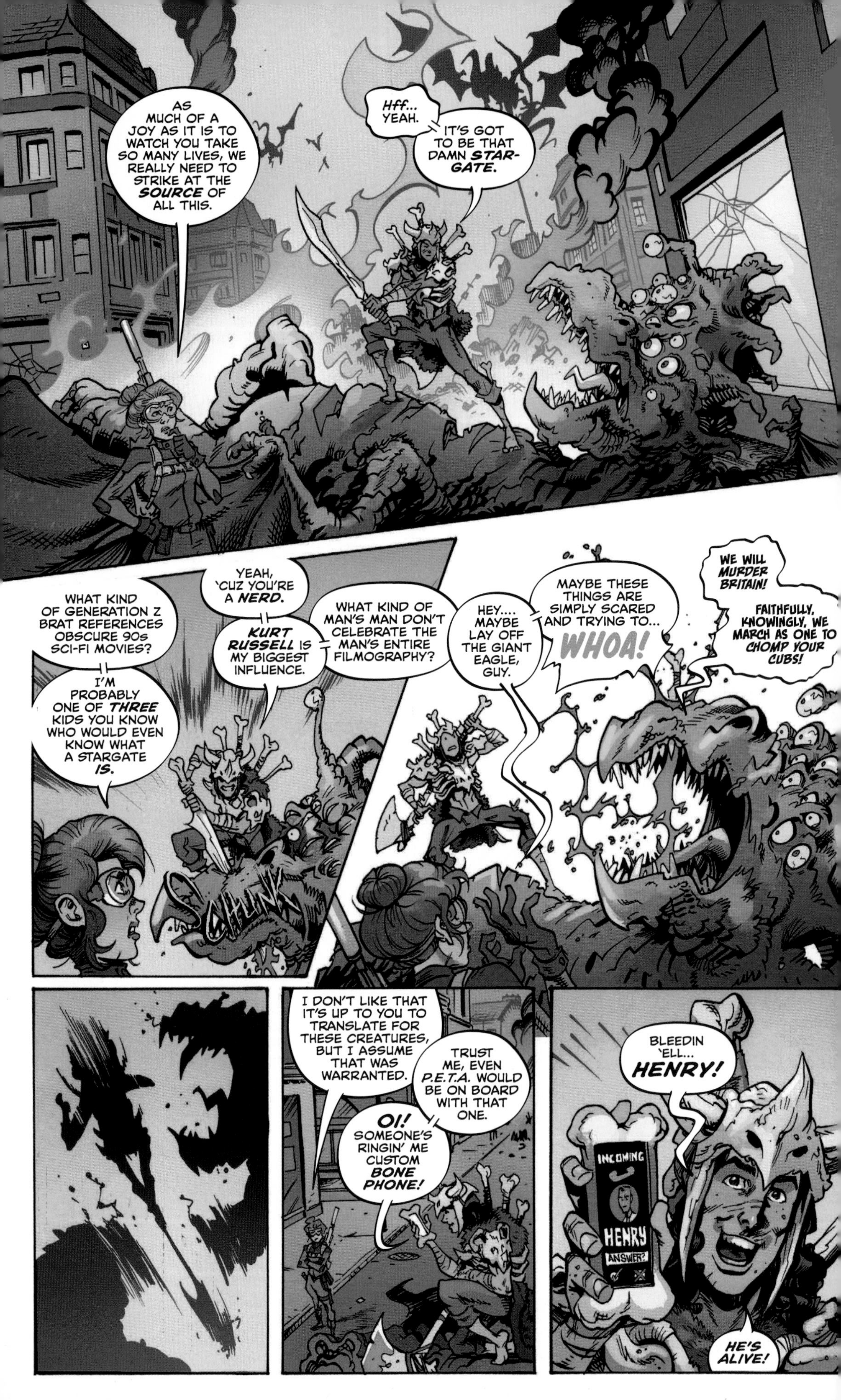
AS MUCH OF A JOY AS IT IS TO WATCH YOU TAKE SO MANY LIVES, WE REALLY NEED TO STRIKE AT THE SOURCE OF ALL THIS.
Hff... YEAH.
IT'S GOT TO BE THAT DAMN STAR-GATE.
WHAT KIND OF GENERATION Z BRAT REFERENCES OBSCURE 90s SCI-FI MOVIES?
I'M PROBABLY ONE OF THREE KIDS YOU KNOW WHO WOULD EVEN KNOW WHAT A STARGATE IS.
YEAH, 'CUZ YOU'RE A NERD.
KURT RUSSELL IS MY BIGGEST INFLUENCE.
WHAT KIND OF MAN'S MAN DON'T CELEBRATE THE MAN'S ENTIRE FILMOGRAPHY?
SCHUNK
HEY.... MAYBE LAY OFF THE GIANT EAGLE, GUY.
MAYBE THESE THINGS ARE SIMPLY SCARED AND TRYING TO...
WHOA!
WE WILL MURDER BRITAIN!
FAITHFULLY, KNOWINGLY, WE MARCH AS ONE TO CHOMP YOUR CUBS!
I DON'T LIKE THAT IT'S UP TO YOU TO TRANSLATE FOR THESE CREATURES, BUT I ASSUME THAT WAS WARRANTED.
TRUST ME, EVEN P.E.T.A. WOULD BE ON BOARD WITH THAT ONE.
OI! SOMEONE'S RINGIN' ME CUSTOM BONE PHONE!
BLEEDIN 'ELL... HENRY!
INCOMING
HENRY
ANSWER?
HE'S ALIVE!

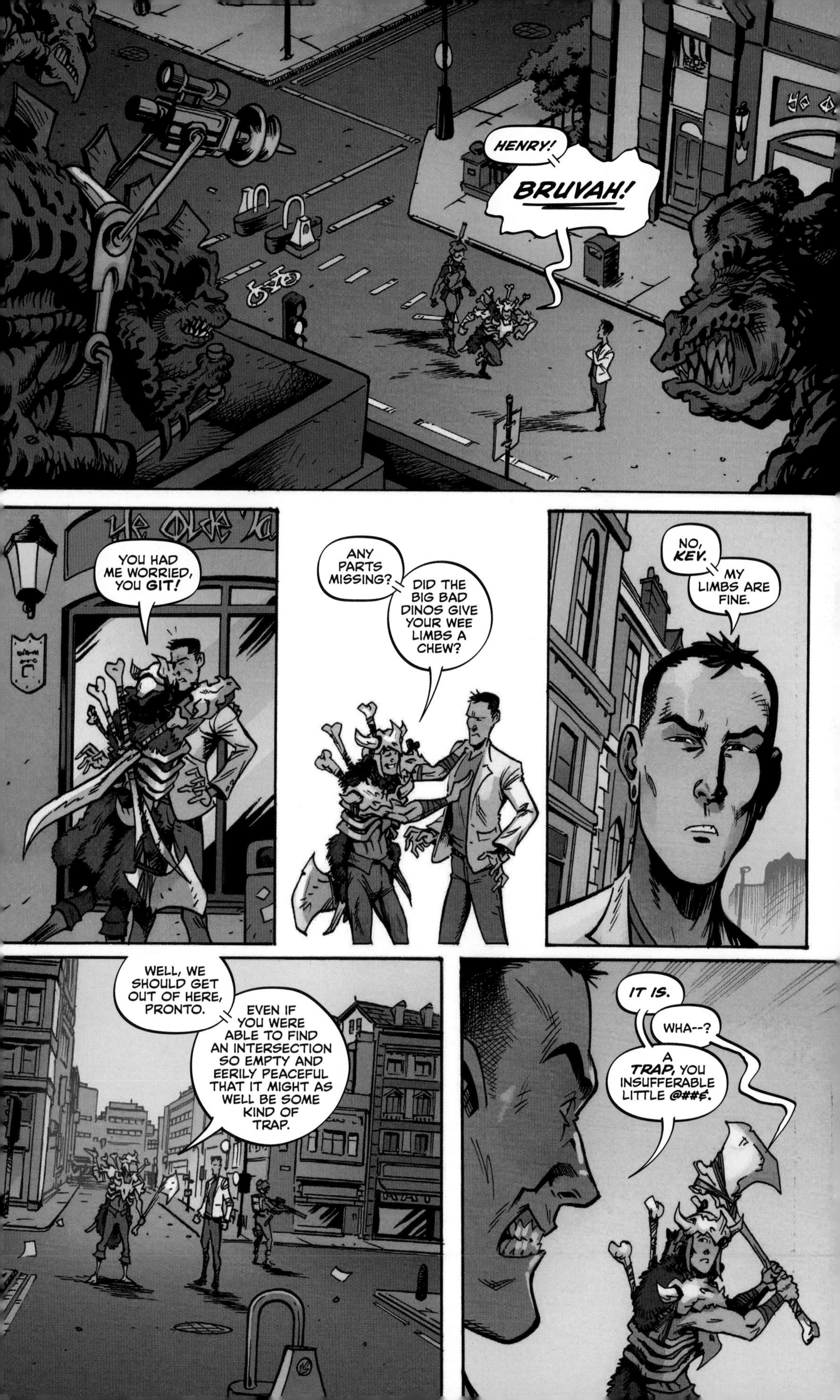
HENRY!
BRUVAH!
YOU HAD ME WORRIED, YOU GIT!
ANY PARTS MISSING?
DID THE BIG BAD DINOS GIVE YOUR WEE LIMBS A CHEW?
NO, KEV.
MY LIMBS ARE FINE.
WELL, WE SHOULD GET OUT OF HERE, PRONTO.
EVEN IF YOU WERE ABLE TO FIND AN INTERSECTION SO EMPTY AND EERILY PEACEFUL THAT IT MIGHT AS WELL BE SOME KIND OF TRAP.
IT IS.
WHA--?
A TRAP, YOU INSUFFERABLE LITTLE @##¢.

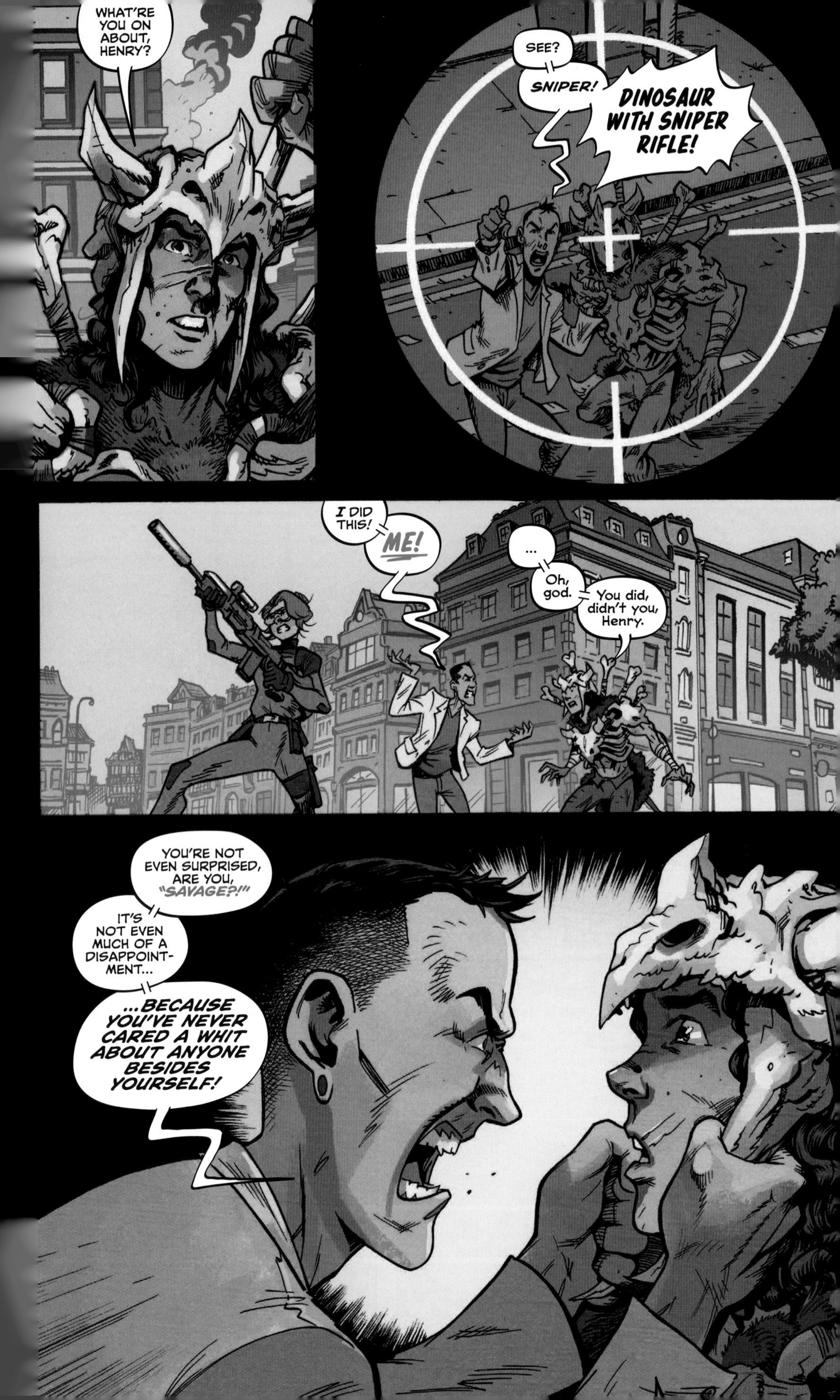

WHAT'RE YOU ON ABOUT, HENRY?
SEE?
SNIPER!
DINOSAUR WITH SNIPER RIFLE!
I DID THIS!
ME!
...
Oh, god.
You did, didn't you, Henry.
YOU'RE NOT EVEN SURPRISED, ARE YOU, "SAVAGE?!"
IT'S NOT EVEN MUCH OF A DISAPPOINT-MENT...
...BECAUSE YOU'VE NEVER CARED A WHIT ABOUT ANYONE BESIDES YOURSELF!

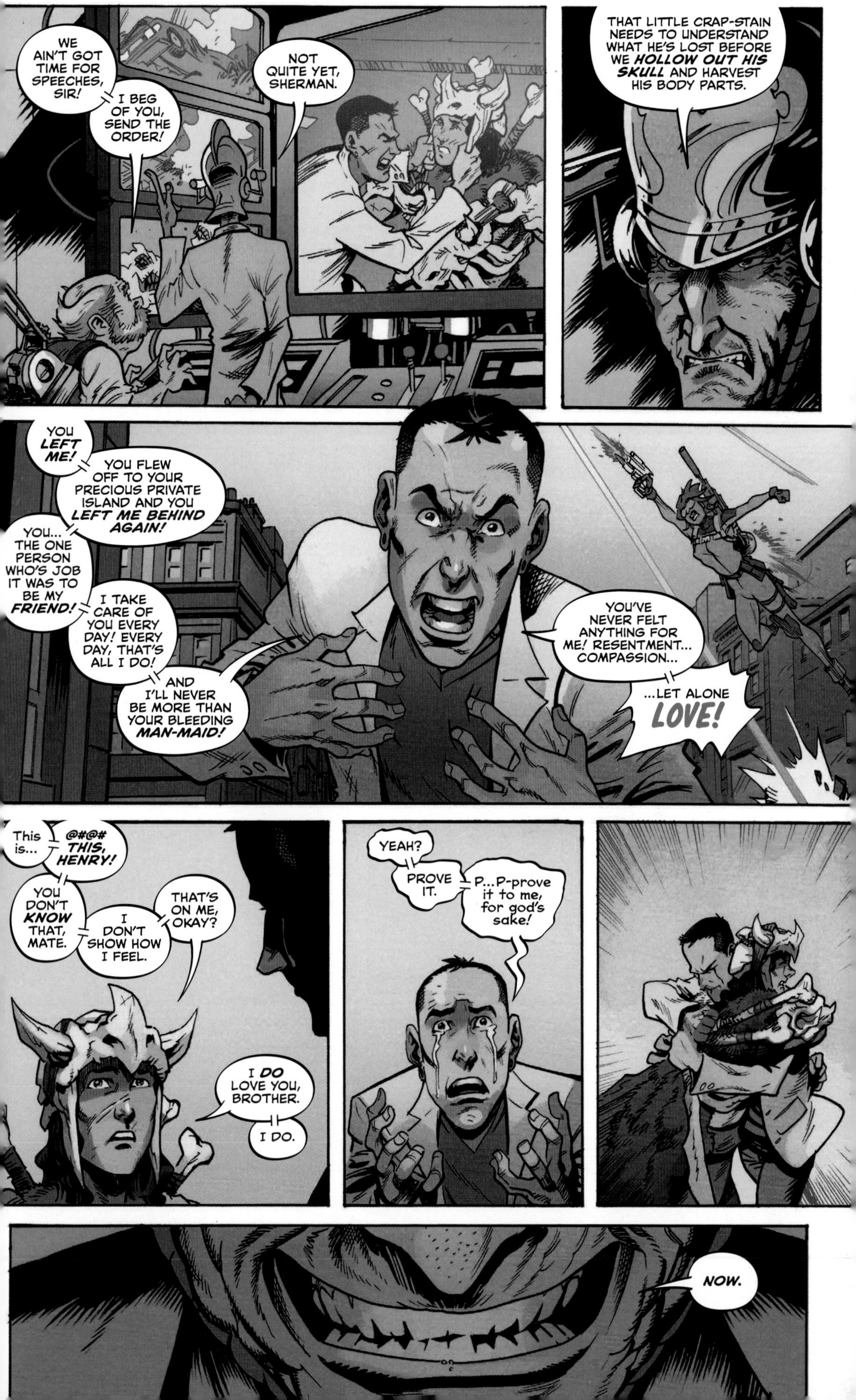
WE AIN'T GOT TIME FOR SPEECHES, SIR!
I BEG OF YOU, SEND THE ORDER!
NOT QUITE YET, SHERMAN.
THAT LITTLE CRAP-STAIN NEEDS TO UNDERSTAND WHAT HE'S LOST BEFORE WE HOLLOW OUT HIS SKULL AND HARVEST HIS BODY PARTS.
YOU LEFT ME!
YOU FLEW OFF TO YOUR PRECIOUS PRIVATE ISLAND AND YOU LEFT ME BEHIND AGAIN!
YOU... THE ONE PERSON WHO'S JOB IT WAS TO BE MY FRIEND!
I TAKE CARE OF YOU EVERY DAY! EVERY DAY, THAT'S ALL I DO!
AND I'LL NEVER BE MORE THAN YOUR BLEEDING MAN-MAID!
YOU'VE NEVER FELT ANYTHING FOR ME! RESENTMENT... COMPASSION...
...LET ALONE LOVE!
This is...
@#@# THIS, HENRY!
YOU DON'T KNOW THAT, MATE.
I DON'T SHOW HOW I FEEL.
THAT'S ON ME, OKAY?
I DO LOVE YOU, BROTHER.
I DO.
YEAH?
PROVE IT.
P...P-prove it to me, for god's sake!
NOW.

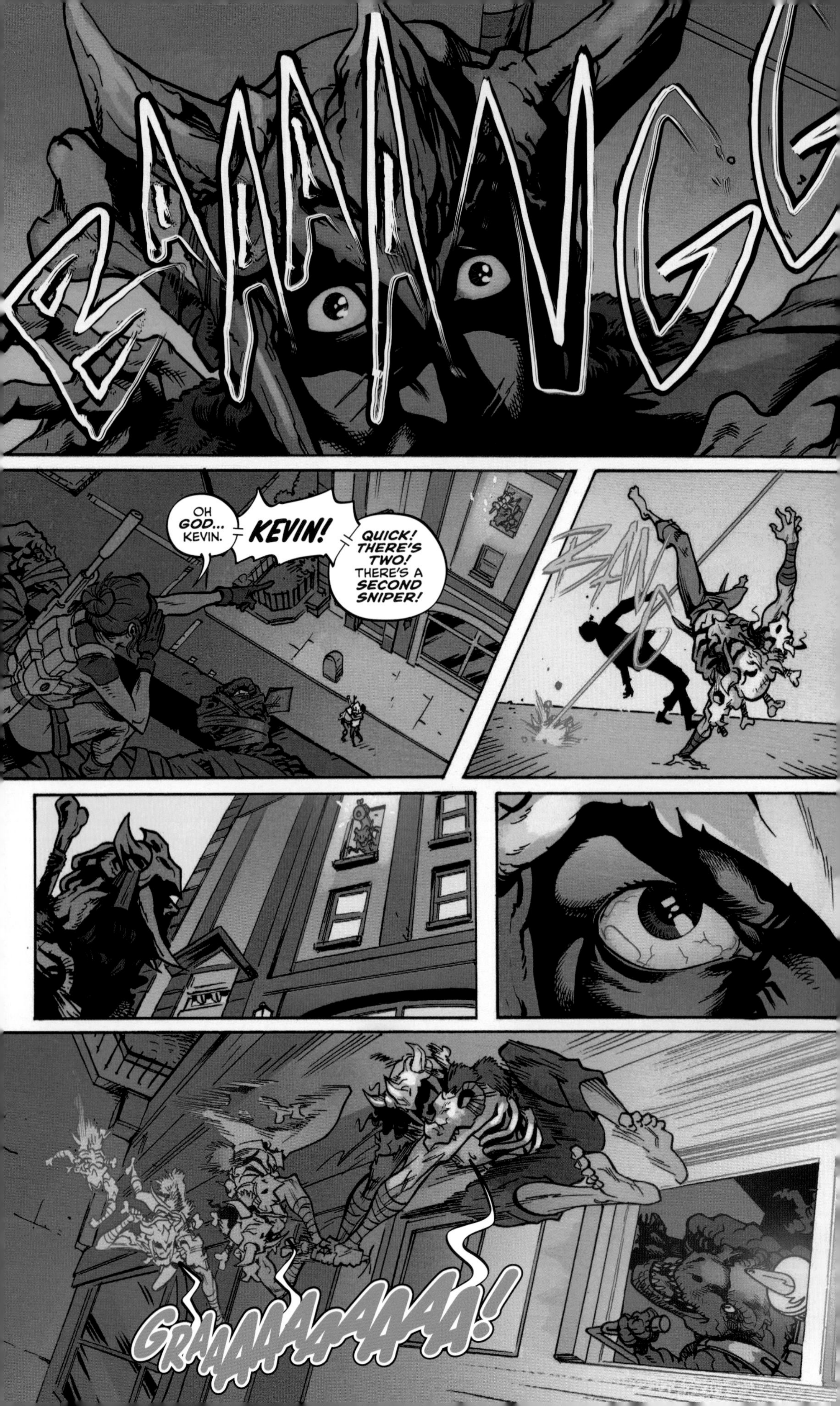

ZAAANG!
OH GOD... KEVIN.
KEVIN!
QUICK! THERE'S TWO! THERE'S A SECOND SNIPER!
BANG
GRAAAAAAAAAA!

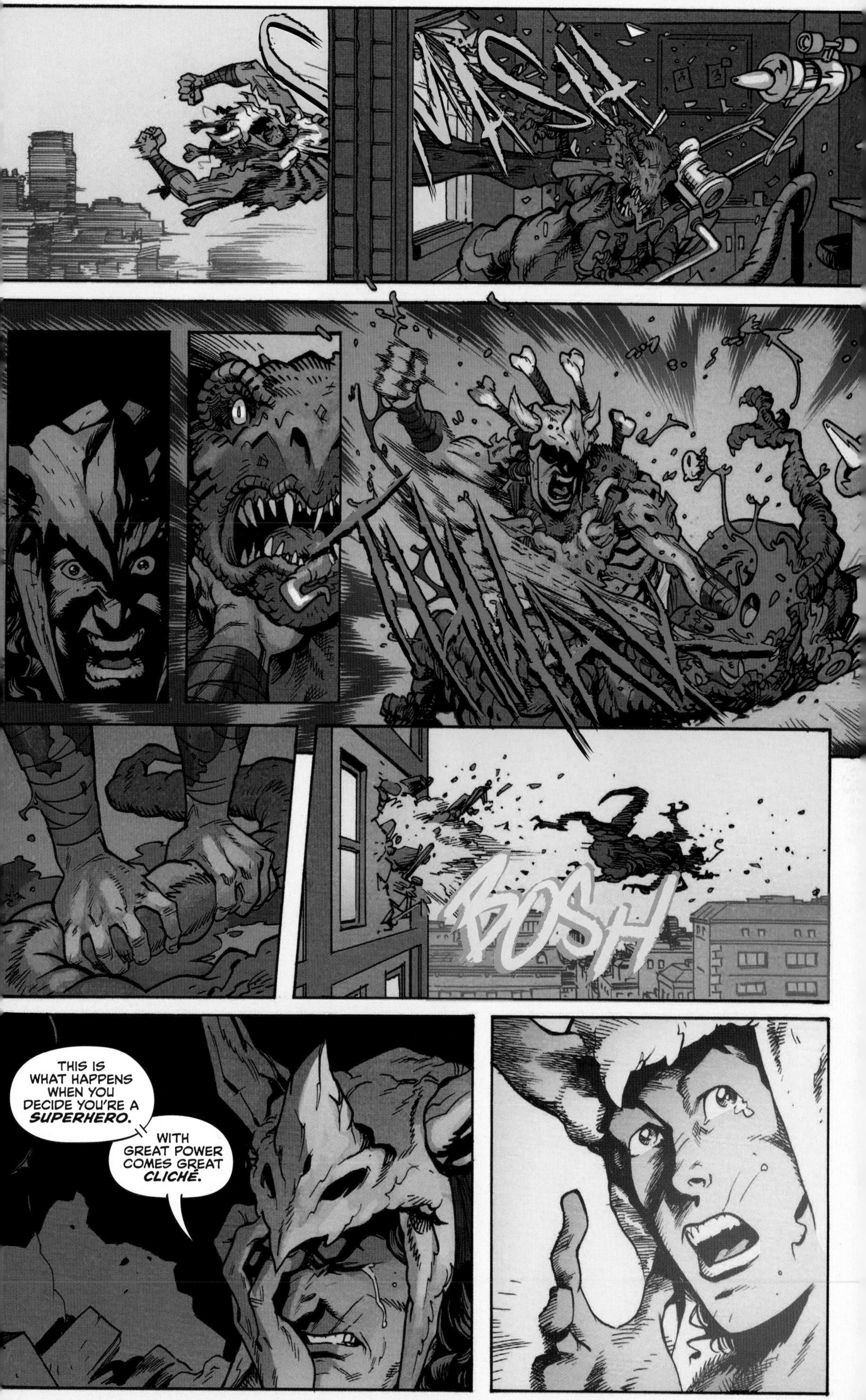
SMASH
BOSH
THIS IS WHAT HAPPENS WHEN YOU DECIDE YOU'RE A SUPERHERO.
WITH GREAT POWER COMES GREAT CLICHÉ.

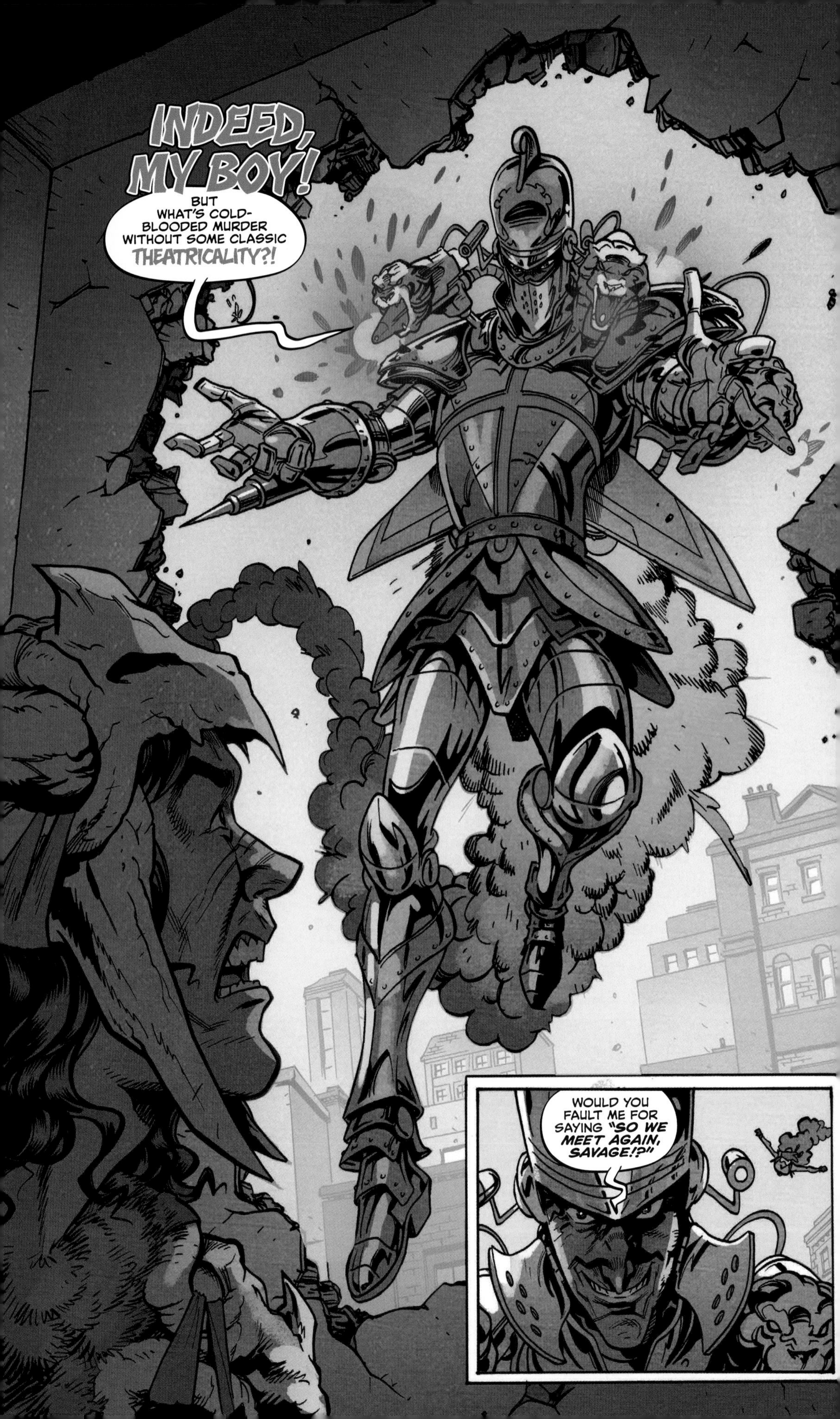
INDEED, MY BOY!
BUT WHAT'S COLD-BLOODED MURDER WITHOUT SOME CLASSIC THEATRICALITY?!
WOULD YOU FAULT ME FOR SAYING "SO WE MEET AGAIN, SAVAGE!?"

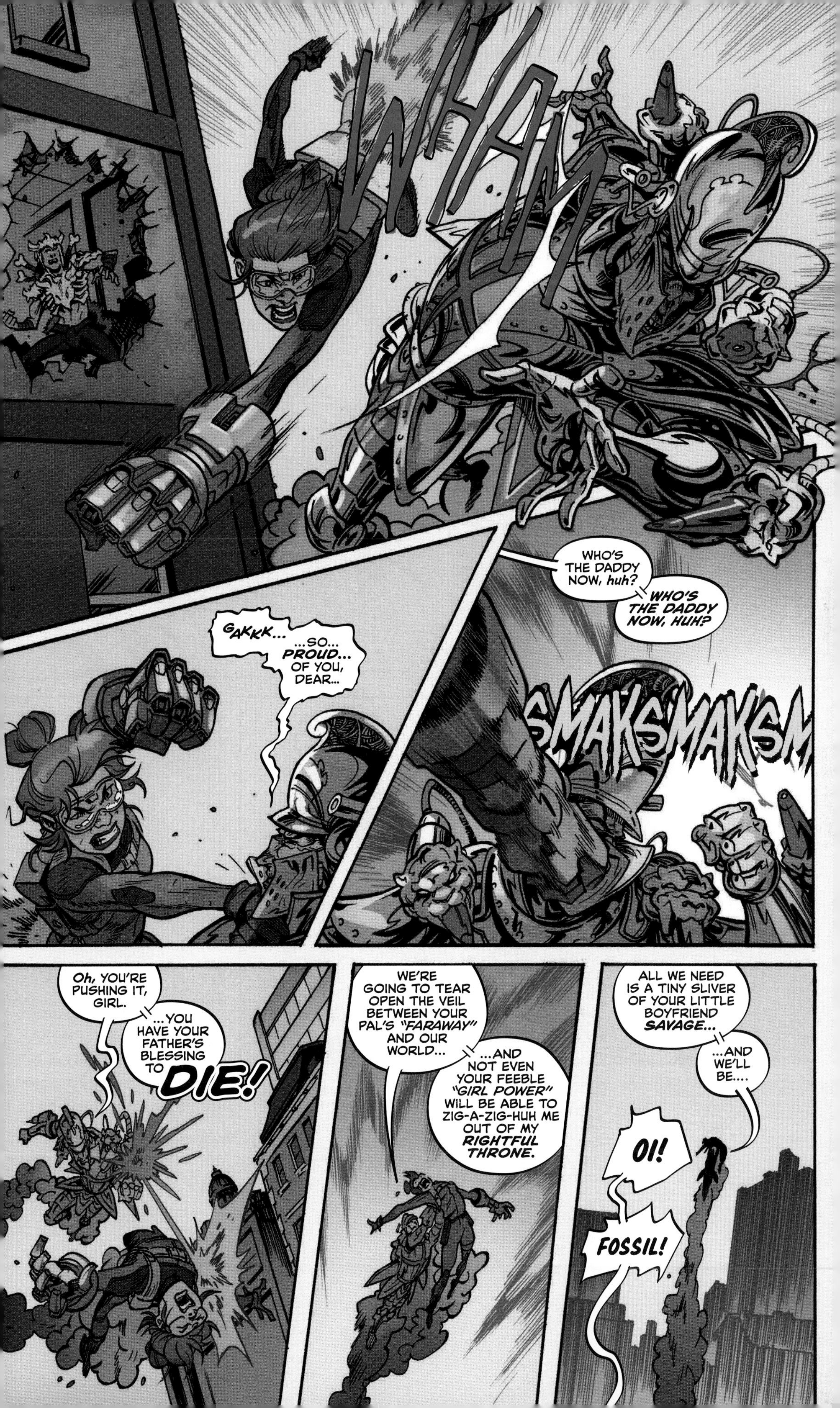
WHAM
WHO'S THE DADDY NOW, *huh?*
***WHO'S THE DADDY NOW, HUH?***
GAKKK...
...SO... ***PROUD...*** OF YOU, DEAR...
SMAKSMAKSM
*Oh,* YOU'RE PUSHING IT, GIRL.
...YOU HAVE YOUR FATHER'S BLESSING TO ***DIE!***
WE'RE GOING TO TEAR OPEN THE VEIL BETWEEN YOUR PAL'S ***"FARAWAY"*** AND OUR WORLD...
...AND NOT EVEN YOUR FEEBLE ***"GIRL POWER"*** WILL BE ABLE TO ZIG-A-ZIG-HUH ME OUT OF MY ***RIGHTFUL THRONE.***
ALL WE NEED IS A TINY SLIVER OF YOUR LITTLE BOYFRIEND ***SAVAGE...***
...AND WE'LL BE....
OI!
FOSSIL!

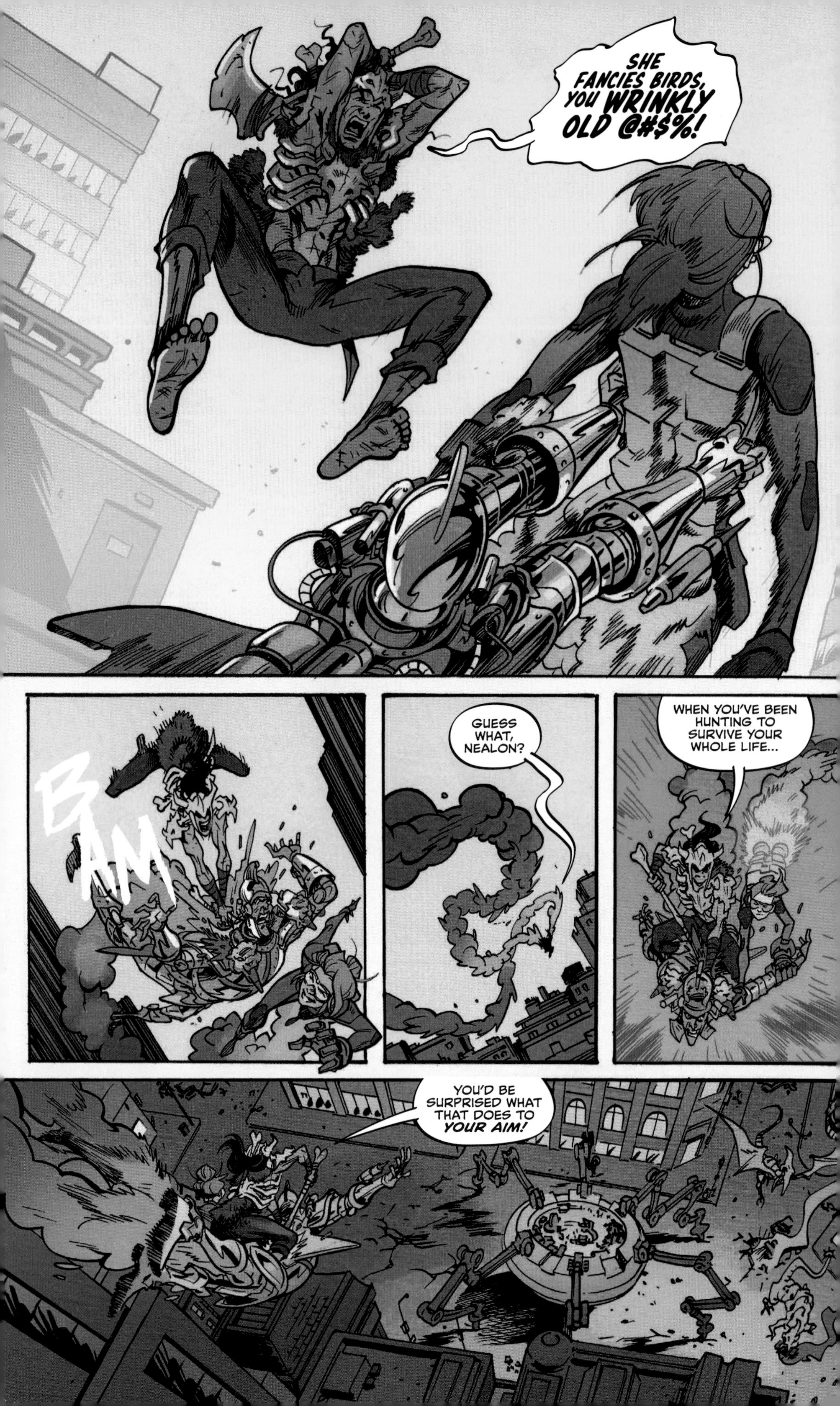
SHE FANCIES BIRDS, YOU WRINKLY OLD @#$%!
BAM
GUESS WHAT, NEALON?
WHEN YOU'VE BEEN HUNTING TO SURVIVE YOUR WHOLE LIFE...
YOU'D BE SURPRISED WHAT THAT DOES TO YOUR AIM!

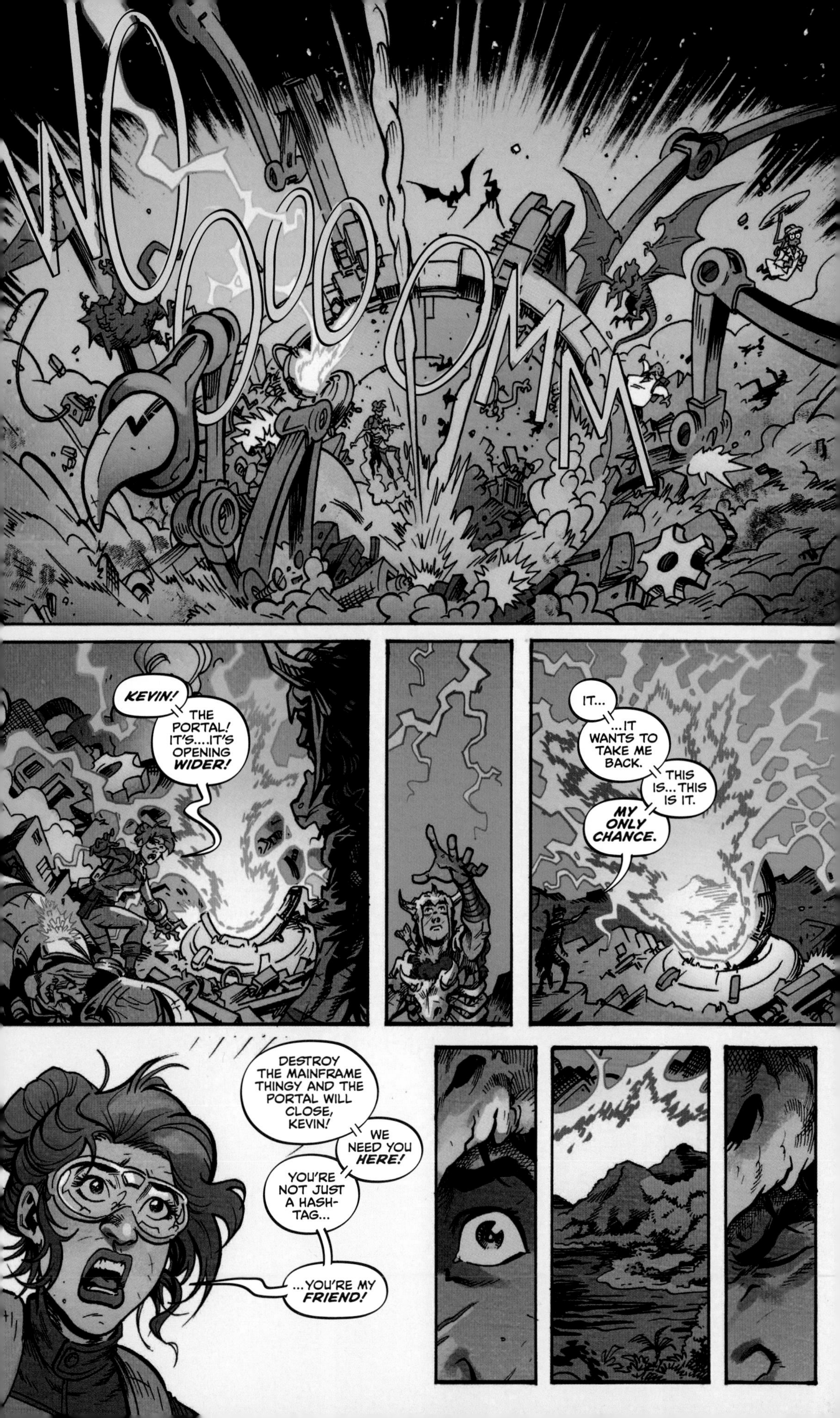
WOOOOOMM!
KEVIN!
THE PORTAL! IT'S....IT'S OPENING WIDER!
IT...
...IT WANTS TO TAKE ME BACK.
THIS IS...THIS IS IT.
MY ONLY CHANCE.
DESTROY THE MAINFRAME THINGY AND THE PORTAL WILL CLOSE, KEVIN!
WE NEED YOU HERE!
YOU'RE NOT JUST A HASH-TAG...
...YOU'RE MY FRIEND!

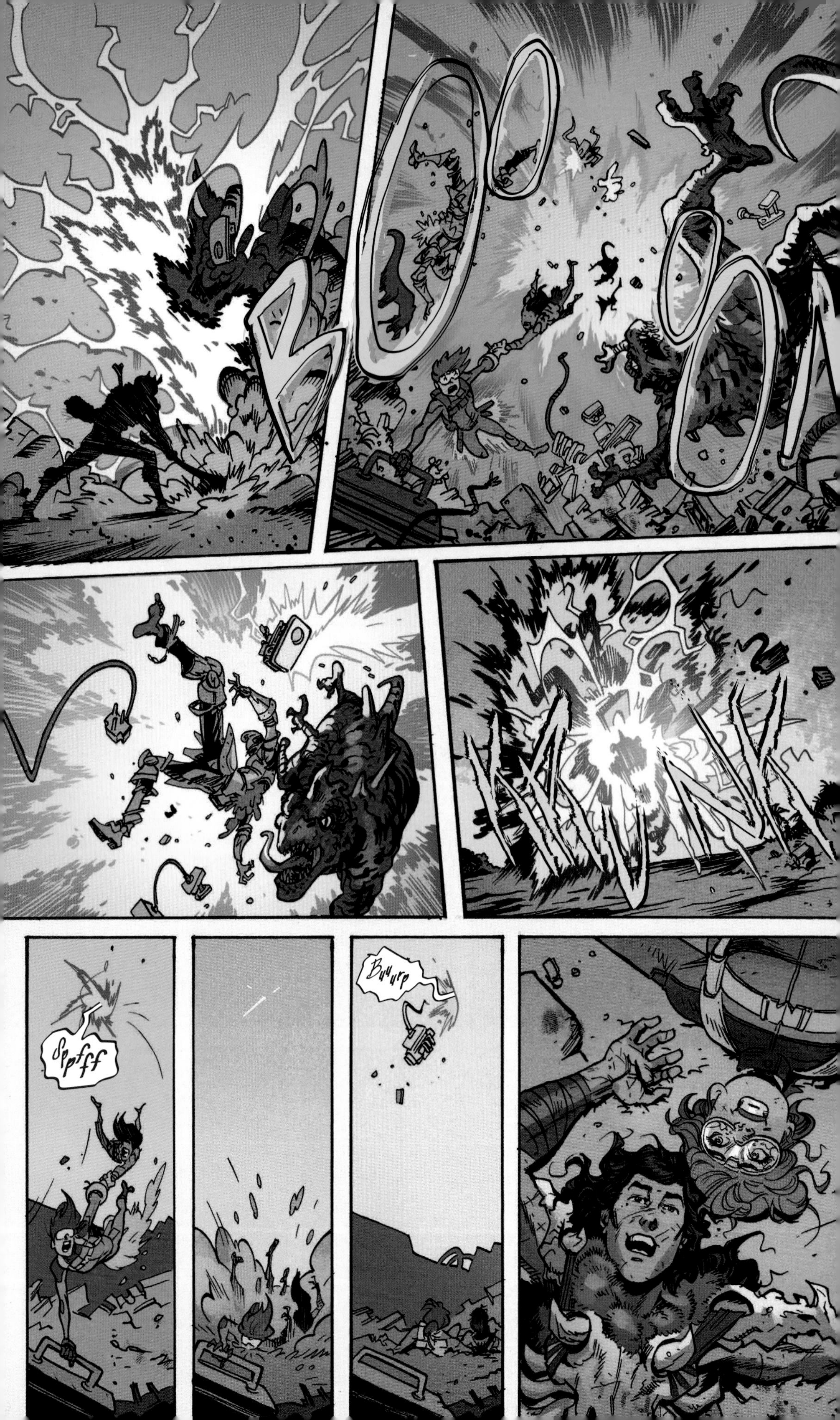
BOOOOM
Sppfff
Buuurp

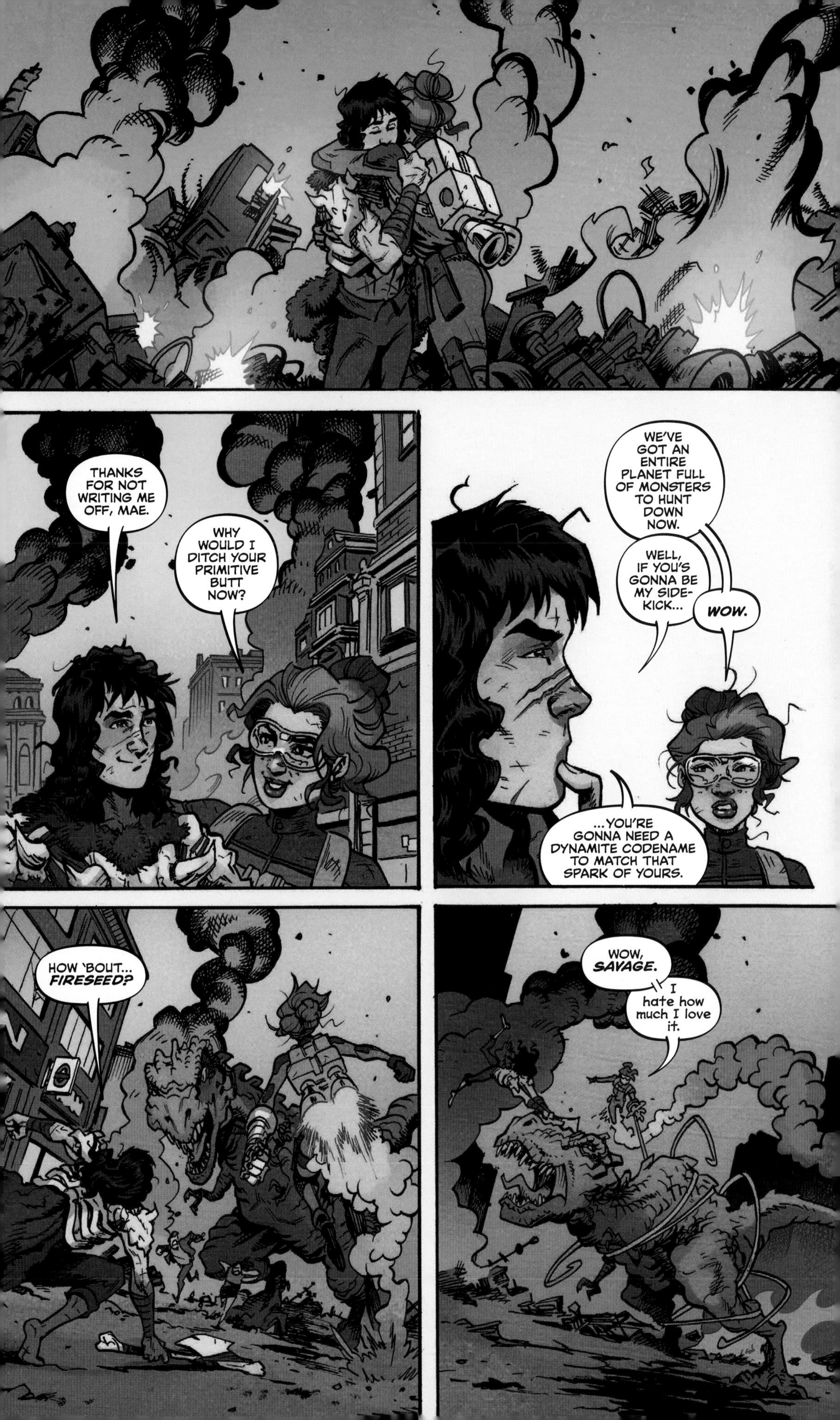
THANKS FOR NOT WRITING ME OFF, MAE.
WHY WOULD I DITCH YOUR PRIMITIVE BUTT NOW?
WE'VE GOT AN ENTIRE PLANET FULL OF MONSTERS TO HUNT DOWN NOW.
WELL, IF YOU'S GONNA BE MY SIDE-KICK...
WOW.
...YOU'RE GONNA NEED A DYNAMITE CODENAME TO MATCH THAT SPARK OF YOURS.
HOW 'BOUT... FIRESEED?
WOW, SAVAGE.
I hate how much I love it.

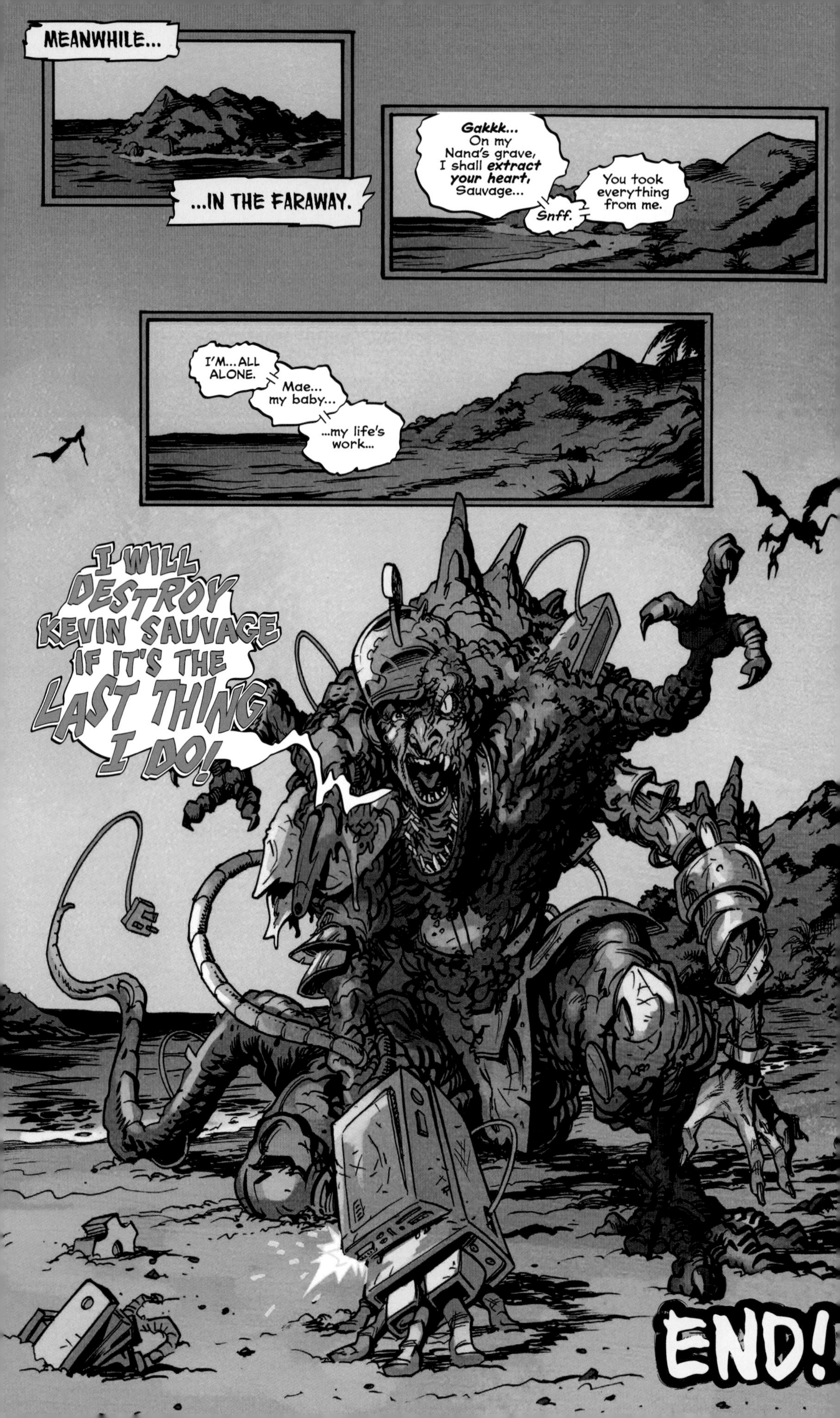
MEANWHILE...
...IN THE FARAWAY.
Gakkk... On my Nana's grave, I shall extract your heart, Sauvage...
Snff.
You took everything from me.
I'M...ALL ALONE.
Mae... my baby...
...my life's work...
I WILL DESTROY KEVIN SAUVAGE IF IT'S THE LAST THING I DO!
END!

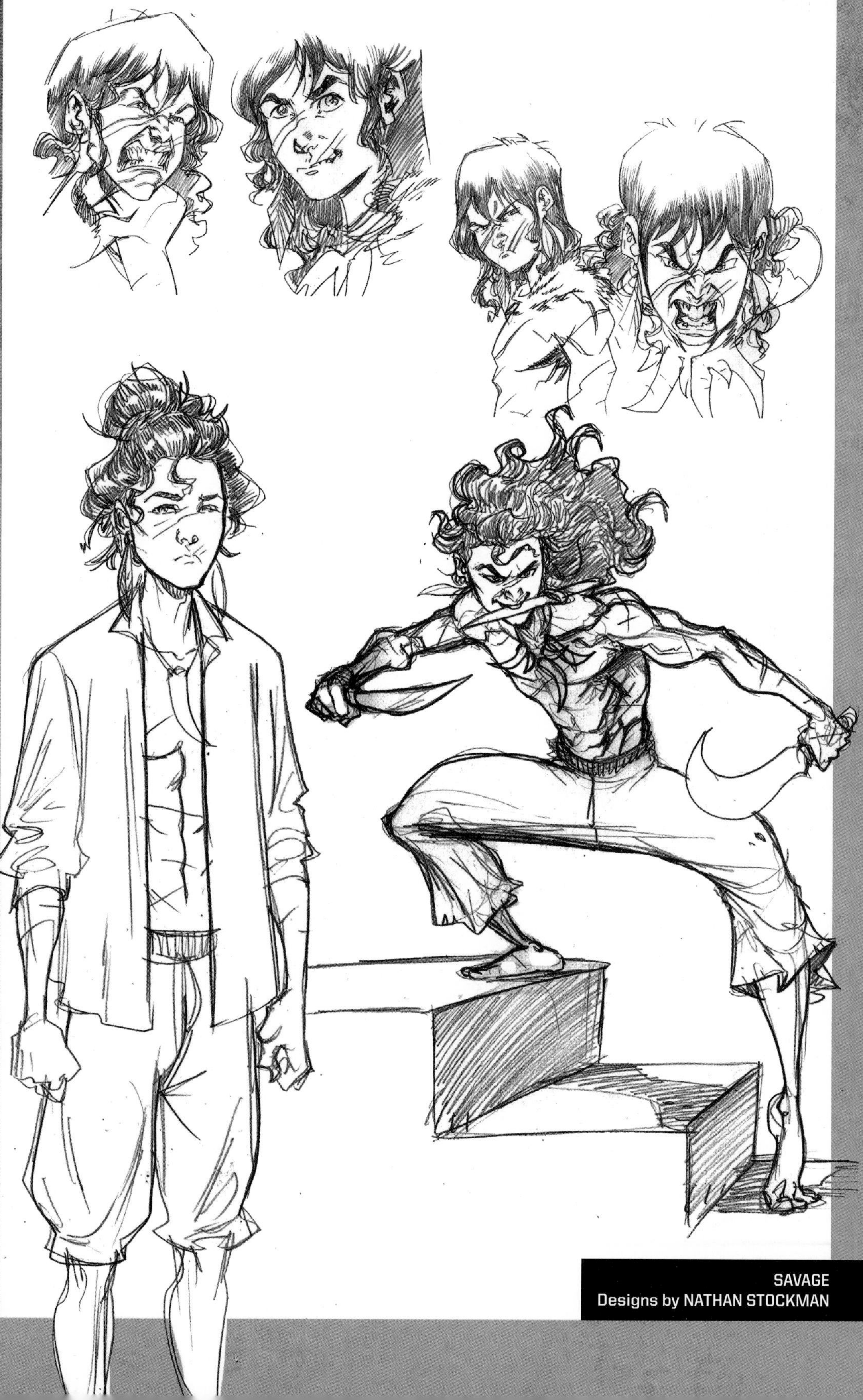

SAVAGE
Designs by NATHAN STOCKMAN

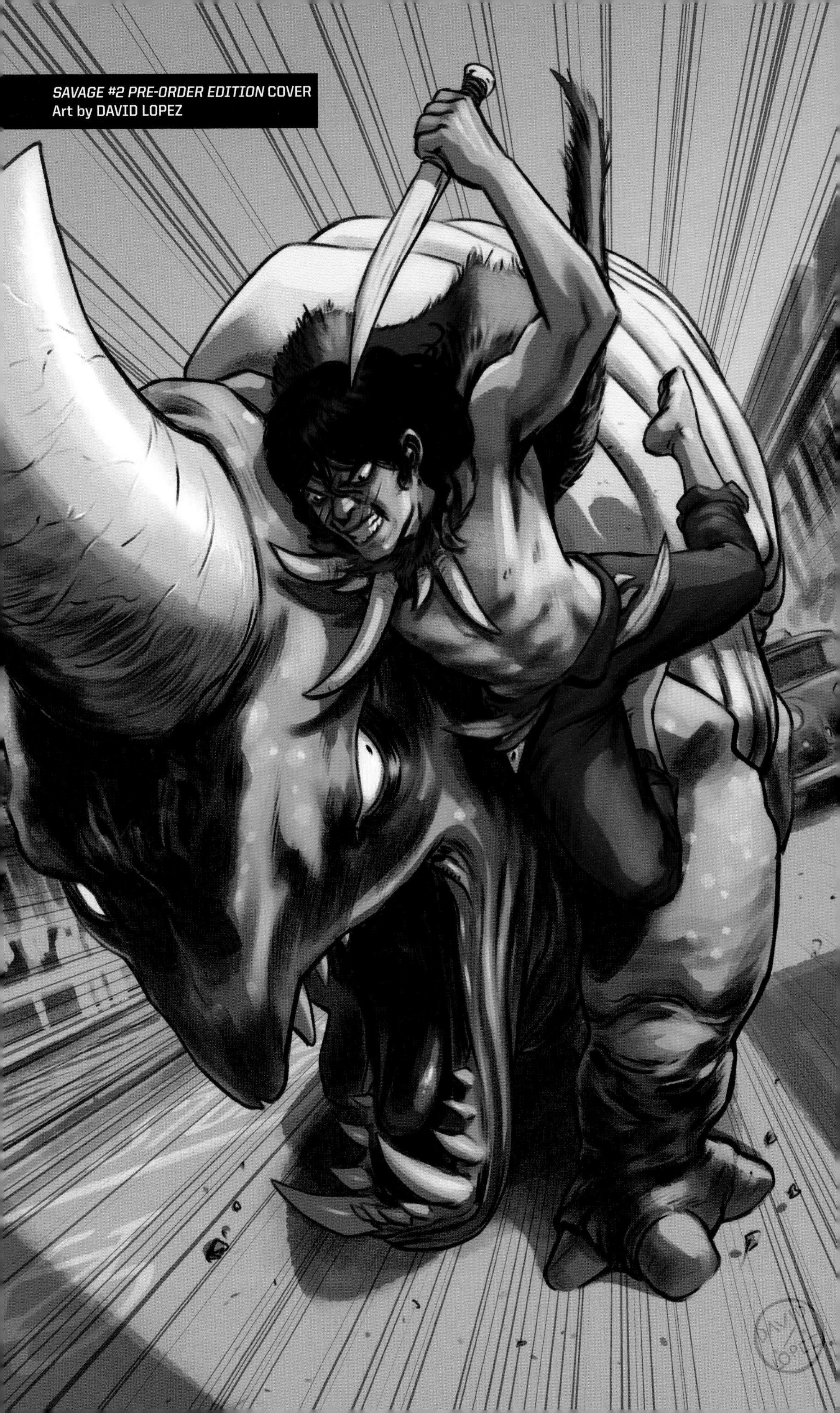

*SAVAGE #2 PRE-ORDER EDITION* COVER
Art by DAVID LOPEZ

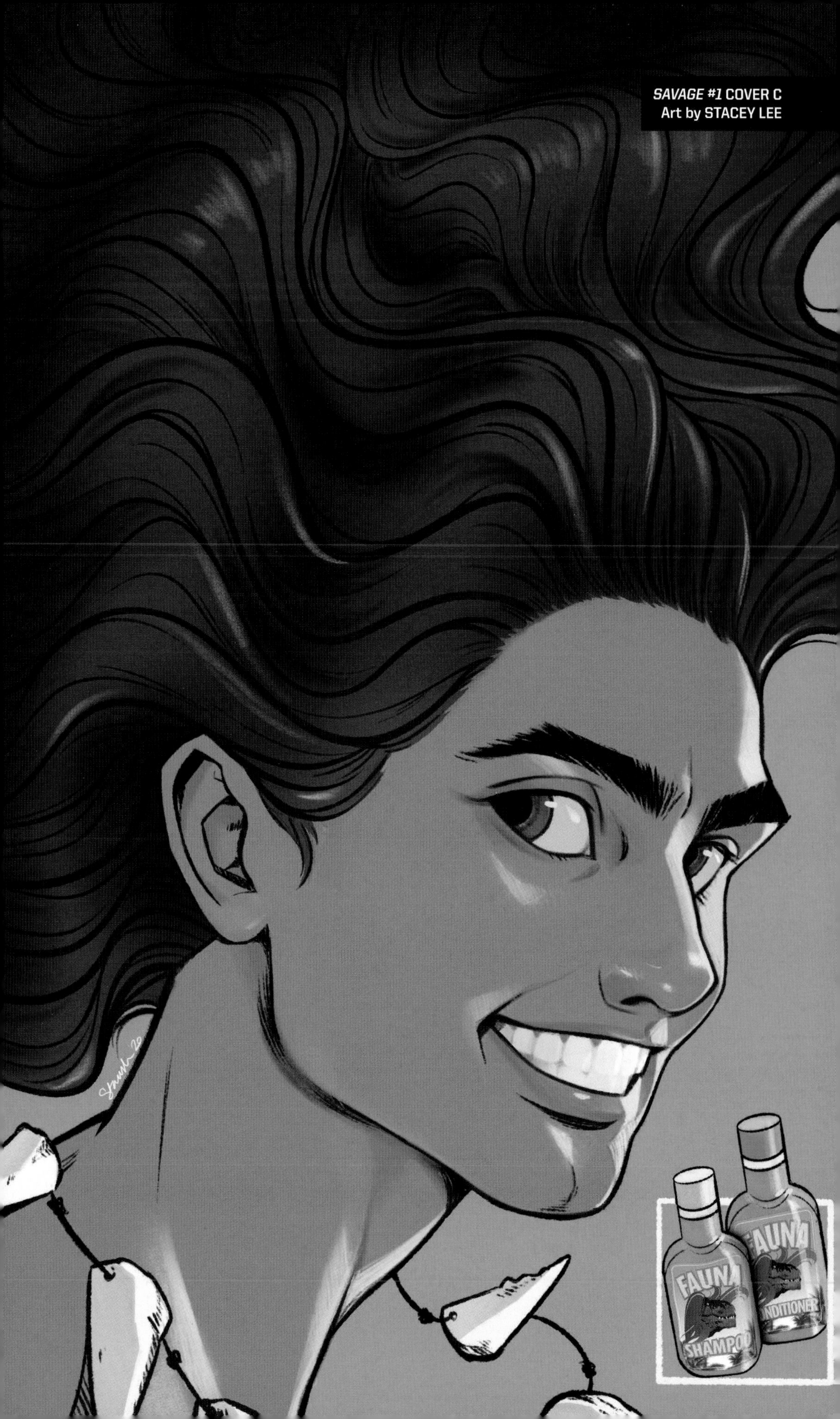
FAUNA
SHAMPOO

*SAVAGE #1* COVER C
Art by STACEY LEE

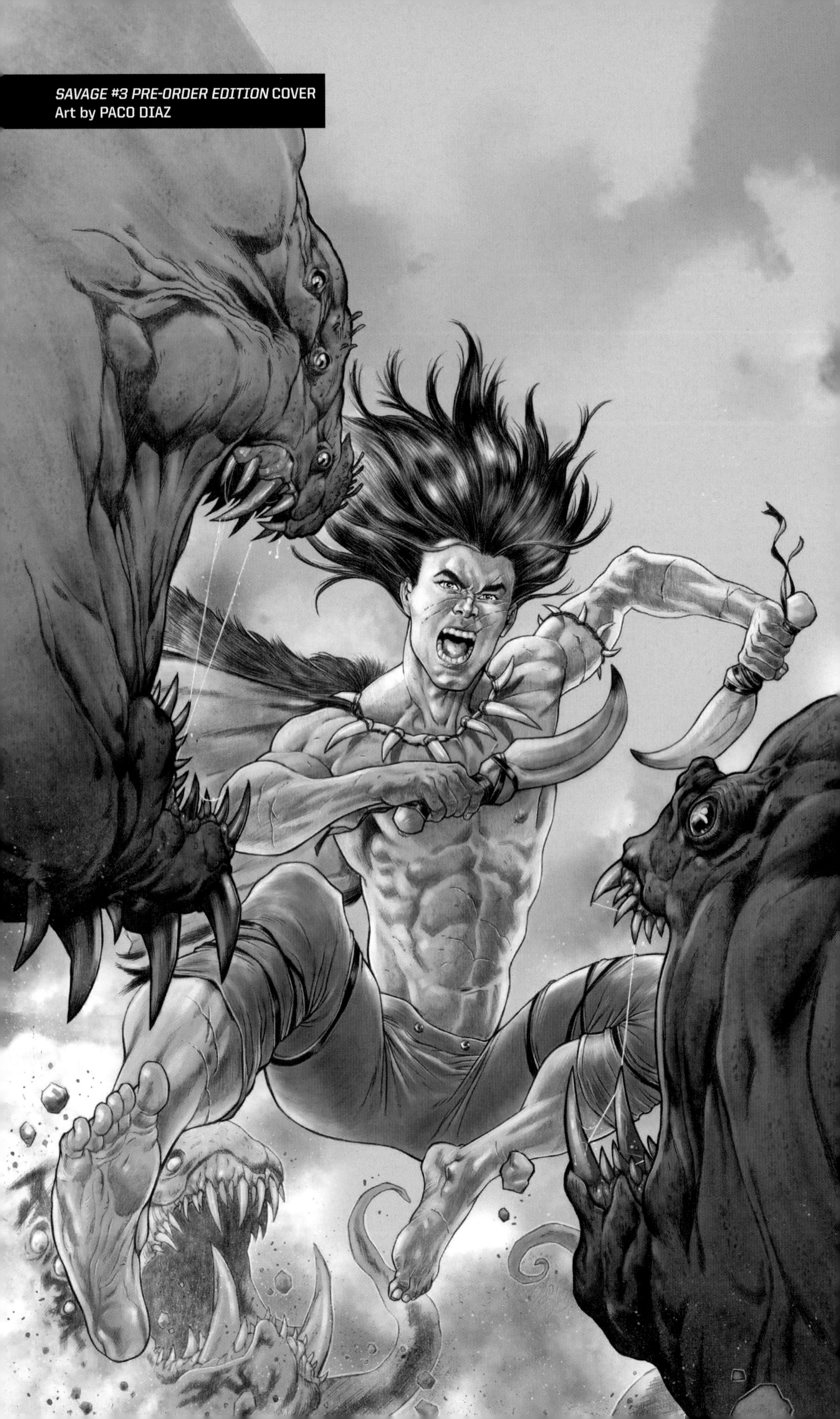

*SAVAGE #3 PRE-ORDER EDITION* COVER
Art by PACO DIAZ

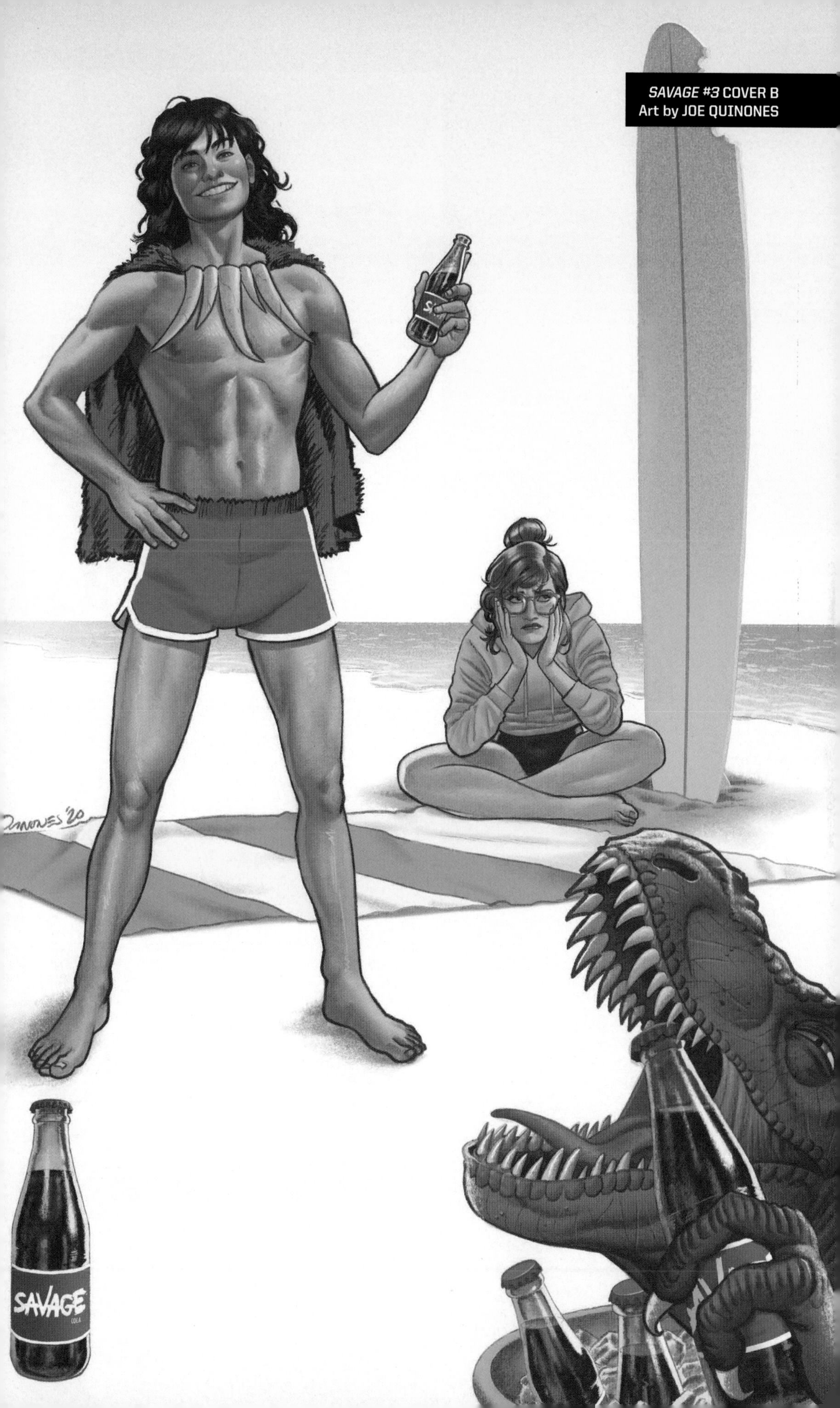
QUINONES '20
SAVAGE
COCA

*SAVAGE #3* COVER B
Art by JOE QUINONES

*SAVAGE #1*, p. 18, 19, and (facing) 20
Art by NATHAN STOCKMAN

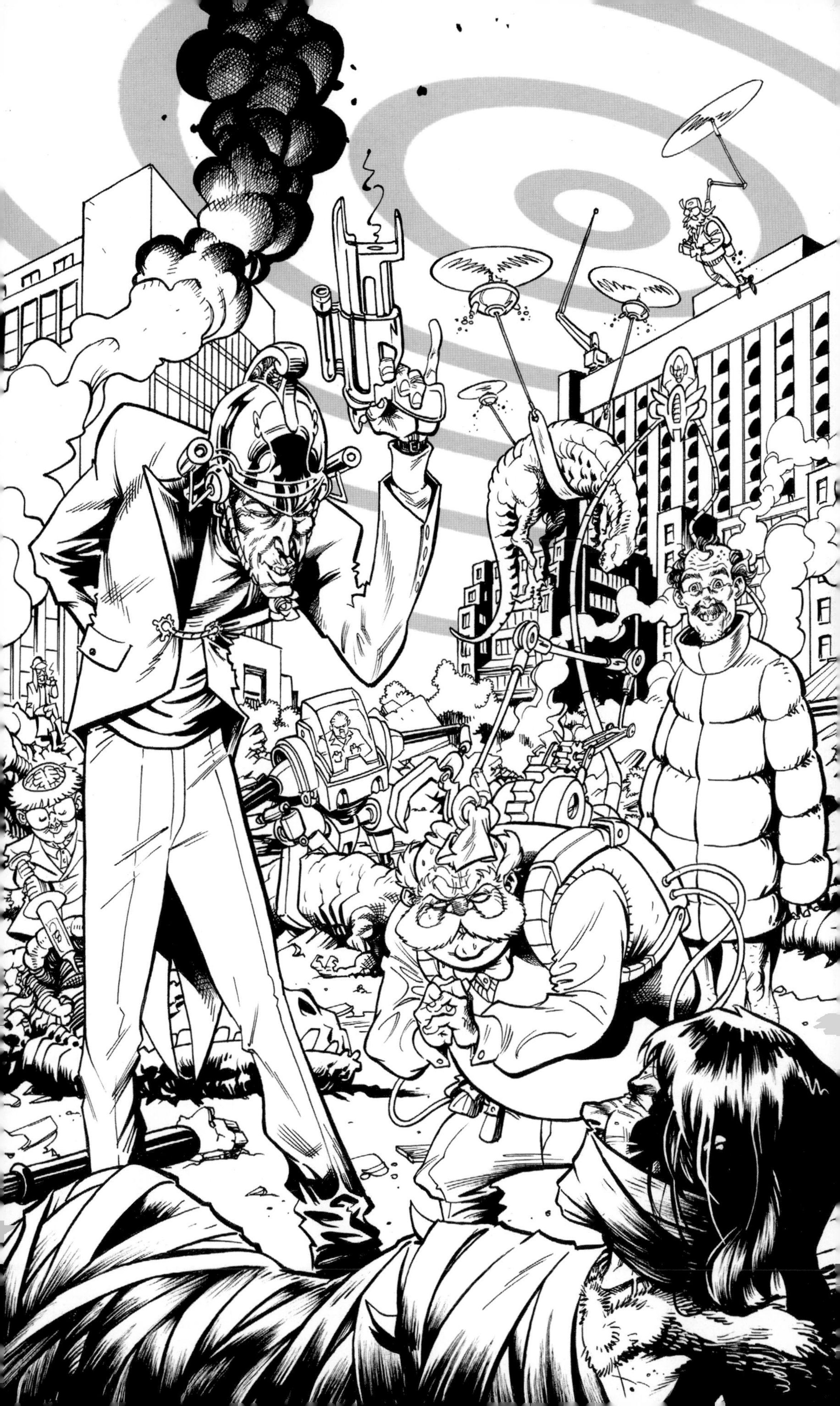

*SAVAGE #2*, p. 4, 5, and (facing) 6
Art by NATHAN STOCKMAN

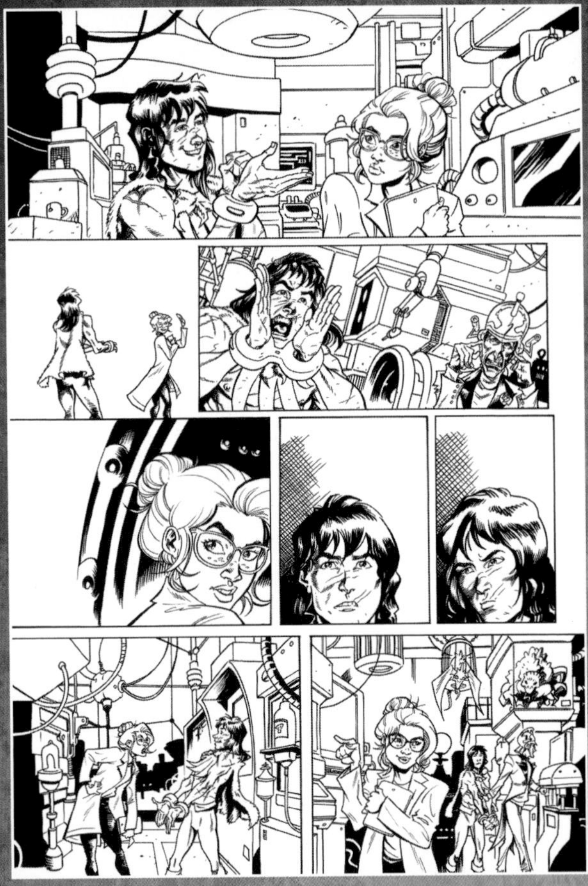

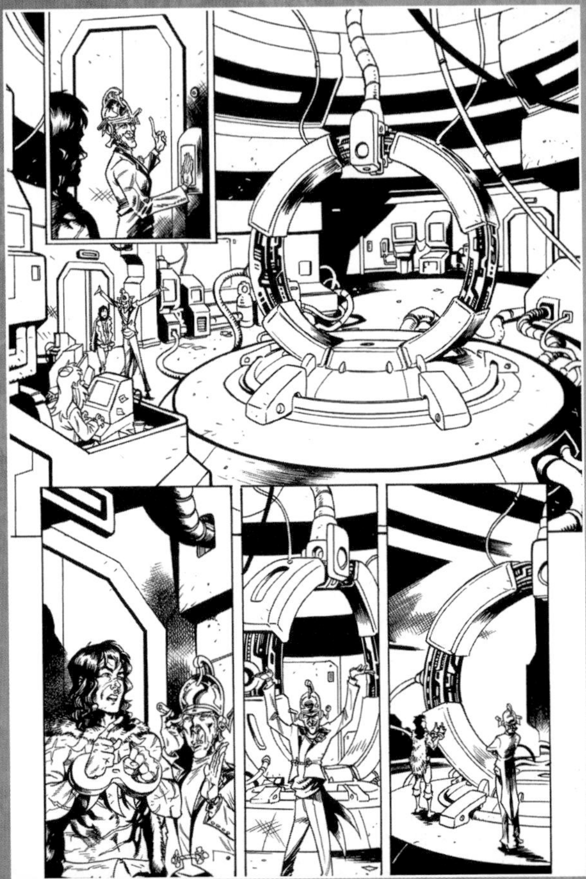

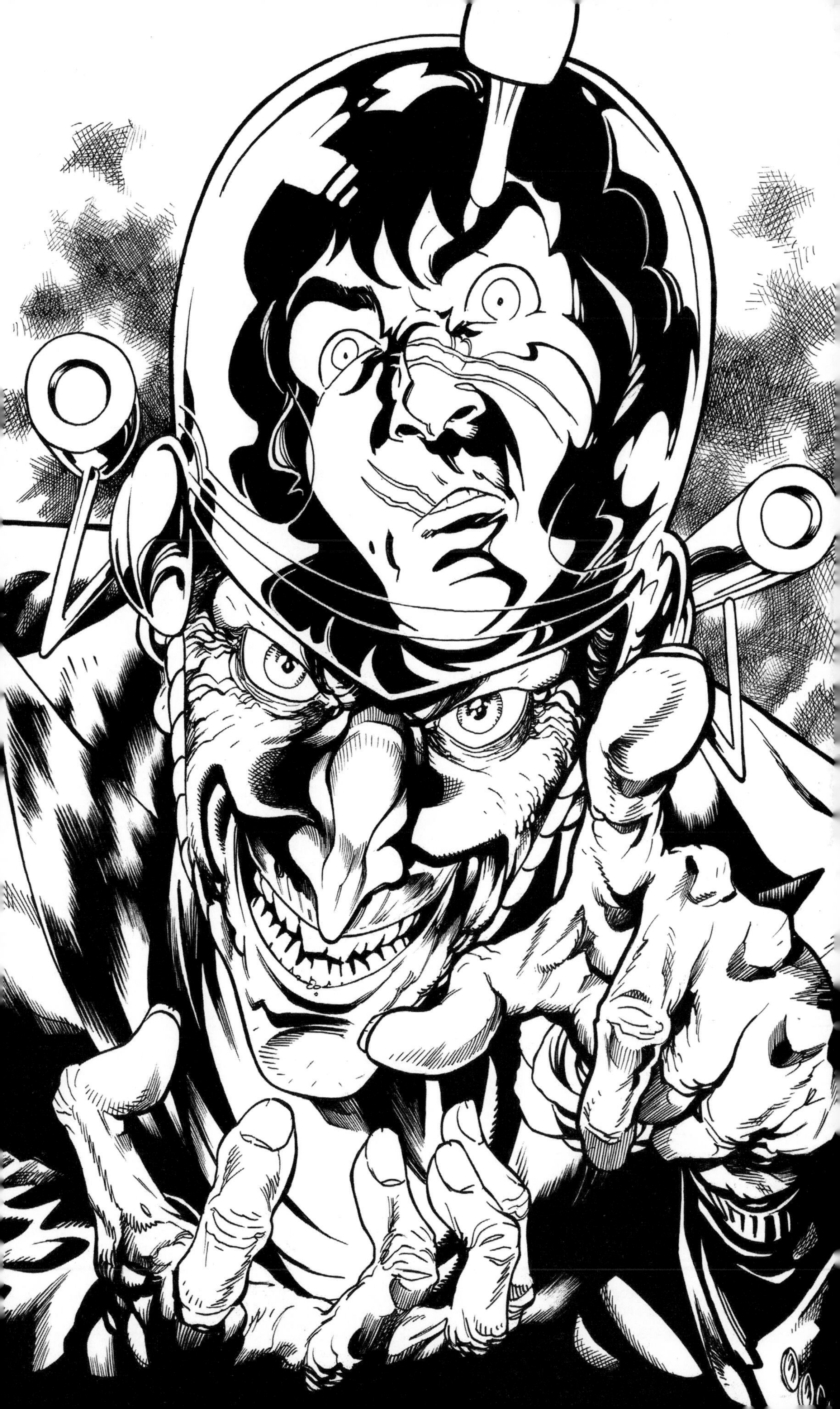

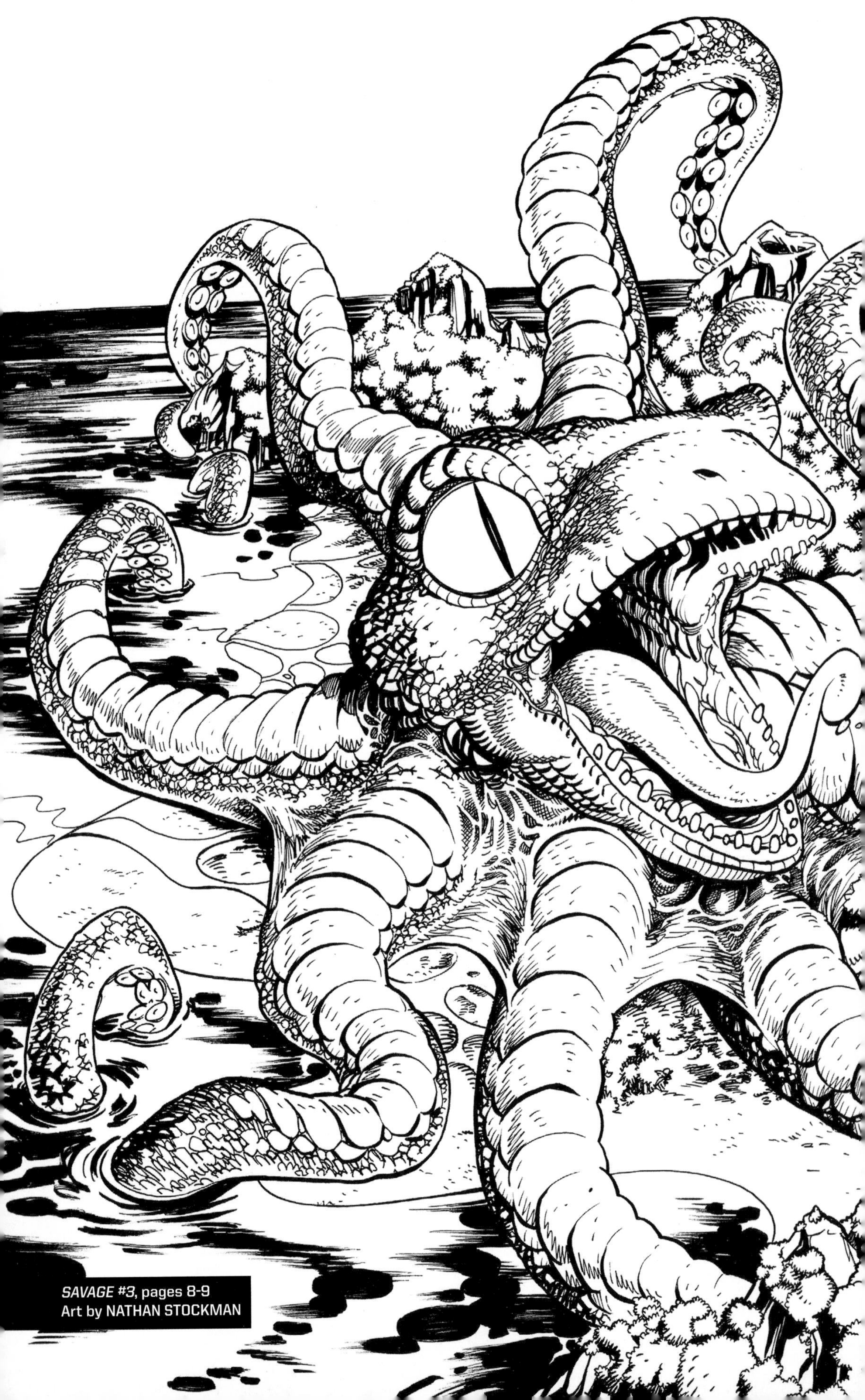

*SAVAGE #3*, pages 8-9
Art by NATHAN STOCKMAN

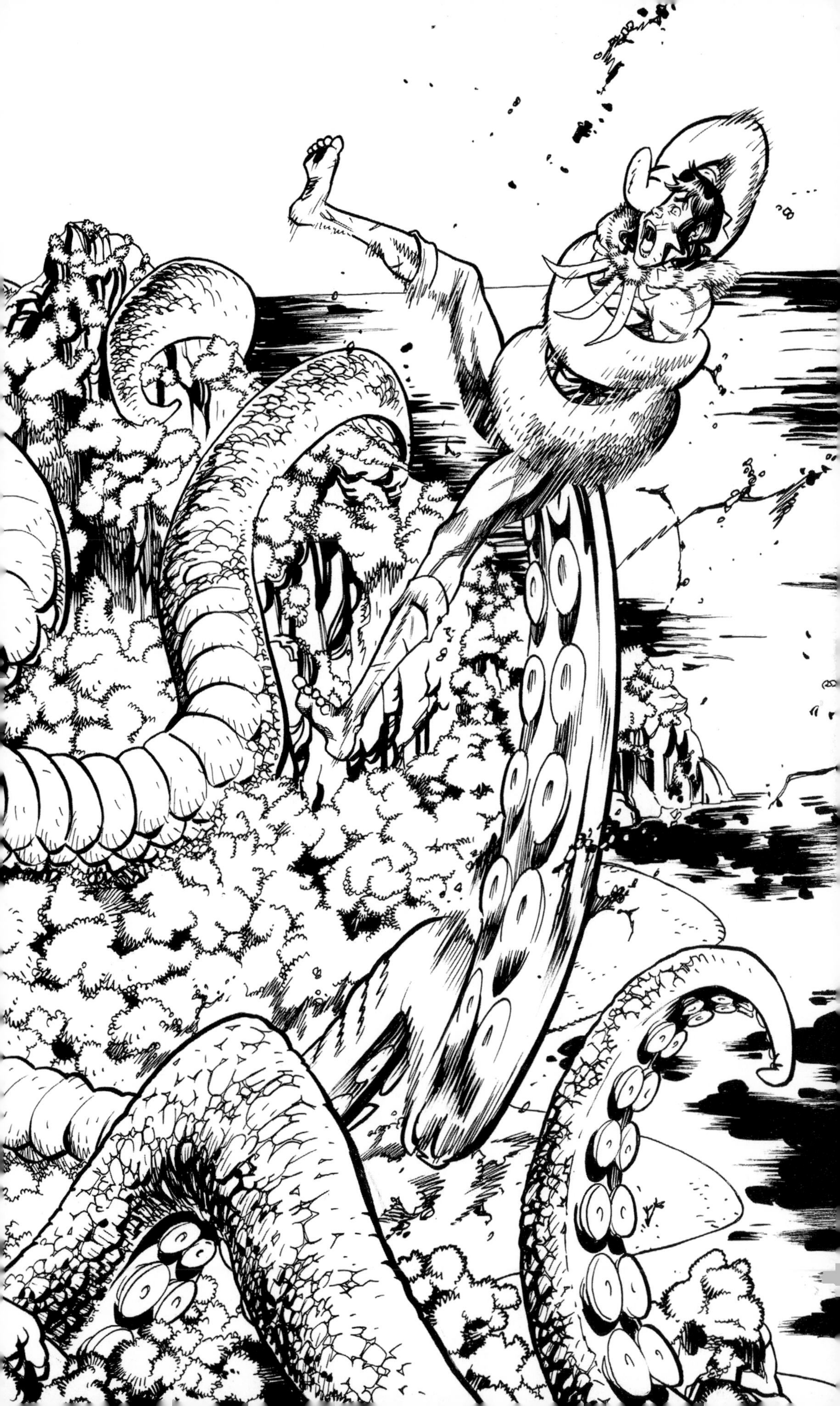

*SAVAGE #3*, p. 18, 19, and (facing) 20
Art by NATHAN STOCKMAN

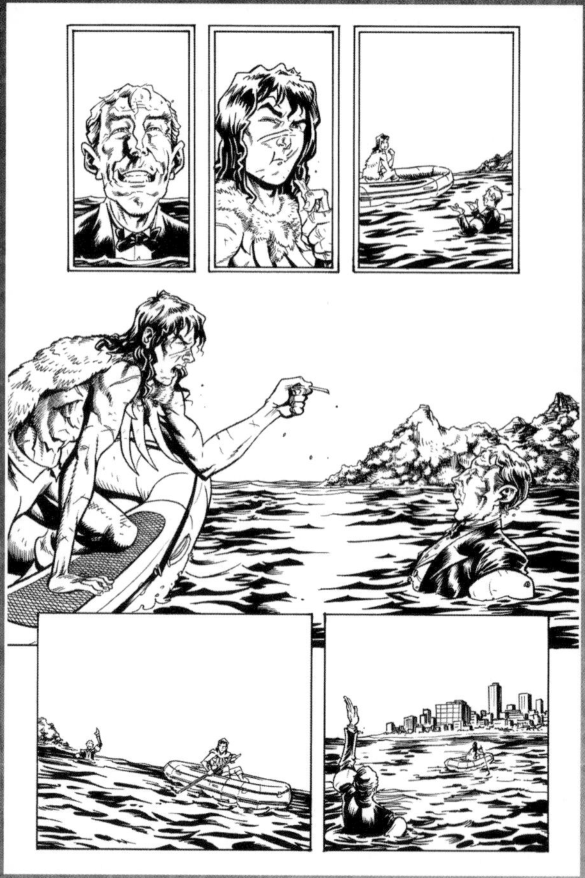

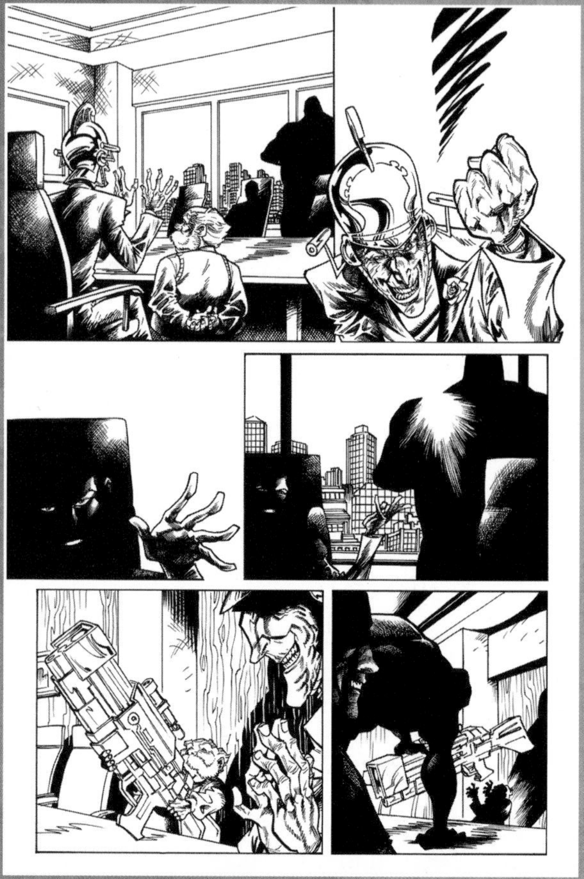

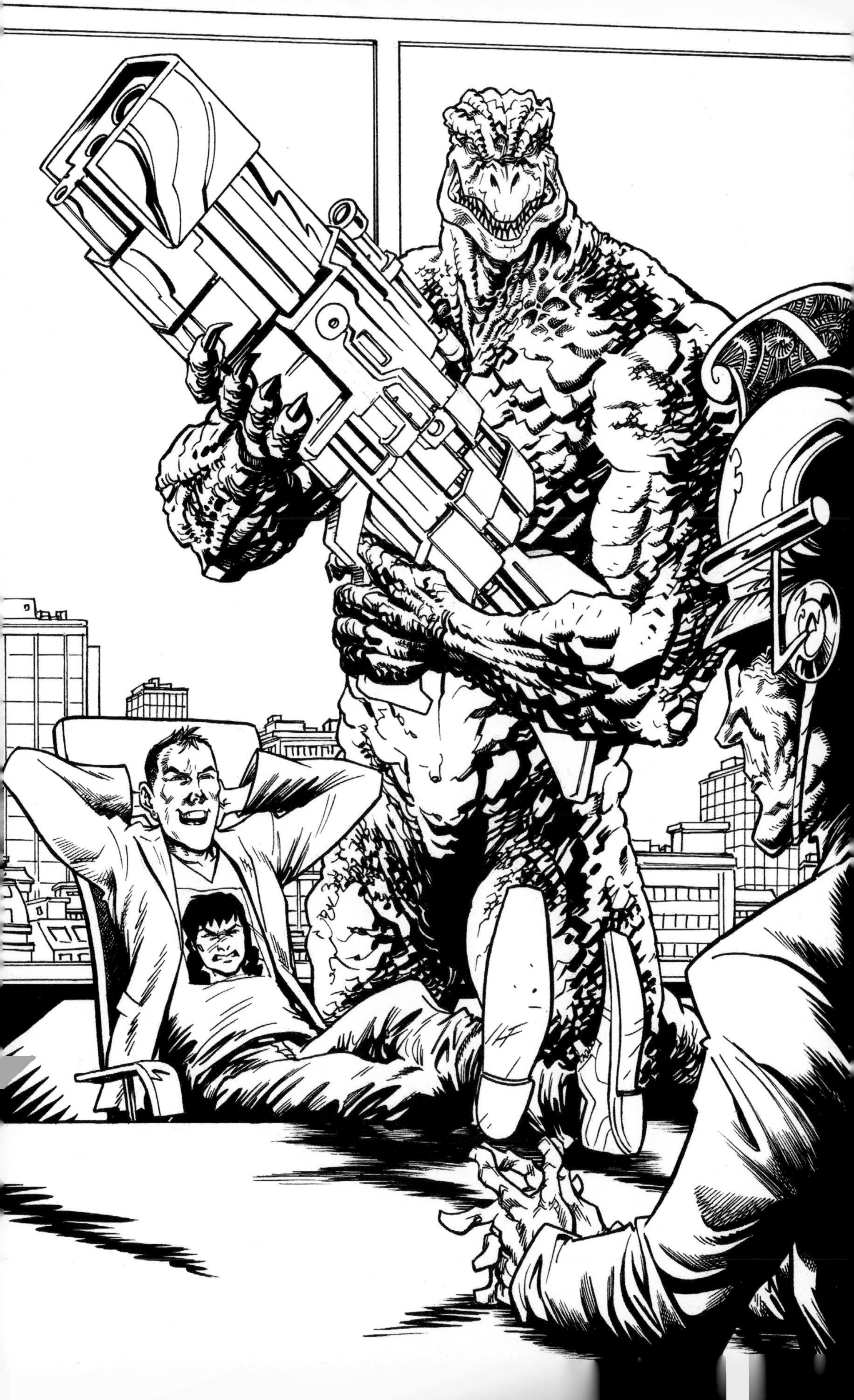

*SAVAGE #4*, p. 12, 13, and (facing) 14
Art by NATHAN STOCKMAN

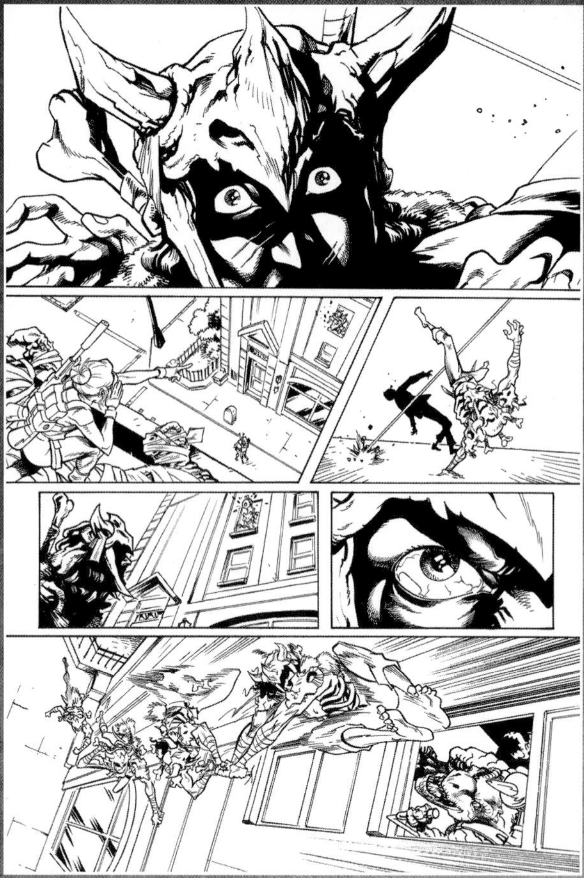

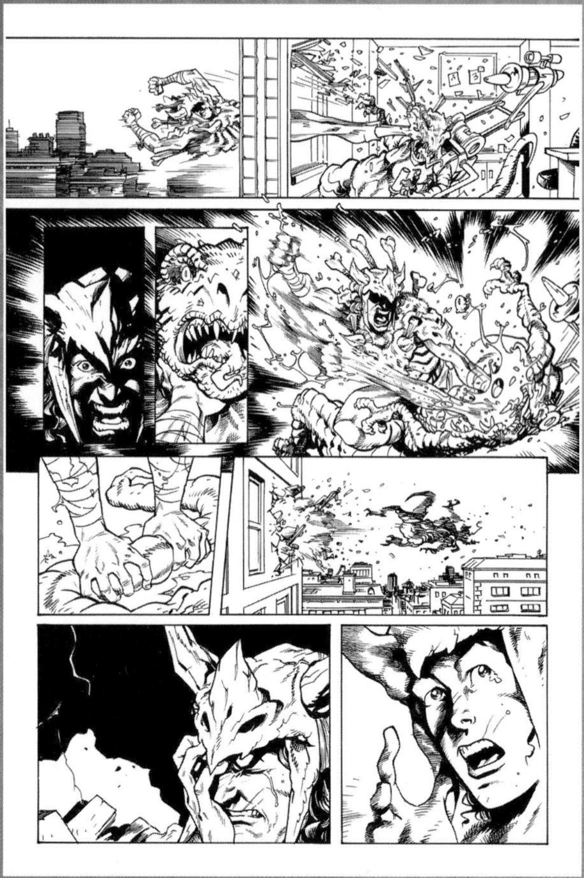

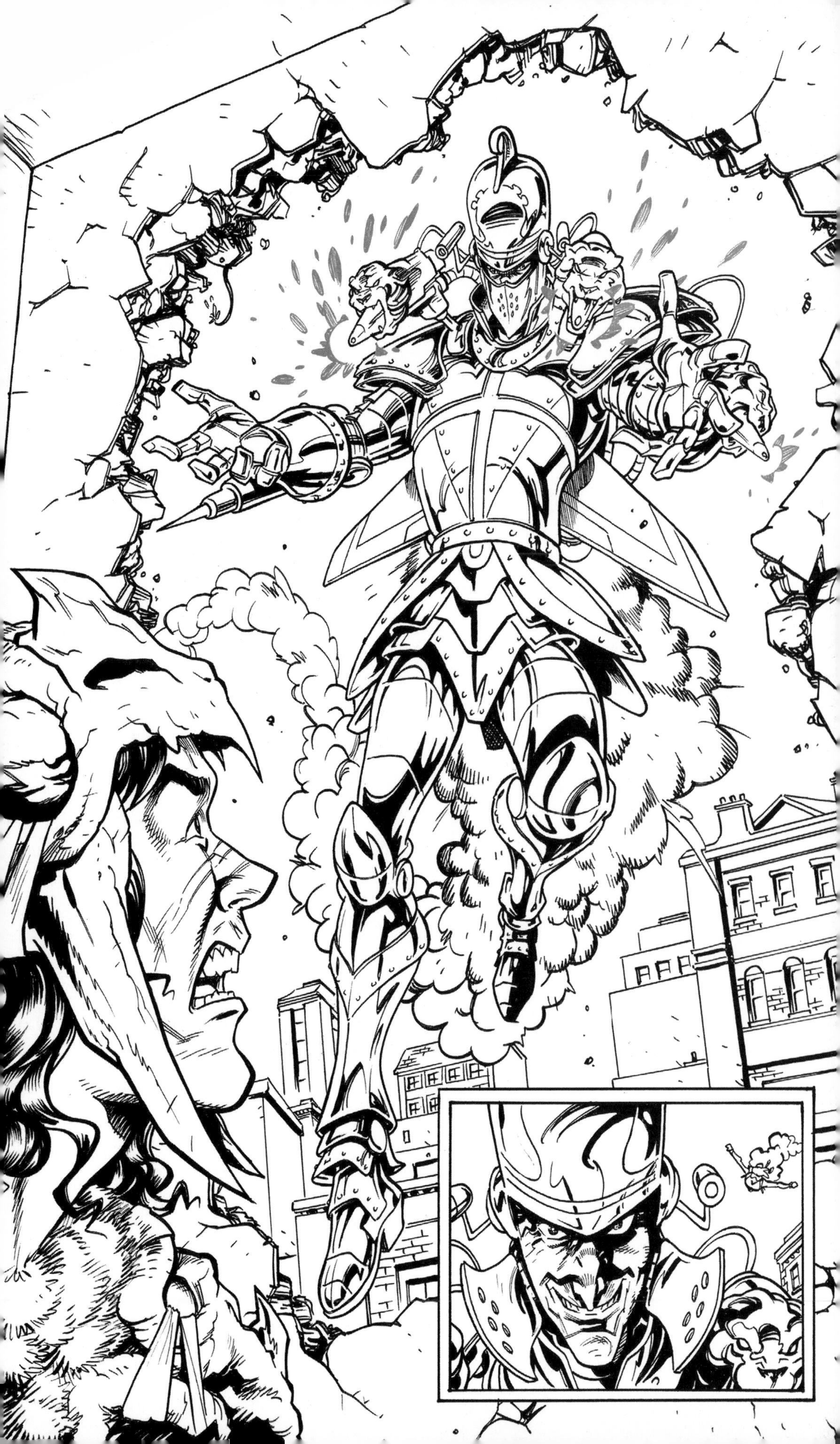

# EXPLORE THE VALIANT U

## ACTION & ADVENTURE

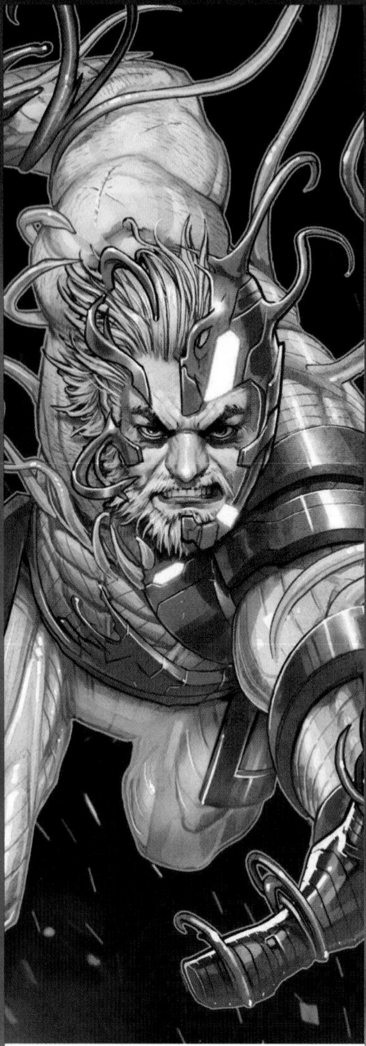

**BLOODSHOT BOOK ONE**
ISBN: 978-1-68215-255-3
**NINJA-K VOL. 1: THE NINJA FILES**
ISBN: 978-1-68215-259-1
**WRATH OF THE ETERNAL WARRIOR VOL. 1: RISEN**
ISBN: 978-1-68215-123-5
**X-O MANOWAR (2019) BOOK ONE**
ISBN: 978-1-68215-368-0

## COMEDY

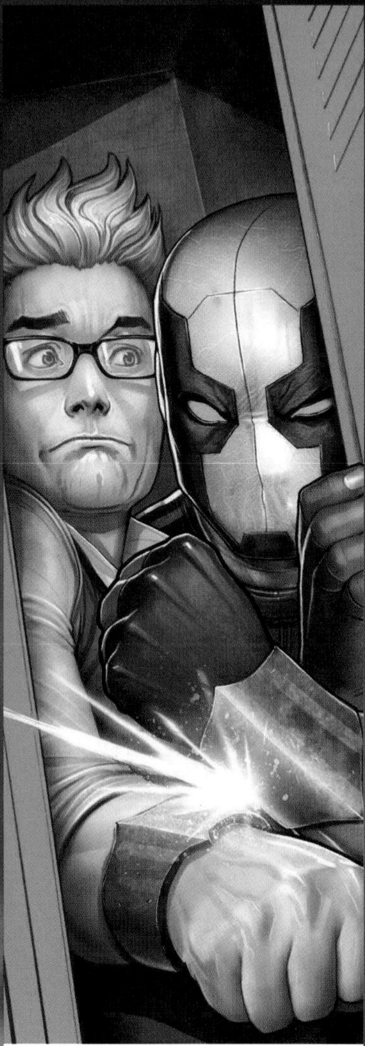

**A&A: THE ADVENTURES OF ARCHER & ARMSTRONG VOL. 1: IN THE BAG**
ISBN: 978-1-68215-149-5
**THE DELINQUENTS**
ISBN: 978-1-939346-51-3
**QUANTUM AND WOODY! (2020): EARTH'S LAST CHOICE**
ISBN: 978-1-68215-362-8

## BLOCKBUSTER ADVENTURE

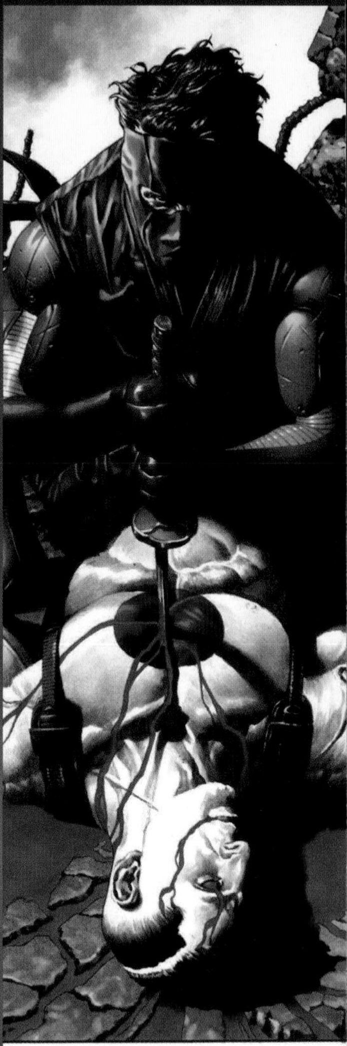

**4001 A.D.**
ISBN: 978-1-68215-143-3
**ARMOR HUNTERS**
ISBN: 978-1-939346-45-2
**BOOK OF DEATH**
ISBN: 978-1-939346-97-1
**FALLEN WORLD**
ISBN: 978-1-68215-331-4
**HARBINGER WARS**
ISBN: 978-1-939346-09-4
**HARBINGER WARS 2**
ISBN: 978-1-68215-289-8
**INCURSION**
ISBN: 978-1-68215-303-1
**THE VALIANT**
ISBN: 978-1-939346-60-5

# VERSE STARTING AT $9.99

## HORROR & MYSTERY

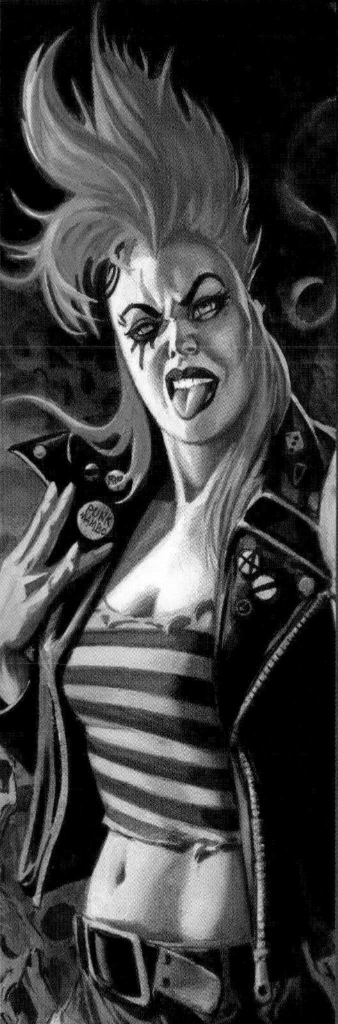
PUNK MAMBO

**BRITANNIA**
ISBN: 978-1-68215-185-3
**DOCTOR MIRAGE**
ISBN: 978-1-68215-346-8
**PUNK MAMBO**
ISBN: 978-1-68215-330-7
**RAPTURE**
ISBN: 978-1-68215-225-6
**SHADOWMAN (2018) VOL. 1: FEAR OF THE DARK**
ISBN: 978-1-68215-239-3

## SCIENCE FICTION & FANTASY

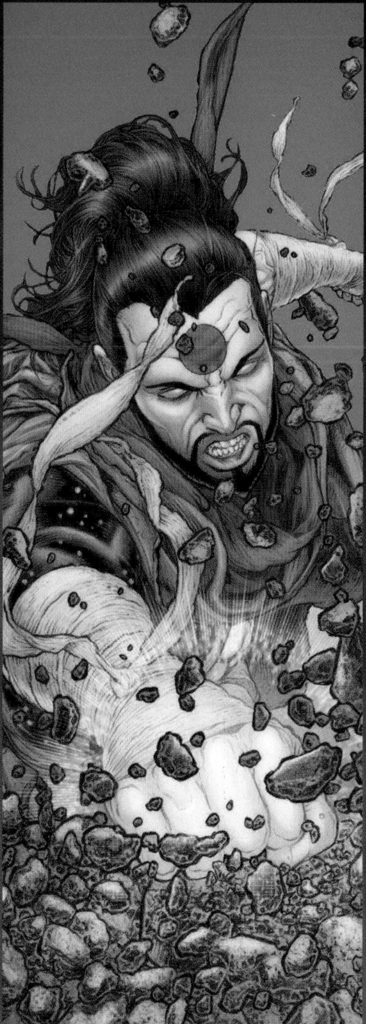

**DIVINITY**
ISBN: 978-1-939346-76-6
**THE FORGOTTEN QUEEN**
ISBN: 978-1-68215-324-6
**IMPERIUM VOL. 1: COLLECTING MONSTERS**
ISBN: 978-1-939346-75-9
**IVAR, TIMEWALKER VOL. 1: MAKING HISTORY**
ISBN: 978-1-939346-63-6
**RAI BOOK ONE**
ISBN: 978-1-682153-60-4
**WAR MOTHER**
ISBN: 978-1-68215-237-9

## TEEN ADVENTURE

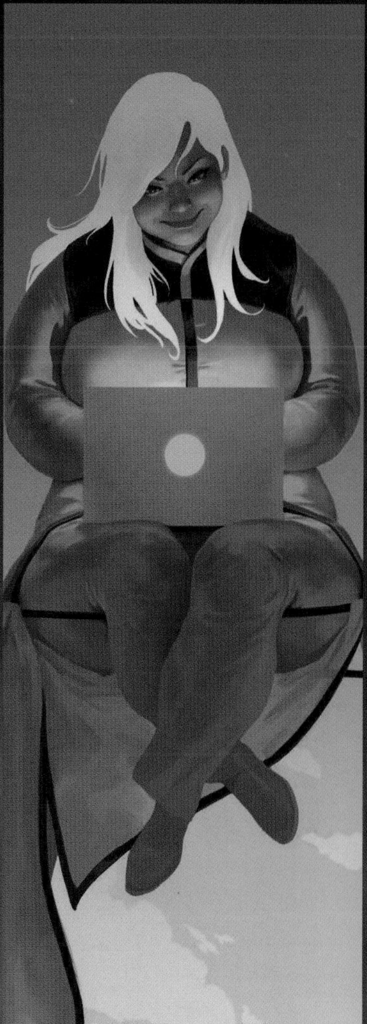

**DOCTOR TOMORROW**
ISBN: 978-1-68215-370-3
**FAITH VOL. 1: HOLLYWOOD AND VINE**
ISBN: 978-1-68215-121-1
**GENERATION ZERO VOL. 1: WE ARE THE FUTURE**
ISBN: 978-1-68215-175-4
**HARBINGER RENEGADE VOL. 1: THE JUDGMENT OF SOLOMON**
ISBN: 978-1-68215-169-3
**LIVEWIRE VOL. 1: FUGITIVE**
ISBN: 978-1-68215-301-7
**SAVAGE: THE WILD**
ISBN: 978-1-68215-384-0
**SECRET WEAPONS**
ISBN: 978-1-68215-229-4

Discover the entire Valiant Universe of titles at VALIANTENTERTAINMENT.COM/ALL-SERIES

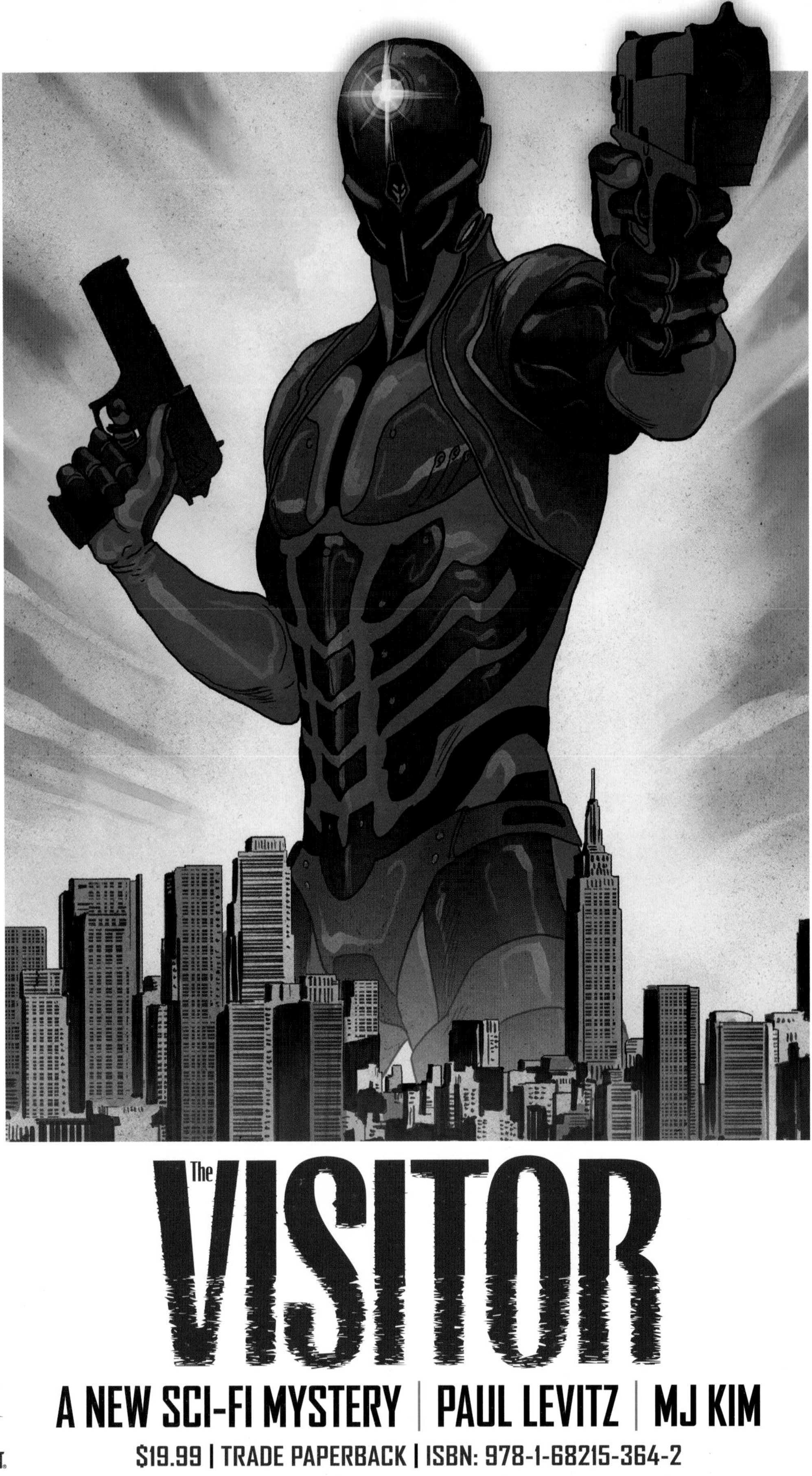